FRIGHTENING, YES, BUT THRILLING IN A STRANGE WAY . . .

That was how Stuart Compton affected Louisa—ever since the moment when they first met, when he drove up in his magnificent black Bentley and, without introduction, encircled her in his arms and kissed her forcibly. He was the most despicable man she had ever known—and the most attractive.

But now, a terrible danger threatened from Compton Hall. Murder lurked in its shadows, a ruthless killer who would stop at nothing to achieve his aims. Caught between the two rival Compton heirs, Louisa fled to America in search of her own shadowy past, only to be plunged into a spiraling maze of passion, intrigue, and long-buried secrets.

In bustling, aristocratic New York, a fated passion called to her, a love such as she had never known—and danger such as she had never dreamed. . . .

SLEEP, MY LOVE

ELIZABETH NORMAN

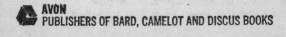

AVON
PUBLISHERS OF BARD, CAMELOT AND DISCUS BOOKS

SLEEP, MY LOVE is an original publication of Avon Books.
This work has never before appeared in book form.

AVON BOOKS
A division of
The Hearst Corporation
959 Eighth Avenue
New York, New York 10019

First Avon Printing, February, 1980

AVON TRADEMARK REG. U.S. PAT. OFF. AND IN
OTHER COUNTRIES, MARCA REGISTRADA, HECHO EN
U.S.A.

Printed in the U.S.A.

For Kota, who wanted
to read the original

Chapter One

EVERYTHING WOULD HAVE BEEN DIFFERENT if the stranger hadn't come into our midst. Greed and duplicity came with him, and horror and death: first Nanny Thompson's, then Lord Bude's. My name was third on the list. Why in the world should he want to kill me? For the longest time I was unaware, even, that he did.

My story begins on the afternoon of Wednesday, May 25, 1927, in the village of Ledington, near Bridgehampton, Dorset. The day was chill and gray. A thick mist hugged the ground. But my spirits were buoyant.

All England's spirits were buoyant, as were spirits all over the world. Charles Lindbergh had landed safely in Paris. Aunt Grace, Uncle Andrew, and I had listened to the account on the wireless the Saturday night before. During the days since, we had continued to listen to the festivities: last night we heard all about the banquet at Le Bourget Field.

Just now Aunt Grace was entertaining Miss Ormsby and Mrs. Collins, and I had an hour or two to myself. Much too lighthearted to stay indoors, I had decided to see if the wild hyacinths were blooming near the marsh at the head of the millpond. The pond had long since lost its mill. Indeed, no one in Ledington remembered it, but a bramble-shrouded foundation testified that it had once stood there. The dam, however, remained intact. Its lichen-encrusted stonework rose dry beside the lane. A ruined sluice gate allowed much of the pond's water to escape.

The sun now glowed brightly through the mist, and

suddenly the afternoon was humid. I removed my sweater, climbed the embankment, and laid my sweater on the dam.

When I reached the hyacinths I stood marveling at the wide purple frame they made around the marsh marigolds, yellow as lemons, that grew in the mire. Every year I made a pilgrimage to see this sight.

Suddenly the mist thickened, blotting out the sun. It was chill again, and I turned and walked back toward the lane. When I was again in sight of the dam, I saw a long black Bentley gliding silently toward me.

The Bentley was a low, open racing car, and as it drew steadily nearer—one curtain of mist after another parting for it—I began to discern the driver. He was a large man with huge shoulders, and he wore a black leather helmet and dark goggles. They looked like deep black holes in place of eyes. His cheeks were sunken beneath high bones, and his chin was prominent. He sat easily in the car, holding its wheel expertly in those large hands.

Finally he drew alongside the pond, stopped the car, and got out. He walked up the embankment, and when he reached my sweater, he picked it up.

I began to run toward him. "Leave that alone!"

He started, turned, and saw me. I had obviously taken him by surprise, but then his astonishment at finding me there turned at once to amusement. He did not replace my sweater, however. He stood there clutching it with an arrogant smile while he watched me stumble along the narrow path toward him.

There was a roughness about him that I did not like. "There's nothing amusing about invading another's privacy or in stealing her clothes," I said breathlessly, as I reached him.

"I had no intention of stealing your sweater," he said, "or invading your privacy. But now that I apparently have, I find the experience gratifying." He examined me from head to toe in the most humiliating manner.

"You are rude!" I said.

"And you are delectable." His bright blue eyes widened.

"How crude!" I reached for my sweater. "Give it to me."

He deliberately held the sweater beyond my grasp.

"Stop staring at me like that!" I said. "You have no right to be here. Give me my sweater and go away."

"Well then, since I'm crude, and a thief, and a trespasser, I shall have to behave badly. Now let me see, what would a scoundrel do now?"

As he spoke, his hand shot out and he grasped me tightly by the wrist.

"What are you doing?" I cried, outraged, trying in vain to wrench my wrist from his grasp. "Let me go!"

"Perhaps you will tell me what other abominable qualities I possess."

Quick as a cat, he pulled me to him and grasped the back of my head. Then he tilted my face to his, bent his head, and fastened his mouth on mine. He held me motionless as he continued to kiss me.

Then, abruptly, he let go. Immediately, shaken and breathless though I was, I drew back my arm in fury and slapped him across the face with all my might. The blow must have stung him, but he did not flinch. He merely grinned disdainfully down at me before whirling about and walking to his car. Then he drove up the hill toward Compton Hall.

I picked up my sweater from the ground, where he had dropped it, threw it about my shoulders, and walked home. My day had been ruined. I was furious with the stranger for what he had done and the whole world for allowing it to happen.

As the day and evening passed, my anger grew. And long after I should have been in bed, I found myself pacing the floor. Why could I not sleep? I had not been hurt that afternoon. The experience was past. Why could I not simply forget it? Why this unreasonable anger?

I was forced to admit that I was not angry only with the stranger. I was angry with myself. I had not found the man entirely unattractive. There was something magnificent in his maleness, something disturbing in the way he had held me—frightening, yes, but also thrilling.

Was there a streak of badness in me? Had I inherited it from my mother?

"Was my mother bad?" I whispered to myself. I remembered the men who visited her at night. But that had been a long time ago—before the war. "Does one inherit these things? No! I will be as I want to be. Nice. Decent. I will see to it."

With this declaration my anger collapsed. I lay down then and fell asleep.

The next day, Thursday, was my day to read to Lord Bude. I had read to him every Monday and Thursday afternoon for years—almost ever since I had come to live with Aunt Grace and Uncle Andrew at St. Clement's Rectory. Even then, a milky film had clouded Lord Bude's eyes, though not as densely as it did now.

At half past one I left the rectory and climbed the path that wound up Compton Hill to the gates of Compton Hall. Above me clouds of deep lavender and cream floated languidly. A crisp breeze made the spearwort and brooklime dance where they grew in sunny places along the way.

The gates of Compton Hall marked the beginning of the grounds of the house, though not, of course, of Lord Bude's estates; his holdings included the town of Ledington, all the land between it and Compton Hall, heaven knows how many hundreds of acres in the other direction, and large parcels in other parts of Dorset and Somerset as well.

The main gates were kept closed and locked. But since I walked when I came to visit Lord Bude, it was unnecessary for Herbert, the gatekeeper, to come out of his lodge to open them, because he always left the door of a little archway in the wall unbolted for me.

I passed through it, and, not seeing any evidence of Herbert or of his wife, Anna, I proceeded down the long drive toward the house.

Compton Hall was a wide, three-storied, Georgian house of gray-pink stone. I guessed it contained fifty-five or sixty rooms, though I could not be certain. The building would have looked down on the town of Ledington if it had not been placed so far back on its high, flattened hilltop. But though one could not see the village from there, one looked out across the emerald park to the distant Dorset cliffs, sometimes pearl, sometimes misty violet, and to the sea.

Since the Hall stood almost half a mile away, I had plenty of time to think as I walked, and I savored the marvelous thing that had happened to me almost a week before. Lord Hartley, Lord Bude's son, had noticed me.

For years we had spoken politely when I had come to Compton Hall, but that had been all. Once in a great while I had met him there, and as he had passed me, walking straight and lithe and handsome, he had said, "Good afternoon, Louisa. Isn't it a perfect day?" or, "Isn't it dreadful weather?" or something of the sort.

And I had answered, "Good afternoon, Lord Hartley. Yes, isn't it."

But then, last Thursday, without any warning, he asked me to dine at Compton Hall. Mr. Livermore, an American financier, Mrs. Livermore, and their daughter, Salvia, were visiting him. Lord Bude's solicitor, Mr. Winterthorn, was staying the night as well. Lord Bude had been ill and would not be coming down to dinner. Still, it had been necessary to invite another woman to make the correct arrangement at the table. So Lord Hartley had asked me. At least I had thought at the time that was the reason. And I thought too, since Lord Bude's solicitor had obviously liked me when we met previously, that perhaps Lord Hartley had invited me to please Mr. Winterthorn.

This had been partly true, since Lord Hartley had asked me to play the piano after dinner. He asked me to play Beethoven, who was Mr. Winterthorn's favorite composer. I agreed, of course, though I would much rather have danced.

But it had been more than that. Lord Hartley had suddenly become attracted to me, or so he told me later. "When I saw you sitting at the piano after dinner on Thursday night," he said, "I thought, 'What an absolutely beautiful girl Louisa is.' And then all of a sudden I felt I wanted to be with you—often. Do you mind?"

I had not minded at all, but Mrs. Livermore had. She had hoped that Salvia would marry Lyle. Lyle, however, had been more fascinated by Mr. Livermore's stories of high finance than by Salvia. And when Mrs. Livermore found out that Lyle was interested in me, she left Compton Hall in a huff, taking her daughter and her husband with her.

To my relief, Salvia had not seemed to mind. She had even come to the rectory to say how much she had enjoyed the dinner party on Thursday, to wish me good-bye, and to invite me to visit her if ever I got to New York.

I had enjoyed the party too, but one thing had spoiled it for me: Lord Bude had been taken with a nervous seizure in his room, and Lyle had had to attend him almost all the while I played the piano.

But that had been a minor thing. It hardly bears mention alongside my delight over the way things had turned out.

I had thought I was doomed to marry a local farmer; I was twenty-two—high time to think of marriage. After all, I had no family or worthy background. My mother had been a millworker until she died, and I had become something of a foster child of the rector of St. Clement's parish. But now, miraculously, here I was, dining at Compton Hall and being called upon by Lord Hartley himself! I could hardly believe it.

Lyle had gone to London, but he would return in a few days. Then he would call at the rectory.

At that point my thoughts were interrupted by a figure hurrying alongside the house toward the drive. It was Bertha Bailey, my childhood friend, who was now a parlormaid at the Hall. When she reached the drive, she began to walk in my direction.

"I came to meet you!" she cried, when I had drawn near enough to call to. "I have news!"

"It must be very special to bring you out here like this."

"It is!"

Bertha said nothing more but stared pop-eyed at me instead. Finally I said, "Well, aren't you going to tell me?"

"It's nerve-racking," she said, "positively nerve-racking."

"What is?"

"Lieutenant Compton! His lordship's nephew!"

"I did not know he had a nephew."

"His lordship and his lordship's brother were estranged long ago. Oh, it was a beastly affair. Mr. Keating and Mrs. Merrymede told us about it at lunch, but it is not to be discussed ever at the Hall. And Lieutenant Compton has never been to Compton Hall or even met his lordship. And now, after all these years, he suddenly appears. He is here now. It's nerve-racking, positively nerve-racking."

"Why?" I asked.

"I don't know, but it is."

I walked along silently thinking about this rather strange new development, and Bertha stared at me as I did so, gauging my reaction. But she was bursting with gossip and could not be quiet long.

"We are ever so glad his young lordship is away from home," she said suddenly.

"Oh?"

"He has gone up to London for several days."

"Yes, I know. Why are you glad of that?"

"Because they hate each other."

"Lord Hartley hates his cousin?" I asked.

"That is what Mr. Keating said, but Mrs. Merrymede said his young lordship wouldn't hate anybody. They were at Harrow and then at Cambridge together. Lieutenant Compton must have done terrible things to his young lordship. He would come home in a proper state because of it."

"What did he do?"

"I don't know. Mr. Keating or Mrs. Merrymede wouldn't say, but they were always at each other's throat by the sound of it. So that's why we're glad they're not going to meet."

"Well, then I'm glad too. Have you heard from Mr. Salt?"

Mr. Salt was Mr. Livermore's valet. He and Bertha had fallen in love, she declared, and he had promised to persuade Mr. Livermore to employ Bertha too, so they could be together. Bertha told me that she had not yet heard. Then we talked about Mrs. Merrymede's injured ankle (Mrs. Merrymede was the housekeeper at Compton Hall), and about other things until we reached the house.

There Bertha left me, skirting the building toward the kitchen. I walked to the entrance door.

John, one of the footmen, opened the door for me. "Good afternoon, miss," he said. "His lordship is still at luncheon, but I will go up and tell Mr. Keating you are here."

He went off and returned quickly, saying that Keating, Lord Bude's butler, would be down directly. Then I heard voices and footsteps enter the hall above. Two men were talking. I recognized Lord Bude's voice, but not the other.

Lord Bude called, "Oh, Keating, would you kindly tell . . ." but I could not distinguish what else he said.

As he spoke, I heard footsteps on the stairs. I looked up, expecting Keating to appear on the landing. But it was not Keating who came into view; it was the man I had met at the millpond the day before.

I think he was shocked to see me. He started as he rounded the landing and saw me standing there looking up at him, but this reaction lasted only an instant. Then, apparently composed, he continued toward me.

"The millpond lies back in that direction, miss," he said, pointing toward the drive. "It is ill-mannered to wander into other people's houses and disturb them at lunch simply to ask directions." Then he added, "Or am I mistaken?" He smiled that disdainful smile.

If I could have struck the man dead with my glance, I would have. As it was, I gave him a look of undisguised loathing, but I did not deign to answer.

At that moment I saw Keating appear on the landing, and I hurried to him.

"If you will follow me, miss," Keating said. "His lordship is in the library."

I was only too happy to follow Keating up the stairs. He led me to the library door and announced me.

Lord Bude sat in his usual chair by the window, a thin crane of a man, bent with age, topped by a mass of straight white hair.

"You are late!" he said. "Thank you, Keating."

Keating left the room, closing the door behind him. I approached Lord Bude, glancing at the little clock on the chimneypiece.

"I don't think so, Lord Bude," I said. "It's just two o'clock. I hope I've not interrupted your luncheon."

I smiled at him. Somehow I had come to like this crotchety old man very much.

"It was high time we finished," Lord Bude said. "Kept me sitting there for hours—all about cars and so forth."

"The man who came down the stairs?" I asked.

"My nephew. Army. Lieutenant, Grenadier Guards. Military Cross for gallantry. Racing driver! Won at Le Mans last year, and the Italian *and* European Grand Prix in 'twenty-five. A *man*, that."

"Yes. Well, shall we begin?" I said, as I walked to the bookshelf to fetch Boswell's *Life of Samuel Johnson*, which we were reading.

"Tough! Spirit there. Direct—no beating about the bush. Says what he means. But if he doesn't like you, he will say so. Aggressive. Chip on his shoulder." Lord Bude chuckled. "Like to see the man to knock it off."

By this time I had taken the book from the bookcase, and as I walked back to my usual place, across from Lord Bude, I could see that he was now lost in his thoughts.

I sat down, opened the book, and waited. Finally Lord Bude looked up at me through his clouded eyes and said, "Oh, yes. Well, get on with it."

"We were reading about Mr. Savage," I said. I read: "He told Sir Joshua Reynolds that one night in particular, when Savage and he walked round St. James Square for want of a lodging . . ."

A while later, I had gotten to: "Not withstanding all the support of such performers as Garrick, Barry, Mrs. . . . ."

"Mind of his own!" Lord Bude cried.

"Mind of his own?" I asked.

"Knows what he wants—going to get it. Ruthless, that."

"Who?" I asked.

"Compton, of course. Ruthless!" Again Lord Bude chuckled. "Positively ruthless. Determination! Ideas of his own! Has to be done his way, or else . . . Knock you down if you do not do it his way, I'll wager. Dangerous! Doesn't like people. Bad—very bad, that. Don't you agree?"

"About what, Lord Bude?"

"A man who doesn't like people. Bad!"

"I don't believe I've ever met a man—"

"Tough as stone. No feelings! Argumentative. Impudent! How dare he turn up here after all this time? Cheek!" Lord Bude chuckled again. "Can you imagine? Cheek!"

"Would you rather we continue on Monday, Lord Bude?" I asked. "I really don't think you have heard a thing I've read."

"I have heard every word," he said. "Now, get on with it."

I continued to read until four o'clock, when we usually stopped. Lord Bude did not interrupt me again, but I am sure he paid no attention to Mr. Johnson.

I left him, and as I opened the library door, I glanced back at him. He sat slumped in his chair, his fist to his chin, deep in thought.

From the library I walked across the huge hall to the staircase and down it. But when I reached the landing, I stopped short. Lieutenant Compton stood at the base of the stairs, waiting for me. I paused for only a moment, and then continued down the steps.

"Ah, Miss Little," he said, as I approached him. "Keating told me you finish reading to my uncle at about this time."

I swept past him but he followed me across the vestibule. "I decided to wait for you," he continued, "and see you safely back to the rectory."

John opened the entrance door for me, and as I sailed through it, I said, "Thank you, John." Then, looking straight ahead of me, I walked quickly down the drive away from the house.

Lieutenant Compton walked beside me. "There is no need to be frightened," he said.

I flashed him a poisoned look and then stared straight ahead again.

"You need not fear a repetition of yesterday's . . . encounter. We both know who the other is now, and that places certain . . . restraints . . . upon our actions."

I did not look at him or speak, but continued walking briskly.

"If such a thing occurred again," he continued, "you'd certainly tell my uncle. So, you see, you're safe! You have told him all about yesterday?"

I continued to ignore him.

"Good! Then I can discuss it with him at dinner tonight."

"I certainly have not!" I spat the words at him.

"Why not?" he asked. "Perhaps you're not so safe after all. If you didn't tell him the first time, why should you tell him the second?"

I flashed him my most withering look. It seemed to have no effect on him. "No, you are safe. That is, unless you provoke a similar encounter again."

I turned, outraged.

"What do you expect when you wantonly provoke a man?" he asked. "You'll find it advantageous to be more careful in the future."

I did not look at him now, but I knew he grinned in that arrogant way.

"Yesterday I thought an accident might have happened at that pond. That was why I looked at the sweater. I don't suppose *that* occurred to you, did it? Then my fears for your safety were rewarded by a vicious attack. That was wrong, and you were punished for it. It's only just, you know."

He waited to see if I would speak. I did not.

"The score is settled now, and we'll let bygones be bygones."

Then, after a moment or two of silence, he said, "Good. That's settled." And after another moment, "Beautiful country, isn't it? Lived in Ledington for long?"

When I still did not answer, he fell silent. He continued to walk beside me, however, until I had stepped through the arch in the wall. And even after that he walked beside me on the grass as I hurried along the path down the hill toward the wood.

Once there, we were obliged to walk single file; Lieutenant Compton walked ahead of me. Now he said, "You have a beautiful little church here in Ledington. Is the rector a close relative of yours?"

He held a low branch aside for me to pass, but I did not look at him or speak.

"You do not seem very communicative today, Miss Little. It is just as well. Sometimes one can enjoy the beauties of the countryside better in silence. And conversation isn't necessary for two people to enjoy one another's company. Let's not talk, then, but concentrate on the enjoyment of nature."

I ignored him, willing myself to feel entirely alone. As we neared the town, we reached a fork in the path. Lieutenant Compton took the more traveled way and I marched off in the direction of the rectory. He realized his mistake and followed me. And when at last we reached the rectory, I opened the door to the house and entered it without looking back, leaving him standing on the portico alone.

May, the maid, stood just inside the door.

"Mrs. Cuttlebuck wants you, miss," she said. "She's been calling for you. She's quite upset that you are so late."

"Thank you, May. I'll go right up."

"She's been wondering where you were. Well, far be it from *me* to tell her you were out mooning about with a strange man. One after another, it would seem."

I whirled and faced the girl. "What do you mean by that, May?" I said. "What are you trying to say? You have made several remarks lately—as though you want to hurt me. What is it?"

"Nothing, miss. Only I'm glad *I* don't go about stealing people from other people, and then tossing them aside for somebody new. Ruining people's lives!"

Tears appeared in her eyes, and she turned away, hoping I would not see them.

"Oh, May! You don't think I—that Mr. Thornton and I . . . But I am not at all interested in Mr. Thornton. I have tried to discourage him from coming here, you know that."

"You did it out of spite!" May cried. "You didn't even like him." She glared at me. "He'd have come to see me if it wasn't for you."

"I couldn't help it, May. I'm not responsible for what Mr. Thornton does or does not do. I didn't want him here, and I all but told him so. And it's not your place to comment on what I do or whom I see."

May gave me a disbelieving grunt but she said no more. So I left her and climbed the stairs to Aunt Grace's room.

Aunt Grace sprawled on her bed—a flaccid mountain of flesh. A beaklike nose jutted from beneath a mop of dun hair. Beady eyes stared at me. Her thin lips were set with disapproval.

"Louisa, my dear, where have you been?" she called. "I have been worried to death."

"You know perfectly well, Aunt Grace. I've been up to the Hall reading to Lord Bude."

"I saw you walking with a strange man."

"You *saw* me?" I asked.

"My dear, I am obliged to leave this bed occasionally, you know, and even though I go no farther than the foot of it, I can see the path from the wood quite clearly from there. God has at least spared my eyes, though they tire so terribly easily nowadays. And May came and told me you were coming with someone."

"It was Lord Bude's nephew, Lieutenant Compton. He is staying at the Hall and asked to see me home."

"Alone?" She pursed her lips. "Through the wood? Had you been quarreling?"

"No, I— Why should we have been quarreling?"

"I do not know, but there was something definitely wrong there. Louisa, my dear, Mr. Cuttlebuck and I have given you a good home with a proper religious atmosphere. We expect you to behave correctly. I hope we shall not be disappointed in you."

"I don't know what you mean," I said.

"Men are not to be trusted, Louisa. You must not allow them liberties. You understand that, don't you?"

"Yes."

" 'Watch and pray, that ye enter not into temptation: the spirit indeed is willing, but the flesh is weak.' Matthew 26."

"Yes. Couldn't you sleep?"

"No. I just lay here all alone, wide awake, tossing and turning. Fluff my pillows for me like a good girl. They are all packed down and full of hard lumps. Oh, I am so uncomfortable. Gray—so terribly gray. If you knew what it is like to lie here day after day, year after year. Exiled from everything and everybody. And nobody caring. And one's body wasting away. And long afternoons . . ."

"You always take a nap in the afternoon," I said, as I began to fluff her pillows.

"Yes, I know, but I couldn't today. If only you could have been here to read to me—some poetry, perhaps. You read so beautifully. It would have soothed me, and then perhaps I could have slept. Oh, I am not complaining. You have been an angel, truly. And you are a godsend with my medicines. I could not live without you. Dear Louisa! How I miss you when you leave me. How I need you. It is too cruel to be away like that. Why, any girl in your position would be happy to be here with us.

"That is much better. No one could do that but you," she continued, after I had fixed her pillows. "Now, could you smooth out the sheets there? They have gotten quite rumpled, but do not touch the feet!"

"Speaking of medicine, it is time," I said. I reached for the bottle, measured a spoonful of the thick brown liquid, and fed it to Aunt Grace. Then I poured a glass of water for her to drink. "I am afraid I shall soon have to go to the chemist for some more of this. Doctor Carmichael did say you should continue with it, along with the pills, didn't he?"

"And to discontinue the salve," Aunt Grace said. "Just when I think it was doing me some good. He does not know what is wrong with me. He never has. The salve was doing wonders for my poor, burning skin, but just because he could not *see* anything, he has taken it away from me. And that ghastly, dizzy, hotness—that prickly, hot, dizzy feeling—he simply ignored it. He said it was the weather. Weather! Humph!"

"Does your foot still ache?"

"Not so much as it did, but it is still terribly sore, and I think it is spreading to my fingers. But we will not know about that until tomorrow. Now, be an angel and go down to the study and see if Mr. Cuttlebuck has finished the *Times*."

I read to her until she grew sleepy, and then when she said she would nap a little, I escaped to my room. I longed to be alone to think. I had been terribly aware of Lieutenant Compton during our walk. I had never felt like that about anyone before. I did not know what it was. Was it fear? Repugnance? A combination of these? Whatever it was, it had made me tremble a little.

Be that as it may, I was determined not to think about him anymore. He would soon leave Compton Hall, and then he would be completely forgotten.

And then Lyle would return. What would happen then? How does Lyle feel about me? I asked myself. I love his smile. And he is good and gentle. What will happen?

I found no answers to these questions, nor did I make any decisions—none, that is, except to say nothing to Aunt Grace about Lieutenant Compton.

The following morning, I found Uncle Andrew at his usual place at the breakfast table. Thin but still handsome, his white mustache perfectly trimmed, he sat engrossed in a long letter. I did not interrupt him, but helped myself to some eggs and toast, poured myself a cup of coffee, and sat down.

In a minute or so Uncle Andrew looked up at me as he folded his letter and said, "Good morning, my dear. Shall we take a moment to thank the Lord for his blessings?

"Lord," he began without pause, "we thank thee for this bountiful table and for this beautiful day. Look down and bestow thy special blessing on this thy servant, Louisa. Guide her into paths of virtue and moral uprightness. And we humbly ask that thou bestow thy blessing upon those who are sick, and those who hunger and are in pain, and those who are sick at heart. And we thank thee for kind thoughts from old friends. Amen.

"Well, my dear," he said, looking up at me, "did you sleep well?"

"Beautifully, thank you," I said.

"I have just received a letter from an old friend." He waved the letter at me. "I had thought he had forgotten all about me. Dear old Wallburton. He was a character! Oh, the times we had at Oxford." He chuckled. "Poor fellow, he's lost his living in Portsmouth. But it is quite out of the question for him to stay here for any length of time. Quite out of the question."

"How nice," I said. "To hear from him I mean, not that he has lost his living. Have you heard from Mr. Morley lately?"

"Morley?"

"Yes."

"I do not recall . . ."

"Is he still in Manchester?"

"Manchester? Oh, my dear Louisa, you must mean my old friend Martin, rector of St. Stephen's."

"But you said his name was Mr. Morley of St. James's church."

"No, no. It couldn't have been Morley. Jeremiah Morley was an old man. I believe he was secretary to the Archbishop of Canterbury. He died before you were born."

"I've often thought of writing to Mr.—Martin."

"Good Lord, why would you want to do that?"

"To thank him."

"After all these years? He probably wouldn't remember.

But it is a very kind thought. I do not think he is there anymore. Yes, I am quite sure he went to a little town up north—near the Scottish border, somewhere. We lost touch some time ago. Pity, but one can not keep up everything, you know."

"Aunt Grace and I were talking about it a few days ago. You did not know my mother, did you?"

"No, she had died before I went to Manchester to fetch you, but I have told you about it many times."

"Have you told me everything you know about her?"

"Yes, I think so. I never did know much about her. Why do you ask?"

"I don't know. I still think about it sometimes. It seems so strange that you would go halfway across England and bring a perfectly strange little girl back here to live with you. Why did you do it? Why did you want me?"

"What a strange question. Why—you were an adorable child. And Mrs. Cuttlebuck and I were childless. And it was an act of human kindness. We simply could not leave you there all alone, and when Martin wrote about your plight and asked if we could help, we decided to have you here with us. And we hope you have been happy. We have given you a great deal, Louisa. We have spared no expense, no amount of loving care."

"And I do appreciate it," I said. "I don't know what I would have done if you hadn't. But it's natural to wonder about these things."

"Certainly it is, but it does not do any good now, does it?" Uncle Andrew said. "It is best to forget it now. That was all long ago—all in the past." He looked at his watch. "I'm going out to visit Mrs. Bradwick, and then I am having lunch with Stapleton and Mrs. Stapleton at St. Andrew's rectory. Please tell May.

"I wanted to talk to you about that Gordon youngster. You know, a Sunday school is not a regular school. His mother is most upset."

"But I must have discipline," I began. "If—"

"Yes, yes, I quite agree," he said, rising from his chair, "but one can not have members of one's congregation fly-

ing at one's throat. We will discuss it later. Oh, and the
vestry will meet here on Wednesday evening after service.
So tell May, and please be on hand to help her."

Then he disappeared in the direction of his study.

That afternoon as I sat at Aunt Grace's bedside reading
to her, we heard a car turn into the rectory drive.

"I did not expect him back so soon," Aunt Grace said.

"Uncle?" I asked.

"He has been with Mrs. Aimsley. She had been taken
bad."

"Oh, dear. But that can't be Uncle."

The engine sounded different from ours—a deep, powerful purr. I got up and went to the window to see who had
driven up.

"What is it?" Aunt Grace asked.

"It's Lieutenant Compton," I said. "He is getting out.
I—I suppose I'll have to go down. But I won't be long."

Chapter Two

As I DESCENDED THE STAIRS, I REALIZED THAT the odd, shaky feeling had returned. How could he call here after yesterday?

By the time I reached the bottom of the stairs, May had shown Lieutenant Compton into the drawing room and was hurrying along the corridor toward me.

"He says his name is Lieutenant Compton," she said.

"Yes, May," I replied. "That will be all."

But I knew that would not be all—that she would be listening to every word I said to Lieutenant Compton from outside the doorway.

When I reached the drawing room, I found him standing in the center of it. He turned and took a step toward me.

"Good afternoon, Lieutenant Compton," I said, rather more loudly than necessary. "How nice of you to call."

"It is a great pleasure, Miss Little," he replied.

"Won't you sit down?" I said, walking to the chair in the bay window, which was the chair farthest from the doorway.

Lieutenant Compton sat in the chair opposite mine.

"Another lovely day, Miss Little," he said.

"Yes, isn't it." I gazed at him but said nothing further.

After several moments he said, "You do not read to my uncle today?"

"No, Lieutenant," I replied.

"Then you must read on certain days only."

"On Monday and Thursday afternoons."

"That's a pity. I enjoyed our quiet walk so much yesterday, and I had hoped we might have another today."

I did not reply.

"What are you reading to my uncle just now, by the way?"

"Boswell's *Life of Samuel Johnson.*"

"Ah, very good. An interesting man. I might recommend his *Journal of a Tour to the Hebrides.* Now, there is a fascinating account."

"It is Lord Bude who chooses what we read, Lieutenant Compton."

"One day while they were tramping about Skye, I think it was, Dr. Johnson fell off a ledge. When Boswell reached him, he thought Dr. Johnson had struck his head and was dead. But then Dr. Johnson opened his eyes and his friend said, 'Thank heavens. I thought you were dead.' And Dr. Johnson said, 'I did too, at first, but then I knew I wasn't because my feet were cold and I was hungry.' 'Why did you think that meant that you weren't dead?' his friend asked. 'Well,' Dr. Johnson said, 'I knew that if my feet were cold, I could not be in hell, and if I was hungry, I could not be in heaven either.' "

I could not help smiling. "I do not believe that really happened, Lieutenant," I said.

"You have a delightful smile, Miss Little."

I looked at Lieutenant Compton reprovingly, but I did not speak again.

We remained silent then for far longer than I thought acceptable. I was very conscious of May outside the door. What must she be thinking?

"You are in the army, Lieutenant Compton?" I said to break the silence.

"I was, but no longer."

Then another silence descended upon us.

Finally he said, "Is the flower arrangement on the table yours?"

"Yes, it is," I said.

"Very nice."

"Do you like flowers, Lieutenant?" I asked.

"I like rare and beautiful things, Miss Little."

His eyes traveled boldly over me. Then they returned to mine and held them fast. My pulse quickened. I could not look away.

"Would you like to see the garden?" I asked. Somehow I had to get him out of the house—out of May's hearing.

"Very much," he said.

Once we began to walk between the flower beds, I felt more in control of the situation. No one could hear what we said here.

"What is that yellow flower?" he asked.

I did not reply, but continued walking, looking straight ahead of me.

"What is that white one called?" When I did not answer this question either, he said, "You have become meditative. Since you suggested showing me the garden, you might at least tell me about it."

I could stand it no longer. I swung about and faced him squarely. "Lieutenant Compton, why did you come here?"

"Because I think you're the most beautiful girl I have ever seen. I have never seen eyes as blue as yours nor hair with such brilliant lights in it. Nor skin so flawless. Men have always wanted to be with beautiful women, Louisa. That is why I am here."

What reply could I make?

"I am afraid I must be getting back to Aunt Grace," I finally said. "She is an invalid and requires constant care."

I began walking back toward the house then, and Lieutenant Compton walked beside me.

"You care for her?" he asked.

"Yes."

"Is there no one else to help? Your mother?"

"My mother is dead."

"Was she— Did she live near here?"

"No, Aunt Grace and Uncle Andrew brought me here after she died. They are not really my aunt and uncle. They are no blood relation at all. I simply call them that."

"They brought you here? From where?"

By then we had reached the garden gate, and I said, "I really must go now. Good-bye, Lieutenant Compton."

"I will call again tomorrow."

"I'm afraid I'll not be able to see you. Aunt Grace requires all my time, and then I have the flowers to do for the church. So you see, there really won't be any time. Good-bye, Lieutenant."

With that I ran to the kitchen door of the house and stepped inside, leaving him standing there staring after me.

The following day, Saturday, I had begun to arrange the flowers in the vestry of the church, when I heard someone walking through the open door to the south transept. I could see across it to that doorway from the room where I worked, and for a moment as I watched him, Lieutenant Compton paused there, an eerie figure silhouetted against the intense green of the churchyard. Behind him, out among the gravestones, Mr. Collins, the sexton, had begun to dig the grave for Mrs. Aimsley.

Lieutenant Compton saw me, walked to the vestry, and stood in the doorway.

"Hello, Louisa," he said.

"Good afternoon, Lieutenant Compton," I replied.

"Why so formal?" He smiled. "My name is Stuart."

"Very well. Stuart, then."

"I came to offer my services to the parish. If there is anything I can do to help, you have but to command me." He bowed exaggeratedly.

"If that is really why you came, there is a great deal to be done. But the Lord's work lies in the village, not here. Many of our cottagers . . ."

"That would mean leaving your side. So, I confess that is not the real reason I came."

"Oh?"

"I came to see the Compton mausoleum out there in the churchyard. Even more important, I came to see you."

"You found the mausoleum?"

"Yes, I did. And now I've found you. It has been a successful afternoon all around."

I began to strip the leaves from the stalks of the flowers before me.

"What are the pink and white flowers?" he asked.

"Peonies," I said.

"Wonderful fragrance," he murmured, as he came to stand close beside me. He leaned against the table then and lifted one of the blossoms to his nose. "Are all these from your garden?" He gestured to the flowers on the table and those in a pail of water on the floor.

"Some of them, but the peonies and lilies are from Mrs. Malden's garden."

"You are adept at that, aren't you?"

"I've been doing it for many years."

"How many?"

"Six or eight, I don't know."

"Since you came from— Where did you say?"

"I don't believe I did say. Manchester."

We fell silent then, and he watched me work. Finally he said, "Someone has died?"

"Yes, Mrs. Aimsley."

"Fortunate woman."

"Fortunate?"

"To be buried here. My mother wanted to be buried in the churchyard in Ledington—in the mausoleum out there beside her sister."

"And she is not?" I asked.

"My uncle forbade it. Jealous, selfish, vindictive old blackguard. It was a loathsome thing to do. It was little to ask, yet he refused. I hate the ground he walks on. Filthy old bastard."

"That's not true! Lord Bude is the kindest man."

"Is he? Refusing to allow your wife and her sister to be buried in the same mausoleum is kind? It's a huge place. I was just there. There's room for at least twenty more coffins in it."

"There must have been a reason."

"Indeed there was a reason. He never forgave her for not marrying him. That's the kind of man he is—nurturing a grudge all those years." He paused, thinking. Then he said, "But she will lie there one day."

"How?" I asked.

"We shall see."

After a short silence I said, "Then it was your father who was Lord Bude's brother."

"Yes . . . Charles, the youngest son."

"I've never heard him mentioned."

"I should think not! Both he and Uncle William fell in love with my mother, Elizabeth, but she chose my father. So out of pique, Uncle William married Mother's sister, Aunt Anne. They were twins by birth, but Anne was a mere shadow of my mother. Mother was very beautiful. The sisters had always been very close—until after Mother married Father."

"And then they were not?"

"Aunt Anne was also in love with my father."

"Oh. But did they see each other after that?"

"Never, with the exception of one visit. The two couples became entirely estranged. They were separated geographically for some time. My father was in the army also, and was stationed in India. He died there and is buried there. That is why, later, my mother wished to be buried here with her sister instead of lying all alone."

After a while he went on. "Aunt Anne was delicate. Childbirth was especially hard on her. She had two daughters, and both died in infancy. During that time, my mother had me. I was a robust child and a boy, so there was envy there. But then Aunt Anne became pregnant again. This time she was to die because of it. Perhaps she sensed this, because she called for Mother, and Mother went to her."

"And they were reunited?" I asked.

"Yes, I suppose so. It was a very perplexing reunion. Aunt Anne said some . . . She was not in her right mind, probably."

I snipped the last stem to the proper length, stuck it between the flowers, and stood back to observe the finished bouquet.

"Very nice," Stuart said.

"Thank you. Now for the ordinary things," I said, as I poured water into another vase. "I always think of pinks and these cabbage roses as rather commonplace, which is unfair to the poor flowers. But we need some color in the presbytery.

At that moment an enormously fat woman, panting and wheezing, entered the room brandishing a feather duster. She paid no attention to us, but dusted first the row of chairs against the wall and then the paneling above them. Then she brushed her duster across the front of the cabinet in which Uncle Andrew hung his surplices and cassocks and across the tall mirror which he used when he dressed here for services. This seemed to satisfy her as far as the vestry was concerned, and after no more than one minute's work, she walked out into the main body of the church.

Stuart did not take his eyes off her.

"Who is that?" he asked.

"Miss Collins, the sexton's sister," I said.

"Wouldn't you think she would do something about herself? It is positively disgusting! People have no right to inflict their gluttony on others. Revolting!"

"Sh-h-h, she'll hear you."

"Do her good if she does."

"Poor thing. I'm sure she can't help it."

"She certainly can! She can eat less. Gluttony is a sin. And she could bathe. Phew!"

Quickly, to change the subject, I asked, "Has Lyle returned?"

"No, thank God," he replied. "What time is it?" He looked at his watch. "Later than I thought. I must be getting along. Shall I see you in church tomorrow?"

"I attend every service."

"I'll see you there, then."

With that he strode to the other door of the room,

which I had left open. And he disappeared into the church-yard.

By half past four that afternoon I had decided that Lyle had not returned from London. I could not wait for him any longer at the rectory anyway because I had told Aunt Grace I would deliver Nanny Thompson's birthday cake. Nanny Thompson was the oldest person in Ledington: ninety-one years old. She had been Lyle's nanny from the time he was born. Today was her birthday. I walked to Nanny Thompson's cottage, which snuggled beneath its blanket of ivy, wisteria, and clematis at the base of Compton Hill, up the rose-bordered path, and knocked on her door. When my knock was not answered, I knocked again, and when the house remained silent, I pushed open the door and peeped inside. Nanny Thompson sat slumped in a chair on the opposite side of the room staring out the window into her flower garden.

"Nanny Thompson?" I called.

"Oh?" she cried, looking in my direction.

I stepped into the room then and said, "Happy birthday! Aunt Grace has sent a cake!"

"Oh, Miss Little. How good of you to call." She hoisted herself out of her chair then and waddled across the room to me. Taking the basket, she lifted the cloth covering the cake. "Spice? Oh, lovely."

"Yes, with raisins."

"Oh, lovely. I'll put it here and you can take the basket. A lovely spice cake! Umm."

"To wish you happy birthday."

"Lovely," she said once again. She lifted the cake out of the basket and put it in a large, round tin. "Lovely spice cake! Here is your basket. Now sit down. Tea?"

"No, please don't trouble."

Nanny Thompson sank again into her chair and I sat opposite her.

"Have many people called?" I asked.

"No, no. Everyone's forgot. I forgot, myself, until Miss Ormsby— And then *he* called."

"He?"

"He didn't come to wish me happy birthday." She stared at me now with her pale, yellowish eyes. Her head trembled. "Oh, my, no!"

"Who?" I asked.

"Oh, my, no. No, he's found out. He's found out somehow. I don't know how, but he's found out." She sat silently then for a few moments, her poor head bobbing, gazing into the distance. Then she continued, "And questions? Oh, my poor soul, the questions he asked. He had to know all about it—every detail. And what happened to this one, and what happened to that one, and all about everything. Oh, my poor soul, he got me so mixed up. He got me so muddled I didn't know what I was saying half the time. I don't know why he wanted to know all those things. It's all in the past. It's all gone and forgotten about. It's all over and done."

"Who called?"

Nanny Thompson looked at me wide-eyed for a moment. Then she said, "It's made me so tired. It was so terrible. It tired me out."

"Then try not to think about it," I said.

"Oh, I can't. I shall never forget. It comes back in the night sometimes. I hear the poor little scream and then I jump out of bed to go to it, but I can't, of course. And then I see its dear little body all bloody . . . and still . . . and white. Its mouth open as though to cry out again. But it will never make another sound."

She paused, eyes wide.

"Nanny Thompson, please! What is it?"

"The dear little Bainsborough child, of course. It never leaves me be. It cries for me, and when I don't come . . . it never leaves me be!"

"Would it help to talk about it?"

"No! No, it wouldn't help. There is nothing that can ever help." Then she sighed and continued, "Well, it doesn't matter. It was bound to come out. He was bound to find out about it someday. But I am near the end of my road. Oh, yes! It won't be long now, so it doesn't matter."

"Surely not," I said. "Why you're as healthy as anyone in the village."

"But it will come. We are all waiting for it, you know. We're all waiting for the consumption, or the cholera, or the typhoid, or the cancer, or the stroke, or heavens knows what. We are all waiting for it. Every time we feel a little odd, we think, 'Here it is. *It* has come.' Well, why not have it and have done? Hmmm? Why not have it over with and done? Better still, why not end it all now? Then we wouldn't have to wait for it."

"You wouldn't!" I cried.

"No, my dear. No, I wouldn't. But I think about it sometimes, and then things don't seem so bad. Oh, my, no, not so bad at all."

Nanny Thompson looked exhausted, almost ill. "You must be tired." I rose from my chair. "I must go. Enjoy the cake and have many more birthdays. We all love you so."

"Thank you, my dear. But it happened a long time . . ."

I walked softly to the door then, leaving Nanny Thompson gazing out of the window.

Who had called, I wondered. And what dreadful things preyed upon her poor mind? A baby's horrible death? The Bainsborough child, she had said. Lyle would tell me.

But Lyle did not attend church that Sunday morning. Stuart, however, did. As I entered the church, I saw Stuart sitting in the rear directly behind Della Gordon, Thomas Thornton's sister, and her husband and her little boy, Silas —whose unruly behavior was the bane of my existence in Sunday school.

I thought no more about Stuart then because the service began almost as soon as I was seated. It crept along placidly enough until the point at which Uncle Andrew said, "O Lord, open thou our lips."

In the pause that followed this, before the congregation could respond, a voice shouted, "Madam!"

It was Stuart's voice. Every pair of eyes turned then to

look at him. He was clearly visible, even though we were all kneeling. He was such a big man that his head rose above everyone else's.

"Madam!" he repeated, looking at Della. "It is clear that you can not control your brat. I suggest you take him out of the church."

"I'm sorry, sir," Della said, "but there's no one else to take care of him."

"That is no excuse for subjecting others around him to perpetual annoyance. Take him out of here."

"Take yourself out," Della's husband growled, "if you don't like it."

"Then I'll take him out, myself," Stuart said to Mr. Gordon. At this he grabbed Silas by the neck of his jacket and held him in midair. The child was terrified. Stuart's eyes had narrowed to slits and his jaw was clenched. "And I'll give the brat the trouncing he needs."

"Stop it!" Della cried, jumping to her feet. She wrenched Silas away from Stuart and dragged him to the aisle. "Come along, Milton," she said. "I'm going home."

They left the church then, and when they had gone, Uncle Andrew resumed the service, repeating, "O Lord, open thou our lips."

And the congregation answered, "And our mouth shall shew forth thy praise."

"O God, make speed . . ." Uncle Andrew intoned. Morning prayer continued, as though nothing had happened.

After the service the entire congregation stood in groups outside, talking.

"That poor child," Bertha said to me. "Lieutenant Compton has a mean disposition. You know, he almost killed one of the grooms at the Hall yesterday. Really, he almost killed him simply because he was late in saddling a horse. Poor Henry. He is in *bed* with it."

"There must have been more to it than that."

"That's all there was to it. Mr. Keating says he has

been in one fight after another all his life. Making scenes, making trouble, and threatening innocent people with their very lives."

"Threatening whom?" I asked.

"Nellie!"

"Nellie Linton?"

"*Yes!*"

"Why ever should he do that?" I asked, thinking of sweet, shy, little Nellie Linton, who was a chambermaid at Compton Hall.

"He threatened her with her *life!* Lieutenant Compton accused her of stealing one of his ruby cuff links from on top of his chest of drawers. 'I'll slit your throat from ear to ear,' he says, 'if you don't give it to me. My mother gave me those cuff links and I want it back,' he says, grabbing Nellie and practically shaking her to pieces. He almost crushed her to death! And you know Nellie wouldn't steal any more than you or I would."

"Of course she wouldn't," I said.

"And she didn't! The poor girl looked and found the cuff link on the carpet behind Lieutenant Compton's chest of drawers the very next morning and gave it to Mrs. Merrymede, who returned it to Lieutenant Compton. He is a dangerous man! He would *murder* you as soon as look at you."

Then she gasped, "Here he comes! Do you know him? I must go! Come see me tomorrow after you've finished reading."

She dashed away as Stuart approached. "Good morning, Louisa," he called. Then when he stood by my side, he continued, "I apologize for the disturbance, but people can't be allowed to get away with that sort of thing."

"Was it necessary to disrupt the service?" I said.

"Certainly. One must never annoy others or allow one's children to do so."

"What did the child do?"

"He put something down my neck. God only knows what."

"That little devil!"

"Yes. But shall we talk about more pleasant things?"

"What would you like to talk about?"

"About how fortunate I am to find that the most beautiful thing in all the world stands here before me." His eyes bored into mine.

"I am sure you can't be serious."

"I have never been more serious about anything in my life, Louisa. The very lilacs turn their heads in envy."

"There are no lilacs left, Stuart."

"I don't know much about flowers, do I?"

He said nothing more, but looked at me as if to say, "But I know a great deal about women."

At that moment I saw Miss Ormsby disengage herself from the Peterson family and stride toward us. A tall bony woman with glasses, she had a no-nonsense air about her. "Dear Louisa," she called, "isn't it a heavenly day."

"Good morning, Miss Ormsby," I said. "Yes, isn't it." After I had introduced her to Stuart, I said, "Miss Ormsby is one of the pillars of our congregation."

"My dear, how sweet!" Miss Ormsby said. "I have never missed communion in forty years, Lieutenant Compton. Tell me, how is Lord Bude? I understand there were guests at the Hall last week."

"In excellent health, Miss Ormsby. Yes, I believe so," Stuart said.

"A most beautiful young lady and her parents?"

"Yes."

"Americans, I believe."

"Yes."

"Friends of Lord Hartley, I presume."

Stuart did not reply, but managed the ghost of a smile.

"I understand they're very rich."

"Yes. They—I should not mention it, Miss Ormsby," Stuart said. "It must be confidential, you understand."

"Oh, yes, Lieutenant," Miss Ormsby whispered. "I would never breathe a *word*."

"The lady's name is Miss Ting. She is the daughter of

Chang and Wang, the Siamese twins, and their Iroquois Indian bride, Polkahottentot. She has fled America, being suspected of the horrible Trenton murders."

Miss Ormsby's expression turned from awe, to disbelief, to outrage. Turning abruptly to me, she said, "How is your Aunt Grace?"

I hurriedly described Aunt Grace's condition, and then, to my relief, we were rescued by Uncle Andrew.

"Good morning, Rector. I must say I thought your sermon especially fine."

"Thank you, Miss Ormsby. It is most kind of you to say so."

"Dare I make a suggestion, Rector?"

"Certainly, Miss Ormsby."

"A sermon *soon* on Proverbs twelve—particularly verse thirteen."

"Oh?"

"You remember." Miss Ormsby glanced at Stuart as she quoted, " 'A wicked man is snared by the transgression of his lips.' " Then she turned back to Uncle Andrew. "Please tell Grace I shall be in to see her during the afternoon. Perhaps I shall see you later then, Rector. Good-bye, Louisa."

She marched away from us and hurried toward the lane.

"Lieutenant Compton?" Uncle said, extending his hand. He shook Stuart's hand heartily and said, "We had heard you were visiting at the Hall. Please give your uncle my best regards, and say that I was most anxious to know that he is well. I shall be up to see him soon."

"I will do that, Rector," Stuart said. "I apologize for interrupting the service."

"Not at all, my boy. Not at all. 'Discipline your son, and he will give you rest, he will give delight to your heart.' As a matter of fact, you have done us a very great service. We have had a considerable amount of trouble with that Gordon child, especially in the Sunday school. As I said to Louisa, the child should have a thorough thrashing. Discipline, you know."

"Yes, sir."

"Have you been enjoying yourself, Lieutenant?" Uncle Andrew continued. "Been seeing the local sights? Like our church? It is a gem of a church architecturally—a little gem. And the cross—you have seen our cross?"

"I didn't know you had one. I haven't seen a cross in the village."

"Oh, it is not in the village. It is quite hidden—just beyond the meadow there. Follow the footpath through the north wall of the churchyard and you will come to it."

"Perhaps Louisa will be my guide."

"Certainly! Certainly, Lieutenant. I am sure Louisa will be happy to show it to you."

"But Aunt Grace—" I began.

"I shall tell her you have been delayed. She will manage quite nicely. Now, go along and show Lieutenant Compton the cross. I am sure he is anxious to see it." And please do not forget, Lieutenant, to extend my warmest regards to Lord Bude."

Then Uncle Andrew left us. We stood alone now; everyone else had gone.

"Is it hidden in the wood there?" Stuart asked me.

"Yes. Do you really want to see it?"

"Yes."

"Then let's go this way." I began to walk toward the north gate of the churchyard and Stuart walked beside me.

"Why isn't it at the crossroads in the village?" he asked.

"It stood on the village road at one time. The old road once led past it from an ancient bridge across the river, but the bridge collapsed and was never rebuilt; so the road fell into disuse and disappeared. That was hundreds of years ago. Now the cross stands in that grove of cedars beyond the meadow. It's said to be fourteenth or fifteenth century, but Uncle says the head is much later."

"Do you mind showing it to me?"

"I seem to have little choice," I said, smiling at him.

We reached the gate and Stuart held it open for me to pass through.

I walked along the footpath and Stuart walked in the grass beside me.

"I think you were very unkind to Miss Ormsby," I said.

"She was very unkind to *me*—annoying me with her gossipy questions."

"She can't help it. If it were not for her gossip she would have nothing to live for."

"Then it would be better that way."

"Stuart!"

He seemed irritable that morning. Was he? It might have been my imagination, or he might have always acted that way. I did not know him well enough to be sure. But I soon began to feel that he was especially curious about me.

"Are you happy here?" he asked, after we had walked along in silence for some minutes.

"Yes. Why do you ask?"

"It seems a poor life—nursing a sick woman. And, I suppose, taking the place of a rector's wife."

"Well, I'm not unhappy. So I suppose I'm happy."

"Are you glad they brought you here?"

"I don't know what would have happened if they hadn't."

"Was it as bad as that?"

"It was worse. Oh, perhaps I should not say so. I don't remember it all very well. I was not quite six when my mother died."

"And your father?"

"I never had a father. At least I never knew him. My mother never spoke of him. We were very poor. She worked sometimes in the mills in Manchester, but not all the time. We lived in one dingy room after another. We never remained in one place for very long."

"And then your mother died?"

"Yes. An accident at the mill. She left me one morning, and I never saw her again."

"A tragic death."

"Yes."

"But you still possess her in your memory."

"Not really, I'm afraid. I was only six years old at the time."

"But you must remember her—what she looked like."

"No, only dimly if at all. I remember she had dark brown hair and brown eyes. I think she was pretty, but I suppose all children think that about their mothers. I don't remember much else about her."

"Did you go to the funeral?"

"No. Uncle Andrew thought that it would be too much of an ordeal for me. Perhaps he was right."

"Then you have no proof that she died?"

"Proof? But of course she died. If she hadn't, I would still be there with her—and probably working in a mill, myself. Whatever makes you say such a thing?"

"Doesn't it seem strange to you?"

"What is strange?"

"The rector came for you."

"Yes. Uncle Andrew came and asked if I would like to live with him in the country."

"And you said yes."

"No. I didn't want to leave Manchester. Mother wasn't very kind to me, but she was all I had, and I didn't want to leave."

We entered a grove of trees and stood before the cross, an octagonal stone shaft with a vase-shaped stone ornament on top of it.

But Stuart was not looking at the cross. He was looking at me.

"I think that's rather fascinating, don't you?" I asked.

"Something fascinates me more than that," he said.

"Something?" I said, looking up into his eyes.

He slid his arms around me and drew me to him. He clenched me tightly and his mouth seized mine, draining the breath from my body and leaving me weak. When it was over, I leaned against him for a moment, afraid I did not have the strength to stand alone.

He gazed down at me with a rough smile on his face. It was a smile almost of triumph, and at the same time of possession. Then his hand brushed my breast.

I wrenched myself from his grasp. "Is this why you

wanted to see the cross, Stuart?" I said. "Especially when you found it was hidden in a lonely place? I don't like pretense. And I don't like what you have in mind. It makes me feel cheap."

Then I spun around and began walking back along the path toward the meadow. He did not follow.

Chapter Three

IT WAS WRONG, MY LEAVING HIM LIKE THAT.
I had been unjust. It was perfectly natural for Stuart to
want to be alone with me and kiss me. And I had even
wanted him to do just that. But knowing as little about
lovemaking as I did, I had panicked and run away.

Well, what was done was done, and though I could not
put it completely from my mind, Lyle distracted me. He
called at the rectory that afternoon at three o'clock.

"When did you return?" I asked, after we were seated
and I had poured tea.

"In time for dinner last evening. Why do you ask?"

"Then you didn't go to see Nanny Thompson."

"Nanny Thompson? No, why?"

"Well, yesterday was her birthday, and—"

"Good Lord! I forgot all about it."

"She had only two visitors all day, and I was the third.
Poor soul. Everyone seems to have forgotten her. It is
almost as though she were already gone. Aunt Grace sent
a spice cake and I delivered it."

"I'll have to make it up to her," Lyle frowned. "Dear
old Nanny. How *could* I have forgotten? But I wouldn't
have been able to go anyway because I wasn't here. Well,
I'll do something. How is she?"

"Remarkable. You know she is ninety-one."

"I thought her mind was wandering badly the last time
I saw her."

"Do you know anything about a Bainsborough child?"

"The murder, do you mean? Why do you ask?"

"Because Nanny Thompson told me about it."

"Nanny told you about it?" he asked.

"She was much too upset to explain it plainly, but I gather the child died horribly."

"Yes." Lyle paused, deep in thought for a moment. "I—I become incensed everytime I think of the injustice of it. Surely they could have proved her innocent somehow. Nanny Thompson wouldn't hurt a fly!"

"Proved her innocent of what?" I asked.

"She was accused of the murder. You know as well as I do that she wouldn't murder anyone, let alone a two-week-old baby."

"Nanny Thompson was accused of the murder?"

"Yes. She stood trial for it. There was not enough evidence to convict her, but the jury expressed grave doubts as to her innocence, which is absurd. She is the gentlest, kindest soul who ever lived. Her counsel could have done *something*. If they had concentrated on Lady Angela's whereabouts, her motives, questioned the servants, the guests. The house was full of people on that night."

"What exactly happened?" I asked.

"You haven't heard of it? Well, I'm not surprised. It happened shortly before I was born. It seems that Lord and Lady Bainsborough's daughter, Lady Angela, had been having an affair with someone whose identity was never revealed. The affair was kept secret from her parents. When she found herself with child, she disappeared. Evidently she stayed for months with a girlhood friend in the country somewhere, but then when her time came near, she went to one of the hospitals in London which care for penniless women in that condition. The child was to be put out for adoption and Lady Angela was to return home, her reputation untarnished."

"Good heavens! It's like something you might read in a novel."

"Yes. But that is only the beginning. While all this was going on, Lord Bainsborough employed several private detectives to track down his daughter. They found her on the very day she gave birth to her child, a girl. Lord

Bainsborough then collected his daughter and her child and took them home with him. The baby, of course, needed a nanny, so Lady Bainsborough engaged Nanny Thompson. Nanny had excellent references.

"Well, several days after she took up her duties, the child was murdered in its crib in the middle of the night. It had been stabbed and slashed with a kitchen knife, and to spare you all the gruesome details, Nanny Thompson was charged and tried for the murder."

"But who could have done such a thing?" I asked. "And why?"

"Nanny Thompson blamed it on Lady Angela."

"Horrible!"

"After the trial, Nanny would never have gotten another position if Father had not engaged her for me. He is an excellent judge of character, I must say. We were never sorry. Why, Nanny has been like a mother to me. Completely devoted and so kind. You have no idea." Then after a pause while he gazed into my eyes, he said, "I hope I haven't upset you."

"Not at all, Lyle," I said. "But I feel dreadfully sorry for her."

"I wouldn't upset you for anything, Louisa. I know how sensitive you are. Your peace of mind—your happiness—means everything to me, I'd do anything to increase it."

"Thank you, Lyle."

"Now, I have a favor to ask."

"Name it."

"Will you play for me?"

"Certainly. What would you like?"

"The Beethoven that I did not hear the other evening."

"Very well," I said, smiling at him.

His eyes devoured me while I played.

"I am afraid that was not very good," I said, when I had finished.

"Beautiful!" he exclaimed. "Sheer enchantment. You play like an angel."

"I don't believe angels play the piano."

"There is one angel who does."

I could not meet the intensity in his eyes. It confused me.

"What are these?" Lyle asked, picking up a book of Chopin Nocturnes from the music rack. "Do you play this?"

He held the book open for me to see the page. It was the Opus 27, No. 2.

"I don't know it by heart."

"Then I will turn the pages for you."

"Do you play?" I asked him.

"No."

"But you read music."

"No, I don't do that either."

"Then how could you turn the pages for me? How would you know when?" I asked, smiling up at him.

"Simply nod and I will turn then," he said with a grin.

"Very well, but do not expect a polished performance."

I began to play, and when I reached the bottom of the second page of the music, I glanced up at Lyle and nodded. He was watching me intently. At my signal he quickly stepped nearer, bent, and deftly flipped the page. I smiled my thanks at him then, but instead of straightening up, he bent still further, grasped my chin gently in his hand, and kissed me.

It was a long kiss, and when he finally released me, I gazed at him, too astonished to move.

"You see how I lose self-control? I didn't mean to do that. It was a compulsion. I can't resist you when—"

Again he tilted my face to his and kissed me lingeringly.

"Lyle, I—" I began, when he released me. But then I noticed a bit of black fabric at the edge of the drawing room doorway. "Excuse me a moment."

I jumped up, ran on tiptoe through the doorway into the corridor, and stood facing a very startled May. She backed slowly away from me as I continued to walk toward her.

"You were listening!" I whispered.

"I was not!" she hissed.

"You were! I will not have you spying on me like this, May. I forbid it! If it happens again, I'll speak to Aunt Grace and have you sacked. I simply will not tolerate it!"

"I was on my way to dust Mr. Cuttlebuck's study, miss."

"You know perfectly well that the rector works in his study on Sunday afternoons and is never to be disturbed."

In answer to this, May gave me a poisonous look, and without another word, she whirled about and marched toward the kitchen.

"I'm awfully sorry, Lyle," I said, when I returned to the drawing room. "If there is something I can't bear, it is being spied upon."

"Quite right, Louisa. One can't be too strict about that. That must be a problem you face more than anyone else."

"I can't see why that should be so."

"Ah," he said, flashing that thrilling smile at me and nodding his head as he did so. "I can see why. I can see it only too clearly."

I could not help laughing at this, not so much because I found his remark amusing, but because I was so happy.

"Shall we walk in the garden for a bit before I leave you?" he asked.

There Lyle encouraged me to talk about myself. I told him about my childhood in Manchester and about Mother, what I could remember about her, and how wonderfully it had all turned out. Finally we sat down together on a bench against the garden wall in the shade of an ancient yew. From there we could not be seen from the house or stables.

Now, like a planet moving inexorably through the heavens, his face approached mine. My head tilted and my lips parted to receive his. Then he locked his mouth to mine and crushed me to him in an endless kiss.

When it was over, he stared deep into my eyes for a long time before he spoke. I silently returned his gaze.

"I must go away again for a few days," he said at last.

"Must you go?" I murmured.

"Yes!" Suddenly his eyes blazed with excitement. He drew a gold cigarette case from his pocket, quickly withdrew a cigarette, and lit it. "It's a marvelous opportunity.

I can't let it go by. The Duke and Duchess of Lees are entertaining a group of Americans and among them will be John D. Rockefeller. Rockefeller! And Lord Charles, who was my friend at Cambridge, has asked me down."

"But what is so wonderful about meeting Mr. Rockefeller?"

"I'll tell you one day, but not now. Now I must go."

He kissed me again, quickly this time, and then he rose to leave.

I spent the remainder of the day awash in conflicting desires. Stuart and Lyle were so different.

I knew something dreadful had happened when I saw Miss Ormsby running toward the rectory the following morning. At about eleven o'clock, I looked out toward the lane and saw her dash up the walk.

I ran to the door and opened it.

"She's dead! She's been murdered!" Miss Ormsby cried. She paused, but only for a moment, to catch her breath and watch my reaction. Then she hurried on. "Strangled in her cottage—in her chair, by the fire. *I* found her. Oh, it was horrible. Horrible! The expression on her face and those ghastly black bruises on her throat. So white and stiff and cold." She shivered. "I must tell Grace." Miss Ormsby brushed past me then and dashed down the corridor crying, "Grace! Grace!"

She flew up the stairs, and I followed.

"Grace! Grace!" she cried as she ran into Aunt's room. "Oh, it was horrible. Horrible! Dead and cold—strangled in her own chair. *I* found her. Why I should have to be the one, I cannot imagine ..."

"For God's sake, Dorothy," Aunt Grace shouted. "Who's been murdered?"

"Nanny Thompson! I shall never get over the shock. I found her this morning. She is dead. *Murdered!*"

"Nonsense!" Aunt Grace stated flatly.

"I immediately went and got Constable Westley and *he* said it was murder. And then I went for Doctor Car-

michael, and he said she'd been dead since Saturday night
sometime. She was sprawled out in—"

"Be calm, Dorothy!" Aunt Grace snapped. "What *happened?*"

"Well," Miss Ormsby said, "I was passing her cottage
early this morning on my way to the post office to mail a
letter to Agatha Crowley. Nanny Thompson wasn't there!
You know she is always in her garden in the morning
before the sun gets high. And she wasn't there yesterday
either when I passed before church. So I thought I'd just
look in and see if she was all right. Suppose she was ill
and suffering? And there she was sprawled in her chair by
the fireplace—the rug under her feet all askew and in a
bunch, and her arms flung out as if calling on God himself for help, and her expression: Her dead eyes wide
open, about to pop from her head. Oh, I wish I could
describe it. It was as though the pain was too intense to
bear. Horrible! Dead and cold. And those ghastly black
bruises all over her throat. Strangled! Someone's strangled
her with his bare hands—that's what Constable Westley
said. And there she's sat since Saturday night. Murdered
in her own cottage."

"I can't believe it," Aunt Grace said.

"It's true!" Miss Ormsby said. "I tell you, I saw her
with my own eyes. I found her. And then I went and got
Constable Westley, and . . ."

"Yes, yes," Aunt Grace said. "What did the constable
say?"

"He said she was murdered. It was a marauder or a gypsy
or someone."

"Why did he think that?" I asked.

"Because the window was open and Nanny Thompson's
peonies were all trampled down and there were footprints
—*big* footprints in the ground."

"Someone came in through the window?" I asked.

"Yes, and strangled her," Miss Ormsby said.

"Why should anyone do that?" Aunt Grace asked.

"To rob her, of course," Miss Ormsby said.

"Why should anyone want to rob Nanny Thompson?" I said. "She had nothing worth stealing. And even if they wanted to rob her, why didn't they walk in through the door? She never locked it."

"Yes, but a stranger would not know that," Miss Ormsby said triumphantly.

By afternoon I suppose everyone in Ledington had heard about the murder.

When I asked Keating about his rheumatism that afternoon, he answered, "It is very bad—very painful—especially with the rain. But one must count his blessings, miss. It would seem that one is fortunate, these days, to be left alive at all."

"You have heard about Nanny Thompson, then?" I asked.

"Indeed so, miss. To think that such a thing should occur right here among us in Ledington. I am sure I don't know what the world is coming to, miss."

And when he announced me to Lord Bude, Lord Bude said, "Come in, Miss Little. Come in. Terrible day. Wretched! Wondered if you would come at all."

"Good afternoon, Lord Bude," I said. "Because of Nanny Thompson, do you mean?"

"Yes," Lord Bude said, gazing out the window. I waited for him to speak. Then he sighed and said almost to himself, "I cannot believe it." He shook his head. "No."

"None of us can," I said. "She was such a gentle, *good* person."

"Yes. Well, let's get on with it," Lord Bude said, turning to me and scowling.

"She was talking about dying only that afternoon. Isn't that strange?"

"You saw her?"

"Yes. It was her birthday and Aunt Grace sent a cake."

"Yes, well—"

"The poor dear must have felt forgotten. Only three people came to call, and one of them only wanted to find out about the trial. I wish her last day—"

"The Bainsborough trial?" Lord Bude interrupted.

"Yes."

"After all these years? Who was it?"

"She didn't say. I asked her, but she never answered me. She said he, whoever it was, wanted to know *all* about it. She kept saying: 'He's found out. He's found out.' And then she said, 'Well, it was bound to come out sooner or later.'"

After we had exhausted the subject of poor Nanny Thompson, I read awhile and then it was time for me to leave.

I went to find Bertha. "Have you heard?" she asked, staring at me pop-eyed.

"Oh, Bertha—it makes me so unhappy. Why? Why to poor old Nanny Thompson? And on her birthday!"

"Your Lieutenant Compton didn't help."

"What do you mean? And why do you say *my* Lieutenant Compton?"

"I saw the way you hurried out to him after church on Sunday. And everyone saw you talking and talking to him."

"That doesn't make him *my* Lieutenant Compton. And what do you mean he didn't help?"

"Nanny Thompson came here on Saturday night."

"Here to the Hall?"

"Yes."

"Nanny Thompson has not left the village in years. How would she get here?"

"She was as spry as could be. She was always working in her garden. She walked up here. I saw them myself, standing on the drive together as big as life. And—" Bertha pursed her lips and raised her eyebrows.

"And?" I asked impatiently.

"He was being cruel to her."

"What did he say?"

"Oh, I couldn't hear what they said. I saw them from the landing window. He was saying mean and nasty things to her all right. But Nanny Thompson wouldn't take that from him. She was furious. At one point she started to stamp toward the house, but something he said stopped her, and she went back to him and they had more words. And there she was, flailing her arms around, wringing her hands, and shaking her head till I thought she'd shake her hat off. I hope she told him off good and proper."

"Well, she was a little . . . strange at times. I suppose she came to see Lord Bude."

"His old lordship was not at home on Saturday night. He was dining with Lady Hatchfield at Hatchfield House."

"Oh?"

"Yes. But his young lordship *was* at home."

"Why do you say it like that?" I asked.

"Because after Nanny Thompson stalked off down the drive, Lieutenant Compton came into the house and he was met by his young lordship in the vestibule. There wasn't anyone else there then. I couldn't hear what they said at first because I had to go up to the hall or they would have seen me."

"Bertha! You are shameless!"

"Louisa, when you are in service, you have got to protect yourself from what people say. Everybody's always talking and you've got to protect yourself from what they're saying or you're liable to find yourself sacked for something you didn't do. You must always know what's going on."

"Couldn't you hear anything they said?" I asked.

"Now who's being shameless? No, they were talking too low. But then they started to argue. I could hear every word from then on, let me tell you."

"What about?"

"About Lieutenant Compton's leaving the Hall. Lieutenant Compton said some awful things to his young lordship, and his young lordship was so nice. He simply explained how his lordship has not been well and how Lieutenant Compton had upset him. He said it would be better if Lieutenant Compton could return at some future time, when his father had recovered."

"What did Stuart say?" I asked.

"Oh, it's 'Stuart' is it?"

"Yes."

"Well, he said some terrible things. How his young lordship was a liar and a bloody hypocrite in the bargain, and how it made his flesh crawl to stay under the same roof with him, and I don't know what all names he called him. It was dreadful! And then Lieutenant Compton says that he'll be so glad to leave he can't wait to get out. Well, I can tell you, we all breathed a sigh of relief when he went!"

"Stuart's gone?"

"Yes. He left at about two o'clock yesterday."

Well, I thought as I walked down the hill, I shall not see Stuart again. He had known, then, that he would be leaving on Sunday afternoon. He had known that when he kissed me. Yet he had not said good-bye. Would he have said something if I had not been so abrupt?

Nanny Thompson was buried from the church on Wednesday morning. Almost everyone in Ledington was there. Nanny Thompson would have liked that. The sun shone in a cloudless sky, almost as if God were saying that nothing had impeded her soul in its flight to heaven. The air was cool and sweet, as they lowered her coffin into the ground, and perfumed by the roses that grew in the churchyard. Nanny Thompson would have liked that, too.

After it was all over, I picked a bunch of pink China roses, her favorites, and laid them on her grave, whispering good-bye.

"Come in, come in," Lord Bude called from his usual chair. "You are late, Miss Little. That will be all, thank you, Keating."

"Oh, I don't think so, Lord Bude. I believe I heard the clock on the landing strike two just a moment ago."

"Humph. Miss Little, I am a very busy man. I do not have time to waste in waiting for people. It is very kind of you to come up here and read to me, but I must insist that we begin on time."

He reached down into the crevice formed by the upholstery of his easy chair and its cushion and drew out a small package wrapped in white tissue paper.

"This may facilitate a greater degree of promptness," he said, as he thrust the package at me. "When is your birthday?"

"I—I don't know, Lord Bude. Aunt and Uncle and I have always celebrated it on Holy Cross day, but even they don't—"

"Since you don't know, we will consider this a birthday present."

"Why, thank you, Lord—"

"Open it!"

I sat down in the chair opposite him, which I always used, and removed the ribbon and paper from a thin black velvet box. I was so surprised by all this that I continued to stare at the box in wonder.

"Well, open it!" Lord Bude commanded.

I obeyed. And there in the satin lining of the box lay a rectangular, white-gold wristwatch. Its band was a filigree of white gold, and on either side of the watch face were two triangular sapphires.

"Lord Bude! It's beautiful!" I cried. Impulsively then, clutching the watch, I darted over and kissed him on the forehead. "How can I thank you? I have always wanted a watch of my own. It is the loveliest—"

"Miss Little! That is quite enough! I did not anticipate a mawkish display. Now, get on with it."

"May I wear it?" I asked.

"If you must."

I removed the watch from its box and fastened it about my wrist. Then I took Mr. Boswell's book from the shelf, resumed my seat, and began to read.

Lord Bude interrupted me only once, I believe, during those next two hours. This was to ask me to reread something. Then as four o'clock approached I came to a conversation between Dr. Burney and Mr. Johnson. " 'The morality of an action,' " I read, " 'depends on the motive from which we act . . .' "

"Exactly!" Lord Bude cried.

"I beg your pardon?"

"Exactly! That is just what *I* have always said. It is the *motive* behind the act that determines the right or wrong of it. Nothing is absolute. Don't you agree?"

"No, I don't think so, not exactly. Murder, for instance. I can't imagine murder being moral, or there being a good motive for murder."

"Of course there could. Suppose someone suffered abominably from a disease which could only kill him. Horrible suffering! Would I not be justified in helping that man to a painless peace? I would not mean any harm in this." Lord Bude paced the floor. "We execute criminals. Isn't that correct? And what about war? Those filthy Krauts. Kill them all, I say. Filthy swine!"

I had never seen him so upset. This reminded me of what Lyle had said—that his father had been acting peculiarly of late.

"Well, what else?" Lord Bude went on. "Stealing? I am all alone—no money, not a penny. Children. Lots of children. Cold! Hungry! Steal a loaf of bread to feed my starving children. Is that bad? They would starve if I didn't. Starve or steal, which? *Steal*, of course. Perfectly right!"

There seemed to be something behind all this, and his problem, whatever it might be, was evidently very important to him. He paced back and forth before me wrestling with it—asking himself questions and answering them in a loud voice. I did not know what to do. There seemed to be nothing *to* do.

"Lie?" he continued. "Of course, if one meant no harm. Tell a poor wife she is dying of some terrible disease? Tell her she will suffer the pain of the damned?"

At that moment someone knocked on the library door.

"Yes? What is it?" Lord Bude called.

Keating opened the door.

"Is everything all right, my lord?" Keating asked. "I heard loud voices and I— And Major Seaton-Smith is below in the loggia, inquiring if your lordship is at home."

"A question of ethics!" Lord Bude said. "Miss Little and I were discussing a question of ethics. But I have lost track of my argument now. Well, no matter. It is after four. I think that will do, Miss Little. Thank you."

"Shall I come again on Monday, Lord Bude?"

"Yes, yes. As usual, as usual."

"Thank you for my present."

"Yes, yes. Good day, Miss Little. Good day."

I left Lord Bude then. I wished that Lyle might be waiting for me, but he wasn't.

I was all the more surprised, then, when I returned to the rectory and found him sitting near Aunt Grace's bedside.

Lyle rose as I entered the room and said, "Hello, Louisa."

"Hello, Lyle," I said. "Are you feeling well, Aunt Grace? Is there anything I can get you?"

"No, my dear," she said. "See the beautiful grapes Lord Hartley was kind enough to bring me." She pointed to a shallow basket of huge, yellow grapes, which sat on her bedside table.

"They're lovely," I said to Lyle. "This is a pleasant surprise! When did you return? And was your visit a pleasant one?"

"Yesterday evening," he said. "It was most enjoyable— most interesting and instructive."

"And did you meet Mr. Rockefeller?"

"Indeed I did. Extraordinary man! I think he is the shrewdest fox I have ever met. One look and he knows all about you. Those eyes of his see straight through you. And his mind works like lightning. Why, the Duke was telling him at dinner one night about some drainage problems on one of his farms in Kent. Well, after three questions, Mr. Rockefeller had analyzed the situation entirely and was able to advise him."

"Did Lyle tell you he spent a few days at Eversham Palace?" I asked Aunt Grace.

"It was quite a large party," Lyle said. "Forty of us, I suppose. Even so, we rattled about the place—enormous labyrinth. We were always getting lost in it and having to ask a footman the way."

"That must have been very amusing," Aunt Grace said.

"Oh, yes. I will tell you all about it one day, but now I must go and let you have your nap. I've stayed far too long, but it's been such a pleasant visit that I haven't been able to tear myself away. I can't tell you how I've enjoyed seeing you."

"I have found it equally delightful, Lord Hartley. However, I do tire easily. I seem to have no reserve at all. Yes, I will nap a little now. I shall have pleasant dreams, I know. Walk with Lord Hartley to his car, Louisa. I will lie back and rest awhile. But look in on me when you return to the house."

Lyle and I walked downstairs.

"I suppose you've heard about Nanny Thompson," I said, after we had entered the drawing room and settled ourselves.

"Yes." Lyle looked down at the carpet and stared at it for some moments. When he finally looked up, I thought I saw tears in his eyes. "And I didn't even wish her happy birthday," he murmured.

"But you would have. It simply escaped your mind. And you weren't here. You would have made it up to her."

"But now I can't, can I? We should never put things off, you know."

"But you didn't have the opportunity."

"How kind you are, Louisa." He gazed deeply into my eyes. After a moment he continued, "I came home as soon as I read about it in the newspapers. I wanted to have a word with Constable Westley."

"What did he say?"

"Nothing. There was nothing except one or two footprints. That's not much to go on. Inspector Greg was over, of course, but what could he do? It was a passing vagrant or . . . Well, we shall probably never know. The coroner has dispensed with the inquest, and I suppose the whole thing will be dropped. But it was so *beastly* unfair—so senseless. However—there is really nothing we can do about things like that. We must simply make the most of what we have."

He smiled at me. "I've missed you terribly. You were always in my thoughts while I was away. Suddenly there you would be in my mind—in the midst of dinner, or during billiards, or while we rode out in the afternoon, or at night as I tossed and turned in bed. There you were and I thought, What am I doing *here*? I want to be with Louisa. I want to reach out and take her hand." He took my hand. "Like this. And put my arms around her. Like this." He embraced me. "And . . ." Then he kissed me tenderly on the mouth.

Soon we left the house, and as we sauntered across the lawn toward his car, Lyle said, "I have something to ask you."

"Yes?"

"I am giving a dinner party at the Hall on the tenth. Lord and Lady Charles will be down for the weekend. Thank heaven his father and mother have a previous engagement. Lord Charles is bringing one or two of the Americans I met at Eversham Palace. And several friends will be down from London. Unfortunately, Father disapproves. Rather the wrong set, he feels. And then they are all quite young. You know how older people are. I'm afraid he has decided to isolate himself in his room again during the weekend."

"What can I do?"

"Will you come to dinner at the Hall that evening? You will like my friends. I know you will."

"Thank you, Lyle, but . . ."

"I've asked Mrs. Cuttlebuck for permission. I know how much she depends on you, so I wanted to be sure she could get along without you for the evening. She said yes."

"I'm afraid I couldn't, Lyle. I have nothing appropriate to wear. I'd be terribly embarrassed. Thank you so much, though."

Lyle smiled down at me. Perhaps you can manage something. Don't decide now. Think it over first and let me know later."

By that time we had reached the car. He got in and drove off, waving to me as he turned into the lane.

After he had gone, I walked back to the house and stopped at the door of Aunt Grace's room. "Can I get you anything?" I asked, when I saw that she was not sleeping.

"No, my dear. Come in and talk to me. I can't seem to sleep—too much excitement in the air."

"Is there excitement in the air?" I asked, as I sat down near her bed.

Aunt Grace examined me for a moment. "Lord Hartley is *definitely* interested in you."

"How do you know that?"

"I could tell by some of the things he said. I think it is only a matter of time."

"What is?"

"Until he asks you to marry him."

"Don't you think that's premature? Why, he hardly knows me. And you said yourself that I have no background—no family. Why should he want to marry *me*? No, I think he is probably—just amusing himself."

"Do not take his attentions lightly, Louisa. He is very serious indeed."

"What have you said to him, and what has *he* said to you?"

"Nothing. But I have lived a great deal longer than you, Louisa, and I know. One does not invite a young lady to a dinner party at the Hall to meet one's closest friends for no reason at all."

"Nor does one refuse for no reason at all."

"You refused? Louisa, whatever—?"

"You know perfectly well I have nothing to wear. Why, I would be embarrassed to death."

"Oh, dear, I wish you had talked to me first."

"Why?"

"I think you should have a new evening dress made and a new riding habit, too—just in case you should be asked to go riding during the weekend. Madame Prieur could do them in time, and we will tell Lord Hartley that you have reconsidered."

"But that would cost a fortune."

"We could manage."

"Aunt Grace! It was only yesterday that you were saying that we must cut down. And now you are saying that I should not only have a new dress, but a new habit as well? I can't tell you how much I appreciate it, but I couldn't let you. Why, Madame Prieur's dresses cost a *fortune*."

"I know my dear, but—well, things have changed a bit. We can afford it quite nicely now. Tomorrow afternoon, about three o'clock, Patrick will drive you . . ."

"What has happened, Aunt Grace, that you can suddenly afford to spend all that money?"

"Mr. Cuttlebuck has come into a bit of good fortune."

"How?"

"Well, if you must know, Lord Hartley has very kindly agreed to increase the endowment. So, the annual stipend for the rector will be increased accordingly."

"How can Lyle increase the endowment?"

"After his father dies."

"But that hardly enables you to buy expensive dresses *now*."

"No, but he has kindly agreed to make a sizable contribution until his father dies."

"Providing, I suppose, that you buy me expensive dresses?"

"It has nothing to do with buying you dresses, Louisa. Lord Hartley simply realizes that it is difficult to get along as things are now. He appreciates the valuable work Mr. Cuttlebuck is doing in the parish, and he wishes to express his gratitude. It just happens that this will make it possible for you to have a new dress. I hardly expected you to object."

"It is not the dress, Aunt Grace, it is the fact that Lyle would be buying it for me."

"Oh, Louisa, you are being positively Victorian. These are modern times. We must be liberal in our—"

"Like allowing me to have a shingle?"

"Louisa! You know how Mr. Cuttlebuck feels about that. The bob was indecent. This—this latest is unmentionable. I suppose if current fashion demanded that you parade about naked, you would wish to do it? God did not give us hair to be shorn entirely away.

"And anyway, what about your horse and your gold watch? They were gifts from Lord Hartley's father."

"Samantha and the watch are different. Oh, there's nothing really *wrong* with his buying me a dress. But it's embarrassing."

"You are taking it all much too seriously, Louisa. There is *no* connection between Lord Hartley's token of appreciation to Mr. Cuttlebuck and the dresses *we* wish to buy for you. And heaven only knows you need clothes. Now, we will say no more about it. You will go into Bridgehampton tomorrow afternoon shortly after three and see Madame Prieur. Patrick will drive you. And tell Lord Hartley that you have reconsidered."

But it was not Patrick who drove me, after all. Lyle appeared just as I was getting ready to leave. He insisted on driving me.

Madame Prieur showed us countless clippings from magazines and drawings of her own designs. When I asked her to recommend a design, she was so pleased that she brought out a sketchpad and rapidly began to draw a picture.

"It should be cut very straight, like so," she said, as her hand flew across the paper. "Sleeveless, of course, low vee-shaped neckline, and the skirt just below the knee, like so, with a scalloped hemline dipping to the back. Now the material—" She stalked into another room at the rear of her shop and returned with a bolt of gorgeous silk crepe of the palest gray-green shade. Holding a fold of it against me, she said. "To bring out your color, *n'est-ce pas?* And for the decoration—" She set the material down and went back to her sketch. "Gold and silver sequins about the neck, waist, and hemline in a scalloped design with curlicues and swirls. *Voilà!*"

"Marvelous!" I cried. "Oh, yes—it is going to be lovely. Don't you think so, Lyle?"

"Very beautiful indeed, Madame Prieur," he said.

After that she and I decided on a habit of navy blue Saxony cloth. Then Madame Prieur led me into another room where she took my measurements and asked me to return the following Tuesday for fittings.

Yet another surprise was in store for me. Lyle asked me to go riding with him the next day.

Chapter Four

HE ARRIVED AT THE RECTORY ON HORSEBACK at about three o'clock. It was a delightful ride. We rested for a while at a ruined castle, sitting side by side on a low wall and looking out across the valley, and then we returned, following a track along a stream that led eventually to the base of Compton Hill.

"Aren't you thirsty?" Lyle asked, as we walked our horses. "I am. Shall we stop at the Hall for something to drink? I don't think I could go on without it."

After we had left our horses at the stables, Lyle led me toward the gardens and across the lawn to the rosery. In the center of the rosery stood a bower—a tiny, airy pavilion of metal rods and wire mesh covered entirely with climbing roses. Beneath its dome-shaped roof a footman had already begun laying a white cloth over a table which stood between two rustic chairs.

"What a charming idea," I exclaimed. "You planned this in advance," I smiled at him.

"You like it?"

"It's marvelous!"

By the time we reached the bower, the table was set. And we were no sooner seated than John arrived with the tray. He placed a huge pitcher of lemonade on the table between us, and plates of little sandwiches and iced cakes, and a pot of tea.

"Thank you, Arthur and John," Lord Hartley said. "That will be all, I think." Then as the footmen walked away toward the house, he said to me, "My mother liked lemonade served to her here in the afternoon, sometimes, I understand. That was before I was born, of course. In those days Keating would have served us himself, but he is almost lame with his rheumatism, poor man."

"Yes," I replied, "I feel so sorry for him."

I had no sooner poured his glass than he gulped it down and, grinning, held it out for more.

"You *are* thirsty. So am I." Then when I had poured more lemonade for him and drunk some of my own, and we had helped ourselves to sandwiches, I sighed, "This is heavenly. The garden is a picture. I've never seen such a profusion of roses. That's the maze, isn't it?" I asked, gazing across the lawn. "Do you ever go into it?"

"Not since I was a child. Once I learned its secret, it ceased to amuse me."

"What secret?"

"How to reach the center of it. There is a little marble pavilion there. You can just see the gold ball on its roof rising above the hedges. See it?"

"Yes. What is the secret?"

"One always turns first to the right and then to the left, to the right and then to the left, and so forth. There are four entrances—one on the north, one on the east, one on the south, and one on the west. But no matter which entrance one uses, the formula always works."

"How very clever. It must keep the gardeners constantly busy clipping the hedges inside it. And I suppose they must be especially careful in clipping the figures in front of it. They're called topiary figures, aren't they? One would hardly know they are made of growing yew."

"The maze and the figures were designed by Lancelot Brown in 1750. They are kept exactly as he planned them. All the figures are about to enter the maze, you see."

"They are lovely. Let me see, a lion, an elephant— What is the low shape?"

"A hippopotamus," Lyle said, laughing, "of all things. He was always my favorite."

"And an ox, cart and driver. And three ladies, one with a parasol. And a kneeling camel?"

"Yes, and a bear and a knight on horseback."

"It's like magic—all of this." I gestured to the gardens and the distant glass houses. "And Compton Hall is so beautiful. Not only beautiful, but so full of tradition. It's like a—well, like a great, warm-hearted nanny whose arms you long to have wrapped around you. Do you know what I mean? It must make you very happy."

"You are a romantic, Louisa. It is a fine enough house, as far as it goes, and I shall keep it, at least for a while, but it's nothing extraordinary, you know."

"But you couldn't think of selling it!"

"Why not? Eventually, but not just yet. The acreage yes, but I shall keep the house and the land around it. After all, the eighth Earl of Bude must have a seat in the English countryside. It would be expected of him. And Compton Hall will do until I can build something more impressive."

"*More impressive?* How could you ask for anything more impressive than this? It's positively breathtaking."

"It may seem that way to you, Louisa, but you would not think so if you had seen Eversham Palace, or Blenheim, or Castle Howard, or Hampton Court. No, Compton Hall is merely . . . adequate."

"But you couldn't build anything bigger—not these days."

"No, not in our present circumstances. After taxes, the estates bring in enough to live on in relative comfort and sustain the London house. One does not *want* for anything, and there is still something left over. What you might call a moderate income."

"What more could one want? Will you have tea?"

"Yes, please. I could want a great deal more."

"But you must already have more than almost anyone in England. And you certainly couldn't build another Blenheim."

"Wouldn't is the word." Lyle laughed. "No, not another Blenheim, thank heaven. Horrible, cold, drafty place." He became serious then as he regarded me. "I do not have very much at all, Louisa. Shall I tell you what I want?"

I returned his gaze, but I did not speak.

"I want a large house in Palm Beach and one in New-

port in the States. I want a villa in the south of France—
Antibes, I think. I want a house in Paris as well as our
house here in London. And I want to build the largest
palace in England! In the countryside. In the Gothic style
with an enormous tower." Now his eyes narrowed, and he
said, "I want to be, not only one of the richest men in
England, but one of the richest men in the entire world."

I simply stared at him in astonishment.

"Do you think I'm crazy?" he said. He grinned at me
now. "It is perfectly possible—if one has capital to invest.
But not here in England."

"Where then?" I asked.

"In the States. That is where fortunes are being made.
Men like Rockefeller, Ford, Baker, Livermore. Manufac-
turing, steel, shipping. Wall Street! That is where it's
done."

"Is that why you wanted to meet Mr. Rockefeller?"

"Yes. He told me that I must come and see him when I
get to New York. And Mr. Livermore said the same. Why,
with connections like that—one or two words from men
like that— Buy this, sell that. That is all there is to it. That
is, *if* you have the money to start with."

"That is why you want to sell . . ."

"The farms. Exactly!"

"It seems such a pity," I said.

"What does?" he asked.

"To—to destroy something that has been a unit and so
much a part of the family for, I suppose, hundreds of years."

"Since 1554. That was when Thomas Compton was
created Baron of Ponteford, Viscount Hartley, and Earl of
Bude. He earned it. He was Ambassador to France, Lord
High Admiral in Wyatt's rebellion, Lord Privy Seal, and
to him, more than to any other Englishman, Elizabeth
owed her life and throne. He earned his grant. Someone
had to begin it. Is it so wrong, then, that *I* should want to
begin something—something far more valuable—for my
son? Imagine what the ninth Earl of Bude will inherit
when I die. Imagine what *I* shall create for him, and his
heir, and his heir's heir. Is that wrong?"

"No. How could it be?" I wondered aloud. "Still, it seems so . . . nearly perfect as it is." Again I gazed across the rosery and the lawn to the house, lost in this lovely world.

"Have you seen it from the lake?"

"No."

"We could walk there before we return to the stables. It's quite picturesque reflected in the water. Do you have time? It would only take another ten minutes or so."

"I'd love to. I do have to arrange the flowers for the service tomorrow, but there will still be time enough."

We left the bower then and walked through the rosery and down a gravel walk beside a high, clipped hawthorn hedge. At the left the hedge became a stone wall. Presently we stood looking through an arched opening in the wall where a flight of steps led down to the lake, actually a large pond flecked here and there with pink, white, and yellow water lilies. Amid the lilies Compton Hall lay perfectly reflected in the water.

"Beautiful!" I murmured.

"I believe you have fallen in love with it," Lyle said.

"I have."

"Then we will keep it—as a sort of dower house, perhaps. Would you like that?"

"Yes, but what . . ."

"Father is anxious for me to marry. He would like to see his grandchild before he dies." We began to walk back along the wall toward the stables. "As I plan things, my wife will be one of the wealthiest, most envied women in the world."

He paused now, turned, and gazed at me with his beautiful dark eyes. Instinctively I withdrew a step and found myself standing against a tangle of fragrant honeysuckle and white clematis covering the wall.

"I think you are the loveliest thing I have ever seen," Lyle said simply. He placed two fingers lightly on my cheek and drew them slowly down the side of my face. "Skin so smooth, and warm, and . . . glowing."

His fingers came to rest on my throat. His other arm

slid around me, and slowly he pulled me to him. Then he bent his head and kissed me. And I returned his kiss. I wrapped my arms around him and yielded myself to his affection, his protection, his care. I am safe here, I thought, shielded from unpleasant things. And I am happy. I give myself to this man.

But then I thought of Stuart. Why, I did not know. In that fleeting instant I knew I would give myself to him too, if he asked me! Why was everything so terribly complicated and sad?

"Why do you look so sad?" Lyle asked, when he had finished kissing me.

"Not sad," I said. "Serious."

"Serious in a happy way?"

"Yes," I lied, smiling up at him.

On Monday I read to Lord Bude again, and his remarks that day were to make me wonder still more about whatever mystery lay in the Hall's past. He asked that we begin one of Lord Lynston's novels. I thought Lynston terribly old-fashioned. But we selected *The Prodigal*.

I came to the part that begins:

> "God bless me!" cried Rosedale, with an air of vexation. "You can not mean what you say. My sister? She is but a child and as pure as the snow. You cad! You are not worthy of entering the same room with her."
>
> "But I have changed, Rosedale," cried Dawton. "The glory of her goodness has purified me. Forsooth, I have thrown off my evil ways. I have cast away my greed and hatred and embraced love for all men. Ah, my poor stepfather—how I have wronged him. But I shall atone for failing him and for all the callous things I have done to others."
>
> "Can such a thing be?" Rosedale . . .

"Rubbish!" Lord Bude said.

"I beg your pardon?" I asked.

"I said, rubbish! People don't change like that."

"But he is in love," I said.

"Never mind. He was born of—a low person in the worst part of Liverpool. Wasn't he? And then he was adopted by Lord Brierwood, wasn't he? Saint of a man—loving father! Harrow and Cambridge—did they change him? Look how he turned out—a wastrel, scoundrel, blackguard."

"But surely you do not think that simply because his mother was a poor woman in—"

"She was a strumpet!"

"Well, but that does not necessarily mean he—"

"That is exactly what it *does* mean. Low persons breed low persons. Nothing changes them. They go on being low persons no matter what is done for them, no matter what is given them, no matter what advantages they have."

"No, I do not believe that," I said. "A person can choose the way he will be. No matter what his parent is like, he can be what he wants to be."

"It is in the blood!" Lord Bude was almost shouting now. "There is nothing he or anyone else can do about it. It was there when he was born. Look at Du Barry. She brought up that black devil like her own son. She was even going to adopt him. And how did he reward her for all this? He turned her over to the authorities who cut off her head! It is in the blood, I tell you. What would a child like you know about it anyway?"

We had both become agitated, and I did not think this was good for his health. So I tried to change the conversation.

"And he is in love with Lady Ellen. Don't you think love can change a man?"

"Humph!"

"Well, it is a terribly powerful feeling, isn't it?"

"How do you know? Are you in love with somebody?" Lord Bude demanded.

"If I were, I do not think I would know whether I was or not."

"Stay away from it! It brings only misery, Louisa. Marry

a good, honest man when the time comes and forget about love. Settle down and bring up a family. It is your children that bring happiness. Caring for them, doing for them, planning for them. Knowing that after . . . you are gone . . ."

Lord Bude spoke more quietly now, having turned from me to gaze out the window. I watched him, wondering what was troubling him.

Then, as I had begun to wonder if I should interrupt his reverie, it was done for me by a shape falling past the window, landing with a loud thud. This was accompanied by men shouting.

"What was that?" I asked.

"Part of one of the chimney shafts, I should think. Falling to pieces. I have workmen up there repairing them."

"Are they so old?"

"Old? Ancient! Absolutely ancient. This part of Compton Hall is Elizabethan. Built in 1580. She stayed here, you know. She stayed for several days. She liked it. Left reluctantly. Three kings and two queens have stayed at the Hall: Elizabeth, Charles II, George I, George II, and Victoria."

"Queen Victoria stayed here?"

"When she was a young girl. She wasn't queen then. With the Duchess, who was a friend of my grandfather's. Ah, but if these rooms could only talk, or if we could go back and be here during those early times.

"A house is not a dead thing, Louisa. It lives, and breathes, and changes. It gathers. It absorbs the personalities of its occupants. I often wonder if the old Hall could speak, what it would say.

"*You* feel it, don't you?" he asked. "Well?"

"Yes, definitely," I said. "It's such a lovely place. I hope it will always be safe—just as it is today."

"Put that thing back," he said, pointing to the book I held in my lap. "We will read something else. Something sensible. I am not in the mood for Lynston's foolishness."

We decided upon Robert Louis Stevenson's *Familiar Studies of Men and Books*, and as I read to Lord Bude, he seemed to become fascinated by it. And he did not interrupt again until it was time for me to go.

It was the following Wednesday that Stuart returned. My thoughts were interrupted by the sound of a horse walking up the rectory drive. It was Stuart riding a big black horse. As shocked as I was at seeing him, I could not help observing how beautifully he sat on his mount. And how good he looked in his riding clothes.

I left the house at once and walked to the stables to meet him. By the time I arrived there, Stuart had dismounted, and he and Patrick, who now held the horse's reins, were talking together.

". . . from Sir Arthur Spitalfield," Stuart was saying. "He is closing the house to go—" Then he saw me. "Hello, Louisa."

"Good afternoon, Stuart."

"This is Sultan." Stuart gestured to the horse as he spoke.

"Magnificent!" I said.

"I bought him this morning from Sir Arthur Spitalfield. He is closing Holly Hill and plans to live in Italy. Health reasons. So he is selling off his stable."

"Seventeen point three hands, he is, miss," Patrick said proudly.

"Yes," Stuart said. "Seventeen point three, as I was telling Patrick. Anglo-Arab. By a thoroughbred, Red Robin, out of an Arab mare that Sir Arthur brought over from Egypt. Notice the long front and high withers—fine back, and quarters."

"I can see that, Stuart," I said.

"Yes. Enormously fast," Stuart said. "He would make a show against any thoroughbred."

He and Patrick went on talking about and admiring Sultan. Patrick was delighted. He liked nothing better than to talk about horses.

At length Patrick led Sultan away, and Stuart said to me, "You don't seem happy to see me."

"I had no idea you would be leaving Ledington on Sunday," I said.

"I'm sorry to have disappointed you."

"I did not say that I was disappointed."

"You did not say you were not."

"Where are you staying now?" I said. "Surely not at the Hall."

"Why do you think not?"

"Because I understand you and Lyle don't get on very well."

"Cold-blooded vertebrate! I'd not stay anywhere near him. Class of Reptilia! I own the manor house beyond Bridgehampton. I'm staying there."

"Oh? But you stayed at Compton Hall a week and a half ago."

"My house was closed. Why shouldn't I stay at the Hall? My uncle could accommodate me for a few days. I *am* his nephew. It was a worthwhile visit. Both informative and intriguing. And I came to see a miniature of my mother which my uncle had in his possession. It was painted by Corubini, and shows her as she looked when she was about your age."

"Did you see it?"

"Yes. She was very beautiful. Blonde hair and very blue eyes. I wonder where the artist got the blue pigment."

We walked a few steps away from the stable door, and then pausing, I said, "Strange it should be in Lord Bude's posession."

"He was in love with my mother."

"How did he come to have it?"

"He stole it."

"*Stole* it?"

"He borrowed it while he was courting her and never returned it."

"Then he should give it to you."

"The old bastard would never give anything to anybody."

"Stuart!"

"It's true."

"I should think he would want to be friendly now, after all these years. Perhaps he does."

"Never! He hates me, and the feeling is mutual."

"Perhaps not. After all, if something were to happen to Lyle, you would be his heir. Isn't that so?"

"If there were no will to the contrary. But there must be. He would toss and turn in his coffin if he thought I had inherited a stick."

We fell silent then, as we walked onto the lawn together. He seemed lost in thought.

"Have you heard about Nanny Thompson?" I asked at length.

"Yes," he replied.

"Did you know her?"

"No. Mother mentioned her. She was Hartley's nanny. I—I believe Mother met her when she went to see her sister that last time. That was long ago. No, I never knew her."

"But you talked to her Saturday night at the Hall."

He examined me closely before he spoke. "That crazy old crone? Lot of gibberish."

That was all he said. He seemed extremely casual, unconcerned about it.

"I don't suppose you ride?" he asked at once.

"Of course I do," I replied. "I have a very fine horse. A bright black chestnut hunter. Her name is Samantha. Would you like to see her?"

I led Stuart back toward the stable and Patrick, who had now emerged from it and stood watching us.

"Shall we ride together this afternoon?" Stuart said.

"I am afraid that is quite impossible. My time is occupied with caring for my aunt. She is asleep now, but I expect she will wake at any moment."

"Can she never get along without you? What is the nature of her illness?"

"It has many facets. She is rheumatic. Her arms and legs pain her sometimes so badly that I must write her letters for her, dress her, and help her do almost everything. Her eyes tire easily and pain her, so I must read to her a great deal. And she is weak. She lacks strength to do anything. She suffers from dizzy spells often and she suffers

from a weak stomach. She can eat only certain foods—
never vegetables. Sweets agree with her most. And there
are other things."

"Extraordinary that one person should be tormented so.
These symptoms come and go?" Stuart asked.

"Yes, from day to day."

"According to her moods?"

"What are you implying—that it is all in the mind?"
I said, turning to glance at him. "How can you, when you
have never so much as met her?"

"It is you who suggest it. You must think it possible."

"Might that not be a sickness too? A sickness of the
mind? And would not that require as much care as an
illness of the body?"

"If it were genuine," he said. "But she must allow you
some time to yourself."

As we approached, Patrick sat down on his bench beside
the stable door.

"Ride with me tomorrow," Stuart continued, "and I
will show you the manor house."

"I should like to, Stuart, but I read to Lord Bude tomorrow afternoon." At that point I heard a car draw up before
the rectory, though I could not see it from the stables.
"Is that a car?" I said. "I think May might have gone into
the village, and Uncle is not at home. I shall have to go and
see who it is." I left Stuart and hurried across the yard,
calling back over my shoulder, "I shan't be a moment."

I walked as fast as I could away from him, across the
stable yard, and down the drive toward the corner of the
house. As soon as I passed out of Stuart's view, I would
run. It would be quicker to run around the rectory to the
front of it than to go through it, and perhaps that way I
could intercept Lyle before he entered the house. I felt
sure it was Lyle's car and that he had come to call. And I
knew that I must keep him from learning of Stuart's
presence.

When I came to the corner of the house, I ran around
it, straight into Lyle's arms.

"Well," he said, "this is an unexpected pleasure."

"Oh, Lyle! How did you know—"

"That you were at the stables? May told me. She was washing windows on the portico."

"What did she say?"

"Only that you were out here. Shall we walk in the garden a bit?" he asked, taking a step toward the stable yard.

"No! Not that way," I cried. "Let's go into the house. The sun— It seems so warm today."

"Of course. Are you feeling well?" As he spoke, he turned, took my arm, and began to lead me toward the front of the house.

"I— Well— No! As a matter of fact"—I laid my fingers against my forehead—"I feel quite terribly faint, and I think I should . . ."

"You *are* pale. Why, your heart is pounding. I can feel it. I think you should lie down."

"Perhaps an aspirin and soda . . ."

"Yes, and then lie down. I shan't stay. It's more important that you rest. I left some peaches for Mrs. Cuttlebuck. From the glasshouses. Oh, and Father has a slight upset and asked me to tell you that he will not be well enough to be read to tomorrow, but that he will look forward to seeing you on Monday as usual."

"I'm so sorry," I said. "I hope it's nothing serious."

"No. A stomach upset. A day or two in bed and he will be fine."

We had reached the front of the house by then. May was still washing windows. She looked around at me with a malicious, triumphant look and then went back to work. Lyle walked to the front steps with me, helped me up them, and opened the front door.

"Feel better very soon," he said to me, as I walked through it. He followed me into the house and closed the door behind us. "I don't think I can get down tomorrow, and it would be better for you to rest anyway, I should think. But I'll see you on Friday—sometime during the day."

"That would be wonderful," I said.

Then Lyle tilted my face to his and kissed me lightly. "Feel better at once," he said.

He left. I waited until I heard him cross the portico and descend the steps. Then I hurried down the passage toward the kitchen.

But as I passed the staircase, Aunt Grace called, "Louisa?"

"I'll be up in a moment," I called back.

I left the house by the back door and walked quickly across to the stables, where I found Stuart and Patrick talking together about horses.

"Everything all right?" Stuart asked.

"Yes, but Aunt Grace is calling for me, and I shall have to go up to her. I—that was a message from the Hall. Lord Bude is ill, so I shall not be reading to him tomorrow afternoon."

"Then I'll show you the manor house."

"Yes."

"At two o'clock?"

"Three o'clock would be better." I glanced at Patrick, wishing he had left us. "That would be delightful, Stuart. And Samantha will appreciate the exercise."

Aunt Grace had a visitor the following afternoon. It was Miss Ormsby.

"I have come across some rather significant information," she said, staring pointedly at Aunt Grace and me, "which I believe will be of interest to you, Grace."

"What is it, Dorothy?" Aunt Grace asked.

"It is about Lieutenant Compton, who, incidentally, left the Hall rather unceremoniously on Sunday afternoon."

"What about him?" Aunt Grace asked.

"He *was* in the army, you know. He is no *longer* in the army. He was cashiered!"

"Cashiered?" Aunt Grace said. "For what?"

"He killed a man. Beat him to death. During a drunken card game. And they cashiered him from the army for it."

"But surely they would have done more than that."

"You would certainly think so! It must have been a dreadful sight. The man was covered with blood. But Lieutenant Compton claimed it was accidental. Accidental! Can you imagine?"

"How do you know this?" I asked Miss Ormsby.

"Colonel Fitzcroft told me," she answered. "The colonel has very influential friends in the army and he knows everything that is happening there."

I left Aunt Grace and Miss Ormsby shortly after that, hoping that my absence would hasten the conclusion of their visit and that Aunt Grace might be asleep by the time Stuart arrived.

But Miss Ormsby was still with Aunt Grace when Stuart rode up the drive. I told him at once that Aunt Grace wanted to meet him, begged him to be nice to her, and led him upstairs to her room.

"Aunt Grace, this is Lieutenant Compton," I said. Then I turned to Stuart. "You already know Miss Ormsby."

"Good afternoon, Mrs. Cuttlebuck," Stuart said, as he nodded to Miss Ormsby. Her nod in return was almost imperceptible. "Louisa says you have not been in the best of health lately. I am so sorry to hear that. I hope it will improve."

"How good of you to say so, Lieutenant Compton," Aunt Grace replied. "Won't you sit down? In this chair here, where I can see you without twisting my neck. There," she said, when Stuart was seated near her. "Dear Louisa. I do not know what I would do without her, Lieutenant Compton. She thinks only of my welfare. I could not possibly manage without her.

"No, my health has not been of the best for some time. I am completely bedridden, you know. And under a doctor's care. No sooner does one malady seem to come under control, than another begins. I am sure Doctor Carmichael does not have the vaguest idea what has happened to my neck. It aches so. It simply does not respond to heat. The long cords ache, Lieutenant Compton. They feel as though they are on fire sometimes. And massage does not help at all. It seems to make it worse . . ."

Stuart sat quietly looking at Aunt Grace. Was there the slightest suggestion of a twinkle in his eyes?

Aunt Grace went on, "It is impossible to bear sometimes. And then when I am able to take a few steps, the world spins and tumbles terribly, and if I did not have Louisa to hold onto I should simply fall."

By now Stuart's mouth had lost its smile. His eyes wandered about the room.

"And I am delicate. I must watch every mouthful," Aunt Grace continued. "Thank heavens I can take sweets—to keep up my strength, you know. Though heaven knows, I have no resistance. The slightest draft and I have a chill. And colds? Oh! Constantly. Louisa, hand me a handkerchief from the drawer there."

Stuart's eyes narrowed and a slight twitch began in the muscles of his jaw.

"You must be susceptible to disease then, Mrs. Cuttlebuck," he said. "You should be careful."

"Oh, I am," Aunt Grace said. "The slightest—"

"Never travel," Stuart said firmly. "Especially to the eastern countries."

He glared at me. I could hardly blame him. Aunt Grace could be an impossible bore. Miss Ormsby smirked as she scrutinized Stuart.

"Travel?" Aunt Grace asked. "I couldn't think of it in my condition. The eastern countries?"

"I am just back from India. I was stationed there."

"India?"

"A backward country," he said. He rubbed his eyes quite hard with his fingers. "No concept of sanitation. You have no idea of the poverty and the filth. And the disease. The natives die like flies in the streets. Of fevers, especially malaria, typhoid, yellow fever, and, of course, cholera, diphtheria, typhus, and tetanus. Smallpox is common. And leprosy. Their fingers fall off from it. They fall off in the street—right there in front of you."

"Oh!" Aunt Grace cried, clapping her handkerchief over her nose and mouth.

Again Stuart rubbed his eyes with his fingers. "And a

horrible disease of the eyes called the blind staggers. They catch it from the cows that roam the streets. First itching and burning of the eyes. Then rot sets in and the eyes simply rot in their sockets until they fall out in a runny, slimy, jellylike mass. Appalling. You have no idea."

"Oh!" Aunt Grace cried into the handkerchief which she held clamped over her nose and mouth. "That chair, Lieutenant Compton. I believe its leg is loose, and I would not want it to collapse. Wouldn't you be more comfortable sitting over there?"

"The legs seem firm to me, Mrs. Cuttlebuck," Stuart said. "Thank you." He remained seated, smiling at her. He rubbed his eyes again. Now they looked red and inflamed.

"You are still in the army, Lieutenant Compton?" Aunt Grace asked through her handkerchief. She did not seem to have any intention of removing it.

"No, Mrs. Cuttlebuck," Stuart replied.

"And what of your future plans?"

"I do not know." Again he rubbed his red eyes.

"It would seem you are without purpose, Lieutenant. And I cannot but—"

"I have always believed that prudence and indecision are not incompatible, Mrs. Cuttlebuck," Stuart said, as he rose from his chair and stepped to her side. Quickly and without warning, he leaned over, grasped her hand, and kissed it.

"Aunt Grace screamed, wrenching her hand from his. "Oh! Oh, my heart!" The hand flew to her chest. "Oh, I am having an attack. Leave me! Louisa, my smelling salts!"

Quickly I reached into the bedside table drawer for them and held the bottle under her nose. Then I said to Stuart, "Would you get Doctor Carmichael, please?"

"No! No, it is all right now," Aunt Grace cried. "Go away! Just let me rest."

"I can't leave," I said.

"Go! Go! I shall be all right. Dorothy will stay with me. Go and leave me, both of you."

"But I can't leave you, Aunt Grace."

"I am much better. It was only a flutter. It frightened me

for a moment, but it is all right. I am a perfectly good judge of my own condition, Louisa. Now, go!"

Stuart had already stepped to the doorway. He waited for me there. I followed him reluctantly, and we left the room, closing the door behind us.

"I—I can't bear to leave her like that," I said to him. "But I was afraid if I didn't, she would become angry and that would have been bad for her heart."

"There was nothing wrong with her," Stuart said.

"How can you say that?"

"Do you think there was? Honestly?"

"Well—"

"She pretended an attack to get rid of me. It was obvious."

"Well, I—I think we should go downstairs."

"And out to the stables where Patrick will saddle your horse."

"I can't go riding. Not . . ."

"Leave the ladies to gossip. They will enjoy themselves."

I knew that he was right. And whether he had killed a man or not, I wanted to go riding with him. We left the house together and walked toward the stables.

"I trust your eyes are feeling better?" I said sharply as we walked across the lawn.

"Perfect," Stuart said.

"Stuart, how could you? That will prey on her mind for weeks."

"She deserved it. How can she possibly bore people about her condition like that? Does she really think they're interested, or does she enjoy entrapping them?"

"She needs sympathy. And whatever you think, she *is* ill, one way or another."

I did not say more because by then we had come in sight of Patrick, who sat on his bench beside the stable door. He did not sit there alone, however. May sat beside him. She grasped his arm playfully, tilted her head, and laughed up at him. Then she laid her cheek on his shoulder and gazed up at his face.

It occurred to me then that May often made excuses to consult Patrick about one thing or another. It was not unusual to find her in the stable yard. Since Thomas Thornton continued to ignore her, May aimed herself at another target.

May rose and walked toward us.

"Oh, May," I said. "If anyone should call this afternoon, I shall not be at home."

"Yes, miss," she said. Then she walked on to the house.

Too quickly, it seemed, we had ridden through Bridgehampton, along the coast road for perhaps half a mile, and had come to an ivy-covered stone wall. We rode beside it until we approached a gateway. The gate stood open. One of its hinges had rusted away, and it leaned back against the wall at an angle for support. Its top was covered with ivy, and briar bushes grew at its base.

Here Stuart motioned me off the road, and I turned Samantha to follow Sultan through the gateway onto a rutted drive. Then we walked down it toward a line of trees, and shortly Stuart said, "You will see the house in just a moment. There!"

The manor house stood before us on its weed-and-bramble-choked lawn—a fire-blackened, hollow stone shell covered with ivy, hop, and wisteria all gone wild.

"But it is a ruin," I said, reining Samantha to a halt.

Stuart paused beside me. "It caught fire in a storm thirteen years ago. My mother died in it."

"Oh, Stuart."

"I pray that she was unconscious from the smoke—that she didn't suffer. I wasn't here. I was at Harrow."

"And your father?"

"He died when I was eight years old. He was an officer in the army. Major General, Forty-second foot. He was stationed in London until I was five, and Mother and I lived in the manor house. It had belonged to Mother's father. Mother and her sister, Anne, were the only heirs. When the estate was divided, it was decided that Mother would have the house and that Anne, then Lady Bude, would have acreage. Lord Bude preferred it that way."

"Then you went to India?"

"With my father and mother. For three years. Then Father died. Cholera. And we returned to England. I went to Harrow and Mother lived here until the fire. Then Cambridge and a commission in the army.

"I inherited the manor house and three farms. Not very much land—five hundred acres in all. I rent the farms and keep a few acres around the old house. There are several barns and cottages beyond the trees there. I keep one for myself, and a caretaker and his wife live in another."

"What are the stone heads above the doorway?"

"Elizabeth in the center," Stuart said, "Henry VIII on the right of her and Mary on her left."

"And the inscription above?"

" 'Fugere Pudor, Verum que Fidesque.' Shame, Truth, and Faith have flown."

"Oh? Why?"

"Elizabeth threw Sir Leslie Francis, its builder, into the Tower on suspicion of treason. He never returned. His son, Edward, placed the tablet there—in his memory, I suppose."

"The house must have been beautiful. I can almost see the windows with their little diamond panes reflecting the sun."

"It was. And you *will* see them, perhaps."

"How?"

"If you are here. The windows will be replaced along with the rafters, and the roof, and the floors, and the rooms."

"You are going to restore it?"

"Exactly as it was when Mother lived here."

"What an enormous undertaking! Why, that would mean rebuilding it entirely. There is very little left."

"Yes."

"It would cost a great deal."

"Yes."

I looked at Stuart, wanting very badly to ask him where

he intended to get the money to pay for it. But of course I did not ask.

He must have read the question in my eyes, but he did not answer it. He merely said, "It will be done."

That was all. But as I watched him, his eyes glittered as they traveled over the structure, and his mouth smiled triumphantly. I knew he was seeing it finished.

Then he noticed that I was watching him closely. He pointed ahead. "The drive curves around the house there, and down beyond it is the home farm where I live."

"Beyond the house the drive became a track which led through a fringe of trees and ended in a muddy yard surrounded by barns and sheds and three stone cottages.

"This is where I stay when I am here," he said, as we drew our horses to a halt before the largest of the cottages. "August will look after the horses."

A man ran toward us from one of the barns, scattering a flock of chickens as he came. He grasped our horses' reins, and Stuart and I dismounted. Then I followed Stuart into the house. It was a simple structure composed of a large room, with a smaller one opening off it on the ground floor and a staircase against one wall leading to a sleeping room above.

Mrs. Gouge, Stuart's housekeeper, served us tea. When she had gone and we had finished eating, Stuart leaned over without any warning and kissed me.

"No!" I said, pushing him away.

He grasped my arms then and held them still by the wrists.

"Don't force me, Stuart," I said. "You will regret it if you do."

He stood glowering down at me. But after a moment his eyes softened, and he slid his arm around me. Again he pulled me to him.

"I always get what I want." He smiled that arrogant smile.

"Even when it isn't possible?" As I spoke, I placed my hands against his chest as if to push him away.

"There is always a way."

"You seem very sure."

"You want to be made love to," he said. "You want it badly. Why do you resist so?"

"How very transparent you must find people, to be able to read their thoughts so clearly! And how *very* sure you are of yourself, Stuart. You must believe yourself irresistible."

"Come upstairs," he whispered.

"No."

His hand grasped the back of my head and positioned it to receive his kiss. His mouth attacked mine hungrily. That endless kiss drew the will from my body, leaving me weak and trembling . . . and wanting.

He released my mouth then and smiled that proud smile. He did not kiss me again, but he stood there holding me against him, watching me and waiting.

I waited too—for what seemed an eternity. At length, when he had still not moved or spoken, I said simply, "Yes." Tears came to my eyes then. I have no idea why.

He led the way and I followed him up the stairs and into a low-ceilinged, dormered bedroom. We walked to the window and looked out at the sea. "Far off there is Spain," he said. "Shall we make believe?" His arm slid about my waist, and he drew me close as we looked out over the ocean. "Shall we say that we are there together far away? Where the days are warm and the air is filled with jasmine and myrrh?"

"I would rather be here," I said, turning to him.

He smiled. Then he clasped me in his arms and held me close to him as he kissed my mouth, my eyes, my forehead. I slid my arms around his neck and clung to him.

I cannot describe the rapture I found in that room that afternoon. But I found what I had always longed for . . . though until then I had been unaware of the yearning.

Much later, as Stuart held me still against him in blissful languor, I whispered, "Listen! The rain."

"Yes. And we have found shelter," he said.

"Yes, my darling," I said, wrapping my arms around him and holding him close. "We have found shelter."

Then he kissed me—a long, lingering kiss. At that moment I thought of Lyle and wondered if he could ever make me glow as I did now.

Once more I abandoned myself to the rapture of Stuart's lovemaking.

After a while, when we were quiet again, he asked, "Do you walk at the millpond still?"

"I haven't recently," I said. "Not since I was attacked there by a fiendish brute. But he has gone, and since I now have nothing to fear, I shall probably resume the habit in the late afternoon." As I spoke, I ran my fingers slowly through his hair.

"Why do you do that?" he murmured.

"Because I like the feel of it," I answered.

Then he kissed the base of my neck.

"Why did you do *that*?" I whispered.

"Because I love your daisy," he said, smiling at me.

"My daisy?"

"Your birthmark. It looks like a tiny flower—a deep-rose-colored daisy."

"I've always hated it."

He kissed it again.

"I didn't know there could be such happiness," I continued.

"Would you have fought it if you had?"

"Yes."

"But you won't fight it anymore?"

"I don't know."

"Why do you say that?"

"If I don't, what then?"

"Then we shall enjoy our time together."

"Is that all? Are you playing with me? You will go away one day, won't you?"

"Who can say? Let the future shape itself."

"Without any plans for it? We must go, Stuart. I must get back to Aunt Grace. I've already stayed away too long."

Stuart left me then—a little abruptly, I felt—to find August and to tell him to bring the horses. By the time I had descended to the ground floor of the cottage, Stuart and the horses waited for me outside the door. I was thankful that neither August nor Mrs. Gouge was anywhere to be seen.

The rain had stopped by then, but I was apprehensive about the weather, and I watched the sky carefully. I suppose this was how I chanced to see the man looking down at us from the tallest of the Three Sisters, three bluffs between the manor house and Bridgehampton. As soon as I looked in the man's direction, he stepped back out of sight, so I hadn't time to be sure if it was Lyle or not. Why would Lyle be standing up there?

Still, the thought of that figure looking down at us would not leave my mind. It ceased to trouble me only after Stuart had seen me to the rectory drive and had left.

Chapter Five

MAY MET ME AS I ENTERED THE RECTORY. "Miss, there was a chauffeur from the Hall this afternoon. He brought you a plant and a note to be answered."

"Where are they, May?" I asked. "And what did you tell him?"

"In the drawing room, miss. Why, that you weren't home, like you told me to."

Just then Aunt Grace called from upstairs, "Louisa?"

"I'll be up in a moment," I called back.

May had placed the potted plant on a saucer in the bay window. It was a yellow orchid with pink spots. I had admired it one afternoon in the orchid house at the Hall. Against the pot leaned an envelope with my name on it.

I read:

Compton Hall, Thursday

My dear Louisa,

I hope this finds you recovered.

The orchid is *C. Mendiana*. I think it is one of the plants you admired here.

I'll be driving into Bridgehampton tomorrow morning, and since you are to call for your dress at Madame Prieur's shop, may I drive you there?

Shall I call for you then at eleven o'clock?

Yours,

Lyle

Yes, that would be wonderful, I thought, when I had finished reading the note. Then I went up to Aunt Grace.

"He touched me! He is diseased!" Aunt Grace shrieked. "Or was that some foul trick? He is a beast! Rude and nasty."

"Your heart," I said. "How is it?"

"It is perfectly fine. A momentary flutter, that is all. We will say no more about it. Now bring that chair here and sit down. I want to talk to you."

When I sat beside her bed, she continued, "Lieutenant Compton is a selfish, cruel man. I have heard accounts of him."

"From whom?" I asked.

"Never mind. He *killed* a man! And look how he insulted Dorothy. And that incident in church! Why, he would have killed that poor Gordon child if his mother had not saved him. And look how he has treated *me*—a poor invalid. How could you be so imprudent as to associate with him?"

"I have spoken to him only once or twice," I said. "And gone riding with him once, Aunt Grace."

"And that will be the end of it," Aunt Grace said. "Why, even his family were never accepted. His father was a bounder and his mother a coquette. She caused all kinds of trouble. And what if Lord Hartley should hear that you have gone riding with Lieutenant Compton? What then?"

I did not answer her. He would not like it, of course. He would not like it at all. He must not know.

Aunt Grace went on. "Lord Hartley is interested in you. Do you realize what an opportunity this is? You are not stupid. This is your chance for not merely a decent marriage, but a distinguished one. If you play your cards right, you could be the next Lady Bude! So we will have no more foolishness as far as Lieutenant Compton is concerned."

She took a deep breath and went on. "You know only too well that the living at St. Clement's is endowed by Lord Bude. If you become Lady Bude, Mr. Cuttlebuck's position here will be secure. After all we have done for you, Louisa, it is little enough to ask. I mention this only as one of the many advantages of such a match. Why, every young lady for miles around would give her right arm to become Lord

Hartley's wife. You will *not* see Lieutenant Compton again. That is understood?"

I left Aunt Grace without provoking an argument, rang the Hall, thanked Lyle for the orchid, and said I would love to drive to Bridgehampton with him in the morning.

As Lyle and I approached Bridgehampton, I asked, "Have any of your guests arrived? Uncle Andrew told me he saw one of the cars from the Hall returning from Bridgehampton yesterday with two ladies in it."

"That was the Princess Pildudska. She arrived on—"

"*Princess?*"

"Yes."

"But I had no idea there would be a princess at dinner tonight."

"Does it matter?"

"I wouldn't know how to behave with a princess."

"Princesses are people just like you and me—no different. And often not nearly as nice." He smiled and laid his hand on mine for an instant. "You will soon become accustomed to them. She arrived on the four o'clock train with Mrs. Groombridge, the daughter of Lady Agatha Mersham." My face must have betrayed complete ignorance, for he continued, "She was the daughter of the Duke of Ramsbury. Lady Agatha and Princess Pildudska's mother were close friends. The princess is a guest of Mrs. Groombridge. She has been staying with her in her London house for the past several months."

"Who else is coming? I understand Lady Woolwich will be there."

"How do you know that?"

"Bertha told me."

Lord Hartley grinned. "I might have known. Yes, she and Lord Woolwich are old friends. And Lord and Lady Charles. They are driving down this afternoon. Four Americans and Mr. Rosso and Mr. Sly. Fourteen in all for dinner, counting you and me. The others will arrive later for the dancing."

"Oh, dear."

"What is it?"

"I—I hope I don't embarrass you."

"Why on earth should you? No, you will be a tremendous help. Just be yourself. Your beauty and charm will captivate them all."

Chapter Six

As I DESCENDED THE STAIRS AT SEVEN O'CLOCK, the Hall car drew up with Rodger sitting at the wheel. He drove me to the Hall where Keating waited in the loggia.

"Good evening, miss," he smiled. "His young lordship is in the oval parlor. Please follow me."

Soon he swung open the door to the parlor and announced, "Miss Little, my lord."

"Good evening, Louisa," Lyle said, hurrying toward me. "That will be all, Keating, thank you." After Keating had left us, Lyle said, "I say! You look absolutely marvelous."

"Thank you, Lyle," I said. "Am I the first to arrive?"

"I think the princess and Mrs. Groombridge have come down, as well as Lord and Lady Charles. They are in the drawing room, but we have a minute or two to ourselves before we need join them." He went to a table against the wall and took a flat black box from it. "This is Mother's necklace. I would like you to wear it this evening." He lifted the hinged lid and turned it so that I could see the pearls lying on the white satin lining.

"They're magnificent." I had never seen anything so lovely.

"Put them on. There is a mirror."

I lifted the pearls out of the box, walked to the mirror, and put them around my neck. But I could not manage the clasp.

"I can't seem to close it," I said. "Will you help me?"

Lyle fastened it for me. Then I stood looking into the mirror, entranced by my reflection. Lyle stood behind me.

As our eyes met in the glass, he placed his hands on my waist. Then he kissed the back of my neck.

"Do you like them?" he asked.

"I have never seen anything so beautiful," I said. I turned around and faced him. "I don't know what to say."

"When you smile like that and your eyes sparkle like that"—he put his arms around me—"you are absolutely . . ." His kiss finished the sentence.

He was so handsome in his white tie and tails. And I felt so splendid. I was living in a fairy tale, and here was my handsome prince. He had changed me from a poor village girl into a princess. I clung to him and returned the kiss in gratitude.

"My dear, dear Louisa," he said, as he released me. "But come, they'll be wondering where we are."

We left the oval parlor then for the drawing room. There was no time for me to count the people in the room. Lyle's guests stood about in groups, and as we entered, they ceased talking to one another and stared at us. But the silence lasted only a moment. Then the room buzzed again.

"Come and meet the princess," Lyle said, leading me to a pale lump of a woman with large, florid lips who had sunk into a sofa near the chimneypiece.

"Princess Pildudska," Lyle said, when we stood before her, "may I present Louisa Little."

The princess waved her hand, nodded, and mumbled something unintelligible, which I supposed was in Polish. Then she smiled at Lyle and glued her cowlike eyes to his face.

"The princess does not speak English very well, Miss Little," a tall woman standing nearby said to me. "But she said she is charmed."

"Please thank the princess for me," I said, "and tell her I am delighted."

"Mrs. Groombridge is entertaining the princess while she is in England," Lyle explained. "Now I want you to meet Lady Woolwich."

He grasped my arm then and hurried me away toward a

dark-haired beauty who brandished a long ivory cigarette holder. She was deep in conversation with an olive-skinned man and a large-boned young woman with blonde hair.

After Lyle had introduced me, he said, "Lady Woolwich has just returned from Paris, and Lady Charles has been given Sun Chariot, the Derby winner, by Lord Charles as a wedding anniversary present. What exciting lives we lead! And Mr. Rosso has only just returned from the States." Mr. Rosso was the swarthy man.

"Newport," Mr. Rosso elaborated. "I was a guest of Mrs. Crowinsharp's there."

"I was just telling Lady Charles," Lady Woolwich said to me, "about Antibes. Deauville is positively mundane now, you know. *Nobody* goes to Deauville any more. In Antibes we've Noel. He's doing a devastating new play and painting the most enthralling pictures, and Cecil, and Grace. One can hear her practicing scales all morning. But *all* morning long. Up and down, up and down in that pink and blue barn of hers." She blew a cloud of smoke into the air. "And Gertrude and Elsie, wearing her gloves to the beach, naturally, and—"

"And everyone sits about in the heat and gets tiddly on sidecars," Lady Charles said. "Lovely! Excuse me, my dears, I must speak to Charles."

She left us then to go to her husband, and so did Lyle, to speak with two men who were obviously the Americans. Lady Woolwich continued her lesson on Antibes, and Mr. Rosso seemed lost in thought as he contemplated the princess.

Finally, without warning, he turned to Lady Woolwich and said, "Any money there, do you suppose?"

"The princess?" Lady Woolwich asked. "Tons of it, darling, but I can't imagine why you ask. Really, Aldo, things can't be *that* desperate."

Just then Lyle returned and, excusing us, led me away from them to the window.

"Stupid of me," he said, reaching into his coat pocket for a piece of paper. "I forgot to give you this." He handed me the paper. On it was written a list of the dinner guests in two columns. It was a list of precedence—who would take whom in to dinner. "Mrs. Merrymede made this for you. You see," he continued, indicating the names, "it is really quite simple. I shall go first with the princess. Then Lord Woolwich will take Lady Charles in, and then Mr. Rosso, who claims a connection with Prince Reggio, will take Lady Woolwich, and so forth."

I looked at Lyle in astonishment.

"Well, someone has to do it," he said, "and it would be an enormous help to me if you would."

"I couldn't possibly," I said. "It is always the lady of the house who arranges these things. I am not . . ."

"Let us make believe you *are*," Lyle said, smiling broadly at me. "All you need do when Keating announces dinner is to say to Lord Woolwich, 'Will you take Lady Charles in?' and so forth. The place cards will show everyone where to sit at the table, and then when we have finished dessert, all you need do is rise and the ladies will follow you back here, where Keating will serve coffee for you. Then we will join you later and go into the hall for the dancing. That is simple enough, isn't it?"

"I suppose . . ."

"Good! Don't look so unhappy. It's simple. It's all written down for you there. Just read it off." At that moment Lyle glanced across the room and exclaimed, "Good Heavens!"

I followed Lyle's astonished gaze to the drawing room doorway. Keating had thrown the doors open, and as Lord Bude and a short woman shaped rather like a cube walked through them, he shouted, "Lord Bude and Lady Hatchfield."

"What the devil!" Lyle exclaimed. Already he was striding across the room toward his father. I hurried after him. "Being announced in his own drawing room like that, and arriving with that woman at the last minute. What is he doing?"

Now we stood facing Lord Bude and Lady Hatchfield.

"Ah, good evening, Lyle," Lord Bude said. "Miss Little,

this is Lady Hatchfield. Since it is not my party, I thought it might be amusing to have myself announced."

"Good evening, Father, Lady Hatchfield," Lyle said, rather more loudly than necessary. "You may remember, Father, that a week or so ago I expressed the hope that you would join my friends and me at dinner. But I am under the distinct impression that you refused on the grounds that they belonged to an . . . inferior set. I cannot imagine why you changed your mind at the last minute."

"I think," Lord Bude said, "it is sufficient to say that I *have* changed my mind. We'll let it go at that. And since this is my house, I have every right to come down to dinner if I wish. Now, Roseanna," he said to Lady Hatchfield, "shall we mingle with my son's guests and see if anyone has anything interesting to say?" Then he led his companion past us toward the Princess Pildudska.

Lyle murmured angrily, "Is he trying to ruin my dinner party? Oh yes, Keating, what is it?"

"I should like to ask Miss Little, my lord," Keating said, "about the seating arrangement. It is now necessary to lay two extra places, miss," he said to me. "As to the place cards, I presume that now his lordship will sit at one end of it and—"

"I think you should ask his lordship how he wishes it to be done, Keating," I said.

"His lordship has expressly asked me to ask your advice in the matter of seating, miss," Keating said.

"What the devil!" Lyle exclaimed.

"Then ask Mrs. Merrymede," I said.

"Mrs. Merrymede is temporarily indisposed, miss."

"Lyle," I said, "you must know how this is done. I don't. Couldn't you—?"

"I don't know anything about these things," Lyle said. "Keating, you are an expert on such matters. What's the matter with you? And where is Mrs. Merrymede?"

"There is nothing the matter with me, my lord," Keating said, "and Mrs. Merrymede is indisposed—she has one of her horrible headaches and cannot be disturbed."

"What headaches?" Lyle asked. "Well, take care of it somehow."

"His lordship has expressly asked me to consult with Miss Little," Keating said, "and to be guided by her advice. It is an extremely delicate matter of precedence, my lord." Then he turned to me. "I presume that his lordship will sit at one end of the table and yourself at the other, miss. Now about Lady Hatchfield—"

"I should think Lady Hatchfield would sit at the other end in that case," I said.

"Over my dead body!" Lyle said.

"Oh, no, no," Keating said. "She is simply an old friend. That would not be at all appropriate. And his lordship has suggested that, due to the late hour, we make as few changes as possible. I would suggest that you remain at the other end of the table as planned, miss. But as to Lady Hatchfield, should she take precedence over Mrs. Groombridge and be placed second to your left? Or should Mrs. Groombridge take precedence over Lady Hatchfield?"

"Well, settle it somehow," Lyle said with annoyance. "I've other things to do." And he left.

"Then it is a question of who takes precedence, Lady Hatchfield or Mrs. Groombridge, Keating?" I asked.

"Quite so, miss," Keating said. "Mrs. Groombridge is the granddaughter of the Duke of Ramsbury, while Lady Hatchfield is the wife of Sir Edwin Hatchfield."

"Then let me ask his lordship," I said.

I left Keating then and crossed the room to Lord Bude.

"May I speak with you a moment, Lord Bude?"

"Certainly, my dear." He stepped away from the others and I followed him. "You look upset, which does not suit your pretty face."

"Lord Bude, I understand you asked Keating to consult me about the seating arrangement at dinner. I don't know about these things. Evidently—"

"But you are acting as hostess for the evening, and the hostess should know about these things."

"Yes, but I don't. I didn't want to be hostess, but Lyle

begged me to be. Evidently it is a matter of who takes precedence, Lady Hatchfield or Mrs. Groombridge. Mrs. Groombridge—"

"My dear, that is your responsibility for the evening. Now, if you will excuse me, I must get back to Lady Hatchfield."

After that I returned to Keating. "It would seem to me, Keating," I said, "that the wife of a baronet would take precedence over the granddaughter of a duke. The latter seems rather far removed, don't you think?"

"Very good, miss," Keating said. "Then I shall place Lady Hatchfield second to your left at the table. Thank you very much, miss."

He left me then, and it did not seem like more than three minutes before he returned to announce that dinner was served.

This was my cue to arrange the procession into the dining room. I did this without difficulty, placing Lady Hatchfield as the fourth lady in line on Mr. Rosso's arm, followed by Mrs. Groombridge on Mr. Mayworth's. Then feeling very proud, I placed Lord Charles and myself at the rear of the procession and we went in.

The table was beautifully set, and one would never have known it had been rearranged at the last minute. However, the arrangement of the diners was not completely satisfactory: Mr. Sly, Lord Hartley's solicitor, was the only gentleman not flanked by ladies. Mr. Mayworth sat on his left. And Mrs. Groombridge was not flanked by gentlemen: Miss Moore, an American actress who was traveling with Mr. Sipp, sat on her right. Mr. Sly did not seem to mind, but Mrs. Groombridge actually seemed angry.

I wondered about this, of course, but only briefly. Because of the constant flow of conversation, I had too many other things to think about. I was not able to converse easily with Lord Bude, the princess, Lady Charles, Mr. Rosso, or Lord Woolwich—as they all sat at the other end of the table. But occasionally I was able to hear snatches of their conversation. And once I heard Lord Bude only too plainly. Was it that he spoke in an unnecessarily loud voice? Or was it simply that there had been a lull in the conversation?

". . . at the rectory with the Reverend and Mrs. Cuttlebuck," he said. "But she is no relation to them. As a matter of fact her mother was a millworker in Manchester! When she died, it was arranged that the child be brought here to live with Mr. and Mrs. Cuttlebuck. And she has been a godsend." Lord Bude looked at me then, and when he saw that I had heard, he smiled. "Our dear Miss Little has been an enormous help to the rector and Mrs. Cuttlebuck, and company for me. She reads to me on two afternoons a week, for which I am grateful." He stared at me then with raised eyebrows, demanding a reply.

"I'm only too happy to do so," I called down to him. "And I'm delighted to see that you have recovered from your illness."

"Yes, yes, quite," he replied.

Then he turned to Lady Charles. I could not hear what he said because Lyle and Lady Woolrich, on either side of me, were talking. "Tell us about London. What have you been doing?"

"Oh, the usual thing, Lyle," Lady Woolwich said. "Who do you suppose we saw at the Ritz Bar on Wednesday afternoon?" She turned to me. "Always remember, darling, the mixed bar is on your right." Then she turned back to Lyle. "With Noel, of all people. Swathed to the chin in monkey fur? Gwen! I nearly dropped my cocktail. Ivor was there with Jack, and . . ."

Thus began another long list of people she knew, with explanations to me, as though to a child, along the way.

During dinner, I noticed Miss Moore lean across the table to speak to Mr. Rosso. She was very animated and flashed her brilliant smile at him repeatedly. Mr. Rosso, however, seemed to have eyes only for the princess, who continued to gaze with her cowlike eyes at Lyle—even though she was forced to lean forward constantly in order to do so.

Lady Charles was, as I have said, too far away to speak to easily, but our eyes met two or three times during the meal, and each time this happened, she smiled quickly and instantly turned away. It seemed she felt obliged to be nice to me, but didn't wish to be. Or was it Lord Charles's attention to me that was responsible for her attitude?

By the time dessert was handed round, I was certain that Lord Bude had been watching me a great deal during the meal. It made me uncomfortable, and I was glad that dinner was almost over. Somehow I felt that everyone at the table was secretly evaluating me and waiting for me to make a blunder.

Also, there had been so much conversation about things that I had no interest in or knowledge of. For instance, I understood nothing about American business, and Lyle, Mr. Mayworth, and Mr. Sipp discussed it continually.

Now as I ate one last yellow grape, Lyle said to Mr. Sipp, "It would not matter then, with someone like Mr. Livermore on one's side. One would automatically recoup at the market. But I must make something of an announcement." He glanced around the table then and in a loud voice said, "Now, I have something to tell you all." He spoke louder still. "I have something to tell you all, which, I know, will be delightful news." Now all turned their attention to Lord Hartley. "We are going to have a ball here at Compton Hall."

This was greeted with great enthusiasm.

"Yes, it will be fancy dress," he continued, "and we are going to make it as much like the once-famous Compton Hall balls as we can. It will be on June twenty-first. Everyone here will receive an invitation, of course. Mr. and Mrs. Mayworth, I hope you and Mr. Sipp and Miss Moore will stay on for it."

Now everyone exclaimed at once.

Through it all Lord Bude sat at the other end of the table, watching Lyle and me with an expression of tolerant surprise on his face. I wondered if this were a surprise to him as well as to the rest of us.

Finally, when the excitement had subsided somewhat and the room had become quieter, he looked across at me, nodded, and said, "I think it is about time now, my dear."

"I was just about to do so, Lord Bude," I said.

I stood then and, followed by the ladies, left the room. I was even more uncomfortable as we drank our coffee in the drawing room than I had been at dinner. At least at dinner I had had Lyle nearby to provide encouragement. Now I was alone with the ladies. It was not so much Lady Woolwich's patronizing manner that disturbed me, or the way Lady Charles avoided me, or the disagreeably cutting remarks that passed between Mrs. Mayworth and Miss Moore. No, it was the venomous glances that Mrs. Groombridge gave me when she thought I wasn't looking. She had decided to hate me, and it was part of her conversation with Lady Charles, finally, that told me why.

". . . my mother, Lady Agatha Mersham, was the daughter of the Duke of Ramsbury," she said. "Why, I grew up at Washam Hall Palace. And the dukedom, as you well know, is one of the oldest. It was on the accession of his cousin, Richard II, that John de Mauntland was created the first Duke of Ramsbury in 1380. Now, really, Lady Charles, how would *you* feel—especially when Lady Hatchfield is the daughter of some obscure squire down in Dorset? I have never been so humiliated!"

Later, when I asked Mrs. Groombridge if she would like more coffee, she pretended she had not heard me and turned abruptly to speak to the princess, who sat silently beside her. I was sure then that I had been wrong about the order of precedence that evening and, thus, had insulted Mrs. Groombridge and embarrassed Lady Hatchfield.

I felt terribly ashamed and longed for the men to join us. It was only after they did and we went into the hall for the dancing that I began to enjoy myself a little.

As we left the drawing room, I chanced to overhear a scrap of conversation between Lyle and Lady Charles which I remember almost word for word.

"You distinctly promised to be nice to Louisa, Elinor,"

Lord Hartley said. "I must count on your keeping that promise."

"But I *am* being nice to her, Lyle," Lady Charles said. "I am!"

It was only later that I was to think very much about that conversation. Just then, I was anxious for the dancing to take me out of the limelight, which it did.

The dancing took place in the enormous first-floor hall of the house. The small orchestra, which Lyle had brought down from London, included a marvelous saxophonist. Other guests, local people, arrived after dinner for the dancing. Among them were Lord and Lady Lownsden, Lady Lilly Lindley, Lady Hewingham, Mr. Denby, and Colonel and Mrs. Fitzcroft from the Grange. Thirty or so people danced in the hall that evening—not enough to necessitate using the long gallery.

It had been six months since the last time I had danced. That had been at the Railway Ball, at the assembly rooms in Bridgehampton. I loved dancing, so I enjoyed myself thoroughly. I do not remember what my partners and I talked about, however, or even if we talked at all. But I remember the dance that followed the waltz with Lyle. It was a tango, and I danced it with a stout, ruddy-faced man whom I had never met before and whom I learned was Sir Arthur Spitalfield.

"So kind of you to give an old man one of your dances," he said, as he began to guide me, rather breathlessly, about the floor. "But I had to ask for one—had to. Like living it all over again—twenty years ago."

"Living it over again?" I asked.

"Yes, yes. Twenty years ago. You look not unlike her, you know."

"To whom are you referring, Sir Arthur?"

"To Lord Hartley's mother, the late Lady Bude. Yes, you remind me of her, definitely. And that necklace wouldn't be hers, would it?"

"Yes," I said. "Lyle suggested—"

"I thought so—the diamond clasp, you know. It was her

favorite, I believe. How many times we danced—here in this very room. And now you have taken her place, and I feel that twenty years have slipped from my shoulders."

"Hardly taken her place, Sir Arthur!"

"Well, you know what I mean, my dear. I am not blind, you know. Ha, ha, ha. Now, please do not take offense. You have given a dying man more pleasure than you can—"

"Surely not! You must be in the pink of health."

"No, no! Heart. I have always enjoyed myself, and I shall continue to do so. Carmichael says I must not be upset. I must rest. Rest? Humph! But it is the winter that I cannot bear. Going to Italy. Have a villa at Capri. Won't be back—no, no. But I don't mind. Sold my stable entirely, except for one or two horses and a team of hackneys. Quality! A lot of Andalusian blood there. Selling them to a local man on Sunday afternoon, I shouldn't wonder."

While he finished telling me about his horses, I had chance to look about the room. Where was Lyle? I found him standing near the stairway with Mr. Mayworth and Mr. Sipp. No doubt they were talking about the American stock market or some such thing. The princess sat against the wall with Mr. Rosso by her side. She paid no attention to him, however. She was gazing at Lyle.

But then Sir Arthur and I stopped dancing and he led me to the railing of the stairwell. Our dance was not yet finished, but I was very glad we had stopped dancing since Sir Arthur had become red in the face and breathless.

It was while he stood leaning against the balustrade and I stood beside him that I overheard part of Lady Woolwich's and Lady Charles's conversation as they climbed the stairs behind us.

"Wouldn't you think she would have done *something* with her hair," Lady Woolwich exclaimed.

"She probably would not know *what* to do with it," Lady Charles said. "She is obviously a low person. And like all low persons, she is, I am afraid, entirely unaware."

I turned my head so that they would not discover me watching them. I looked across the hall toward the drawing room and saw Lord Bude watching me, as he had all evening.

He asked for the next dance. I was amazed. I had never associated dancing with this thin, bent, old man. But he was amazingly agile for his age, and danced well indeed.

After he had silently guided me about the hall several times, he inquired, "Enjoying yourself, Miss Little?"

"Very much, thank you," I replied.

"Humph! I take it you approve of the . . . assemblage this evening?"

"I do not think it is my place to approve or—"

"Quite right, quite right. But I can tell you without reservation that *I* do not. I have never witnessed such a conglomeration of low types. Especially those Americans, and particularly that actress, Miss Moore. Notice how she playacts being at ease? But nothing could be further from the truth. She is like a fish out of water here, and she knows it perfectly well. And some of the others feel the same. They could never fit in. Don't you agree?"

"I do not think I can judge."

Lord Bude stopped dancing then and led me to stand against the wall near the library door.

"No, I suppose not," he said. "One must be born to our society—bred in it—in order to fit in. You can always tell, no matter how hard they work at it. Sticks out like a sore thumb. They can look the part; that is easy. Any woman can put on a necklace." He paused while he stared at the necklace around my neck. "Or wear a dress." Now he examined the dress I wore. "It does not matter how she came to have it. One can always tell that she is not used to it. Ill at ease. Obvious! Well?"

"I do not think it matters, Lord—"

"Matters? Of course it matters. People cannot go about making other people miserable. Well, can they?"

"No."

"Of course they can't. Cannot have people unhappy. And that is what happens when common persons mix with people accustomed to good society. They do not mix. They do not know what to say, and they do not know what to do. One has to be born to it. One cannot acquire it. Don't you agree?"

"I suppose so, Lord Bude." I had decided that the best way to end this conversation would be to say as little as possible and agree with him.

"Yes!" he said. Then looking out across the hall at the dancers, he continued, "Ah, there he is."

"Who, Lord Bude?" I asked.

"Lyle, of course. He is dancing with Lady Lilly Lindley. See him? Ah. They have known each other all their lives. Now, the manners of a young lady of quality—of aristocratic background such as she is—would always be above reproach. She would be perfect for him. And Lord Lownsden is immensely rich. She would be perfect. Perfect!"

That was when the music stopped for good. I was never so grateful to see an end to anything.

Lord Hartley and I stood at the top of the stairs and said good night to those who were leaving the Hall. When they had departed, he and I descended the staircase together and walked out onto the drive to Lyle's car.

I had expected that Rodger would drive us to the rectory, but evidently Lyle had decided to drive us himself. "Where is Rodger?" I asked, when Lyle had gotten into the seat beside me.

"I suppose he is driving Lady Hatchfield home," Lyle said.

We drove down the drive then without speaking, and it was only after we had passed the lodge and driven through the gates that Lyle spoke again. He grasped my hand and squeezed it.

"You were a great success," he said.

"Was I?" I asked.

"Definitely! Both Lady Woolwich and Lady Charles made a particular point of saying how charming you are."

"Oh?"

"Yes. And no wonder." He squeezed my hand again. "You were an absolute delight—perfect!"

"Not so perfect," I said, disengaging my hand. "And before we forget, let me return your mother's necklace."

"I had forgotten about it," Lord Hartley said. "It looks so right on you. It seems to belong around your neck. You must wear it often."

I removed the pearls and slipped them into his coat pocket.

"Why not so perfect?" he said.

"I am afraid I made a ghastly mistake in placing Lady Hatchfield before Mrs. Groombridge. It should have been the other way around, but I don't know anything about precedence. It must be terribly complicated. Mrs. Groombridge was livid."

"It doesn't matter and you will learn. I can't imagine why Father brought the woman—why he came down at all. Unless it was to spoil the evening, or try to. But he didn't try. All he did was to watch us like some bird of prey," he mused. "Did you notice?"

"Yes."

"What were you and he talking about just before the last dance ended?"

"I think he was telling me how . . . unsuitable I was this evening."

"*What?* Unsuitable? What do you mean?"

"Not in so many words, but—"

"What?"

"Well, he made it seem as though he was talking only about Miss Moore, but he wasn't. He said she was . . . common, and that she could never be at ease in good society. That one must be born and bred to it. That clothes and jewels did not matter. It was manners that made the difference, and that they could *not* be acquired."

"Rubbish."

"He was telling me that I should not have been there this evening."

"Rubbish! Of course you should have been there and you will be again."

"He said he has always had great hopes for you and

Lady Lilly. That she is a lady of quality and would be perfect for you."

"Lady Lilly? If he has, he has never said anything about it to me. Why, I have never paid the slightest attention to Lady Lilly. My God, she's a bore. This is all ridiculous!" Then after a pause he said, "Oh, I think I see."

"What do you see?"

"Nothing. Forget all that nonsense. You were simply marvelous, and I am very proud of you." Again he took my hand and held it.

He seemed lost in thought after that, and we did not speak again until we drew up before the rectory.

As we walked toward the house together, he said, "You are coming riding with us tomorrow, then?"

"Yes, I would love to," I said. "What time are you leaving?"

"About two, I should think. Would that be all right?"

"Lovely. Then I shall see you at about two o'clock tomorrow."

"A little before that would be even better," Lyle said, flashing his smile at me in the moonlight.

Then we climbed the steps to the portico, and before he opened the door for me, Lyle took me in his arms and kissed me. "Sleep well, my darling," he whispered. "You have made me very happy tonight."

The following day, Saturday, I rode out with Lord Hartley, Lord and Lady Charles, and Lord and Lady Woolwich.

I returned to the rectory at about five o'clock in the afternoon, intending to change into a dress and go to the church to fix the flowers for the service the following day. But as soon as I entered the house, Aunt Grace called, "Louisa, is that you?"

"Yes, Aunt Grace," I called up to her. "I'll be up in a minute."

I climbed the stairs then and went directly to Aunt Grace's room. I was surprised to find Uncle Andrew there, pacing the floor in front of the window.

"Can I get you something?" I asked Aunt Grace.

"No, my dear," Aunt Grace said. "Lieutenant Compton called."

"Oh?" I said. "When?"

"About fifteen minutes ago—"

Uncle Andrew interrupted. "Louisa, I do not think it appropriate for that man to call here."

"Appropriate?" Aunt Grace cried. "It is downright foolish. Dangerous! Suppose Lord Hartley should find out that you encourage Lieutenant Compton to call. Do you want to put your relationship with Lord Hartley in jeopardy? Think of the future, child! And if you cannot think of your own future, think of ours."

"You went riding with Lieutenant Compton Thursday," Aunt Grace went on. "You spent the whole afternoon with him, didn't you?"

"It was just a ride."

"Louisa," Aunt Grace said, "you said you would forbid that man to call here."

"I said nothing of the kind, Aunt Grace. But don't upset yourself."

" 'The wise man's eyes are in his head; but the fool walketh in darkness,' " Uncle Andrew said. "You are an intelligent girl, Louisa. You must realize the folly of entertaining Lieutenant Compton. We think only of your happiness, my dear. Since you are to marry Lord Hartley— Ah, yes, we pray for that blessing, and the Lord hears our prayers. Then you will forbid Lieutenant Compton to call?"

"Very well," I said.

"Let us pray," Uncle Andrew began. "Oh, Lord, look down on this thy humble servant, Louisa. Guide her footsteps into paths of wisdom and forethought . . ."

When he had finished, I left them and went to find May.

"May," I said, when I had found her in the kitchen, "I understand Lieutenant Compton called."

"Yes, miss," she said.

"What did you tell him?"

"Why, that you were not at home, miss. That's all I told

him. I didn't say another thing to him, honest, I didn't. I just said that you were not at home. That's what you told me, wasn't it? That you were not at home? That's all I said."

Both Lyle and Stuart attended church the following morning. I do not believe I heard a word of Uncle Andrew's sermon, nor did I pay very much attention to the rest of the service. I was too busy trying to decide what to do when it was over.

When I left the church, stepping out onto the stone walk, I looked about to see where Lyle stood and where Stuart stood. You can imagine my surprise, then, when I found that they stood together, talking.

It was not an amicable conversation, at least not on Stuart's part.

"Good morning, Louisa," the two men called in unison, when I approached.

"Good morning, Lyle, Stuart," I said. "One could not ask for a more beautiful day, don't you agree?"

"Quite!" Lyle said to me. "I was just telling Compton about the ball up at the Hall and how much I hope he will come." Then he turned to Stuart. "I sent an invitation to the manor house, Compton. I didn't know whether you were still at Sandhurst or not, so I thought it safer to send it there. I do hope you will come."

"Why the devil should I?" Stuart asked testily. "It was not very long ago, Hartley, that you couldn't wait to get rid of me. Now you invite me back to a ball and expect me to attend?"

"It was not that we did not want you, Compton. It was Father's health. I explained it to you at the time. Nothing personal, you understand. Always good to see you again, you know that."

"Of course Stuart will come," I plunged in. Then I turned to Stuart and said, "Why, the balls at Compton Hall are almost legendary, Stuart. It will be a marvelous evening. Say you will."

Stuart looked at me. Then after a moment he said to

Lyle, "Frankly, Hartley, being in the same room with you is more than I think I can stomach. What are you up to, anyway?"

"Nothing!" Lyle said. "My dear cousin, we have very little family left. There is no reason why we can't be on cordial terms. After all, we have known each other since we were in school together. I simply wish to provide a pleasant evening. There is no reason to make a great thing about it."

"Very well," Stuart said. "I have nothing to lose, Hartley. God only knows what you are up to, but rather than wonder about it, perhaps I shall come to your ball to find out."

"You were always the suspicious one." Lyle shook his head. "Now, if you will excuse me, I must get back to the princess. Good day, Louisa, Compton. Remember me to Mrs. Cuttlebuck."

With that, he strode off toward his car, where the princess and Mrs. Groombridge waited.

"Who is the cow-eyed woman?" Stuart asked me.

"The Princess Pidudska, I believe," I said.

"Louisa," he said, turning to me, "I went to the millpond yesterday, but you weren't there. Then I called at the rectory, and—"

"Good morning, Lieutenant Compton." Uncle Andrew had announced himself before we had seen him. I had not even heard his footsteps.

"Good morning, Rector," Stuart said.

"It is always good to see you at morning service, my boy. And I am particularly happy that you were able to attend this morning. The eighteenth psalm has always been one of my favorites. As beautiful in its way, I think, as the twenty-third. But unfortunately it is neglected."

While he spoke, I noticed that little Catherine Pomery stared at Uncle Andrew. She had stood behind a box bush while Uncle talked to Miss Ormsby. I had noticed her peering in his direction a few minutes before. Now she peeped out from behind the trunk of an oak tree which stood not ten yards from us. She was staring expectantly at him. Did she think he was about to ride up to heaven on a cloud, or something equally spectacular? "Strange child," I thought.

"Oh, Louisa, my dear," Uncle continued, "Mrs. Cuttlebuck seemed to have taken a turn for the worse just before I left the rectory. I think she will want you nearby. Would you mind running along and seeing if she is all right?"

"Of course, Uncle. I will go right along," I said. "Don't you love the eighteenth psalm?" I turned to Stuart. " 'He sent from above, he took me, he drew me out of many *waters. Late in the day*, he delivered me from my strong enemy . . .' "

"I do not believe the time element—" Uncle began.

"Now I must go to Aunt Grace," I said. And I left them.

Chapter Seven

LATE IN THE DAY—AT ABOUT FOUR O'CLOCK in the afternoon—I stole away from the rectory and walked to the waters I had mentioned: the millpond. It stood deserted in the late afternoon sun. I sat down on the ruined foundation and waited. In only a few minutes his car approached. Moments later he strode along the path toward me. Now he stood, legs spread apart, hands on his hips, glaring down at me.

"Good afternoon, Stuart," I began.

"I came to the millpond yesterday, but you weren't here," he said angrily. "Then I called at the rectory. May told me you had ridden out with Hartley. Is that true?"

"Yes. I went riding with Lyle and some of his—"

"And Friday night you played hostess at Compton Hall. You wore an expensive dress and Lady Bude's pearl necklace. Is that correct?"

"Who told you that?"

"Sir Arthur Spitalfield. I have just returned from Holly Hill."

"You went there to buy his horses?"

"Clever girl. You are taking Hartley for all you can get, aren't you?"

I jumped to my feet then and stood facing him. "How can you say such a thing?" I said.

"You're a fair match for him," he went on, paying no attention to me. "How far do you intend to go? I warn you: don't go too far. You will find you have made a mistake if you do."

"What do you mean by that?"

"You will find out," he said, his eyes narrowing and turning to blue ice. "You will find out that you have made the biggest mistake of your life."

A shiver of fear ran through me suddenly. "Are you threatening me? You are trying to frighten me. What do you mean? Tell me!"

"I'll let you find out for yourself."

"Stuart, what have I done? I have every right to attend a dinner party at Compton Hall. And I have every right to ride with—"

Stuart grasped the skirt of my dress near the waist and pulled me roughly to him.

"Don't!" I glared at him as I tried to wrench free. "I won't be taken by force like this."

"You don't have to pretend any longer," he sneered. "You take your pleasure where you can, don't you? And you take as much of it as you can get. Compton Hall or the millpond, what does it matter? Lieutenant Compton one day, Lord Hartley another."

"I will scream," I said.

"I wouldn't, if I were you," he growled.

I did not scream. There was a note in his voice that warned me not to. Nor did I struggle further as he kissed me. I had no wish to. Almost as soon as his mouth fastened on mine and his great arms tightened about me, I felt that thrilling glow deep within me. And as he continued to kiss me, the glow swelled and spread through my body. I trembled with delight.

But then, without warning, he thrust me away from him. "Do you think Hartley can do that?" he snarled. "Slut!"

Then his hand struck my cheek, wrenching my head back and hurling me to the ground. I lay there, too stunned and frightened to move. He stared down at me for a moment, an expression of loathing on his face. Then he flung himself about and stalked back along the path toward his car.

In a minute or two the engine started, and the car roared off down the lane at what must have been full throttle. I listened to it until the sound disappeared. Tears sprang to my eyes. Then I lay my head in the crook of my arm and wept.

My tears were not only tears of heartache, but tears of outrage and humiliation as well. How could he have done that to me? He was a brute. Everyone was right about him. He was loathsome—vile. I *hated* him.

I slept little that night and did not feel at all like myself the following day. I would have given almost anything not to have to read to Lord Bude that afternoon, but I have never avoided duty.

As I read, I wondered why Lord Bude had decided to resume reading *The Prodigal*. But I did not wonder after I had read the following passage:

> "By G--, sir. You can not mean what you are saying."
> "With all my heart, Father. Miss Glenville is the sun, and the moon, and the stars to me. She is the very air that I breathe, the very bread of my life. I cannot live without her everlastingly at my side. Yes, I shall marry her. And she has pledged herself to me as mine alone forever."
> "But she is a low person," cried Lord Claredon. "You know nothing of her. Who were her parents? Where did she come—"

"Dawton's sister!" Lord Bude exclaimed.

"I beg your pardon?"

"Dawton's sister, that's who she is! Miss Glenville is Dawton's sister."

"How do you know that?" I asked.

"It is obvious. Their mother was a strumpet! Low persons breed low persons. Lord Claredon is right—absolutely right. Cannot have his son marrying out of his class like that. Impossible!"

"If they love each other, I do not see why—"

"Love? Humph! Love does not mean a thing. It is over like that." Lord Bude snapped his fingers. "Does not mean a thing! It is background and breeding that matter. Look what happened on Friday night. Mrs. Groombridge was furious. Retired to her room in tears. And Lady Hatchfield was mortified. Mortified! It does not work, I tell you."

"But surely one can *learn*," I said.

"Learn? Humph! Takes a lifetime. You have got to be born to it. I tell you, Miss Little, if my son ever considered marrying a low person, I would—I would not permit it. I would not *permit* it! Do I make myself clear?"

"Yes, perfectly. But please do not excite yourself, Lord Bude. Shall I call Keating?"

"Certainly not. I am perfectly all right, Miss Little. Go on. Let us get on with it, then."

" 'Who were her parents?' " I continued reading. " 'Where did she come from? I will not permit it!' "

"Quite right! Never!" Lord Bude cried.

" 'But Father, I cannot live without her . . .' "

I read on then without any further interruption from Lord Bude. But as I read, I was aware that he watched me in the same hawklike manner he had used on Friday night. I was glad when four o'clock came.

From the library I went directly downstairs and ran straight into Bertha.

"It's a good thing you're here," she told me. "I have something to tell you about his young lordship. He was furious on Thursday."

"Was he? Why?"

"You got the orchid he sent you?"

"Yes."

"And the note?" she asked.

"Yes, I did."

"Well, there was to be an answer to it. Rodger took it down to the rectory, but you weren't home. So he talked to May. And May says that she hopes the note don't need an answer right away because you were out riding with Lieutenant Compton. She says he was going to show you the manor house and the rest of his property over beyond

Bridgehampton, and that being the case, you would probably not get back to the rectory till late in the afternoon."

I was too stunned by this to speak. I simply stared at Bertha.

"But that's not all," she continued. "Rodger comes back here, where his young lordship is waiting for your answer to his note, and tells him what May said. Well, his young lordship was *furious*! He storms out of the house, goes to the garage, gets his car out, and zooms off in the direction of Bridgehampton. And he was gone the rest of the afternoon."

"Oh, no," I murmured.

"Did you see him?"

"I think so," I said, as much to myself as to Bertha. "I think I saw him watching us from the top of one of the Three Sisters, when we were riding home. I wondered at the time if it could be he. But it might not have been Lyle, because he has said nothing about it since. Not a word. He has never even seemed angry."

"He knows about it, all right. May told Rodger, and Rodger told his young lordship."

"And I suppose Rodger told Keating," I said, "and Keating told—"

"No, Rodger told Elvira, and Elvira told Mrs. Merrymede, and Mrs. Merrymede told Mr. Keating. And then it all came out because you were coming to the Hall on Friday night."

"So everyone knows," I said.

"Yes. Louisa, you cannot go on seeing Lieutenant Compton when it makes his young lordship so angry. It's *foolish*! Why do you want to see him, anyway?"

"Ur—humph!" Keating stood in the doorway. "Miss Little?"

"Yes, Keating?" I asked. "What is it?"

"It is his young lordship, miss. He has been asking for you and wishes to know if you will join him in the drawing room."

"Thank you, Keating," I said. "I'll come right along."

Then I said to Bertha, "Thank you for telling me, Bertha. Good-bye for now. I'll see you on Sunday, if not before."

Then I followed Keating to the drawing room doorway, where he announced, "Miss Little, my lord."

"Hello," Lyle said, as he hurried across the room to me. "I'm so glad I caught you. Thank you, Keating."

Keating left us then, closing the drawing room doors behind him.

"Hello, Lyle," I said. "I'm glad too. I was having a chat with Bertha. How have you been? Have your guests been keeping you occupied? Are they all staying on for the ball?"

"No, neither Mr. and Mrs. Mayworth, nor Mr. Sipp, nor Miss Moore are staying. They must go back to New York. Business, you know. They have stayed away far too long as it is, according to Mr. Sipp. Lord and Lady Charles and Lord and Lady Woolwich motored back to London yesterday afternoon. And the princess and Mrs. Groombridge and Mr. Rosso left on the half past two train. That is why I was not here when you finished reading to Father. They will all be down for the ball, though."

"I'm so glad Mrs. Groombridge has gone. I don't think I could face her again."

"That was not your fault, you know. Didn't the whole thing strike you as being a little odd?"

"How do you mean, odd?" I asked.

"Well, Father arrives at the last minute, creating the problem by bringing Lady Hatchfield. Now, he specifically directs that you solve it. How could you know Lady Hatchfield's background? And then he had made sure that no one would help you. Mrs. Merrymede had one of her 'terrible headaches.' *What* terrible headaches? She has never had a headache in her life. And Keating would not help, though he knew very well you were making a mistake. He is an *expert* on such matters."

"But both Mrs. Merrymede and Keating like me. They wouldn't do such a thing."

"Don't forget they are in Father's employ."

"I see. Then that is what you realized on the ride home Friday night?"

"Yes. Don't you agree?"

"I suppose so. And Lord Bude continued to make me feel uncomfortable by saying those things to me while we danced on Friday night. And a little while ago when I was reading to him, he did the same thing."

"Oh? What happened?"

I explained. "He must have known what was about to happen. It was an excellent way for him to—express some of his sentiments."

"All of which means that Father has learned that we are seeing quite a lot of each other."

"And disapproves," I said.

"Does it matter if he does?"

"I . . . don't know."

"My dear Louisa, I have long since come of age, and I am free to act with or without his approval. And I am sure that Mr. and Mrs. Cuttlebuck are delighted." He grinned at me.

"Yes. But . . ."

"I know how you feel. He'll come around, I promise you. He's been behaving very strangely of late, erratically. But in a rational moment, he can't possibly object. Now, don't think another thing about it. How are Mrs. Cuttlebuck and things at the rectory?"

"She is better today." Then after a pause I asked, "Why did you ask Stuart to the ball?"

"Why?"

"Yes. I thought you and he didn't like each other very well."

"Oh? I can't say that I have an overwhelming affection for him. He is not the kind of person one can feel affection for. I'm sure you can sense that. How one can go through life insulting people and striking out at them both physically and mentally, as he does, is beyond me. I don't know where that ugly streak came from—certainly not from the Compton side of the family. He is cruel, Louisa. I know. I grew up with him. We went to school together. I could tell you some things he has done that would make your skin crawl, but there's no purpose in that. Don't get too near him."

"Why did you invite him to the ball, then?"

"Why? Perhaps I shouldn't have, but after all, he is my cousin. And I thought he might like to see what a ball was like at Compton Hall. He has—an obsession—about his mother, and she attended balls here. And I thought he might enjoy it. That's all. Did you receive your invitation?"

"Yes, it arrived in this morning's post. It was beautifully done. Thank you so much."

"And have you decided on your costume?"

"I thought I would come as a gypsy."

Lyle looked at me with disapproval, I thought. But he said nothing.

"You don't approve?"

"What on earth made you decide that?"

"It would be an easy thing to do. One of Aunt Grace's old skirts, and a bandanna, and some big earrings—"

Lyle raised his eyebrows.

I continued, "I can't sew very well, and we have no costumes at the rectory."

"Not a gypsy," Lyle said, smiling at me. "Please, not that. They are so dirty and . . . common. No, it must be something beautiful. Something . . . entrancing. A queen, or an empress, or something like that. We have trunks of costumes in the attics. I used to play with them sometimes when I was a child—swords, and armor, and mustaches." He laughed. "Many of the dresses are magnificent. Shall we see if we can find something for you there?"

"Could we?"

"Of course. We'll go up now!"

And we did.

We rummaged through several trunks before we found a green and gold Cleopatra costume with a matching wig. They were in surprisingly good condition.

"You will be breathtaking in this, Louisa," he said as he held the dress before me. "Yes, that is *exactly* the thing.

Exactly . . ." He glanced at his watch. "But we'll work it all out later. I have an errand to do this afternoon. I shall be meeting Aunt Leonora at the station soon."

"Who is Aunt Leonora?"

"Father's sister. He has decided that if we must have a ball, it will be done with perfect decorum. Consequently, Aunt Leonora."

We put back the other costumes and left the attic. "You don't seem to like her very well."

"I don't dislike her but she is rather strange. I have met her only three or four times in my life. Edinburgh, where she lives, is some ways off."

"Strange?" I echoed.

"She is particularly conscious of the social amenities, on the one hand; everything must be done strictly according to etiquette."

"Oh, dear."

"But on the other hand, she is a clairvoyant, a spiritualist."

"You are not serious," I exclaimed.

He began to laugh. As he did so he pointed all his fingers at me and popped his eyes. "She brings the spirits back to earth."

I laughed too. "No, you can't be serious."

"Yes! Which is just the opposite of being proper, somehow. And she does astrology. The first thing she will probably ask you is when you were born."

We both laughed again.

"At any rate," he continued, "she attended many balls at Compton Hall while she was growing up and when she was a young lady, and she knows exactly how they were done."

"It's going to be wonderful. I am looking forward to it so much—especially now that I have a beautiful costume."

A bit later Lyle drove me down to the rectory. We had not spoken of my afternoon with Stuart.

I did not see Lyle for a few days because he was off collecting the estate rents.

On Thursday I hoped that Lord Bude would say nothing about Lyle and me. If only he would let me read to him without interruption. But Lord Bude was not alone in the library. Across from him, in the chair I usually occupied, sat a tall, thin white-haired woman who I was sure was Lady Leonora Compton, Lyle's Aunt Leonora.

"I am so sorry, Lord Bude," I said. "I didn't mean to interrupt, but I thought we were to read together this afternoon."

"Quite right, my dear," Lord Bude replied. He turned to his sister and said, "This is the child I was telling you about, Leonora."

"How very sweet," she said to me. "I am delighted, Miss Little. May I ask your birth date, my dear?"

"June second," Lord Bude said promptly. "Can you make anything of that?"

"I am so glad to meet you, Lady Leonora," I said.

"Oh, let me see," Lady Leonora said. "The sun is eleven degrees of Gemini, I believe . . . and both Saturn and Neptune are directly on your sun. Oh, dear . . ."

"Something wrong?" Lord Bude asked.

"No, not wrong . . . I would need to do a chart, of course," she said, "but I am afraid close relationships will be very tricky, very risky for some time to come, my dear. Be very careful, and do not form any permanent relationships—especially ties of the heart. Romantic connections should be avoided at all costs. Dangerous at this time. Terribly dangerous."

"Precisely!" Lord Bude exclaimed.

"That is very good of you, Lady Leonora," I said. "But I'm afraid that is not really my birthday. I—we don't know exactly when it was. Wouldn't it have to be the exact day?"

"Oh my, yes," Lady Leonora said. "And the exact hour and minute to do it perfectly. Really, William," she said to Lord Bude, "you should know better. What was the point of that?"

"As good a day as any," Lord Bude said.

"It is perfectly obvious that it must be the correct day,"

Lady Leonora said. "Sometimes I think you do not take this at all seriously."

"Of course I do, Leonora. Of course I do. I wish you would tell that to that young scoundrel Lyle. *He* is the one who should beware of romantic relationships! I had thought he would marry that Livermore girl. That would have been disaster enough, but at least he would have settled down. He seemed captivated enough by her at the time, but then something went wrong, as it usually does, and he sent her back to America in tears."

"But you wrote that you disliked her intensely, William," Lady Leonora said.

"So I did, but you cannot have the boy chasing this one one week and that one the next like a bloody rutting goat."

"William!" Lady Leonora exclaimed. "Not in front of this child."

"Well, it is true," Lord Bude said. "Bloody rutting little goat . . ."

"I will not sit here and listen to such language." Lady Leonora rose from her chair. "What has gotten into you, William?"

"All right, all right! Sit down, sit *down*. I wish you would do Lyle's chart or whatever it is you do and straighten him out a little. Tell him to stop running after women and to forget his crazy ideas of making quick, easy money on the American stock exchange, of all places. He will end up a pauper, which will serve him right. I pity the young lady who marries him. He will end up selling potatoes in the streets, mark my words."

What was he trying to do? Discourage me from marrying Lyle? Or was Lord Bude truly concerned about Lyle's schemes?

Lady Leonora was saying, "I have no intention of going to all that work when neither you nor he has any faith in the stars. Do you know how long it takes to do a chart? And how you can be so blind is beyond me. Go out and look at the stars some night. And then ask one of your farmers what he plants by. It is the *moon* that he plants by. And ask a fisherman about the tides. It is—"

"I know, I know. The moon makes the tides," Lord Bude interrupted. "There may be something in it. I have told you there may be. But not that other nonsense!"

"They *do* return sometimes, William," Lady Leonora said. "And your ridicule doesn't deter them. They do. But I hope you never experience it. It is terrifying! It would be far better for you to go on doubting." Then she turned to me and said, "Our mother came to me one night, my dear. That was ten years after she had passed on. She was terribly troubled over something that—" She glanced quickly at Lord Bude. "Well, she was terribly troubled, though I could not quite understand what it was she was trying to tell me. I saw her as clearly as I see you now. And of course communication with the other side is common. I have done it many times.

"Nonsense!" Lord Bude said.

"You may think what you please out of ignorance and obstinacy, William. But I have no intention of sitting here and listening to you ridicule the truth." She rose now and walked toward the door. Halfway across the room she paused and said to us, "I shall leave you and Miss Little alone to do your reading. Miss Little, I shall see you at the ball, no doubt, and possibly before. I am delighted to have met you, my dear, but now you really must excuse me. Mrs. Merrymede and I have so much to do." Then she left.

After I had read to Lord Bude without interruption. I hurried up to Lady Bude's room. There Elvira, one of the sewing maids, waited to alter my costume. Afterwards we agreed to try it on again on Monday.

Monday was a gloomy, gray day. By a quarter to two in the afternoon one would have needed a lamp to read by— so dark had the day become. But I did not think it would rain because a heavy, wet mist had blown in from the sea. It seldom rained when this happened.

When I had finished reading to Lord Bude, I left him and went up to Lady Bude's room for the final fitting. The costume fit perfectly now, and Elvira had pressed it beautifully. I had just finished telling her so when Bertha arrived.

"Louisa, I have news!" she said.

"If you won't be needing me any more now, miss," Elvira said.

"Oh, no, Elvira," I said. "Go along, and thank you ever so much."

Elvira hurried out of the room then, leaving Bertha and me alone.

"What is it, Bertha?" I asked.

"Nellie Linton! She's been sacked! And just when we're so busy."

"Whatever for?"

"Stealing!"

"Nellie wouldn't steal anything. You said so yourself."

"That's what we thought. But she wasn't as honest as she seemed. I was shocked! She stole lots of things from time to time. She stole a gold letter opener from his young lordship's room just before he left the Hall, and he had the house searched, and they found it in a box with other things in Nellie's trunk—jewelry and money, mostly. She was a thief! We were all shocked! And Mrs. Merrymede sacked her, and she's left Ledington, and nobody knows where she's gone. I think she stole Lieutenant Compton's cuff link that time, and then she got so frightened that she gave it to Mrs. Merrymede to give back to him. But I must go!"

"Will you peek in at the ball?" I asked.

"Yes," she said. "Bye-bye." Then she opened the door, slipped out into the corridor, and closed the door behind her, leaving me alone.

I turned back to the mirror then and posed for myself— this way and that. Yes, it was a marvelous costume. I felt like the empress of the Nile. "Soon the flood waters will come, my people," I whispered to my imaginary subjects, "to bring us a bountiful harvest." How they cheered me! How they admired and loved me!

I thought of Stuart then. How I loathed him. What a contemptible man he was. I hoped he wouldn't attend the ball. I never wanted to see him again. I would dance with

Lord Hartley. I could almost feel his arms around me as I began to waltz. I hummed as I whirled about the room. As I danced, I noticed that the bedroom door was slowly opening.

When the door had swung open wide, Lord Bude took a step into the room and stood staring at me. He was dressed in a raincoat. The dim light from behind me reflected off thousands of tiny drops of rain that covered his coat and hat and beard.

"Who is it?" he cried suddenly. "Elizabeth? Is it—? Oh, it is *you.* What do you want?"

I was so astonished that I could hardly decide what to say. "I don't want anything," I stammered. "I—"

"I didn't hurt her," he cried, paying no attention to me. He shrank back a step, frightened. "She is all right! She— she will get everything. What more do you—? Leonora!" he screamed. He turned and ran into the corridor and out of sight.

No sooner had he disappeared than Lyle dashed into view from the other direction. "What the devil has been going on here? What was all that screaming about? What did you say to him?"

"I didn't say anything to him," I exclaimed. "He asked me what I wanted, and I said nothing. That was all."

"Did he say anything?"

"Well, yes. But it didn't make sense. Shouldn't you go after him? He was acting very peculiarly."

"Keating and Blessing and Aunt Leonora will look after him. And there is a whole house full of servants. What *did* he say?"

"It all happened so fast, I—I don't think . . ."

"Oh, my poor darling, I am so sorry," Lyle said. "You've had a shock. Here, sit down."

"I'm all right, really," I said, as I sat down on the edge of the bed.

"Try to remember."

"He came into the room and asked who I was. Then he said, 'Elizabeth?' And then he said, 'Oh, it is you. What do you want?' That is when I said I didn't want anything."

"And then?" Lord Hartley asked.

"That is when he said the strangest things, something about not having hurt somebody and that she would get it all. Then he started to say something else, but he didn't finish it. He began calling for Lady Leonora."

"I see."

"Who is Elizabeth?" I asked.

Lyle didn't answer immediately. He seemed deep in thought. Presently he said, "I think . . . my mother's sister."

"Stuart's mother? But she has been dead for years."

"Yes."

"Then it couldn't be she."

"Oh, yes. His mind has been going. I told you that. And Aunt Leonora has been filling him full of her nonsense. I can't be sure, of course, but I think he thought you were her . . . umm . . . her spirit."

"Oh—yes. But then Lord Bude thought I was someone else."

"I don't know, but I wouldn't be surprised if he was talking about my mother, that she would get the family jewelry. Aunt Elizabeth had coveted it at one time. And my mother and father had a rather bad accident when a carriage overturned before they were married, I believe. Who knows? Did he say anything else?"

"No. How do you suppose he knew that I was here?"

"From the lighted window, I gather. He was walking on the drive when we arrived a few minutes ago. Are you sure he didn't say anything else?"

"No, I'm certain. Why do you ask like that?"

"Only to try to figure it out. Who knows what went on in his . . . demented mind? But that is as near as I can come to it." Then Lyle sat down beside me and took both my hands in his. "Now tell me, how have you been?"

"You think he will be all right?" I asked.

"Certainly."

"I've been fine. Do you like my costume now that it has been fitted and pressed?" I got up then, stood before him, and turned around slowly so that he could see it. "Don't you think Elvira has done it beautifully?"

"Beautifully," he said, rising from the bed. Then he stepped close to me, took me in his arms, and kissed me. "And you are beautiful, my darling."

"I must get back to the rectory now," I said. "Aunt Grace will be wondering where I am."

"But you don't need to go back quite yet. You can stay here with me for a bit."

"No, I'm afraid I can't, Lyle. I don't think I should." I said this with firmness, though I smiled at him as I did so.

"I see," he said. "Then may I be permitted to drive you home?"

Chapter Eight

UNCLE ANDREW HAD BEEN INVITED TO THE ball. He came, after all, of a good family, being the youngest son of Sir Erasmus Cuttlebuck, Bart. He was one of several Ledington inhabitants who were invited. Among the others were Mr. and Mrs. Dickerson, Major Seaton-Smith of the Grange, and Miss Annabella Ardsley of the Manor.

Almost a hundred people had been invited. But there is a great difference between thinking about such a number and actually experiencing the confusion resulting from so many people descending upon a country house at about the same time!

I began to suspect this as Patrick drove us up Compton Hill shortly before nine o'clock that Tuesday evening. When we had passed through the gateway to the Hall my heart beat wildly. I had never seen such a sight. There must have been twelve cars lined up on the drive waiting to discharge their passengers at the door of the house. Engines throbbed and wheels crunched the gravel as the procession moved slowly down the drive. And the air was filled with talk and laughter. Compton Hall stood before us, ablaze with light.

Finally the car ahead of us pulled up to the doorway. Punch and King Arthur helped Judy and Queen Guinevere out of it. Then it was our turn. Uncle helped me down and we followed the royal couple up the steps and into the loggia.

Part of the lower hall off the loggia had been converted into a cloakroom. Costumed guests left their wraps with maids there while others shouted greetings and laughed and talked together before climbing the staircase to the first floor and the long gallery.

The long gallery was opulent with lights and flowers. The large furniture and the rugs had been removed, and small chairs had been placed along its walls. The floor had been polished to a mirror. The emormous room was already filled with people when Uncle Andrew and I approached it. Lord Bude and Lady Leonora stood just inside the doorway to receive. We said good evening to them, and then Uncle left me as a Roman soldier approached me.

"Ah, Cleopatra, I have found you at last," he said.

"Oh, Marc Antony," I said, "I have waited, lo these many years, for your return to Egypt."

At that point the orchestra began to play "Sometimes I'm Happy."

Lyle danced beautifully and so did Lord Charles. After Lord Charles and I had finished our waltz, we went into the refreshment room for a glass of champagne. Then he left me with Uncle Andrew. But almost instantly, Uncle Andrew went off to find a partner—a Miss Hallburn from Bridgehampton. Miss Hallburn was barely sixteen years old. But I did not remain alone for long. I had no sooner sat down than I saw Lady Leonora weaving her way through the crowd toward me.

"I am so glad you are not dancing this dance, Miss Little." She smiled when she had sunk into the chair beside me. "Now we can talk for a moment. Doesn't it seem terribly warm in here? I must ask Keating to have some of the windows opened."

"Yes, it does seem a trifle warm," I agreed.

"Especially with your wig," she said. "But it is a marvelous disguise. I would never have known you."

"Then how did you know who I was? Did Lyle tell you I was Cleopatra?"

"Not Cleopatra, my dear."

"Oh?"

"No, you are one of the Twin Queens of the Nile. Didn't Lyle tell you?"

"No, we thought it was a Cleopatra costume. Who were the Twin Queens of the Nile?"

" 'Upon their barges would they lie/ Beneath night's starry canopy?' "

"What is that?" I asked.

"You do not know William Lord Inman's poem?"

"No, I don't believe so."

"But everyone knows it. It is his most famous." Then she quoted:

> Though each was regal in her air,
> Still none who saw these maidens fair
> Could choose for beauty 'twixt the pair—
> Their bosoms white, their perfumed hair.
> The Twin Queens of the Nile.

> Upon their barges would they lie
> Beneath night's starry canopy
> To hear the harp and sweet lutes cry
> Of love and lovers' perfidy.
> The Twin Queens of the Nile.

"It's lovely," I said.

"Yes. I knew who you were because I saw you and Lyle talking together in Lady Bude's room yesterday afternoon after the—"

"You mean after Lord Bude . . . left me?"

"Yes, my dear. As soon as we found out what had happened, I tiptoed to her room for a peek. Well, I had to. If Anne had returned, I would most certainly want to have known about it."

"Anne?" I asked.

"The late Lady Bude. Didn't Lyle tell you? Or doesn't he know? Oh, dear, I wonder if he does."

"Know what, Lady Leonora?"

"It is a rather long story. But briefly it is this: The last ball held at Compton Hall took place almost twenty-five years ago to this very day. It may have been exactly twenty-five years ago, I cannot remember.

"Well, Elizabeth and Anne Francis, two daughters of a local squire, attended that ball dressed as the Twin Queens. They were twins, so naturally they wanted to be dressed alike, as they always were. Actually it was their mother who had always insisted that they dress alike, but that is neither here nor there. The point is that it was during the ball that night that William asked Elizabeth to be his wife. She refused, however, in favor, as it turned out later, of William's younger brother, Charles."

"Now," she paused, "I would not have mentioned this at all were it not for the fact that I have a message."

"A message?"

"A message from the other side."

I did not know what to say. So I said nothing.

"Yes, I have had a message from the other side," she continued. "It came to me last night, as clear as can be, with a terrible urgency about it. It is from Elizabeth, and I believe it is meant for you."

"But I never knew her," I said.

"That does not matter. She obviously knows about you. I must tell you. I cannot rest until I do. The message is that you will soon receive a proposal of marriage. I think she meant that it will happen tonight, that history will repeat itself, somehow. Yes, I am sure that is what she meant. And you are to refuse it *at all costs*. It is terribly important that you refuse it."

"Oh, but Lady Leonora, I can hardly believe . . . Oh, no, I am afraid that is all wrong."

"You do not believe it? I know. One doesn't . . . until one receives the revelation. Until one is permitted to experience the *realization*—that is the closest word I can think of—of the hereafter, of the other side. We are all skeptical at first. But you will see, my dear. And take Elizabeth's advice! They are all-knowing over there, and I am sure she wishes only to help. Now, I must go and find Keating, and unless I am mistaken, the approaching Napoleon is about to ask you for a dance." She rose then and said, "Enjoy yourself, my dear." She turned and hurried away.

I was very daring, and agreed to do the Charleston with Napoleon if he would show me how. It was marvelous! But Uncle, I am afraid, watched and was scandalized. The next dance, a tango, I danced with Mr. Winterthorn, who had come as Merlin.

As we danced, I continued to look for Stuart, but I did not see anyone whom I thought might be he. Finally I decided that he had not arrived. But while I looked for him, I could not help noticing that Lyle had seemed to be looking for someone too. And several times I found his eyes on me and my partner as if he were trying to determine with whom I was dancing.

It was not long before Lord Bude approached me.

"Well, uh-umm," he began. "You must forgive me for startling you so yesterday afternoon. I saw the light in the window from the drive, and I could not imagine who could be there. So I went up to find out. You gave me quite a start. And I—" He chuckled. "I must have given you one too, eh?"

"Yes, I was surprised to see you standing there," I said.

"No more surprised than I, I can assure you." Again Lord Bude chuckled. "Thought you were an old friend come back from the dead! Can you imagine? Well, it is not surprising, what with all of Leonora's nonsense about spirits materializing in front of people. Quite unnerving actually. And who is to say that they don't, hmm?"

"Well, I suppose they . . ."

"Quite. So it is not surprising that I should think so when I found you in her room. Nobody ever uses it, you know. And there you were with the lamp lit. Quite a shock, I must say. Marvelous joke, though." He laughed a forced laugh. "Couldn't have been better if you had planned it. Quite perfect. Perfect, you know."

"I was so sorry to shock you like that," I said. "I did not dream that anything like that would happen. Mrs. Merrymede said that Elvira and I might use the room to alter my costume."

"Of course, of course. Well, what do you think of our ball, eh?"

"Wonderful! I have never been to—"

"Yes, yes. It is exactly like they have always been. Always held in the long gallery, you know, and we have always had the plants and flowers brought in from the glasshouses. One might think time had rolled back twenty years, except for that music. I can remember a ball at our dear old Hall—let me see, that would have been in 'ninety-seven, I think—when the Duke and Duchess of . . ."

He reminisced until the waltz was over and a Chinese mandarin claimed me for the next dance.

It was just as the mandarin and I finished it that my heart sank: Stuart stood just inside the doorway of the room. Though masked, it was obviously he. He had come as a harlequin—a harlequin as huge and powerfully made, I thought, as any that had ever existed.

A Norseman asked for the dance that followed. I did not know who he was. I was almost sure we had never met. He was a middle-aged man with a gray mustache, and his head reached only to Stuart's shoulder.

I was able to compare their heights shortly after I had exchanged greetings with the Norseman. It was then that Stuart marched straight through the milling couples that cluttered the floor and stood beside the Norseman, facing me.

"The lady and I have this dance," Stuart announced to the Norseman.

"You must be mistaken," I said to Stuart. "This gentleman and I have this dance."

"You and I have it," Stuart said flatly.

The orchestra began to play, paradoxically, Gershwin's "The Man I Love." Stuart stepped forward, placed his arm around my waist, and grasped my hand.

"Stop it!" I said, tensing and drawing back from him. The Norseman left.

"How dare you?" I hissed to Stuart, as he danced me onto the floor.

"I would have done a great deal more than that to talk to you."

"You could have waited. Besides, I don't want to talk to you."

"You are doing so, nevertheless."

"Please take me off the floor."

"Very well," he replied.

We passed Lyle, who danced by with a young woman dressed as a fairy queen. He grinned a rather odd, self-satisfied grin at us.

But I had little time to think of that because Stuart guided us through the open doorway of the long gallery and out into the little, oval-shaped anteroom. Here he stopped dancing, grasped my arm, and began to pull me toward the corridor.

"What are you *doing*?" I cried, wrenching my arm from his grasp.

"I want to talk to you," he said.

"If you must, talk to me here."

"Not among these people." He grasped my arm again.

"Stop it!" I cried.

"I'm not going to hurt you. I want to talk to you—somewhere where we can't be overheard."

Everyone nearby, I noticed, was watching us. They included Lord Bude and Mr. Winterthorn, who stood at the entrance to the long gallery talking together. So I began to walk toward the hallway with him.

"You love being high-handed," I said.

"Sometimes it is the only way," he replied.

After this we didn't speak again until he had led me down the staircase to the loggia. Then he grasped my arm tightly and pulled me past two footmen stationed there and the maids who tended the cloakroom in the sub-hall, through the deserted breakfast room, and out the door at the far end of it onto the terrace outside.

Then I faced him and said, "You are a brutal beast! Now, what is it you want to say?"

Instead of answering me, he pulled me roughly to him, locked me tightly in his arms, and kissed me.

Finally he released me, and I said, "We have been

through this before, Stuart. Are you going to beat me here on the lawn?"

"No."

"Then if you have nothing further to say, I'll go back to the ball."

"Not yet. I—I suppose I have made a mess of this. You are very angry with me, aren't you?"

"Angry is not the word for what I feel, Stuart. I have never been treated in such a loathsome, humiliating manner before. You handle me as though I were a possession. You have embarrassed me, insulted me, and bruised me."

"You have a right to be angry." Now he grasped both my shoulders and stared down into my eyes. "I love you, Louisa. I love you so much that when I heard you were seeing Hartley—riding with him, wearing his mother's jewelry, permitting him to buy you expensive dresses—"

"That was none of your affair. He didn't buy me that dress."

"No? Where would Mr. Cuttlebuck get the money to buy a dress like that? Or are you a lady of means with a fortune hidden away somewhere?"

I turned toward the doorway, but he held onto me tightly.

"I don't care! I love you!" He almost shouted the words. "I was—jealous. I tried to put you out of my head. But I couldn't stop thinking about you—day and night. I had to see you. I had to. I *love* you!"

As he said those last words, he clasped me in his arms again. Then he kissed me until my heart pounded and I thought I would not be able to breathe.

"Marry me!" he said, when he finally released me. "To-night!"

"You must be mad," I said.

"Come away with me. Now!" As he spoke, he grasped my wrist. "We'll motor up to London tonight. We'll be married there."

"You can't be serious."

"Deadly."

"I couldn't."

"Why not?"

"Well, I—"

"You love me."

"But—"

"That is all that matters, then. Come!" He began to pull me toward the breakfast room door. "My car is outside the stable yard."

"No!" I pulled away from him. "Listen to me. I can't go off to London looking like this. I have nothing to wear. What would people think?"

"We'll find you something."

"No, I can't. It—it is all so unexpected. It's not—it's not proper. There should be an engagement. These things take time."

"Why wait?"

"It's not right. You're asking me to drive up to London looking like this? You're asking me to elope? And what about Aunt and Uncle? After all they have done for me, I can't just run off."

"Ah, here you are." Lyle spoke softly.

He had appeared suddenly in the doorway of the breakfast room. Neither Stuart nor I had heard him coming, which I thought odd.

He came toward us, saying, "Ah, Compton old chap, I'm so glad you could come." When he stood beside me he continued, "I had been hoping you would manage it. I suggest you release Louisa. She doesn't seem to want your attentions." Then he turned to me. "May I have this dance? I think it is about to begin." He offered me his arm.

"Just a minute, Hartley," Stuart said, laying his hand on Lyle's shoulder. "Louisa and I haven't finished our conversation."

"Finish it later, Compton," Lyle said. "And please remove your hand from my shoulder."

But Stuart did not remove it. Instead he grasped Lyle tightly and said very firmly, "Will you excuse us, Hartley?"

"Certainly not, old boy," Lyle replied. "Whatever has gotten into you? Is this the way you thank me for inviting you? Now, let us pass. Or shall I call John and Albert? They are just inside there, you know."

Stuart glared at Lyle. Then he released him, stepped aside, and bowed exaggeratedly to me.

Upstairs the waltz had begun and Lyle swung me onto the floor.

"Are you all right?" he asked. "He didn't hurt you?"

"Of course not," I said. Then after a few moments I asked, "Did you think he would?"

"He might have."

"What do you mean by that?"

"He has a violent nature."

"Perhaps, but not as violent as that."

"Don't be fooled. He is a dangerous man." We danced on rather breathlessly for a few moments. Then Lyle said, "He might try to kill you."

"Oh, Lyle! That is absurd."

Lyle led us to one of the bay windows. We stopped dancing.

He looked at me seriously then and said, "He tried to kill me once."

"How? How did he try to kill you?"

"It was when we were at Cambridge together. We were members of the same racing crew. I was at number five, and Compton's oar was at number seven. We were pulling down the river late one afternoon on a training run when a stiff breeze blew up from the southeast, which made the river very choppy. It was so rough, as a matter of fact, that if we had known how bad it would become, we would never have gone out in the first place. And then Madox, the coxswain, began to urge us to the utmost, and during all this the number two oar came loose. One of the chaps stood up to retrieve it. This played havoc, and we capsized."

"Frightening," I said. "But what does that have to do with Stuart?"

"You will see. Ordinarily, I can swim very well. But that day I remember hitting the water, and then I was in the dark. And someone was pushing me under and holding me there—trying to drown me. Luckily I reached out and felt the inside of the boat and realized that the boat had overturned on top of us. Somehow I was able to get away from my assailant and I came up outside the boat in the daylight. The rest of the crew were there, so I was in no danger. I had been hit on the head, you see, and was dazed."

"And you think it was Stuart who tried to drown you?"

"I know it was. I could see the rest of the crew. They were swimming about in the water. Only Compton was missing. Then after a few moments his arm appeared from beneath the boat and he ducked his head and came out from under it."

"Why should he do such a thing?" I asked.

"He had been sleeping out of college regularly—a local barmaid—and I knew about it. She was quite beautiful— Spanish, black hair, but terribly low. He was afraid I would let the cat out of the bag, which I would never have done. He threatened me about it, and we had a terrible row. Of course, there was no proof of what he tried to do to me, and I would not have used it if there had been. Poor fellow. I am afraid he is, purely and simply, a rotter. Always has been. It is not really his fault—that's just the way he is." He smiled. "I am sorry you ever met him."

I glanced around to see if Stuart had returned. He had. He stood across the room, watching us. Did he know we were talking about him?

I tore my eyes away from Stuart then and looked back at Lyle. He had followed my gaze and seen Stuart.

"Why didn't you tell me this before?"

"There was no reason to," Lyle replied.

"And yet you asked him to the ball."

"Why not? All this happened long ago. And one must try to help people like that. I thought this might bring a little pleasure into his life."

Now the orchestra stopped playing, and the dancers milled about with their partners, waiting for the master of ceremonies to announce the unmasking.

Lyle led me across the room. In a moment the drummer

played a drum roll and the master of ceremonies announced: "Ladies and gentlemen, the moment has arrived. We will all please remove our masks." The room fell silent for a moment. Then it was filled with laughter, applause, and cries of surprise. The drummer played another drum roll, and the master of ceremonies cried, "Ladies and gentlemen!" As the guests quieted and turned their attention to him, he said, "Ladies and gentlemen, I believe Lord Hartley has an announcement. Lord Hartley."

Now everyone looked at us. "Thank you, Mr. Middleton," Lyle said, with a smile at the master of ceremonies. Then he turned to the people before us and, still smiling, said, "My dear friends, I hope you have been enjoying the music of Mr. Sandy Vein and his orchestra as much as I have." He gestured to the orchestra leader, who sat at the piano. He rose and bowed to enthusiastic applause. "Mr. Vein will soon be appearing at the Savoy Grill. We are very fortunate to have him here with us tonight." Everyone applauded again.

"My Aunt Leonora tells me," Lyle continued, "that it has been almost twenty-five years since we have held a ball at Compton Hall. That is much too long." This was followed by murmured agreement. "We know how much everyone enjoys these things, and it is a great pleasure for Father, and my Aunt Leonora, and me to plan them. So we will, I assure you, be planning another one in the very near future." Cries of pleasure and delight followed.

"And now, I wish to share with you my great personal joy." Lyle grasped my hand. "I can't tell you how happy I am to announce that Louisa has consented to become my wife."

I remember vividly the expressions on Stuart's face. Our eyes met, our gaze interlocking. At first, during those few seconds, his eyes told me that he was astonished by what Lyle had just said. Then he was confused, then speculative, then enraged. Lastly, his expression turned to hatred. Across the room Stuart's eyes sent a message of such violent enmity that my blood turned cold.

I wanted to run to him and tell him that it was all a horrid mistake, that I had known nothing about it. But he had left the room too quickly. And anyway, how could one leave the side of a man who has just announced one's engagement? What would people think?

I suppose I was in a mild state of shock; much of the rest of that evening passed in a blur.

But I remember "As soon as possible," Lyle was saying to Lady Lilly, who did not seem at all pleased. "Mr. Cuttlebuck will perform the ceremony, quite naturally, here at St. Clement's. But we haven't decided on an exact date. Have we, my dear?" He looked down at me and smiled.

"No—no," I replied.

"Of course there will be the wedding gown and all the arrangements," Lyle continued. "And then a reception here at the Hall afterward. So there is a lot to be done."

He led me toward a group of well-wishers. "Happy, my dearest?"

"Yes—yes."

Someone asked about a wedding trip.

"Louisa has an intense curiosity about Italy," Lyle said. "Isn't that so, my dear?"

I looked up at Lyle, rather puzzled, but I did not speak.

"You remember," he said, "in the drawing room that afternoon when you said how much you would like to see Venice? Well," he said to whoever had asked the question, "we plan to visit Italy and then travel back into the south of France and over into Spain. And then simply wander."

"And then return to Compton Hall, I suppose," Lady Charles said. "How lovely."

"Yes," Lyle said, "for the present. Of course we'll open the London house. That is, if you would like to, my dear," he said to me.

"Yes," I said. "Whatever you wish."

I remember asking myself then, "Why did I say that?" My mind was in such a horrible muddle that I did not know what to say. So I was just as glad, as the ball progressed, that Lyle and I hadn't the opportunity to talk. I wanted time to think before that happened. But even then,

I believe, something in my mind seemed to say, "No. No. I will not marry you, Lyle."

We danced, and talked with his guests, but the evening is a blur even today. Except—except for the library incident.

It happened long after supper, as I stood beside the dance floor surrounded by local people. While I listened to their chatter, I noticed Lord Bude speaking angrily to Lyle. They stood near the door of the long gallery, and almost as soon as I saw them, they marched out of the room, Lyle following his father.

I should never have followed them, but I did. I excused myself and hurried after them. To justify this, I can only say that it was a time of stress for me. I suppose we all tend to forget our manners at times. Perhaps it was a self-protective measure of some kind. I don't know. Nevertheless, that night I followed Lord Bude and Lyle to the library, and I listened to what they said from outside the door.

". . . know I don't approve of it," I heard Lord Bude say. "And yet you continue to pursue her. And now you announce your engagement to her, in spite of my wishes."

"I'm sorry you feel that way, Father," Lyle said. "You know I've always tried to do as you wish. But I love her, and I can't give her up. I won't give her up."

"You will do so," Lord Bude said. "I will not permit this marriage."

"As I say, I am sorry you feel that way," Lyle said. "I think it's an unreasonable attitude. Louisa is a sweet, kind, good person who would make me a perfect wife. Why do you object so?"

"I have given you my reasons."

"And I'm afraid I can't accept them. I love her. She is the most important thing in my life, and I intend to marry her."

"Remember, young man, that these estates are not entailed. I can do with them as I please."

"I know that, Father," Lyle said.

"If you marry that young woman, I shall leave you without an acre."

"Is that an ultimatum, sir?"

"It is!" Lord Bude replied.

"Then that is the way it will have to be. I love Louisa. She is more important to me than life—far more important than an inheritance."

"Do you think you fool me, young man?" Lord Bude asked scathingly. "I know you better than you think I do. Now leave me."

Almost instantly Lyle opened the door and stepped out into the hall. He saw me at once and must have realized that I had been listening. I had had no time to move away from the door.

"You heard?" he asked.

"Yes," I replied without pretense.

He smiled. Then he offered me his arm. I took it, and he led me away from the library—back across the hall toward the long gallery.

"Then you know how much I love you," he said, still smiling at me.

"But he will disinherit you," I said.

"That doesn't matter. I can't give you up!"

Lyle and I danced the last dance of the evening. We spoke little. Then, at last, it was time to go home. After descending to the loggia, Uncle Andrew and I waited amongst the crowd for some time for Patrick to bring the car around. We had no sooner gotten into it than Uncle began to tell me how pleased he was.

"You are a most fortunate young woman," he said happily. "I hope you realize how very fortunate you are."

"Yes, I do. Thank you, Uncle," I said.

"Let us pray, then. Heavenly Father, bless this thy servant, Louisa, and thy servant, Lord Hartley. Let them come together in the spirit of love for each other and for those who love them so much, who would lay down their very lives for their happiness. And let them . . ."

I was too tired to listen. Luckily, Aunt Grace was asleep when we reached the rectory, leaving me free to go to bed.

But in spite of being exhausted, I did not sleep. I sat in the chair by the window waiting for the first gray hint of dawn. And as I sat, I savored the blessed solitude. Peace and quiet at last.

And I wondered how I could tell Lyle that I would not marry him. Strangely, it would be more difficult to tell Aunt and Uncle than Lyle. I would simply not see Lyle again after I had told him. Nor would I see Lord Bude, who would be delighted by the news. I could not go to the Hall to read to him because this would mean seeing Lyle. But I could not simply leave Aunt Grace and Uncle Andrew and try to put them out of my mind, as I would Lyle and Lord Bude. The marriage would have meant financial security to them. They would be terribly disappointed. Yes, it would be very difficult.

Chapter Nine

Ever since I had last seen Stuart, I had known I would go after him at the first possible moment. That was why I sat at the window waiting for the dawn. When the night at last began to lighten, I rose from my chair and began to dress for riding. I would creep out of the house to the stables and saddle Samantha. If Patrick heard me and came down from his room above to see what was happening, so much the better. Then he could help me. I would tell him I could not sleep after all the excitement of the ball and that an early morning ride would calm my nerves. Then I would ride straight to Stuart.

Taking my crop from the shelf in the wardrobe, I tiptoed to the door and slipped out into the hall. I paused to listen. The house slept.

I tiptoed to the back stairs, and was about to take my first step down them, when a voice cried, "Is someone there?"

It was Aunt Grace. I stood stock-still, not moving, not even breathing.

"Who is it?" Aunt Grace cried. "I heard you!" Then she began screaming, "Andrew! Andrew! Come quick! Andrew! We are being robbed!"

I must run down the stairs and out of the house, I thought. But I had no sooner decided to move than May appeared on the landing above me and Uncle dashed from his room into the hall.

They saw me at once, but neither spoke. They simply stared at me, too surprised, I supposed, to speak.

"Andrew! Come quickly!" Aunt Grace called.

"Yes. Yes, my dear, I am coming," Uncle Andrew called. Then he said, "Louisa," and motioned me to follow him into Aunt Grace's room.

I obeyed, glancing at May, who looked down at me now with a smirk. When Aunt Grace saw me, she exclaimed, "Louisa! What are you doing?"

"I am not doing anything, Aunt Grace," I said.

"Do not be smart!" she snapped. "I heard you. What were you doing at—" She paused, examining me. Then she said, "You were trying to creep out of the house, weren't you? Where were you going?"

"I was going for a ride."

"For a *ride*? At this hour of the morning? Oh, no. You were going to meet someone, weren't you. You were going to meet Lieutenant Compton! You were going off with him, weren't you?"

Uncle Andrew exclaimed, "Lieutenant Compton? Why, that's absurd."

"Absurd, Andrew?" Aunt Grace said. "I should think a man with your experience—"

"She is going to marry Lord Hartley," Uncle said. "He announced it last night at the ball."

Aunt Grace's eyes popped. She sat up in bed quickly. "Well! Well!" Then she smiled broadly at me and held out her arm, wiggling her fingers at me.

I walked over to her bed and took her hand. Then she pulled me down beside her with surprising strength and embraced me. "Oh, my dear Louisa. I am *so* happy for you. Oh, you sweet child."

"I was only going riding," I said, when I was able to disengage myself. "I could not sleep, and I thought a ride might calm me."

"At this hour of the morning?" Aunt Grace said. "What did he say?" she asked, looking at Uncle.

Then Uncle Andrew told Aunt Grace almost word for word how Lyle had announced our engagement the night before. And when he had finished, she turned to me. "We will do it quickly. Madame Prieur will make your dress." Then, with her mouth pursed, she thought for a moment.

"Four weeks should do it easily. We will start publishing the banns next Sunday, and you will go see Madame Prieur tomorrow."

"No," I said. And in spite of my recent decision, I stood, looking first at Aunt Grace and then at Uncle Andrew, and continued, "I am not going to marry Lord Hartley."

"Don't be silly," Aunt Grace said.

"I'm not being silly," I said. "I am *not* going to marry him, and you cannot force me to."

"Louisa!" Aunt Grace began.

"But the engagement has been announced," Uncle Andrew interrupted.

"I shall *un*announce it," I said.

"You cannot do that," Uncle said.

"I can and I will," I said.

Uncle Andrew did not reply to this. Instead he stood staring at me with an expression on his face that I had never seen there before. It seemed one almost of malice, but it was so mixed with astonishment that I could not be sure. Nevertheless, it intimidated me a little.

So I said hurriedly, "You don't understand. Lord Bude objects to our marriage and has threatened to disinherit Lyle."

"He can't do that," Aunt Grace said.

"He can," I said. "The estates are not entailed. Lord Bude can do anything he wants with any of it," I said. "Anyway, I would never fit in up there. I know nothing about precedence . . . or anything else. Lord Bude told me I was a low person and could never learn the things that matter."

"*He* said *that*?" Aunt Grace said.

"He implied it. And then there was a message from Lyle's mother. She doesn't want me to marry Lyle either."

"Lady Bude has been dead for more than twenty years," Aunt Grace said.

"Do you think I don't know that?" I said. "Lady Leonora is a spiritualist, and she received a message from Lady Bude telling me not to accept Lyle's proposal of marriage."

"Rubbish!" Uncle Andrew sneered. "You're not serious?"

"Ridiculous!" Aunt Grace cried. "Louisa, you are much too intelligent to believe anything of the sort. You are imagining things. Lord Bude is very fond of you, and he would certainly not disinherent his only son. What ever gave you that idea?"

Then I told Aunt Grace and Uncle Andrew about the conversation I had overheard.

"He was only annoyed for the moment," Aunt Grace said. "He did not mean it. You will make a splendid Lady Bude—eventually. Now we will have no more of this hysterical nonsense. We will proceed."

Exhausted, I now lost patience. "I told you, Aunt Grace and Uncle Andrew," I screamed, "that I will *not* marry Lyle. You do not own me. You cannot make me marry him. And that is *final*!" Then I whirled about and stalked to the door.

But I did not reach it. Aunt Grace's scream made me freeze in my tracks.

"Oh!" she cried. "My heart!" She clutched at her chest, moaning, "Oh, the pain!" Then as she fell back upon her pillow, she looked at me with saucerlike eyes and cried, "How could you? You want to kill me! You want to kill your dear old aunt. How ever could you? Oh, the pain." Then she turned her head away from me and moaned.

"Aunt Grace!" I cried. I ran to her, sank to the side of her bed, and took both her hands in mine. "Aunt Grace!"

"Marry Lord Hartley," Aunt Grace whispered. Her eyes were closed. "Promise me you will marry him. Promise me before I die. Promise your dear old aunt before she dies."

But all I could think of was getting Dr. Carmichael. So I rose from the bed and dashed to the door.

"I'll get Doctor Carmichael," I called back to Uncle Andrew. Then I ran.

I ran down the stairs and out of the house and across the yard, calling for Patrick as I went. He appeared in his nightshirt and helped me saddle Samantha. I rode off to Dr. Carmichael's house at the edge of the village.

It was the middle of the morning before the doctor arrived at the rectory. He had spent most of the night with Mrs. Gurney, who had finally given birth to twins almost an hour after I had arrived at her cottage—seven miles or so beyond Ledington. Mrs. Carmichael had told me where her husband was. After seeing him at Mrs. Gurney's, I rode home and waited.

I paced anxiously outside Aunt Grace's room while Dr. Carmichael attended her. Uncle Andrew waited with me for a minute or so, but then he left, saying that he would be praying in his study and would I ask the doctor to see him there when he had finished?

The doctor finally stepped out into the hall, closing Aunt's door quietly behind him. "A mild attack, perhaps. Nothing to worry about," Dr. Carmichael said. "Pulse seems strong as ever, but I have given her a sedative to keep her quiet. She will sleep for most of today, and I will stop by to see her this evening."

I knew I must find Stuart. So I asked Patrick to saddle Samantha. I mounted her and rode down the drive, alongside the rectory. When I reached the front of the house, I saw Uncle Andrew and Dr. Carmichael step out of the doorway and begin to walk across the portico.

"Louisa!" Uncle Andrew called. "I wish to talk to you."

But I rode on as though I had not heard.

"Louisa!"

At the lane I turned Samantha, and we cantered off toward the village. The day was sunny and cool; I enjoyed the ride. I had even begun to feel hungry, and I hoped Stuart would give me lunch. I thought of the orange cheese and the delicious-smelling bread that Mrs. Gouge had left for us the last time I had been there. And then I thought of being in Stuart's arms. I wanted that more than anything. I wanted that more than I had realized.

The farmyard was deserted. Not even a chicken was to be seen, and it was more than ordinarily quiet.

The quiet was broken then by the sound of a door opening. August emerged from one of the smaller cottages. I suppose he had been eating. He wiped his hands on his trousers as he walked slowly toward me.

"Good afternoon, August," I called. "Is Lieutenant Compton at home?"

"No, miss," he said.

"Oh? Do you know when he will return? Or where he is now?"

"No, miss," August said.

"Do you think he will be gone long?"

"Aye, miss."

"Oh?"

"Aye, him be gone a long time."

"How do you know that if you don't know where he has gone?"

"Him told me so." August paused while he examined me and considered, I supposed, how much he should tell. Then he added, "Him take his things with him."

"His things?" I asked.

"Aye."

"When did he go, August?"

"This morning, miss."

"In his car?"

"No, miss."

"Then how did he go? Where is he? August, you must tell me."

Now August looked troubled, annoyed by my discomposure. He turned away from me and began to walk quickly toward his cottage. As he went he called back over his shoulder to me, "Him be gone, miss. Him be gone a long time."

I walked Samantha after him. "August!" I cried. "Tell me! Please tell me about it. It is terribly important."

At this, he stopped walking. I suppose it was the urgency in my voice that made him do it. And then he turned and faced me.

"How did he go? On the train?" I asked.

"Aye," he said.

"And he did not say when he would be back?"

"Him say, 'Take care of the farm while I be gone.'"

After I had thought about this information quickly, I asked, "Do you know where to reach him, August?"

"No."

He did not look at me when he said this, and I wondered if he were telling the truth.

"Does Mrs. Gouge know where to reach him?" I asked.

"No, miss. I be going now. There be work to do."

With that he turned his back on me again, and as I watched, he walked back into his cottage and closed the door behind him. I was left alone in the silent farmyard.

There was nothing to do then but turn Samantha around and go home.

When I arrived back at the rectory, Patrick told me that Lyle had called and was still in the house.

I hurried across the yard to the back door and into the kitchen.

May stood near the kitchen table. "Miss Ormsby called, miss," she said.

"Yes?"

"She called to see Mrs. Cuttlebuck, but Mrs. Cuttlebuck was asleep. So she talked to the rector."

I did not reply but hurried across the kitchen to the corridor doorway.

"She saw you ride through Bridgehampton in the direction of Binsley," May said. I stopped walking then and looked back at her. She leered at me now. "And she wondered where you were going. Where could you *possibly* be going, riding that way?"

"That is none of your concern, May," I said. "Nor of Miss Ormsby's either."

Then I sailed through the door and hurried down the corridor toward the drawing room, as May called after me, "His young lordship has called."

Uncle Andrew met me halfway down the corridor. He must have been talking to Lyle in the drawing room and rushed out to speak to me. "Do not say a thing to him about—what we were discussing this morning," he whispered. "I forbid it! I want to talk to you further . . ."

But I did not wait for him to finish. I brushed past him, walked on to the drawing room doorway, and stepped into the room.

Lyle stood at the bay window. As soon as he saw me, he hurried toward me with both arms outstretched. "My dearest," he said. When he reached me, he put his arms around me and kissed me lightly, smiling as he did so. Then he held me away from him and murmured, "Happy?" When I did not answer him, he continued, "My poor dear, you are out of breath. Did you have a good ride? Where did you go? Come and tell me about it."

We sat side by side on the sofa. "I was just giving Samantha some exercise. Nowhere."

"Rector has been telling me how happy he is about our marriage. So am I, my dearest." He took my hand and kissed the back of it. "Happy is a poor little word to express how I feel. I am the happiest man in the world! And everyone is delighted."

"Except your father," I said.

"Poor Father. It will pass. It is simply one of his moods. You know how unstable he has been lately. His mind—"

"Lyle, I can't marry you."

"Why do you say such a thing?"

"Because it is true. Oh, my dearest, I don't want to hurt you. I don't want to make you unhappy. I wouldn't do that for the world. But it is impossible. Lord Bude is completely set against it. And it is *not* just a passing mood. He has his reasons and they are logical ones. I would not fit in up there." May is listening to every word of this, I thought in an instant. Well, so much the better. Let the word spread. "I could not shoulder the responsibility," I continued. "I don't have the knowledge or the background. People would either laugh at me or hate me—as Mrs. Groombridge does."

"That is pure and utter nonsense," Lyle interrupted. "You are under a very great emotional strain, and I know you haven't slept. Rector told me so. You are seeing things all out of proportion because you are exhausted. Father is not being rational at all. On the contrary, what he says is nonsense. You have been a great success. Everyone has been enchanted by you. They have all told me so. And the few little things you will need to know, you will pick up easily."

"Your mother doesn't want us to marry. She warned me against it."

"My *mother*?"

"Lady Leonora had a message from her. Your mother warned me not to accept your proposal."

"Tommyrot! There are no ghosts. Aunt Leonora is a ridiculous old woman. I told you she was odd. She and Father have formed a conspiracy. She made that up to discourage us from marrying. It is such an obvious plot. I should think you would have seen through it at once."

"All the more proof of how much he objects to it, then," I said.

"But I have told you, I am of age. I don't need his permission to marry you. Let him object. He can't do anything about it. I will marry you anyway."

"He will disinherit you if you do."

"Let him. I don't care."

"Then where would all your plans be?" I asked. "Where would all your houses be? Where would the vast fortune be that you plan to leave your son? How would we live? Would you go into business? You would soon come to hate me because you would be miserable. I could not let you give all that up because of me. I am much too fond of you for that. I couldn't let you be so unhappy. Don't you see? No, it is impossible."

"My darling Louisa, there are many ways of achieving one's goals. My plans would not be affected, I can promise you that. But I must have you by my side. Without you there, I could do nothing."

"No," I said. "I would only hinder you every step of the way."

"You don't love me," he said.

"Yes, of course I do, but I can't make you unhappy."

"If you loved me, your only thought would be to be at my side."

"My only thought would be for your happiness."

"You say you want me to be happy, but you make me miserable. You say you love me, but you will not marry me."

"I can't."

He pushed me roughly away from him then and rose, glowering down at me.

"You have other plans, don't you?" he said. "What are they?"

I was too startled by his abrupt change of mood to answer him.

"You will not get away with it!" he said. "You will not get away with it, I promise you that."

Without another word, he spun about, grabbed his hat, and strode from the room.

I realized then how utterly exhausted I was—how faint and almost ill. I wanted a cup of tea. If I could only sip hot tea and then hold the warm cup between my hands, I thought, I would feel stronger.

So I got up and went into the kitchen. Mrs. Moore had just come in from the village, I suppose, and was removing her hat. May stood near the stove.

"Put the kettle on, May," I said. "I want a cup of tea."

"Did you tell his young lordship what you were doing riding out toward Binsley this morning, miss?" May asked.

"You know perfectly well what I told him," I said.

"How should *I* know what you told him? Tell me that, Lady Know-it-all."

"May!" Mrs. Moore said. "I will not have rudeness or disrespect in my kitchen."

"You were listening to every word from outside in the corridor," I said to May. "You always do."

"I did not!" May cried. "I could never have gotten any-where near it!"

"What prevented you?" I asked, weary.

"Mr. Cuttlebuck. He was standing there all the time."

She smiled triumphantly, but the grin vanished instantly because the kitchen door opened and Uncle Andrew stalked through it.

"Louisa," he said. "I would like a word with you in my study, please."

With that he turned and retreated down the corridor. I followed him to the little front room.

As soon as Uncle had closed the study door behind us and we stood facing each other in the center of the room, he said, "Louisa, what did you say to Lord Hartley?"

"I believe you know what I said to Lyle, Uncle."

"I expressly forbade you to say anything about it."

"Uncle, I had to tell him."

"That was a rash thing to do without giving it careful thought. My dear child, you are exhausted from lack of sleep, and you are overwrought. And it is perfectly natural for a young lady to—to rebel at the prospect of womanhood. How we would *all* like to preserve the irresponsibility of childhood! But alas, we must take our place in the world of adults. It has its own rewards, I assure you. You will see."

"That has nothing to do with it," I began.

"No, of course you don't think so now, my dear, but when you have thought it over properly, you will see that I am right. Do not worry. We will simply tell Lord Hartley that you were overwrought. He will understand. I shall explain it all to him. I will do anything to assure your happiness, you know. You must realize that is all your aunt and I think about."

"No, Uncle," I said. "I have made up my mind. I told you this morning. I will not marry Lyle."

"Because of Lieutenant Compton?"

"Why do you say that?"

"Because you were seen riding in the direction of the manor house beyond Bridgehampton this morning."

"You need not concern yourself about that. Stuart has gone away, and I shall never see him again."

I could not keep the tears from gathering in my eyes as I said this, and I turned from Uncle so that he would not see them. Then I ran to the door, opened it, and fled from the room.

I dashed back to the kitchen for my tea. I felt almost as if I might lose control of myself. May, thank heavens, was not there. But Mrs. Moore was, and the kettle was steaming.

By that time I was openly weeping, which made Mrs. Moore exclaim, "Why child! What is it? Sit down here, and I'll make you that cup of tea. Why, you can't have eaten a thing all day. Have a slice of warm meat pie and some bread and butter."

I ate the pie and the bread and butter and drank my tea, and I cried all the while. But kindly Mrs. Moore did not question me. And when I had finished eating, I thanked her, climbed to the second floor of the house, looked in on Aunt Grace, and then retired to my room.

The next day, after Keating had shown me into the library, Lord Bude motioned me to my usual chair. "Miss Little, I wish to talk to you."

"Yes, Lord Bude?"

"I shall come directly to the point. No doubt you have surmised that I do not approve of your marriage to my son. You should know the consequences of that marriage. If it takes place, I shall—"

"I have no intention of marrying him," I said.

"What? No intention?" Lord Bude said. "No intention of marrying him after announcing your engagement to him?"

"*I* did not announce the engagement. Lyle announced it. He announced it without having first asked me. It was as much a surprise to me as it was to you."

"You are not going to marry Lyle?"

"No, Lord Bude. Hasn't he told you so?"

"No. Then you have told him?"

"Yes, I told him yesterday afternoon. And I told Uncle Andrew and Aunt Grace. And that is why I particularly hoped to see you this afternoon."

"Why?"

"I beg your pardon?"

"Why have you decided this?"

"Because I knew you would not approve, and you were quite right. I would *never* fit in here. And then there was Lady Bude's message."

"What message?" he said.

I explained.

When I had finished, Lord Bude said, "Of course she would not approve. Absurd!" Then after a long pause while he stared at me, he continued, "A wise decision, Miss Little. Now tell me the *real* reason."

"The real reason?"

"Yes, the real reason."

"But I have told you."

"Humph."

We sat without speaking for some moments after that. And Lord Bude examined me continually with that expression that was so like a milky-eyed hawk.

"I think, under the circumstances," I said at last, "that it would not be seemly for me to come to the Hall to read to you."

"Why not?"

"I should not be placed in a position to see Lyle."

"Rubbish! He probably would not be about anyway. Certainly you will read to me. I look forward to it. We shall have no more of that nonsense."

"Well, I . . ."

"Not this afternoon, though," Lord Bude said. "Neither one of us in the mood, eh? I shall expect you on Monday as usual."

"Before I go, Lord Bude, I should like to ask something."

"What is it?"

"Have you Lieutenant Compton's address? I mean, do you have any other address than the manor house? Is there anywhere I can reach him?"

Lord Bude looked at me shrewdly now. Was there the suggestion of a smile about his eyes? "Why do you want it?" he asked.

"I wish to write to him," I said.

"About what?"

"Why, I wish to ask him about—a question of history that we were talking about once."

"That is not the reason. I have been watching you. I watched you closely at the ball, Miss Little. It won't do any good. Take my word for it."

I did not reply to this, but continued to look straight into Lord Bude's eyes.

"He is not at the manor house?" he said.

"No, he has left it."

"Then I do not know where he is. How should I? I want to talk to Lyle. Ask Keating to send him to me on your way out, please. Thank you for coming, Miss Little."

Chapter Ten

KEATING TOLD ME THAT LYLE WISHED TO SEE
me. So I followed him to the oval parlor. There was nothing
else to do. I could not very well refuse to see Lyle in his
own house.

"Dearest," he said with a smile. He embraced me and
kissed me. I did not kiss him back.

"Can you ever forgive me?" he asked.

"There is nothing to forgive," I replied.

"Yes, there is. I am so desperately sorry I was angry
yesterday. Though I'm afraid I'm only human. I was hurt."

He gazed fondly at me then. I smiled back at him. There
was a long silence.

"Tell me you have changed your mind," he finally said.

"No, I have not."

"It doesn't matter about Father. I want to marry you
anyway. I told him that only a few minutes ago. I am free
to marry whom I like. You would be perfect in *every* way.
A beautiful and gracious hostess. You would charm everyone. Why, only this morning I received a letter from Lady
Woolwich saying how marvelous she thought you were."

"I am sorry, Lyle. I cannot marry you. And I am afraid
my decision is final. *Please* let us not discuss it further."

"I am sorry," he said. "I didn't mean to distress you. But
you will change your mind. I will be patient."

"No, I never shall."

"Shall I have Rodger drive you down?"

"No, please don't bother. I enjoy the walk."

I left him.

Lyle went up to London a day or so later. He would be gone a week or more.

Nothing important happened during that week—with one awful exception.

It all began innocently enough with the arrival of Uncle Andrew's new surplices on Saturday, sent from London. May pressed them, and Uncle carried them across to the church to put them away in the vestry. He was terribly vain about his appearance, and I remember thinking that he would probably try on each new vestment and pose in it endlessly before the mirror.

As it turned out, morning church service the following day had not been as uneventful as it seemed to me. Colonel Fitzcroft and his wife and little Amelia, their daughter, had left the church just after Uncle began his sermon. And it was extraordinary that after the service was over, Miss Ormsby had hurried away immediately without waiting to speak to anyone.

Both Mrs. Fitzcroft and, later, Miss Ormsby called to see Aunt Grace that afternoon. Mrs. Fitzcroft called while I was talking to Mrs. Moore in the kitchen, so I did not see her arrive. But I saw her depart just as I entered the drawing room.

"Good afternoon, Mrs. Fitzcroft," I called, as she passed the drawing room doorway.

But she seemed in a great hurry and did not reply. She rushed to the front door, and I heard it close with a bang. I watched her from the window as she ran across the portico, down the steps, and out to her car.

No sooner had she done so, than I heard someone else descending the stairs. Aunt Grace must have received another visitor while I was in the kitchen, I thought. Judging from the sound, whoever it was must have been a very large person indeed. The entire house actually trembled. So I ran to the doorway to see who it could possibly be.

It was Aunt Grace herself.

"Andrew! Andrew!" she screamed, as she stamped down the steps. "Andrew!"

She strode down the hall toward me now, her bed robe

flying open with the speed of her approach, displaying the nightdress beneath. This revealed her enormous girth, which rose and fell, despite its quivering, in a single mass with every step. It was like watching an enormous boulder hurtle down a mountain toward me.

"Aunt Grace!" I cried. "You have come downstairs! You are walking!"

"Where is he?" she shrieked. "Out of my way. Andrew!"

She lunged past me, hurled herself at the study door, flung it open, and vanished into the room, slamming the door.

May slipped past me, glancing at me wide-eyed. She stopped at the study door to listen, but before I could motion her away, the doorbell rang and she was obliged to admit Miss Ormsby.

"Oh, Miss Little." She hurried toward me.

But then she stopped to listen. We could hear Aunt Grace shouting in the study, but it was not possible to understand all of what she said. An occasional word reached us, such as: "Promised! . . . never happen again, yet . . . all these years! . . . fool I was!" Suddenly she lowered her voice, and we could distinguish nothing more.

"I came to see Grace," Miss Ormsby said.

"I am afraid Aunt Grace is with Uncle in his study at the moment, Miss Ormsby," I said. "Would you care to wait in the drawing room?"

"In his study?" Miss Ormsby cried, as we walked into the drawing room together.

"Yes. She walked. Yes, I know. I was just as surprised as you are. I didn't know she could do it."

"I *see!*" Miss Ormsby said. "Yes, well, under certain circumstances . . . Lady Worburton *ran* all the way up to the nursery during the terrible fire at Clifton Hall and rescued her infant daughter. And she had been paralyzed for years. Well, it is not surprising . . . under the circumstances."

"What circumstances?" I asked.

"I really don't think I can say. You should not know anything about it. You are much too young."

"But I will certainly know about it sooner or later. Whatever is it? Perhaps I can help."

"Perhaps you might. Yes, Lord Bude might listen to you. It is really *too* unfortunate. Too distressing. Oh, your poor aunt. Whatever will we *do*?"

"Please tell me," I begged.

"Well, only because Lord Bude might listen, you understand. I knew all about it at church this morning. At least I knew *most* of it. I sit in the pew directly behind Colonel and Mrs. Fitzcroft." She paused, a smile hovering about her eyes and mouth.

"Please go on," I said.

"Well, just as Rector climbed to the pulpit for his sermon, I heard little Amelia say to her mother, 'Mamma, what does he wear under those long white and black things?' Then Mrs. Fitzcroft said to Amelia, 'Why he wears trousers just like your father.' 'No, he doesn't,' Amelia said. 'He doesn't wear anything at all.' 'Whatever gave you that idea, Amelia?' her mother whispered back. 'And young ladies do *not* think about such things. Sh-h-h, now. He is about to begin.'

"Then after a few moments," Miss Ormsby continued, "Amelia said, I heard it quite distinctly, 'He doesn't wear anything under there. I know he doesn't because I saw it.' 'Be quiet!' Mrs. Fitzcroft hissed. Then Amelia said, and this is word for word, 'He *showed* us. Me and Dorothy were playing in the churchyard yesterday and he pulled them up and *he showed us.*' The Colonel and Mrs. Fitzcroft whispered together. I could not hear what was said. Then they left the church."

I was stunned. But thinking quickly, I said, "But Amelia is only a child. And a very imaginative one."

"That is exactly what I thought," Miss Ormsby said. "And I made up my mind to tell Mrs. Fitzcroft so. That is why I hurried over to the Grange directly after the service."

"What did Mrs. Fitzcroft say?" I asked.

"They were not at home. They had gone to Mrs. Dawson's cottage."

"How do you know that?"

"Because I returned to the Grange again after luncheon, and Mrs. Fitzcroft told me. She was *furious*!"

"What did she say?"

"She told me the whole story. She said she is going to tell *everyone* about it. The colonel had already gone up to the Hall to tell Lord Bude about it and to demand that the rector be replaced."

"What exactly does Amelia say happened?" I asked fearfully.

"Well, little Amelia and her friend Dorothy Dawson—that is why they went to see Mrs. Dawson. She had not been to church, of course. To corroborate Amelia's story. It was true. Dorothy was frightened at first and did not want to talk about it, but they finally persuaded her to, and she told exactly the same story Amelia had told. The girls were playing in the churchyard early Saturday afternoon, when they happened to glance through the open door into the vestry of the church. There stood Reverend Cuttlebuck. He was dressed in his vestments. Well, as they looked at him, he lifted up his cossack and surplice."

"And?" I prompted.

"He lifted them up high. He had nothing on underneath. He *exposed* himself to them!"

I could think of nothing to say to this, so I simply continued to look into Miss Ormsby's eyes, and she continued to look into mine.

That was when we heard Uncle Andrew's study door open, and in a moment Aunt Grace appeared in the drawing room doorway.

Miss Ormsby rose and rushed toward her, crying, "Grace! I must talk to you."

"Oh, it is you," Aunt Grace said. "I might have known. Well, come up and talk, then."

Their conversation must not have been a particularly congenial one because Miss Ormsby did not look at all pleased after she left Aunt Grace. She paused to speak to me as she passed the drawing room.

"I was only trying to *help*," she exclaimed.

"How is she?" I asked, walking to her.

"Perfectly well, I am sure. I hope she will be able to cope with this unfortunate, disgraceful situation alone. That is what she seems to wish. Good day, Miss Little."

With that, she marched out of the house.

I went up to Aunt Grace. She had returned to her bed.

"The Lord gives us strength when we need it, Louisa," she cried. "But it was all I could do to haul myself back up the stairs to my bed. I almost called for help. I never thought I could do it. And now I am exhausted.

"I can hardly move. And my legs pain me so from all that effort. It is a miracle! But it is gone now. The Lord giveth and the Lord taketh away. I shall never rise from my bed again, I know it."

"But if you did it once, you can do it again. Wouldn't it be wonderful not to be—"

"No, I shall never walk on these poor legs again."

I felt strongly that Lord Bude would be the key to all this. He could demand that Uncle Andrew leave Ledington; he owned the very land the church was built on, and he endowed the living. There would be no church if it weren't for Lord Bude and his family.

This is what I was thinking as I walked up the hill to the Hall the following day. Even after I had begun to read, I continued to wonder how I could broach the matter.

But Lord Bude solved the problem for me by saying, "You are stumbling over your words today, Miss Little. You are feeling well?"

"I . . ." I could not phrase the words.

"You are distracted. You have not been paying attention."

"No."

"What is the matter?"

"I—Lord Bude, I am terribly concerned about Uncle Andrew."

"Yes?"

"Yes. You must know by now about—about the incident with the Fitzcroft child."

"How do you know about that? Things like that are of no concern to a young lady. Good Lord! He has not molested you, has he?"

"No! He has not molested anyone."

"Well, what do you call it, then? Exposing himself like that. If that is not molesting, I do not know what is. Disgusting! The man is a pervert."

"Oh, surely not!" I cried.

"He is! What else would you call it? A man of God! Humph! If there was anyone I thought I could rely upon, it was the parish priest."

"You can!" I said. "We all rely on him—terribly. We always have. He is always there when one is sick or needs him. And he works so on his sermons. He is a *good* man."

"Humph."

"The children must have been imagining it. After all, they are only children. Perhaps a reflection in the glass . . . ?"

"He was standing in the doorway. There wasn't any glass there. I will have a talk with them, of course. We can't be too careful about these things. We mustn't take anything for granted. There must be some truth in it though. They couldn't have imagined it—not when they both told the same story. But we will see. We will see. Now, let us get on with it. You may continue reading, Miss Little."

"But suppose it was true?" I said. "I am sure there is nothing to it at all, but suppose it *was* true?"

"He would have to leave, I suppose. We couldn't have him preaching. My God! He might do it right there—in front of everybody! Who knows what he might do? But there is more than Cuttlebuck to think about. There is Mrs. Cuttlebuck. And what about you?"

"Me?" I asked.

"Yes. If I removed him, what would happen to you?"

"Why, I would go along with him and Aunt Grace, of course."

"Where?"

"To his next living."

"He would never get another. Word gets about. A thing like this spreads like the plague. I have already had visits from Fitzcroft, and Mr. Denby, and Lady Hewingham. And Miss Ormsby, of course."

"Miss Ormsby?"

"Certainly. She is shocked—humiliated by it all. She says something must be *done*! I don't know. I shall have to consider the matter carefully—investigate. We shall see. We will not discuss it further, Miss Little. A young lady does not concern herself with such things."

I had a great deal to think about that night. And because my mind was troubled, I did not fall asleep until hours after midnight.

So I was late in rising the following morning, and by the time I went down to breakfast, Uncle had long since closeted himself in his study. I did not regret his absence. I had been uncomfortable in his presence since the awful story began. And I was especially glad to be alone because, almost as soon as I entered the room, I saw the letter lying beside my plate.

Chapter Eleven

IT WAS ADDRESSED IN AN UNFAMILIAR HAND, and at once I thought it was from Stuart. I wished to read it immediately and without distraction, so after I sent a very curious May off to the kitchen to fetch a soft-cooked egg for me, I tore open the envelope.

Old St. James House
July 5

My dear Louisa,

How long I have dreamed of writing this letter. I had hoped to write it to you and Nancy, your dear mother and my beloved wife. But I know now that she is no longer with us, and we shall never see her again.

But I have found you, my dearest child. I shall never forget that June 2nd, so long ago, when I waited in agony for your birth at the St. Marylebone Samaritan Free Hospital for Women and Children. How I waited impatiently outside your mother's room to hear your distant cry—those twenty-two years ago. Since that day I have searched for you. And many have been the heartbreaks I have endured when I thought I was at last about to find you, only to have my hopes dashed yet again.

Now at last my dream has come true, and I have found you, my dearest daughter. I rush with all speed to be with you.

I shall arrive at the rectory in Ledington on Friday, July 8th, in the afternoon. Would that it could be this very minute! I can barely endure the delay. On Friday we will be together.

Your loving father,
Richard Kean

I stared at the letter for several moments, and then I read it again, and then again. My father? I thought. Surely this can't be true. I have no father. I have never heard of a father. Surely Mother would have mentioned him to me.

At that moment May announced Lyle. After we had exchanged greetings, I said, "I have just received a letter from a man who claims to be my father."

"*What?*"

"Yes."

"All of a sudden—out of the blue like this? Your father? But you said you have no father."

"I don't." I took the letter out of its envelope, and handed it to Lyle. "Will you read it please?" I asked him.

He took the letter and began to read.

"What shall I do?" I asked, when I thought he had finished.

"You have shown this to Mr. Cuttlebuck? What does he say?"

"I haven't shown it to him yet."

"Then I suggest you do, and I think you should do so at once. Why, this is monstrous! Come along."

When Lyle and I arrived at the study door, he knocked loudly.

"I said I was not to be disturbed," Uncle Andrew called through the closed door.

"It is very important, Rector," Lyle called back.

"Lord Hartley? Is that you?" Uncle cried. "One moment."

It was almost a minute before Uncle opened the door. In the meantime we could hear him walking hurriedly back and forth, as though he were tidying the room.

At last he opened the door. "What has happened? Come in. Come in."

"Louisa has had a letter," Lyle said, "which we think you should read without delay."

Uncle looked suspiciously, I thought, at both of us. He took the letter and began to read it.

He had almost finished reading it when we heard a banging on the floor above us and the distant voice of Aunt Grace calling, "Louisa! Louisa, come here this minute."

"This was at the table this morning?" Uncle asked me. "Has your aunt seen it?"

"No."

"Then I think we should show it to her immediately," Uncle said.

Still holding the letter, he hurried from the room. We followed him. On the landing I hurried past the two men, thinking that I might be able to warn Aunt Grace that Lyle was on his way to see her.

But I was not able to, because as soon as I entered the room, Aunt Grace cried, "You have had a letter from that man. I have forbidden you to see or hear from him again. He is the cause of all—"

"No!" I cried.

"Yes! May told me. I have forbidden—" But then her eyes opened wide as she glanced at the doorway. "Lord Hartley!"

"Good morning, Mrs. Cuttlebuck," Lyle said. "I must apologize for calling unannounced like this, but something important has occurred."

"What is it?" Aunt Grace cried. "What has happened? Andrew?"

"Nothing! Nothing, my dear," Uncle Andrew said soothingly. "Louisa has received a letter."

"Not in front of Lord Hartley!" Aunt Grace cried.

"Lord Hartley has read it," Uncle Andrew explained. Uncle handed the letter to Aunt Grace.

"I don't understand," she said, when she had finished reading it. "Who is this man?"

"That is precisely what we are wondering, my dear," Uncle Andrew said.

Aunt Grace continued, "Louisa's father? He never mentioned a father." She said this to Uncle.

"Who?" I asked. "Who never mentioned a father?"

"Why—why that man in Manchester. The rector whatever his name was. A mother, yes. But not a father. I think we should have an explanation. You must ask Lord Bude about it at once, Andrew."

"Why should you ask Lord Bude about it?"

"Can you think of anyone better to ask?" Uncle said to me. "This is an extremely grave matter. Neither your aunt, nor I, nor Lord Hartley, I dare say, has the expertise to deal with such a thing. One must take counsel. '*Every* purpose is established by counsel . . .' Proverbs 20:18."

"Oh, how stupid of me," Lyle said. "*That* was one of the reasons I called—to tell you, Rector, that Father is feeling ill and has asked to be excused this afternoon. He asked if your meeting could be postponed for a few days. He is not fit to see anyone—high fever, you know."

"Of course I would not mind postponing our conference," Uncle Andrew said. "Certainly it should be postponed if Lord Bude is ill. Postpone it as long as he likes—indefinitely. Fevers must be looked after closely. They take a long time to recede, and are apt to return if one is not especially careful."

"Precisely!" Lyle said. "I agree with you about taking counsel, and ordinarily I would say that father must be consulted at once. But . . . I hardly think it necessary in this instance. We can perfectly well take counsel together. Four excellent minds should be more than sufficient, don't you think?"

"But . . ." Uncle began, frowning.

"It is perfectly obvious what must be done," Lyle said firmly.

"What?" Uncle asked.

"Verify the man's story," Lyle said. "Surely there must be records of some kind at the St. Marylebone Hospital. We shall have a look at those records and see if there is any mention of a Nancy Little giving birth to a child on June 2, 1905.

"Yes, of course!" Uncle said.

Lyle continued, "But I am sure we will find no such thing. If there should be such an entry in the records, we shall . . . But I am sure we will find it is all a fabrication. If this man *is* your father, Louisa, what could have kept him away from you for twenty-two years? And how could he have lost you in the first place?"

"Then we shall have to go to London," I said.

"*I* shall go," Lyle said, looking at his watch. "And I'll have to hurry if I am to catch the four o'clock train. I'll go at once to the hospital, and if I can't see the records this evening, I'll see them in the morning. There may be other places to look—it all depends on what I discover at the hospital. I should return by late afternoon or early evening tomorrow."

"Even if you come in late," I said, "won't you please come and tell me? I don't think I could sleep if you didn't."

"Very well," Lyle said. He smiled. "You see, it is entirely unnecessary to bother Father with this. I really must insist that it not be mentioned to him—especially as it is so unnecessary." Looking first at Uncle, then at Aunt Grace, then at me, he waited for our responses.

"Certainly, Lord Hartley," Aunt Grace said.

"You have my word," Uncle Andrew said.

"Of course," I agreed.

"Good!" Lyle seemed relieved. "Now, I must hurry if I am to catch my train. I shall see you, then, tomorrow, and we will be certain of this once and for all. Good-bye until then."

He hurried to the doorway. Then he ran from the room and presently we heard him run across the portico. Uncle and I watched him from the window as he bounded down the walk, jumped into the Rolls, and was driven away.

I don't know how many times I read Mr. Kean's letter that afternoon and evening and the following morning. I felt, somehow, that by reading and rereading it, I could become closer to this incredible thing and understand it better.

Even as I walked up the hill path to Compton Hall the following afternoon, I carried the letter with me in my bag. And shortly before I reached the brow of the hill, I sat down on the branch of a fallen oak and read it once again.

After I had been shown into the library, I said to Lord Bude, "I hope your fever is better."

"Fever?" he asked. "It was nothing—nothing at all. It would seem that the most minute facts concerning my health, and probably everything else, are widely circulated. Now, let us cease speculation and get on with it, shall we, Miss Little?"

As if he wanted us to begin again on a new footing, Lord Bude asked me to read Shakespeare's *Richard II*, a play which, I must confess, I did not find very interesting. Added to this, I found it difficult to read.

These things and the fact that my mind was occupied with Mr. Kean and his letter made the time pass slowly. When we reached Act II and "This nurse, this teeming womb of royal kings,/ Feared by their breed and famous by their birth," I looked at my watch, hoping that it would soon be four o'clock. Suddenly my watch and the word "birth" drew to the center of my mind something that had been puzzling me.

"You told Lady Leonora that my birthday was June second." I said. "And you gave me this watch on June second. How did you know that was my birthday?"

"Birthday? Birthday? One day is as good as another. You said so yourself."

"But Mr. Kean also said it was the second."

"Mr. Kean? Who is Mr. Kean?" Lord Bude stared at me now, his eyes narrowed.

"Well . . . I . . ."

"I asked you a question, Miss Little. What does a Mr. Kean have to do with your birthday?"

"He wrote me a letter, Lord Bude. In his letter he states that he is my father and that he was present at the hospital on June second, the day I was born."

"*Father?* You do not have a father, Miss Little."

"How do you know whether or not I have a father?"

"You do not have a father who is alive."

"How can you be sure of that?"

"I am positive of it."

"Then perhaps you can explain this, Lord Bude." I reached into my bag and withdrew Mr. Kean's letter.

I read it to him very slowly and deliberately. As I read (I knew it almost by heart now), I watched him closely. I could tell that he was utterly astonished. When I had finished, he asked me to read it to him again.

After I had done so, he extended his hand toward me and said, "Let me see it."

I handed the letter to him. He held it very close to his eyes and peered intently at it for almost a minute. Then he said, "Why didn't you tell me about this at once?"

"We know how wretched you have been feeling, and we didn't want to bother you with it. And Lyle knew exactly what to do."

"And what might that be?"

"He has gone to London to look at the hospital's records. There will probably be nothing there. But if there should be—"

"Yes!" he said. "Quite right! Yes, I see. Hmm. Well, we shall see what he has to report. And we shall mount a thorough investigation of this—this person, whoever he is. We shall go to the heart of the matter, and ascertain precisely what fraudulent scheme is behind it all. We shall find out. Never fear, we shall find out *all* about it. Now, I think that will do for today, Miss Little."

"But you haven't answered my question."

"What question?" he asked.

"How you knew my birthday was June second."

"What makes you think it is? Mere coincidence. Now, that will be all for today, Miss Little. We will resume on Monday as usual, shall we? Ask Keating to come in as you go out, please."

"But, Lord Bude, I—"

"That will be all, Miss Little. We shall resume on Monday. Thank you."

I returned to the rectory. I was now even more anxious to talk to Lyle.

He arrived, finally, at about a quarter past nine, having come straight to the rectory from the train. I ran to the door and opened it. Lyle stood there, but he was not smiling.

"It is true," he said.

"Oh?" I gasped.

"It is all true," he repeated when I had led him into the drawing room and we stood together. "It is all written in the records. They could not have been more obliging at the hospital. The date is exact: June 2, 1905. Mother's name: Nancy Little."

"Then he *is* my father." I said. "How else could he know where I was born? No one else knew. And Mother never mentioned it to me."

"We must not assume just yet that he is your father."

"Ah, Lord Hartley!" Uncle entered the room. "What did you discover?"

Lyle told Uncle about the hospital records, and then he said, "As I was telling Louisa, we must not assume too much too soon. Though this verifies the few facts that Mr. Kean stated in his letter, he has a great deal of explaining to do before we can believe he is actually Louisa's father."

"I should hope so," Uncle Andrew said.

"Quite!" Lyle continued. "Now, I have thought a great deal about what to do, and I suggest that we—you and I, Rector—interview Mr. Kean *before* he is allowed to see Louisa. I think we can determine with a few adroit questions whether or not he is bona fide, don't you?"

"Well—yes, I should think so," Uncle said.

"And it would save Louisa much mental turmoil. It is one thing to approach a man whom one suspects may or may not be one's father, and quite another to meet a man whom one *knows* is one's father. Now, I believe, and I am sure you will agree, Rector, it is essential that Louisa hear the entire discussion we have with Mr. Kean from a concealed place. She should hear it all first hand."

"Yes, if you think so," Uncle Andrew said. "Though I don't at all approve of eavesdropping, I suppose Louisa has a right to know. I think we can arrange that. We could interview Mr. Kean here in the drawing room, leaving the doors into the parlor there ajar. Louisa could sit behind them and hear everything."

"I think that would be an excellent arrangement," Lyle said. "Don't you, Louisa?"

"Yes, I suppose so, but shouldn't we consult your father?"

"There is no need to annoy him with this. Mr. Cuttle-buck and I can handle it."

"But he will want to know what you found out."

"Why should he—? You haven't told him, have you?"

"Yes, I had to. You see, the strangest—"

"But you promised not to."

"I know, but the strangest thing occurred to me while I was reading to him this afternoon."

"Why on earth did you do that? I strictly forbade it!"

"If you would let me explain! It occurred to me, while I was reading to him, that he gave me my watch on June second as a birthday present. And he told Lady Leonora that my birthday was on June second. Well, don't you see? Mr. Kean said in his letter that my birthday was June second too. Yet I myself have never known when it is."

"What did he say to that?" Lyle asked.

"He was most interested in the letter when I read it to him."

"You read it to him?"

"Yes, I had carried it with me. He was most interested. Terribly surprised, of course, and he said he would get to the bottom of it—that he would mount a thorough investigation—that it was all a fraudulent scheme of some sort."

"Did you tell him that I had gone to look at the records?"

"Yes."

"What did he say to that?"

"He agreed that it was the right thing to do."

"Did he say anything else?"

"No, except that his calling June second my birthday and Mr. Kean's calling June second my birthday was a coincidence. But I can't believe that."

"What else could it be?" Lyle replied somewhat testily. "These things do happen, you know. Only once in a blue moon, but they do—strange as it seems." He paused then, deep in thought.

"I had no idea you had told Lord Bude about this, Louisa," Uncle said. "It is just as well, though, don't you agree, Lord Hartley?"

"Yes—I suppose so," Lyle said. "Though I hate to have him annoyed. He is in no condition to be disturbed by anything perplexing like this. I'm sure he will be vexed by it and upset. Doctor Carmichael won't like it at all.

"But I'll go over it all with him, and we will see what he has to say. I am sure he will agree that Mr. Kean be interviewed as we have planned, Rector. I'll come down in the morning and tell you what he says about it."

Lyle left us almost immediately afterward to return to the Hall.

Friday morning dawned cloudless and cool. Our canopy of sky was the color of a robin's egg. Beneath my window dew drops flashed in sharp contrast with the soft, misty greens of the meadow beyond the garden wall.

The stage was set for sweet joy.

But the setting deceived us.

"I think something's happened!" May announced after she had gazed out of Aunt Grace's bedroom window for several moments. "A while ago Rodger drove past like the wind—like he was being chased by the devil himself. He was going into the village. And a few minutes later I saw Constable Westley driving his car like he was being chased too. Only he was driving out—toward the Hall. And then a little later Rodger drove back again. And now who drives past but Inspector Greg. From Bridgehampton?"

"I know perfectly well who Inspector Greg—" Aunt stopped to listen as a car approached. "Who is that?"

"It's one of the cars from the Hall," May said. "Yes, it's Rodger driving. There's his young lordship getting out."

"Go and let him in May," I said. "I'll be down in a moment."

Promising Aunt Grace that I would return shortly and tell her what Lyle had to say, I left her and followed May downstairs. By that time Lyle was waiting for me in the drawing room.

"Good morning, Lyle," I said, as I walked into the room. "Isn't it a beautiful— Is something wrong?"

"Louisa," Lyle said, "I have something dreadful to tell you."

"What is it?"

"Father is dead."

"Oh, no!" I was too shocked to say more.

"Is Rector here?"

"I'll go and fetch him," I said.

When I returned with Uncle Andrew, Lyle said, "Rector, I have terrible news. Could you come up to the Hall? Father is dead."

"My dear boy," Uncle cried. "Of course I will come."

"I'm awfully sorry, Lyle," I said. "How did it . . . Was he ill?"

Lyle looked deep into my eyes and said, "He was murdered. Strangled in the middle of the night."

I could only stare.

"In his bed. Whoever did it came in through the breakfast room window." Lyle spoke without emotion—almost as though he were telling us about something that had no connection with him at all. "Keating noticed it was open when he was laying breakfast. There were muddy footprints on the carpet. We thought it was a burglar, and Keating went to see if anything had been stolen. I had breakfast and waited to hear what he had to say.

"And I was waiting for Father. He had not yet come down, which was unusual. We discussed Mr. Kean's letter last night and the whole business. Father ageed we should interview the man, but he said he would think about it more and we would discuss it again at breakfast. So I was waiting to talk to him.

"Then Blessing came running into the breakfast room, shouting my name and saying to come quickly. So I followed him up to Father's room, and . . ."

"Dear Lyle," I said.

"It was ghastly!" Lyle said. "He—he had been strangled to death." He paused as though his mind had gone blank. Then he continued, "Of course we sent for Constable Westley and Inspector Greg. They're up there now. I came to ask you to come," he said to Uncle, "and to tell you that Father agreed that we interview Mr. Kean. The man said that he would call this afternoon."

"But you can't think of that now," I said.

"I must!" Lyle said. "You have to be protected. And it was Father's wish. Mr. Kean said he would call this afternoon. I should think that means he plans to arrive in Bridgehampton on the half past two train from London. It could only be the Old St. James House in London—that he was staying there. He will hire a car from Hobbson's, most probably, or someone will drive him out from there, which will put him here at a quarter to three or three o'clock. I think I should be here at half past two, just in case he should arrive early."

"I can't allow you to do this, Lyle," I said.

"I must, Louisa! Father specifically said it was the only thing to do."

"How very brave you are."

"It has nothing to do with bravery," he said. "I can't help Father now. But I can help you, and Father would wish me to."

A few moments later Uncle and Lyle were driven away toward the Hall. I went upstairs to tell Aunt Grace the grim news.

As soon as Uncle returned to the rectory for luncheon, he climbed to Aunt Grace's room.

"Lord Hartley and I prayed together at the bedside, of course," he said. "It must have been a particularly violent attack, judging by Lord Bude's appearance. Ghastly! Perfectly horrible! After I had consoled him with First Corinthians, 15, 1 through 28, he thanked me—he was most appreciative! Such a modest, humble young man. He has asked, by the way, that we continue to address him as Lord Hartley for the present. The funeral will be on Tuesday morning. Lord Bude will be layed out in the drawing room. The coffin will be closed, however.

"Well—after I left him, I had a word with Keating and Constable Westley, who were talking in the loggia when I came down. It seems that the murderer entered the house by the breakfast room window. He must have been a big man—there were large footprints outside in the flower beds beneath the window, according to Constable Westley. He thought it significant, for some reason, that that particular window was the only one in the house with a broken catch, and so could be opened from the outside. Well, the murderer evidently crept through the house and strangled Lord Bude with his hands."

"Robbery!" Aunt Grace cried. "It must have been robbers."

"No, I do not believe so, my dear," Uncle said. "You see . . . nothing was stolen. Keating and Mrs. Merrymede have done a thorough search and accounting. Nothing is missing —except for one thing: a miniature of the Honorable Mrs. Charles Compton, painted, evidently, by Corubini. Mrs. Merrymede distinctly remembers seeing it on Lord Bude's desk in his study yesterday afternoon."

Chapter Twelve

MR. KEAN ARRIVED AT THE RECTORY AT three o'clock. Lyle, and Uncle, and I had waited quietly in the drawing room for him.

It was a difficult waiting time. We spoke about Lord Bude, how hard it was to believe he was gone, and how much we would miss him. Uncle quoted some Scripture and then offered a short prayer.

Finally a strange car turned into drive and parked just inside the gateway. And while Mr. Kean walked to the house, I seated myself in a chair behind the doors that separated our little parlor from the drawing room. They had, as planned, been left open a crack so that I could peek into the room and hear everything that was said there.

As Mr. Kean entered the rectory, I heard his voice and was struck by its resonance and beauty. The men introduced themselves and then came into the drawing room.

Uncle was saying, "Lord Hartley is a close friend of the family. We are so pleased to have him here on this occasion."

"How very nice," Mr. Kean said.

I could see him easily through the opening between the doors. He was a rather short man with wavy, blond hair and powerful shoulders. Though his features were regular, one might even say handsome, he had pockmarked skin.

"Louisa will be down shortly," Uncle said. "You must realize that this is a most—ah—unsettling experience for her."

"It must have been more than unsettling," Mr. Kean said. "I should think my letter must have come as a great shock. But I decided that a letter would be preferable to my appearing without any warning. I am sorry that all this is so trying for her, but I could think of no less painful way of going about it."

When they were seated, Lyle continued, "You say your name is Richard Kean?"

"My stage name," Mr. Kean said. "Harry Little would hardly do, you know. No relation to Edmond Kean, of course. A mere coincidence. Kean was my mother's name."

"Not *the* Richard Kean—the most famous Romeo of them all?" Lyle said. "And other roles too numerous to mention?"

"You are too kind," Mr. Kean said.

"You are on the stage, Mr. Kean?" Uncle Andrew said.

"Yes," Mr. Kean said. "I am pleased to say that I have been called to that gentlemanly profession, Mr. Cuttlebuck."

"But—" Uncle began.

"Of late I have retired from the theater to contemplate and study," Mr. Kean said. "Acting is an art. Like all arts, there exists always the danger of going—uh—flat. So for the past two years I have gone into seclusion to revitalize—to add new dimensions."

"Mr. Kean," Uncle said, "we have naturally wondered . . . Perhaps you would be kind enough to set our minds at rest as to how you could have lost track of Louisa. How can we be sure that you—"

"That I am indeed her father?" Mr. Kean said. "But it is perfectly natural that you should wonder. Indeed, I should think the less of you if you didn't. I shall recognize her."

"But you say you have not seen her since the night of her birth," Uncle said.

"That is correct," Mr. Kean said.

"Then how could you possibly recognize her?" Uncle asked.

"By the resemblance to her mother, whom I dearly loved," Mr. Kean said. "And, if need be, by a birthmark."

"What kind of a birthmark?" Uncle said.

"The child had a red birthmark," Mr. Kean said, "on her shoulder—her left shoulder, I believe it was. I remember it clearly because it was in the shape of a tiny flower—a daisy."

"Would you kindly tell us, then," Lyle said, "how you could have lost track of Louisa, Mr. Kean? And why you have not bothered to trace her until this late date?"

"Sir," Mr. Kean said, "I have constantly endeavored to find my daughter. For twenty-two years I have searched for her unremittingly—never neglecting the most minute clue. To find her has been my obsession. Fate has constantly thwarted me. But it is a long, heartrending tale with which I shall not bore you. The stage, you know, is but a poor, inadequate mirror next to the real. Suffice it to say that I have searched constantly for her for twenty-two long years."

"We should not be bored in the slightest, Mr. Kean," Lyle said. "Indeed I believe we are entitled to a detailed account of this quest."

"Very well," Mr. Kean sighed. "Then I will begin at the beginning. Before our marriage, Louisa's mother's name was Nancy O'Malley. Did you know her?"

They both replied in the negative.

"So that you will understand this," Mr. Kean continued, "I must tell you that she was a very beautiful woman. I met her when we were performing in Newcastle. I was still acting minor parts: Edmond in the *Twelve-Pound Note*, the young Charles Stanley in *The Valentine*, and Max in Sudermann's *Magda*.

"Well, Nancy had decided she would become an actress. And somehow, through the acting manager, I suppose, she had obtained one or two small parts in the plays we performed during our engagement there. She possessed no talent for the stage, I am afraid, and was poorly received.

"But to make a long story short, we fell in love, and when Mr. Henry Harris, one of the Haymarket managers, engaged me to play the part of Winfred in the production of *The Wolves* at that theater, Nancy came to London with me. Shortly after the first performance of the play, we were married in the little church of St. Andrew's Axe in Soho. Do you know it?" Mr. Kean asked Uncle Andrew.

"My dear fellow," Uncle said, "there must be at least five hundred churches in London. One could not possibly know more than a handful of them, one's living being here in Ledington."

"Yes, quite," Mr. Kean said. "But this must be a dreadful bore for you both."

"Not at all, Mr. Kean," Lyle said quickly. "Under the circumstances, we find it most interesting. Kindly continue."

"Well," Mr. Kean said, "Nancy and I were blissfully happy for the first few months. But then her ardor began noticeably to cool and we began to quarrel. And I soon suspected that she had become interested in someone else. Almost five months after we were married, she left me. I arrived home from the theater one night and she was gone. She left no note—nothing. She was simply gone. This wounded me deeply. I was heartbroken, as you can imagine, and for weeks I could barely perform.

"I heard nothing further from her until I received a note which she wrote to me from the St. Marylebone Samaritan Free Hospital for Women and Children in Marylebone Road. This was almost a year to the day after our marriage and two days before I was to leave London. Engagements from country managers had poured in because of my performance at the Haymarket, and I had accepted an engagement to perform in Dublin, where I was to act in *The Rivals.*

"In her note Nancy begged me to come to see her, which I did at once. In spite of everything, I still loved her desperately. I hurried to the hospital, where I found that she was going to bear our child at almost any moment.

"If I had hoped that she still loved me, I was to be disappointed. To be blunt as well as brief, she wanted money. She was about to bear our child and she thought it only right that I support her now that she was to be a mother.

"I said I would gladly do so if she would return to me. She refused, saying that she could not again bear the boredom which she had endured during her marriage to me.

This angered me, and we quarreled heatedly. I left the hospital in a fit of bitter resentment, vowing I would never see her again. But early the following afternoon, on June second, I returned to the hospital, my love for Nancy overcoming my anger and resentment. I was told that she was in labor and that the birth of our child was imminent. I asked to see her, but of course I was not permitted to. I was, however, allowed to wait in the corridor outside her room. Her labor was evidently a difficult one, and it was not until seven o'clock in the evening that Louisa was born.

"I could not leave the hospital without seeing my wife, especially since I was to leave for Dublin the following morning. So I waited. At last, about nine o'clock, I was told that Nancy was calling for me.

"She had changed her mind. She vowed that she loved me and wished to return to me with our daughter. I was overjoyed. I told her about my Dublin engagement, and that I would cancel it and remain in London with her. But she said that I must not—that my future in the theater was very important, now that we were a family. She would wait in London for me until I returned if I could provide a place for her to live and leave enough money for her to care for our daughter. She said that she could do this perfectly well, since the nurses at the hospital had assured her that she and the baby might remain there until she was quite well.

"So that very night I placed Nancy in the care of my closest friend, John Morris, whom I would have trusted with my own life. We had known each other since boyhood—had been through Rugby together and had grown ever closer since. He gladly accepted the charge. And I also made arrangements for Nancy to stay at the accommodations I had engaged for myself—two handsome first floor rooms at a boardinghouse in Soho Square kept by a Mrs. Barker, the mistress of the Soho School.

"Before I left the hospital that night, I told Nancy what I was about to do, left her money, and said that I would send her more from Dublin. Finally I asked to be shown my daughter."

"How fortunate for you," Lyle interjected, "that it all worked out so well. Can't you tell us perhaps more briefly what happened next? Louisa will be joining us shortly, I think."

"Certainly. Certainly," he said.

"Briefly then, Morris and Nancy ran off together. I had been in Dublin only two weeks when one of my letters to Nancy was returned to me with a note from Mrs. Baker—But that is not important. The important thing is that they ran off together and, enquire as I might, I was unable to ascertain where they had gone.

"It was three years later that I found out where they had gone. Morris's father, Sir Anthony, owns a great deal of acreage in the midlands, and they had gone to live in a small farmhouse on one of his estates. I doubt if Sir Anthony even knows of the existence of the place, let alone that the couple stayed there. It is near Edgebaston, just outside of Birmingham.

"I know this because I came across Morris at Claridge's, quite by chance, when I was lunching there with Harris. He told me, during a short and very strained conversation, he had discovered that Nancy was secretly seeing a Birmingham millworker. When he found out, he ended the affair with Nancy and returned to London. He supposed, he said, that she was still with this Mr. Basta. And he volunteered that Mr. Basta worked in the Craig Mills, if I should be interested in tracing my wife.

"I found Mr. Basta, a sullen, filthy brute of a man. But Nancy had taken up with yet another millworker named McGraff. Mr. McGraff and Nancy had left Birmingham because of a strike at the Craig Mills."

"A tragic story, Mr. Kean," Lyle said. "Would you mind telling us how you found out that Louisa was here? You must have traced her mother, finally, to Manchester."

"Yes. What *did* happen in Manchester?" Uncle asked.

"I was coming to that," my father said. "I was not able

to find McGraff in Liverpool. But, to be extremely brief, I continued to search for the man. During all those years I never gave up hope of finding him. You must realize that during that time my engagements were primarily in London with some tours of the Continent and the United States. And of course during the war, performances for the troops. But there were occasional provincial engagements, and when in Glasgow, or Bristol, or Sheffield, or Leicester, or Newcastle, etc., I always made inquiries at the mills and factories concerning Mr. McGraff."

"Finally, not two weeks ago, while in Manchester discussing the possible production of Othello for Chetham's Hospital there, I inquired through the good offices of a Mrs. Cooper-Inwood, a socially-influential lady of that city, as to the existence of Mr. McGraff. It was through her introduction to several of the mill owners there, who were most cooperative in looking into their records, that I discovered that a Mr. McGraff had indeed been employed in one of the mills there eighteen years ago."

"Your tenacity is to be admired, Mr. Kean," Uncle said. "Did you find this Mr. McGraff?"

"No, Mr. Cuttlebuck," my father said. "He died some years before Nancy's death. She had taken the name of McGraff while she lived with him. But upon his death, she reverted to Nancy Little. This mitigates my unhappiness somewhat. Surely she must have felt some affection or regard for me to have continued to use my name."

"How did you discover all this, Mr. Kean?" Lyle asked. "Since they are both dead."

"By inquiring at the house where Mr. McGraff had lived, and at neighboring houses. That was how I came across Mrs. Schultz. Did you know her?" Both Uncle and Lyle shook their heads. "Louisa will remember her, no doubt," he continued. "She lived in the house two doors away and was friendly with Nancy. It was Mrs. Schultz who told me about Nancy's tragic death and that little Louisa had been taken under your wing, Mr. Cuttlebuck. Mrs. Schultz remembered the town was Ledington because her mother's sister's husband had lived here once."

I did not hear what was said next because I had decided it was time to join the men. I had heard enough. I was convinced. Mr. Kean was certainly my father.

I walked quickly and quietly around to the open doorway which led from the corridor to the drawing room and stood there quite still, without speaking. My sudden appearance startled the men, but they stood almost immediately.

My father took a step or two toward me, held out his arms, and said, "Louisa. My dearest child. How very like your mother you are."

"Even the same color hair and eyes," I said, smiling.

"No, my dear," he said, smiling in return. "Your mother's hair was brown and so were her eyes."

"Can you forgive me for that?" I asked as I allowed him to embrace me. "I had to."

"You wanted to be sure," my father said. "My dearest, dearest child."

He hugged me and then quickly held me away so as to look at me. Tears sparkled in his eyes.

"You must wonder why I did not come sooner. I have searched and searched for you all these years, but it was not until two weeks ago that I—"

"I know," I said. "I heard everything from behind the doors there." I pointed to the double doors leading to the parlor.

"I thought perhaps you did." He grinned.

"You did?" I asked. "Why?"

"Because I noticed Lord Hartley and Mr. Cuttlebuck glance in that direction often enough to arouse my curiosity."

"We thought," Lyle said, "that Louisa had a right to hear what was said."

"I agree," my father said. "And that saves me the ordeal of telling the long, dreary story all over again. We must try to forget all that now, I think."

My father looked from one of us to the other then, but no one spoke. In order to break the silence, I said to my father, "You must come up and see Aunt Grace. She is anxious to meet you."

"I believe your father would rather be alone with his daughter just now, Louisa," Uncle Andrew said. "I shall tell your Aunt Grace what has happened."

"Yes, stay with your father, Louisa," Lyle said. Then he turned to Uncle and asked, "How is Mrs. Cuttlebuck? May I see her? Perhaps we could tell her together."

"Excellent!" Uncle said. "And I am sure she will wish to express her condolences personally. Come along then. Louisa, show your father the church. It is a very fine example of the perpendicular, Mr. Kean, and I am sure you would like to see it."

I led my father out of the house. As we began to walk toward the church, he said, "It is a pretty building, isn't it? I am sure it is equally charming inside. But somehow on such a beautiful day my mood requires the sunshine rather than the solemnity of the sanctuary. Don't you agree?"

"Yes," I said, returning his smile. "Shall we walk in the churchyard? It is quite pretty on the other side of the church. There is a lovely meadow beyond it."

As we strolled along, my father asked, "Mr. Cuttlebuck mentioned condolences. Has someone in Lord Hartley's family died?"

"His father. Lord Bude was murdered. Last night. Strangled, in fact. I can't believe I shall never see him again! We read together only yesterday. I have been reading to him every Monday and Thursday afternoon for years. And now to think that I shall never read to him again."

"Do they have any idea who killed him, or why?"

I told Father everything I knew and he listened intently. When I had finished, he exclaimed, "Terrifying! To think it might just as well have happened to you or to me. So Lord Hartley is Lord Bude now?"

"Yes, but he has decided to continue using his second title for the present. I suppose he can't bear—the change just yet. I simply *can't* believe Lord Bude is dead."

"No." Then after a rather long and awkward silence, he said, "Are you happy? I mean, are you happy that I have come into your life—after all this time?"

"Oh, of course," I said, trying to reassure him. "It has been such a shock—such an enormous surprise! When I become accustomed to the idea, I know I shall be terribly pleased. I am already! I have wondered so many, many times . . ."

"Who I was? What I would be like?"

"Yes."

"And now that I have finally arrived, what do you think?"

"I—I think it is wonderful." He smiled his wide, infectious grin at me, and I smiled back at him, almost laughing. "I don't know *what* to think. I am too surprised to think at all."

"My dearest child, how very sweet you are." He patted my wrist as he said this. "You can not imagine how happy I am today—how filled with joy. How I have hoped and prayed to find you. And how often I have despaired of ever being able to."

We had rounded the church by this time, and I said, "Shall we take this path? There's a bench beyond the yews. We can sit there."

"If you like," he said. "What is the little chapel?"

"It's not a chapel. That is the Compton mausoleum. It is where Lord Bude will be buried and where his family are all buried—at least, most of them. He wouldn't allow his brother's wife to be buried there. There was an estrangement."

My father did not respond. He gazed at the mausoleum in admiration. I was not surprised. It was lovely.

As we strolled along, Stuart leapt into my mind. What would he think if he knew that my father had entered my life? Why, he would not think anything at all of it, I answered myself. Stuart is not interested in me. I was never of any importance to him.

"A penny." My father interrupted my reverie.

"I beg your pardon?" I said.

"A penny for your thoughts."

"I was just thinking about Lord Bude and his family." Then after a moment I said, "What else did Mrs. Shultz say?"

"Nothing very much," my father said. "She told me what a tragedy it had been, and how sorry she had been for you—going off to a strange place like that, with strangers. Do you remember her?"

"Mrs. Shultz? No."

"Gray-haired, pale, thin . . ."

"No. Did she mention a Reverend Morley or Martin? Did you see him?"

"No, she didn't mention anyone by those names. Why do you ask?"

"For no reason, really. He was instrumental in Uncle's coming to get me. They were old school friends, I believe." We approached the bench. "Shall we sit for a bit?"

When we were seated, my father said, "Tell me about yourself. Have you been happy here?"

"Yes, I think so," I replied.

I told him about my life at the rectory and about Aunt and Uncle.

My father listened intently to every word, and when I was finished, he asked, "But what about the lighter side?"

"The lighter side?" I asked.

"Yes, your friends. Surely there must be parties and dances and the like. For such a pretty girl there must be young men. A good many, I should think."

"No, not really. Ledington is a rather quiet place. There are dances at the Assembly Rooms in Bridgehampton. And there was a ball at the Hall not long ago, to which I was invited. I have one or two friends—Bertha Bailey, who is a parlormaid up at the Hall."

"No—ties of the heart?"

"No. Why do you ask?"

"I'm afraid I am already becoming a protective father. Which I have no right to do, of course."

"There is nothing for you to protect me *from*." Then

after a pause, I changed the subject. "Have you always been an actor? What is it like?"

"Always. Ever since our theatricals at Rugby. My father managed a theater in Newcastle, and he supplied the costumes and some scenery for them. Our first play was *The Castle Specter*, and then the next year we did Dr. Young's *Revenge*, in which I played Motley.

"But my father did not wish me to be on the stage. His dearest wish was to see me at the bar. That, however, was not to be. He had leased the new theater in Sheffield. The cost of fitting it out, his partner's reneging on his part of the contract, and a disastrous season all left him minus a very considerable amount. So I was not able to return to Rugby, but decided to become an actor and be of some help to my father financially.

"I was sixteen. I took lessons in fencing, and I learned by heart the lines of those characters which I thought would suit my age and ability. It was not long before I began to play some of those small parts. And that's how my stage career began.

"What is it like?" he continued. "One becomes another being on the stage. Sometimes one can so mesmerize one's audience as to regulate their very breathing."

"I think I can understand that," I said.

"Can you?" he asked. "How?"

"I don't know. But I do."

He looked at me intently then for some moments. At last he asked, "Do you think you would like to act?"

"I don't know. I have never thought about it. But it is a very exciting question."

He smiled broadly at me then, but he did not speak.

"Did you know Sarah Bernhardt?"

"Ah," he said. "Her acting was perfection. I never performed with her, of course, but when I was a young actor, she came to see a performance of *The Fortune Hunter*, in which I played Nat Duncan. Afterward she came to my dressing room to give me a few words of advice. 'You are in the right way,' she said, 'but remember what I say: study, study, study! And do not marry till you are thirty.'"

"What a delightful story!" I exclaimed. "What an exciting life you must lead. You travel everywhere."

"Not everywhere, my dear. But to most of the Continent, and to the United States and Australia. Travel is acting and acting is travel."

"Everyone must know you wherever you go. What is it like to be famous?"

"It is gratifying to be appreciated for one's work, of course, but fame is short-lived and it has its disadvantages as well. Sometimes it is rather like being a goldfish swimming about in a glass bowl."

I laughed aloud then because my father mimicked a goldfish hilariously.

He told me many stories during the afternoon and evening, alone together, as we sat on the churchyard bench and strolled together in the garden after dinner. We were with Aunt and Uncle in Aunt Grace's room late that afternoon.

I heard stories about the actor George Cooke, and how the more he drank, the more he would insult his audience; about a prompter who was so sensitive to criticism that he was apt to become insulted over nothing and intentionally give the wrong lines; about one of Father's dressers who ran off with his costumes to pay for drink; about playing once to an audience of two in Berwick when everyone else in the town had gone off to see Ramon Novarro in *Ben Hur*.

He told me about visiting India, where his brother was a colonel stationed in Calcutta. And he described such people as Shaw, Duse, Henry James, and the king and queen.

He was such a witty and charming man that before the evening was over he had begun to get on well with Uncle, bewitched Aunt Grace, and completely captivated me.

So my father was urged to stay at the rectory and was given one of the spare rooms. I heard him retire to it long after I had gone to bed. He and Uncle had probably sat up late talking.

The next morning's *Times* carried an account of Lord Bude's murder, noting that the Corubini portrait was the only missing object, and mentioning that the portrait's subject had been the mother of Lieutenant Stuart Compton, now second in line for Lord Bude's title.

During breakfast, Father asked if I would like to travel to New York to see his next play. I was astonished. I decided not to go, of course. I knew Uncle and Aunt would object to my going, and I did not see how I could oppose them.

Then I had a visitor: Police Inspector Greg. He asked if he might speak to me alone, so I showed him into the drawing room, where he promptly closed the doors behind us.

Inspector Greg was a short, round, shiny-faced man who punctuated words of importance by rising on his toes.

"Would you be seated please, Miss Little?"

I sat on the sofa and Inspector Greg stood facing me, his hands clasped behind his back. "You knew Lord Bude well?"

"Yes," I said. "I have read to Lord Bude every Monday and Thursday for years. His eyes—"

"I am well aware of that, Miss Little," the inspector said, rising on his toes.

I said nothing further for a few moments and neither did he. He examined me, though, with his watery gray eyes.

"You knew him well?" he said finally.

"Yes, quite well."

"Did he ever discuss personal things?"

"Yes, I suppose so."

"Why do you *suppose*?"

"It depends on what you mean by personal."

"His personal affairs."

"Sometimes he did."

"Did he ever speak of enemies?"

"Not that I can remember."

"Anyone who might wish to harm him?"

"No."

"Do you know his nephew, Lieutenant Compton?" the inspector asked.

"We have met."

"How well do you know him, Miss Little?"

"Casually. I don't really know him at all."

"Did he ever discuss *his* personal affairs with you?"

"His personal affairs? Hardly."

"Did he ever malign his uncle?" The inspector rose on his toes again.

"No. They hardly knew each other, from what I gather."

"We are not at all interested in what you gather, Miss Little. We are interested in facts."

I made no reply.

At last Inspector Greg said, "I think that will be all, then. Thank you."

He turned his back, walked to the doors, and opened them.

"Inspector Greg," I called, getting up. "Will there be an inquest?"

"Certainly there will be an inquest," he snapped.

"Shall I be asked to attend, do you suppose?"

"I hardly think so, Miss Little. I cannot imagine what significance your testimony could possibly have during such an important proceeding."

After he had gone, Father and I drove to Bridgehampton in his hired car. We shopped at the draper's and the chemist's for Aunt Grace, and then my father suggested that we walk together on the quay, since it was a beautiful, warm morning.

A brigantine lay anchored in the harbor, and as we walked arm in arm along the sea wall, we watched it set sail and depart, gliding slowly across the glassy water toward the harbor entrance and the open sea. During that time my father told me of his last voyage to the United States, describing it so that I almost felt I was there—the bright days on deck and the nights canopied with stars.

Finally I glanced at my watch. "Twenty minutes past eleven. Why does time always fly so quickly when one wishes to hold it still? Already our morning is gone. What train will you take tomorrow?"

"I believe there is a train after luncheon," my father said.

"Couldn't you take a later one? The half past four? You could still get to London in time for dinner. *Please* stay the afternoon with us. I cannot bear to see you go."

"Come with me, then. I was not joking about that. Come to New York with me. We would have a delightful time together. We could stay at the Ritz-Carlton, the finest hotel in the city. Wouldn't you like to travel? You say you never have. You should, my dear. You have no idea how it broadens the perspective. And we could be together. I have searched for you so long, and now that I have found you, I can't simply let you go. Come with me. Say you will."

"I would love to, but it's impossible."

"Why?" my father asked. "Why is it impossible?"

"Why—because it is so sudden. It's tomorrow, and we have only just met. And—and I couldn't leave Aunt Grace. And Uncle Andrew would never permit it."

"He could not prevent you from going if you wanted to, my dear. You are of age. But it is your wish, of course, that should guide us all. And it would not be forever, you know—two or three months perhaps. Mrs. Cuttlebuck could get along without you for that time, couldn't she? And afterward, if you wish to return to the rectory, well . . ."

"I suppose she could," I said. "It is not so much that, as—well, it would be like saying that I don't care about them now."

"They must know by this time that you care, and they would want you to have a holiday—to have the experience of traveling."

"Oh, I would love to," I said, looking into his smiling face. "It would be so exciting! I have always wanted to sail on a ship, and I have always wanted to see New York. Do you think I really could?"

"Then you would like to come with me?"

"I would love to!"

"Then you shall."

"Oh, but Lord Bude's funeral is on Tuesday. I must go to that. Couldn't you stay until Tuesday afternoon?"

"I am afraid not, my dear. Rehearsals begin in New York on the nineteenth."

"Oh."

"A funeral shouldn't keep you here. Lord Bude would not want you to give up your trip on account of it. That would not help him. Of course you want to show your regard for him, but isn't it more important to do so in one's heart?" He looked into my eyes and smiled at me. "Everyone knows how good and sweet you are—especially Lord Bude, wherever he is now. He would want you to come with me."

"Perhaps you are right."

"You know I am."

"But I have nothing to wear. I have *nothing*, really."

"Then we will buy you pretty things along the way."

"I would love to come," I said, hugging his arm. My thoughts raced for a while. Then I made my decision. "I *will* come." As I spoke, a thrill shot through me, and I looked into his eyes and saw that they mirrored the excitement in my own.

"But there will be so much to do. And I must pay my respects to Lord Bude. We could stop at the Hall on my way home. We would have time. Would you mind? And you should see Compton Hall."

During our drive back to Ledington and up the hill to Compton Hall, my father talked about the things we would do and see in the United States. As my excitement mounted, so did my determination.

After we drove slowly down the drive toward the Hall and I told Father briefly about its history, we drew up before the entrance front. Father preferred to wait in the car, so I went in alone.

No sooner had I said good morning to Keating, than I saw Lyle coming toward me.

"This is a surprise," he said, smiling.

"Hello, Lyle. I came to see Lord Bude."

"I am afraid Mr. Griever isn't done yet—the coffin has not been delivered. Things will not be ready until tomorrow afternoon. There will not be a viewing, you know."

"Yes, I know. But I wanted to come anyway. I am sure everyone will. I'll come up to the Hall tomorrow, then, before we leave."

"Leave?"

"Father has asked me to go to New York with him, and I have decided to go."

"*What?*" Lyle exclaimed.

"Yes."

"Louisa! You have only just met him."

"I don't see that that matters. He is my father."

"Yes. But—but, my dear . . . Well, that is, just because the man is your father, doesn't mean that he . . . he is, er—"

"He is a good, kind man."

"Yes, of course he is," Lyle said. "Of course. I like him enormously. But you have just met him, Louisa. You can't go off, traveling thousands of miles, with someone you have known for less than a day. That's not sensible."

"I don't care, Lyle. I am going with him. And Lord Bude would not care if I didn't go to the funeral. He would *want* me to go with Father." I pleaded with my eyes for him to agree. "Please don't try to spoil it."

"My dearest Louisa," Lyle spoke slowly and deliberately. He grasped one of my hands in both of his. "I wouldn't spoil anything for you. You must know that. Of course Father would understand. Of course you shall go if you want to. No one will try to prevent you. You must do what you think will make you happy. We want that—all of us. We want only your happiness. You want to go very much, don't you?"

"Yes."

"It could be a very foolish thing to do. Have you thought it over carefully?"

"Yes. It would only be for two or three months."

"I don't think it is wise, but if you want so very much to go, then you shall. No one will try to prevent you, Louisa."

"Uncle will try, and so will Aunt Grace."

Lyle did not reply. He led me out to the car and opened

the door for me. While I got in and settled myself, he spoke briefly to Father. Then we drove away.

Strangely, Uncle Andrew did not object too much to my going. He told us, after much discussion, that he did not think it advisable for me to go, but that if I wished to, he would say nothing more.

It was Aunt Grace who made a fuss.

"How could you think of leaving me here alone?" she moaned. "You have never experienced illness a single day in your life. You do not know what it is like to lie here day in, day out—an invalid, practically paralyzed, not able to do a thing for oneself. I *depend* on you.

"I am old. I have not much time left. I shall leave you soon enough. *Then* you can travel. There is plenty of time for that. But how can you be so selfish as to even think of leaving me in my last days? How could you be so cruel? I will not permit it. It is out of the question!"

As she finished, May came to tell us that Lyle had arrived.

"Lord Hartley!" Aunt Grace cried out as he entered the room. "You cannot imagine what this child wishes to do. She wishes to go off and *leave* me!"

"Yes, I know, Mrs. Cuttlebuck," Lyle said. "May I sit here?"

"You know?" Aunt Grace said.

"I know that Louisa wishes to accompany her father to New York and be with him there during his acting engagement. I am sure that their accommodations will be the finest available."

"Most certainly!" Father said.

"I think it is a rather short acquaintance for such a trip," Lyle said. "It might best be delayed until later, but—"

"Precisely!" Aunt Grace cried. "It is ridiculous!"

"But," Lyle continued, "it would only be for a few months, Mrs. Cuttlebuck. I know how much you depend upon Louisa, but surely you could arrange for someone to come in and take care of you while she is gone. After all, I have made a sizable contribution, in excess of the living, toward the expenses of the rector. Father was seriously considering increasing the living as well, and so am I. I would hate to feel the increase was not put to good use. It would be meant to provide for your well-being as well as the rector's, you know.

"And I think," Lyle said, "that Louisa has a right to go if she wants to."

"Very well, then," Aunt Grace sighed. "I hope you will have your journey without accident and do not contract any contagious diseases along your way."

I spent most of the afternoon examining my clothes, deciding what I would take with me, washing out underclothes and stockings—which would be dry by the following noon—and even packing a few things in a trunk which May helped me carry down from the attic. The next morning Father and I attended service together. But as if to allow us our time alone together, neither Lyle nor Bertha came to church that Sunday.

Before setting out for the station in Bridgehampton later that afternoon, I had only to say good-bye to Lyle and Bertha at the Hall. This I would do after luncheon, and then Father and I would set out for London.

So after the meal I walked up the hill to Compton Hall.

"Louisa, have you heard?" Bertha said, her eyes popping. "It was that monster!"

"What monster?" I asked.

"You know perfectly well what monster! The monster I saw quarreling with Nanny Thompson the night he murdered her. The monster who made those big footprints. The monster who stole the miniature of his mother the night he strangled his own uncle to death."

"Bertha!" I cried.

"It was him! Who else would have taken the Corubini miniature? It was Lieutenant Compton's mother, and he wanted it."

"Enough to murder for it?"

"He didn't murder *for* it. But since he was here, he took it."

"But you don't know that he was here," I said.

"Of course he was here. It's been *proven*. Mrs. Merrymede found his cuff link in the bed beside the body. Well, she found it in amongst the bedclothes after Mr. Griever had taken his old lordship out. There must have been a terrible struggle, and he lost it while he was choking his lordship."

"What cuff link?"

"Lieutenant Compton's cuff link—the same one that Nellie found when the lieutenant was staying at Compton Hall in May. Didn't I tell you how he accused Nellie of stealing it and how he almost killed her when he threatened her about it? Mrs. Merrymede recognized it right away."

"Are you sure it was Stuart's cuff link that was found in his lordship's bed?"

"Mrs. Merrymede is. She is positive. It was a very unusual design, a snake's head with a ruby eye."

"But Stuart's mother was supposed to have given him the cuff links—isn't that what Nellie said? She wouldn't give him a snake's head."

"They *were* very odd . . . but they were the ones all right. And Mr. Blessing said he thought he saw Lieutenant Compton in the village the night of the murder, but it was too dark to be sure. Constable Westley says they'll hang Lieutenant Compton if they ever find him."

"You seem to know a great deal about it," I observed.

"Yes! Constable Westley spends a great deal of time in the kitchen. He's told us all about everything."

"I am sure he does—spend a great deal of time in the kitchen, I mean. Heavy men are often found in kitchens."

"That doesn't change the facts."

"Bertha, I can't believe it."

"Louisa! Be reasonable! Of course he did it. He hated his old lordship. Everybody knows that. It goes way back and we don't know how deep. It's a fact!"

"I don't know, Bertha. I don't know. But strange things have happened here at Compton Hall—other than Lord Bude's murder. I feel it, and I don't like it. I am going away, and I'm *glad*."

"Going? Where?"

"New York."

"*New York?*" Bertha exclaimed. "How can you?"

"Father asked me to go with him and I am going," I said.

"Just like that?"

"Yes. Just like that."

"How exciting! Then you will see Miss Livermore."

"No, I hardly think so."

Then I asked about Mr. Salt, and Bertha said she had heard nothing more from him, and had almost given up hope that any arrangements could be made for her to join him.

"What time are you leaving?" she asked finally.

"We are taking the half past four train to London. Father wants to leave the rectory at half past three so that he will have plenty of time to return the car. What time is it now? Heavens!" I cried, looking at my watch. "It is half past two already. I must go!"

"I'll come down and wave you off," Bertha said. "Mrs. Merrymede won't mind."

"That would be lovely," I said. "But I must run!"

Then I turned and ran from the servants' hall, almost colliding with Mrs. Merrymede. I said good-bye to her and then hurried to the vestibule and Keating, who would take me up to Lyle.

We found him in the library. "You are more than half an hour late," he said. "I had almost decided that you wouldn't come up to say good-bye at all. Aren't you leaving the rectory at half past three? This is cutting it rather thin, don't you think?"

"Yes, I shall have to hurry," I said. "But you knew I would not go without saying good-bye to you—and Lord Bude."

"We can say good-bye at the rectory," Lyle said. "I will drive you down. Keating, I will take Miss Little in to Father. Will you please order my car—at the entrance front as soon as possible."

Lyle led me into the drawing room then. Lord Bude lay in his closed coffin, banked with flowers. They filled the room with their intense fragrance.

We stood before the coffin silently for a minute or two while I thought about the gruff, unhappy man who lay within it.

"Is it better for him now?" I asked, thinking aloud.

"Perhaps," Lyle said. "Who knows?"

"Did Stuart do it?"

Lyle turned and looked into my eyes for several moments. Then he said, "I'll see him hanged for it."

That was all he said. We left the room and hurried down to the gravel sweep before the entrance front, where his car stood.

"I am sorry if I have upset you," I said to him as we rode.

"You haven't," Lyle said. He reached over and laid his hand briefly on mine. "Thank you for being so thoughtful."

"It is *you* who are thoughtful. How can I ever thank you for all you have done for me? And you do forgive me for not being here on Tuesday?"

"There is nothing to forgive."

"I don't deserve such a—wonderful friend."

"You do. You *do* deserve it. Louisa, dearest, enjoy your holiday. And when you return . . . perhaps . . . But I promised not to annoy you."

We did not say anything more until we reached the rectory.

Father and Uncle had already loaded our bags into the car. It stood in the drive opposite the portico of the house. A little group of people had gathered beside it, talking to Uncle and Father. Bertha had walked down from the Hall and stood there with May and Patrick. Mr. Collins had walked over from the churchyard, I supposed, and joined them, and I was surprised to see Miss Ormsby talking animatedly to Father.

I said a last good-bye to Aunt Grace, and then joined the group at the car.

Immediately Miss Ormsby rushed to me. "I am so excited!" she said. "I could not *believe* it. It is all so sudden!"

"Too sudden," Lyle said to us. Then he said to me (I hope Father didn't hear), "It is not too late. You can still change your mind. I am a little worried. I still don't think you should go. It is too soon."

"Nonsense," I said. "It is perfectly all right. Father will take excellent care of me. But—"

"But?" Lyle said.

"I am worried about Samantha. I know Patrick will look after her, but he is so busy, and—"

"Would you like me to take her up to the Compton stables? She would have every attention there."

"Would you? I wouldn't worry if you did."

"Come, Louisa," Father said. "It is time we left."

Everyone said their farewells at once. Bertha, to my astonishment, kissed me, and Miss Ormsby hugged me, and then Lyle opened the car door for me as Father got in on the other side. Almost at once we rolled away from the group. They waved to us and shouted good-bye, and I waved back as we drove out of the drive toward the village.

As we left I glanced up at Aunt Grace's window, but of course she was not there to wave good-bye.

I felt tremendous relief at leaving Ledington. Of course I would miss Aunt Grace, and Uncle Andrew, and familiar places and things. But I desperately wanted to get away from Stuart.

He *had* murdered Nanny Thompson. I knew he had, in spite of the fact that I had not wanted to admit it to myself. And now he had murdered his uncle. He had killed a fellow army officer too, and had attempted to drown Lyle. Something of a pattern had become evident: each attack had taken place after a quarrel. And Stuart and I had quarreled bitterly.

I thought I was free of him now. In actuality, however, quite the opposite was true; I was not free of him at all. I could not know then that the train in which I sat hurtled me toward far greater danger than the danger I had sensed at Ledington.

Chapter Thirteen

MY FATE HAD BEEN CAREFULLY PLANNED: HE would not let me go.

I should have sensed something of this the evening of the following day soon after we had boarded the *Antonia*, the ship that was to carry us to New York. But I did not.

It was not until we were well out into the Atlantic on board the *Antonia* that I was to learn what Stuart had planned for me.

But first I visited the St. Marylebone Hospital. I wanted to see the records, because seeing them might help me to experience something of my past. That was on Monday morning after Father had left me at the Old St. James House with a copy of the *Times*, while he went to engage a stateroom for me on the *Antonia* and take care of some unfinished business.

So after he had gone, I left the hotel, and since I had a few pounds in savings which I had brought along on the trip, I hailed a taxi and directed the driver to take me to the hospital in Marylebone Road.

No sooner had I entered the building than a nurse emerged from a room on my right, closing the door behind her. I said to her, "Can you tell me where I can find the director of the hospital?"

She pointed to the room she had just left. "In there." Then she hurried off.

I walked through the door she had pointed to and into a cluttered room where four or five women worked at desks piled high with papers.

As I approached her, the young woman closest to me stopped typewriting and said, "Yes? What is it?"

"I—I should like to see the director," I said.

"He is engaged," the young woman said. "Perhaps Miss Broughton can help you. Miss Broughton," she called to a tiny, sallow, red-haired woman who sat at a larger desk near the window. "There is a young lady to see Mr. Fergusson."

Miss Broughton got up from her desk then and hurried across the room to me. "Mr. Fergusson is engaged," she said. "Perhaps I can help you. I am the secretary of the hospital."

"My name is Louisa Little," I said. "I—was born here, and I should be terribly grateful if—"

"Louisa Little?" Miss Broughton said, squinting. "Oh, yes, I remember. Mother's name, Nancy, wasn't it? Nancy Little?"

"Yes," I said. "But how could you possibly remember?"

"Won't you come over here?" Miss Broughton said.

She turned from me then and walked to her desk and past it to a chair beside the window on which lay a stack of file folders. These she transferred to the windowsill, and then she dragged the chair to her desk and motioned me to sit down.

"I suppose you would like to see the record of your birth?" she asked. Not waiting for an answer from me, she walked to one of the bookcases that lined the walls of the room, ran her finger across a row of books there, and pulled out the one at which her finger had stopped. "Here it is," she said, as she carried it back toward her desk. "I'm afraid records were kept in a rather primitive fashion in those days." Now she stood before me and began to leaf through the ledger, saying, "June—second—I believe it was? Yes, here it is." She bent forward, placed the open book in my lap, and pointed to an entry. "June second," she repeated. "Mother's name: Nancy Little. Time of birth: seven P.M. Weight of child: five and three quarters pounds."

I was astonished. Miss Broughton seemed to know exactly what I had come for.

"It is not often that we have inquiries reaching back twenty-two years," she said, as she sat down at her desk. "That is very unusual. And then, his manner was *quite* frightening.

"Oh, he was *terribly* pleasant at first. Indeed he had me quite deceived. But then, when I told him that these records are not available to everyone—that only close relatives are ever permitted access to them—then he was most insistent! Indeed, I might say threatening. I was quite terrified."

"Of whom are you speaking?" I asked.

"Mr. Throckmorton," Miss Broughton said. "He became terribly angry when I refused to show him the record of your birth, Miss Little. And please believe me, I would not have if he had not seemed so dangerous."

"Who is Mr. Throckmorton?" I asked. "And why did he wish to see the records of my birth?"

"I am sure I don't know, Miss Little."

"But what about Lord Hartley? You must have shown him the records too."

"Lord Hartley? No, there was no Lord Hartley." She smiled briefly at me. "But of course *he* would have seen Mr. Fergusson, and I am sure that Mr. Fergusson would have cooperated with him."

At the mention of Lord Hartley, Miss Broughton's manner became noticeably warmer. "You must remember, my dear, that I am away a good deal of the time meeting with so many good, kind ladies and gentleman who wish to contribute to the hospital or arrange charitable events of one kind or another."

"Were you—connected with the hospital then?" I asked.

"When you were born?" she asked, raising her eyebrows. "Heavens, no! That was twenty-two years ago. There have been several secretaries since then. Odd that you should ask, however. That was one of the things *he* wanted to know."

"Mr. Throckmorton?"

"Yes. He wanted to know all about her. I hadn't the vaguest idea, and I am sure that no one else does either. There is no one here now who was here that long ago—not even Mr. Fergusson, and he has been here for fourteen years. Her name was Miss Blunt; that is all I know. But Mr. Throckmorton wanted to know all about her. Is she still alive? Where does she live? And so on. Well, no one here could possibly know anything about her. He was most distressed by it."

"This must have happened recently, then," I said.

"Oh, no. A month and a half ago, at least. Yes, it was a day or two after Miss Draper's benefit performance."

"Miss Broughton!" a man's voice called.

A man stood in the doorway.

"Miss Broughton," he repeated. "Excuse me, but could you spare us a moment?"

Miss Broughton hurriedly explained to me that that was Mr. Fergusson, and that Sir Reginald Egan was with him. She asked if I would please excuse her for a few minutes. Then she vanished into Mr. Fergusson's office.

This gave me ample time to examine the record book in my lap. The year painted on the spine of the book was 1905. The date written near the center of page 47 was June 2. As soon as I had read the date, I looked at my watch. It said eleven o'clock. I must hurry. Again I thought of Lord Bude's giving me the watch for my birthday on June second and what a strange coincidence that was.

I returned my attention to the hospital record book. Only two entries appeared there under the heading June 2. One was the name Clara Bonnini, and the other was Nancy Little. The page had been ruled into columns which were labeled: Mother's Name, Age, Occupation, and so on. From the entries in these columns, which were handwritten in ink, I learned that my mother's age then had been twenty-three, her address had been 47 Liverpool Street, her occupation seamstress. She had been married, but her husband was deceased. Strange that my mother should declare my father dead, I thought. But then I glanced at the Husband column of Clara Bonnini's entry. Her husband had been deceased too. And then I looked further up that column to the June 1 entries. Those women's husbands were deceased also. In fact, as I glanced down the column labeled Husband on the opposite page for May 31, 30, and 29, I discovered that *all* the husbands, with one or two exceptions, were described as either deceased or whereabouts unknown.

Returning to my mother's entry, I read that I had been born at 7 P.M. and that my weight at birth had been five and three quarters pounds. The Sex of Child entry, however, was unreadable; it had been obliterated by a blot of blue ink—the same color blue ink in which all the entries on both pages of the book had been written. The final column on the page was labeled: Remarks. Here, opposite Mother's name, was written: "Birth difficult and prolonged."

I read all of the information pertaining to Mother again, and then I looked over many of the other entries on those two pages of the book, and even entries on the preceding and following pages. But I learned nothing more.

Miss Broughton had not returned. I waited for five more minutes, and when she had still not left Mr. Fergusson's office, I gave the hospital record book to the woman sitting at the nearest desk and asked her to thank Miss Broughton for me, and to tell her that I was in a most dreadful hurry, since I was sailing for the United States that evening.

Then I left the hospital and returned to my room at the hotel, where Father paced back and forth waiting for me.

"Where have you been?" he asked, when he saw me. "I have been worried to death about you."

"I am sorry," I said, as I walked to the mirror. While I removed my hat and gloves, I continued, "I decided that since I was in London, I would go to the St. Marylebone Hospital and look at the records."

"And?" Father said.

"A Mrs. Broughton showed them to me. It was all just as you and Lyle said it would be. Except that—"

"Yes?"

"Except that Mother had evidently told the hospital that her husband was deceased."

"When your mother entered the hospital, she had not planned to contact me. It was easier and less embarrassing simply to say that I had died, leaving her alone and destitute. I imagine that is an all too familiar story in such institutions."

"Yes, judging from some of the other entries, it is. There was one other thing."

"Oh? What was that?" Father asked.

"A Mr. Throckmorton went out to the hospital and demanded to see the records of my birth. Evidently he was a brute of a man who terrified the hospital's secretary into showing them to him. The records are kept confidential, you know. Who do you suppose it could have been? Who could possibly be interested in when and where I was born?"

"When was this? Recently?"

"A month and a half ago."

"I haven't the vaguest idea, but you should not have gone out alone. I have been worried sick about you. However, now that you have investigated my story, I trust you are satisfied as to its authenticity."

"I never doubted you for a moment, Father," I said. "I merely went to the hospital because it is part of my past, and I wanted to be close to it. I have so little of it."

"I know, my dearest," he said. Then he came to me, put his arm around me, and kissed my forehead. "I understand completely."

"Were you able to arrange a stateroom for me on the *Antonia*?"

"Yes, everything is arranged. The boat train leaves from Euston Station and arrives in Liverpool at half past six. The *Antonia* sails at seven o'clock. Now, shall we go down to lunch?"

The boat train was late in arriving in Liverpool, and we barely had time to find a taxi in all the confusion of Lime Street Station and reach Pierhead by seven o'clock.

The *Antonia* seemed impatient to depart; smoke rose from her funnel and seamen stood at her lines. She waited only for the boat train passengers from London.

Once on board we found a place at the rail. It was lined with passengers calling and waving to friends and relatives who had come to see them off and now stood on the dock below us waving and calling in return.

"Where are our bags?" I asked Father.

"The porters are taking them below for us," he said.

"I had no idea it would be so crowded."

"The *Antonia* is one of Cunard's smaller ships. I had hoped for a larger one, but she will have to do."

"Oh, look at that funny man with the beard there. Can you read what is printed on that paper? See? He is holding it above his head."

" 'God bless Lena,' " Father read. "Someone in tourist class, no doubt."

"Take care of Edith," a fat woman who stood next to us shouted to someone in the crowd below. The tiny brim of her cloche hat almost hid her eyes. The hat was trimmed with an enormous, pink silk bow. She leaned so far over the rail that I feared for her safety.

"I hope she doesn't fall over," I whispered to Father. "And look! There is a man down there dancing a jig."

"Drunk, no doubt," Father said. "I shall be glad when we are off. I find all this confusion and noise upsetting, to say the least." As he spoke, he drew out his pocket watch and flipped open the lid. "It is after seven. We should be on our way." Just then, one of the ship's officers came to the rail to look down at the dock below. "I say, Officer," Father said to him, "it is seven o'clock. Shouldn't we be getting under way?"

"There will be a slight delay, I'm afraid, sir," the officer said. "The mail has not arrived. I shouldn't think it would be more than a half hour though." As he spoke, he glanced down the length of the dock, and at that moment two vans sped along the dock toward the ship. "Ah, here it comes now. Excuse me, sir." He turned from us then and hurried away.

"Well," I said, "if they still have the mail to load, I think I will go to my cabin for a few minutes. How do I get there, do you know?"

"It may not take as long as they say," Father said. "Stay on deck with me. It is a lovely evening, and you would not want to miss the excitement of getting under way."

"Of course not. I shall come out shortly. But I do want to take one or two things out of my trunk before they are crushed. I shall not be long. What is my cabin number?"

"Number twenty-six—on the promenade deck, but—"

"You stay here. The steward will show me. Steward! Steward!" I called.

But as the steward hurried toward me, my father made a strange, gasping sound, and as I looked at him, his hand flew to his forehead and he slumped, trying to hold himself erect by the ship's railing.

"What is it?" I asked Father, as I grasped him around the waist to try and keep him from falling. "Steward! Help me!"

The steward dashed to Father's side, put his arm around him, propelled him to a deck chair not five yards away, and assisted him into it.

At once I knelt beside the chair and said, "Father! What is it? Are you all right?"

"Yes," he said. "Yes, I shall be all right. A fainting spell. Such an odd feeling. But it is passing now. Yes, I am much better, but don't leave me. Stay with me."

"Of course I will stay with you. I am right here."

It was then, as I looked up thinking there might be someone who could help, that I found we were surrounded by curious people looking down at us. And as I glanced around that circle of staring faces, I realized that one belonged to the fat woman with the pink bow on her hat.

Just then someone shouted, "Step aside! Step aside and let me through. I am the ship's doctor, miss," a man said to me, as he knelt down on the other side of Father's chair. "Stand back there and give the man air," he shouted at the people who surrounded us. "Go along now! Just a fainting spell. Nothing to be alarmed about."

At this the people turned and began to walk away, while the doctor loosened Father's tie and collar. Then he took Father's wrist to read his pulse.

"This is very kind of you, Doctor," Father said. "But I am quite all right now. Just a fainting spell—because of the excitement, you know."

"Any nausea or pain?" the doctor asked.

"No, just a slight dizziness."

I rose then from my cramped position and realized that the crowd had left us completely, except for the fat woman.

"I am Mrs. Alexander Harris," she said to me. "My dear child, you are quite white! Is there something I can do?"

"I am Louisa Little," I said to Mrs. Harris. "That is most kind of you, but I think now that the doctor is with him, everything will be all right. Thank heaven he came when he did!"

"The steward fetched him," Mrs. Harris said. "I am sure your father will be all right now. You mustn't worry. And the rest during the voyage and the sea air will do him good. It did wonders for my late husband, Mr. Alexander Harris, in 1906. He was exhausted. So we traveled to Italy and Greece to see the ruins. He was a builder, you know. He built almost all of Kilburn and Queen's Park single-handedly, not to mention the Iron Exchange, Mervant's Hotel, and the new World and Athenian theaters. My husband was very interested in the theater. Speaking of theater, who do you think is aboard? Lady Craven! She was Delilah Dawn! But that must have been before you were born. There she is! Surely she remembers my late husband. Excuse me, my dear." She turned then and began to walk toward a short, energetic-looking, older woman who still had a beautiful figure. "Do not worry," she called over her shoulder. "Everything will be lovely—lovely!"

Now the doctor stood, and Father said, "Thank you, Doctor. I am perfectly all right, I assure you." Then when the doctor had nodded and turned away, he said to me, "Sit here beside me."

I sat down and then asked, "How do you feel?"

"I feel quite well. Quite well, though I should like to sit

here for a bit. Stay with me, and soon I shall be completely recovered, I promise."

We sat there, quietly watching the growing restlessness of our fellow passengers as the sun sank over the harbor. Finally our whistle began to sound, orders were barked, ropes were cast off, and we began to slide away from the dock amidst final cries of good-bye between the passengers and those who still remained to see them off.

After that, since he assured me that he had fully recovered, Father and I stood at the rail and watched while we slowly pushed out into the middle of the Mersey. Then as we stood there, fascinated, the *Antonia* steamed to the mouth of the great river in the long twilight—past New Brighton, Colwyn Bay, Llandudno, Holyhead, and finally out into Saint George's channel and the Atlantic.

It was just about dark when one of the stewards approached us and said that a buffet was to be served in the dining salon at nine o'clock.

"Heavens!" I said to my father. "It must be almost nine now. We shall have to hurry."

"You go down," Father said. "I should like to have a word with the purser."

"The purser?" I asked. "Why?"

"Just a question or two. Come along, we will find a steward to show you to your stateroom. Then I shall join you in a few minutes."

My stateroom, number twenty-six, was a first-class cabin furnished luxuriously with a spacious single bed, armchairs, thick carpeting, and heavy draperies. It had plenty of closet space and its own lavatory. This is marvelous, I thought as I looked about. My trunk, together with Father's trunk and bags, stood on the floor. The porters had mistakenly left his luggage in my cabin.

He will soon come for them, I thought. And I was right. I had no sooner removed my hat and gloves, and had begun to hang up some of my dresses in the closet, than Father knocked on the door, opened it, and stepped inside.

"The porters left your luggage here," I said. "I thought you would be along to fetch it."

"Louisa," Father said, "a situation has developed which is perhaps—unfortunate. Ah, inconvenient might be a better word."

"Have you been ill again?" I asked.

"No. No, nothing like that. It is simply that the ship is full—every berth occupied. This is highly unusual. Even the purser said so."

"I don't understand," I said. "What does that have to do with us?"

"Well, it is simply that there is no empty stateroom available for you. I am terribly sorry. I was sure that there would be. It is highly unusual that *every* stateroom on board should be occupied. On any other crossing there would be several completely unused."

"But you said that it was all arranged. You told me at the hotel that you were going to book a stateroom for me on the *Antonia*, and that if there was not one available, you would book our passage on another ship."

"There is no other ship. Rehearsals for the play begin on the nineteenth, and I *must* be there for that. The next passenger liner sailing for New York is the *Mauritania*. She sails on Monday and will not reach New York until the twenty-second. That would be too late."

"Then you knew all the time. What am I to do?"

"We will share this cabin."

"*Share* this cabin?"

"There is a bed available in the ship's hospital. The purser said you could—"

"No! I couldn't!"

"Now, please don't get excited. That is what I told him. We will manage here quite nicely."

"Nicely?" I said. "How can we manage nicely? I could not possibly. Where will we sleep? What will people think?"

"They will not think anything at all; only that it is a bit irregular—and they might not notice anything about it at all. Please let me explain what I have in mind before you get upset. It will only be for six days—seven nights. Now, you know that I have my play to work on, and that the lines are difficult. I will need a great deal of peace and quiet to memorize them, and what could be a better time to do this than at night while everyone is asleep? So I shall sit up and study my lines at night in a pleasant corner of the ship somewhere while you sleep, and then I shall sleep during the day while everything is bustle and confusion. We can dress separately here, and it should all work out quite nicely, don't you think?"

"But other people will not know all this," I said. "What will they think of our sharing a cabin? What did the purser think? I shall be mortified."

"He didn't think anything of it, other than that it might be a bit uncomfortable. But he said that he hoped we could make do with it." He gestured to the walls of the cabin. "And that in any case, we would have to as there was nothing else that could be done."

"The purser didn't think anything of it?" I said. "I should think he would be scandalized. A father and his daughter sleeping together in the same bed?"

"I told him we were married."

"You told him we were *married*? *Why*?"

"What else could I do?" Father said. "I asked him if there were another single cabin available—that I would like to book it. When he said that there was nothing, I had to do something. As you say, he would have been scandalized at the idea of our sleeping together. So I told him you were my wife. That, of course, was perfectly acceptable. I told him that at the very last minute it became possible for you to accompany me, and that I had been certain another cabin would be available for you."

"You knew that there would not be," I said. "You have planned this ever since this morning. Were you really ill, or was that to keep me from coming in here and finding out about it? And then you kept me on deck until we were well out to sea, pointing out this and— And then to tell the purser that I am your *wife* . . ."

"Louisa!" Father hissed. "Not so loud. People will hear. What was I to do? Leave you behind?"

"I wish you had."

"No, you don't really wish that, do you? Not to have our time together? Not to try to recover just a few of those long, lost times?" Now tears glistened in my father's eyes.

"No!" I cried. "Oh, Father, no. I don't wish that. But surely there must have been some other way. Two or three days could not have made that much difference."

"It could! You don't understand what this play means to me. It is my return to the stage, a new chance. There may not be another."

"But your *wife*!"

"You said you always wanted to act," Father said. He was grinning that loveable, charming grin of his now.

"I never said anything of the kind. I simply said that the idea was exciting."

"You could do it if you wanted to." He was openly smiling now. "Oh, don't be so serious. It could be amusing if you could look at it that way. A lark! Think what fun we could have. It will only be for a few days. And then we will be in New York at the Ritz-Carlton Hotel. A whole suite of rooms—the finest available."

"I don't suppose there is anything else I can do, is there? I loathe deception, but . . ."

"That's my girl," Father said. "It will all go quite nicely. You will see."

"But what if Mrs. Harris heard me call you 'Father?' I can't remember, but I think I did call you 'Father.' "

"We will think of something. Now we must hurry. We have had nothing to eat since luncheon. Are you almost ready? I will wait outside in the lounge until you are. Then I'll wash quickly, and we will go down to the buffet."

After we had eaten, Father accompanied me back to our cabin. Then, having taken his copy of the play out of one of his bags, he left me, saying that he hoped I would sleep well.

I did sleep well. I was exhausted, and once in bed I drifted off almost at once, thinking about Mrs. Harris and whether or not she had heard me call Father, "Father." We had not met her during the buffet. She sat at the far end of the dining salon talking animatedly to Lady Craven.

Nor did we see Mrs. Harris at breakfast. I had the strangest feeling that the empty seat at our table was hers. It was, as it turned out. And I also had the feeling that the maid who carried breakfast on a tray into stateroom number twenty-eight, the one next-door to ours, was Mrs. Harris's maid carrying breakfast to Mrs. Harris. It was.

Mrs. Harris did not appear at luncheon either, but I met her as I strolled alone on deck during the afternoon.

"Ah, Miss Little," she cried, when she saw me. "Isn't it a lovely afternoon? Quite balmy." Then she turned to her maid, who was the girl I had seen carrying the breakfast tray that morning, and said, "That will be all, now Hébert. Go down and tidy things. Oh, and I shall wear the jade evening dress to dinner." Then as Hébert walked away from us, Mrs. Harris turned back to me and said, "A perfect jewel. I do not know what I would do without her. I suppose one must appear at dinner, though I know I shall feel rather like a tinned sardine, sitting crammed into one of those ghastly tables." Then she smiled widely at me. "But we mustn't complain, must we? It could be far worse, and I understand that the food aboard is quite good and the wines entirely passable."

"Yes, I believe so," I said.

"Are you enjoying the voyage?" she asked. "Oh, if it would only remain like this. So balmy! I feel the tropics! How is your dear father? Tell me that he has recovered completely. I have thought of him so often since yesterday."

"How very kind of you," I said. "But he is not my father."

"Oh?" Mrs. Harris said. "I beg your pardon."

"He is my husband. I—I am *Mrs*. Little."

"Oh, my dear, forgive me. How is your dear husband?"

"Quite recovered, thank you."

"Oh, I am *so* happy to hear it." Mrs. Harris paused then and smiled at me. "You must forgive a foolish old woman, but please let me say that you must have made a perfectly dear, charming, sweet bride. If I had had a daughter, I should have liked her to have been just like you."

"That is most flattering," I replied, feeling rather embarrassed.

"And you were married— Well, you could not have been married very long ago. Such a sweet, young thing Why, I shouldn't think you were twenty yet."

"Twenty-two, actually."

"Oh, twenty-two!" As she said this, she took my arm in hers and began to propel me down the deck beside her. "What a divine age. Why, my dear," she giggled, "I can hardly remember ever being so young. How lovely! You have your whole life ahead of you. And only newly married. How long ago?"

"Ah—just three months ago," I said.

"A May bride?"

"Yes."

"How romantic. And such a coincidence. I was also married in May. It will bring you good fortune and happiness. Now we have something in common already." She hugged my arm. "I knew we would when I first saw you. A church wedding?"

"Oh, yes, of course."

"In London?"

"Yes. In the little church of St. Andrew's Axe—in Soho."

"How very odd," she said.

"How odd?" I asked.

"My dear, St. Andrew's Axe burned to the ground long before you were born and was never rebuilt. A tragedy!"

I did not reply to this, but gazed out to sea.

"It was the jewel of London churches. Sir Christopher Wren, I believe."

"You are interested in architecture?" I asked, hoping to change the subject.

"My husband had a drawing of it hanging in his study,"

Mrs. Harris said. "It was one of his favorite things. I still have it. And I distinctly remember that yesterday you called your husband, 'Father'!"

"It—it is a pet name—because he is so much older than I. An amusing thing between us."

"And was it amusing for him to sit up all night reading while you slept? Hébert saw him." Again she smiled. Now she patted my arm. "Do not be alarmed, my dear. It is no business of mine, and I shall be most discreet about it. I am next to you in number twenty-eight, you know, and one can hear a word or two through the walls now and then. Your relationship with your father is no affair of mine. But, dear child, be very careful. Such a thing could lead to tragic circumstances. I suppose you have really no idea what may lie in store for you."

"Whatever do you mean?" I asked, pulling away from her.

Mrs. Harris did not answer. Instead, she looked at me with intense commiseration.

"But you cannot be thinking—" I blurted. "It is not true! It is not what you think. There was no other way. His work requires him to be in New York on the nineteenth, and there was no other ship. We have just found each other and want to be together."

Then I told Mrs. Harris about Father's letter and how he had arrived in Ledington. And how I had found myself sharing the cabin with him.

"Oh, well, *that* makes all the difference." Mrs. Harris laughed when I had finished.

"That is why he sits up at night," I explained. "I will sleep at night, and he will sleep during the day. So, you see, things will work out nicely."

"Of course they will. I am so glad you told me about it, though. Heaven knows what I would have thought if you hadn't! And you have no mother?"

"No, not since I was six years old. I barely remember her."

"What did she do? Where was your father?"

I told her some of the story—saying merely that my mother and father had lost track of each other.

When I had finished this, Mrs. Harris said, "How unfortunate. Dear Miss Little, how unaware we are of the sufferings of others. Were you happy in Ledington?"

Then I told her something of my life there. I felt I had found a friend. And I wanted to strengthen the friendship.

Finally Mrs. Harris said, "You poor dear. Well, now your suffering is behind you. It is so much better to look back on unhappiness than to have it looming in the future. I believe that we all have just so much of it, and no more. You have already had your share. With such sweet beauty as yours, you could not possibly avoid great happiness. I am convinced of that. Now, I must go. Hébert will wonder where I am. And it is time to be getting ready for dinner. Shall we go down together?"

We did, and she left me at my cabin door.

When Mrs. Harris discovered at dinner that Father was the famous Richard Kean, she asked him countless questions. She had seen him perform many times, and she was intensely curious about his career and especially about the later plays which, I gather, had not been especially successful.

And, possibly because she drank liberally herself, she seemed disturbed that Father did not drink at all.

"You have no wine, Mr. Kean," she said, at one point. "This beaujolais is really rather passable."

"I never touch alcoholic beverages, Mrs. Harris," Father said. "Alcohol destroys the brain."

"Only in excess, Mr. Kean," Mrs. Harris replied. "Doctors prescribe it. But I admire one who takes a definite stand on a subject and never falters thereafter. Tell me, what became of that brilliant star that shined so bright on our London stage?"

And so it went on—question after question until dinner was over.

Then as I left the dining salon with Father, he asked, "Would you care for a stroll on deck?"

"No, I don't think so. I think I'll retire early," I said.

"You should not go to sleep directly after eating," Father said. "It is not good for you. Come for a little stroll in the fresh air."

"No, I think not," I replied. "I am terribly sleepy. It must be the sea air. But I shall leave the door unlatched. If you need anything, don't hesitate to come in and get it. It will not disturb me."

I went directly to our cabin and to bed, leaving the lamp lit in case Father should need it. And I slept almost at once. The sea air had made me drowsy and the gentle roll of the ship lulled me to sleep.

I awoke for a moment or two later in the night. The lamp was still lit. The ship was quiet now except for the throb of its engines as we slid through the Atlantic toward New York. I loved the feel of the ship beneath me—carrying me safely across the sea. I felt it was taking special care of me, somehow.

Thinking about this, I slept again. But shortly I was awakened by someone opening the cabin door. Father stood in the opening staring at me.

"Did I wake you?" he whispered. "I—I hated to do it, but I cannot study my part; I cannot keep my eyes open. I did not sleep a wink yesterday morning or in the afternoon either. How could one sleep with all those comings and goings out there?" He gestured to the passageway outside the cabin door. "It is unnatural!" he cried.

"Please!" I hissed. "Someone will hear."

"One sleeps at night, not during the day," he whispered. "And I cannot risk falling ill—not with rehearsals beginning next week. One becomes ill if one does not get one's proper sleep. You know that. I cannot keep awake any longer. I *have* to lie down and go to sleep. That is all, I have to lie down and sleep."

"Very well!" I whispered. "Be calm—and quiet! People will hear! I will get up and you may have the cabin. Then *I* will sleep during the day. Now, please close the door. I will be out in a minute."

I dressed as quickly as I could, left the cabin, and passed Father in the corridor without speaking. Then I walked through the deserted ship—through the bar to the garden lounge at the stern—and sat down in an armchair where I could look out the windows and watch the long, dim, gray wake of the vessel as it fanned out slowly behind us into the black Atlantic.

I watched it for a while, holding my mind blank—not wanting to think. But I could not suppress for long the thought that pricked my brain: perhaps I should not have come. I had not known Father long enough—not known what kind of person he was. Now I was beginning to find out.

His attitude had changed since we left Ledington. He was no longer kind and affectionate. At times he was almost rude. And he had not been honest with me. He had lied about my accommodations on the ship. And I had found his peevish manner in the cabin a few minutes before distasteful.

But most of all I was perplexed by Mrs. Harris's, "My dear, St. Andrew's Axe burned to the ground long before you were born and was never rebuilt."

I wanted to go back to Ledington—to Uncle Andrew and Aunt Grace and Lyle. Thinking about home, my eyes filled with tears.

Long after my eyes had dried, I sat there waiting for the sky to lighten. Finally the ocean turned to pearl and then the sun rose. It was long after this that a few early-rising passengers began to wander about, and then at last it was time for breakfast. I smoothed my hair and washed my hands in one of the ladies' rooms and went down to the dining salon—not because I was in the least hungry, but because there was nothing else for me to do.

We had nearly finished luncheon that day, when Mrs. Harris asked me, "Do you like the play?"

"The play?" I asked.

"The new play that your—that this dear, great artist of ours is about to appear in."

"I haven't read it," I said. "I really don't know very much about it."

"You haven't read it?" Mrs. Harris asked. Then she turned to Father and said, "But surely you must have told your—this dear child about it."

"A little, I believe," Father said.

"Tell us all about it then," Mrs. Harris said. "What is it like? A romance, perhaps?"

"No," Father said, "It is a tragedy, called *Flannagan's Daughter.*"

I glanced at our dining companions, the Miss Drads, and Mr. Fry. They all listened, wide-eyed.

"It is a new play by Fredrick Lewison—an immensely talented playwright," Father continued. "In it, Aileen kills her father and finally goes mad when her father's ghost returns to torment her."

"Oh! How horrible!" Mrs. Harris said. "I shall be there to see it, of course. I shall be seeing a great deal of my niece and her husband while I am staying in New York, as well as a great many old friends of my late husband. I cannot wait to say that I traveled with Richard Kean, the *star* of the play."

"You are too kind, Mrs. Harris. The part of Flannagan, which I play, is not the longest part in the play. Both Aileen and her husband, Sean, have a greater number of lines, but Flannagan is the most important part, and it is intensely demanding. I am sure you will enjoy it." Then Father turned to me and said, "Shall we sit on deck after luncheon? Perhaps you would test my lines in the first scene to see if I have them down correctly?"

I had no intention of doing so, though I followed him out. I was about to tell him this as soon as we stepped into the sunshine, but he spoke first.

"Have you noticed how Mrs. Harris will not call you my wife, or Mrs. Little, or Mrs. Kean?" he said. "Do you think she suspects?"

"She knows we are not married," I said.

"She knows? How could she know?"

"I told her."

"You *told* her? Why?"

"I didn't mean to, but she asked me how long we had been married and if we had been married in London. And then she asked me what church we had been married in, and I said in the little church of St. Andrew's Axe in Soho. She knew all about it. It burned to the ground long before I was born and was never rebuilt."

Chapter Fourteen

"WHY IN THE WORLD DID YOU MENTION that church?" Father asked.

"You said you and Mother were married there. It's the only church name I know in London besides St. Paul's and Westminster Abbey. I could not very well say we were married in either one of them."

"It was St. Andrew's at Hill," Father said.

"I thought you said it was St. Andrew's Axe." Then after a moment, as I looked out to sea, I said, "Anyway, she had heard me call you 'Father' when you were ill. I am sure she won't say anything about it, though." Then I turned back to Father and said, "I'm going down to the cabin and take a nap."

"But I thought you were going to hear my lines."

"If you are not going to sleep during the day, then I must," I said to him.

Then I hurried away, directly to our cabin, and closed the door.

Immediately I became aware of voices from the cabin next door—Mrs. Harris's cabin.

"She will hear you!" a woman's voice said.

"No, she is on deck with her father, testing his lines," Mrs. Harris said. "Would you like another cup? Isn't it delicious? I simply cannot bear that foul-tasting brew they serve here, can you? That is not coffee. Only the French can make coffee. Hébert gets the beans herself from Smith's in St. James Street, and she grinds them in her own little grinder. Isn't it lovely? Sometimes I can hardly wait for it to drop down into the cup."

"But she is so young," the other woman said.

"Not only that, my dear Lady Craven," Mrs. Harris said, "but she is his *daughter*."

"His *daughter*?" Lady Craven said. "And they are sharing the same tiny cabin?"

"Yes, I am afraid so," Mrs. Harris said. "Sharing it in every respect."

"What do you mean, every respect?"

"I am not a heavy sleeper," Mrs. Harris said, "especially in this rocking, heaving place. How one can sleep while being bounced about is more than I can possibly understand. Well, last night, in the middle of the night, it started."

"What started?" Lady Craven asked.

"They were there—*together*! Such whisperings and moving about. It was most embarrassing."

"Grotesque!" Lady Craven exclaimed.

"I must have drifted off before it was over, but I am sure she enjoyed every moment of it. She is an unprincipled little chit. I knew that as soon as I laid eyes on her. And you should have heard the tale she told me about their being married in a church that has not *existed* for fifty years."

"Well, I am not surprised," Lady Craven said. "He is a bounder. Oh, one cannot deny the magic of those early performances. The Romeo *was* superb. But such a frail talent could not possibly last. It was alcohol and women that destroyed it. You know all about that; it was the talk of London."

"Yes," Mrs. Harris said. "I shall never forget the evening Mr. Harris and I went to see him in *The Bridal*. He was intoxicated! He could barely walk, let alone act. I shall never forgive him for that. He ruined our evening."

"*Melantius* was the end. It was a disaster. Alcohol and Leonora Rosa ruined him."

"Leonora Rosa. They went to France together—somewhere along the Mediterranean. Did you know her?"

"We have met."

"What is she like?"

"Beautiful. But a viper. She lives on the destruction of men's lives."

"And Mrs. Loosely?"

"I would rather not think of her. Now, I must go and have my nap. Thank you so much for the coffee, Mrs. Harris. It was delicious. You must try to nap too. Rest is to the body as the sun and rain are to the flowers, you know."

After that Lady Craven left Mrs. Harris, and then after some rather noisy movement, which I supposed meant that Mrs. Harris was preparing to lie down, her cabin was silent.

I did not sleep for a long time. I lay on the bed thinking about Mrs. Harris and what she had said to Lady Craven. How could I face her? How could I sit opposite Mrs. Harris in the dining salon during meals? I loathed the idea, not because of what she suspected about me, but because I felt that she had betrayed me. I did not wish to talk to her; I did not wish to have anything to do with her—ever.

As it turned out, Mrs. Harris managed to move to the captain's table, where Lady Craven sat. A Mr. Sweeton sat at our table now in her place, gazing constantly, though harmlessly, at me.

Father found me later that evening just as I came out of the cinema where I had seen *Anna Karenina* with my favorite movie star, John Gilbert, and Greto Garbo.

"It is a picture up there," he said, pointing to the ceiling. "Simply glorious. The aurora borealis, lights up the entire sky. You must come and see it."

"I have seen it in England," I said.

"And the flying fish are out."

"Flying fish?"

"Yes. You have not seen *them* in England."

"Fish do not fly," I said.

"They don't really fly, but their fins carry them through the air for quite long distances. They are tropical. One does not usually find them so far north. Come up and see them."

"How very odd," I said. "Can you really see them in the air? What color are they? Are they very large? Let me get my sweater from our cabin. It will only take me a minute."

I fetched my sweater and threw it about my shoulders. Then I rejoined Father. He told me about the flying fish as we walked to the stairway and climbed to the boat deck.

"You can see them quite clearly," he said, as he opened the door for me.

I stepped out onto the deck then. Father said something more, but I could not hear what it was because the wind had come up, and its shriek drowned out his words. I pulled my sweater close about me, and held it tightly. And at the same time I spread my legs to balance myself more effectively on the pitching, swaying deck. But there was no aurora borealis. Nor was there moon or stars; the sky was black. The darkness shrouded the ship and the sea. Only the feeble light from the smoking room portholes illuminated the railing and the ghostly-white lifeboats that swung on davits above us.

"Over here," Father shouted into my ear, as he grasped my arm.

"You said there was the aurora borealis," I shouted back at him. "It is pitch black!"

"It will come again. Come over here."

He led me toward the rail of the ship between two of the lifeboats. As we walked, I looked about hoping to see other passengers nearby, but I saw no one.

"It is so dark!" I repeated, as we reached the rail. "I can't see anything."

This was not quite true. My eyes had become accustomed to the darkness, and I could see huge, glassy mounds of water, each one plumed with foam, sweep silently past us. Their relentless, impersonal procession terrified me. How cold, and black, and endless was that heaving sea.

"Down there," Father shouted into my ear. We stood close together at the rail now. Father's arm was around me and he pointed down into a trough of water below us with his other arm. "See?"

"No," I cried.

"Straight down. Lean over!"

I leaned over the rail a bit, searching the water where it

bathed the steel hull of the ship directly below me, but I could see no flying fish. I felt Father's other hand clutch my waist, then his arm muscles tense, and then the slightest push forward. It was only for an instant, and then he let go of me altogether.

I turned to him and said, "There is *nothing*!"

But Father was not there. He no longer stood by my side. He was only a silhouette now, hurrying toward the doorway. And as I watched, he disappeared inside.

I followed him at once. I could not easily pull open the sliding door, but when I had done so, I found the corridor and the stairway empty. Nor did I find him waiting for me at the bottom of the stairs. He had gone directly to our cabin. I knew this because I went there myself to put away my sweater and found the door locked from the inside.

My immediate thought was to pound on the door until he opened it and then demand an explanation of his behavior on deck.

But I did not do that; I didn't need an explanation. I stood there in the dim passageway facing that locked cabin door and shuddered. How close to me death had hovered! His chill mantle had brushed me as my father pushed me toward the sea.

Why had he stopped? Why had he not thrust me over the rail?

I spent half the night sitting in the garden lounge, as I had the night before. Then I discovered a daybed in the ladies' room near it and lay there until morning.

But I slept only fitfully because a storm had begun and the ship's movements became violent. First it would throw itself onto its side, and then the bow of the ship would rise abruptly and slam down on the sea. At the same time it would toss itself on its other side. Then it would seem to thrust its bow into the depths of the ocean while its stern rose high in the air. And then it would throw itself onto its other side and begin the gyration all over again.

The storm proved to be one of the fiercest in memory,

and it lasted four days. During that time Father was deathly ill and so were almost all the other passengers. They remained in their staterooms. Abbreviated meals were served to those few who came to the dining salon, and all entertainment was canceled.

To make matters worse, rumors began to circulate: the ship was hopelessly off course, and it had sprung a leak which the pumps couldn't control. Rumors ran rampant, and the captain and ship's officers were far too busy to set them to rest. As a matter of fact, we hardly saw an officer, and all during the storm the captain did not appear in the dining salon.

I fared better during all this than most, I suppose. At least I was not seasick. And the ladies' room was left almost entirely to me.

The storm lasted until Monday morning. As we entered the Narrows on our approach to New York harbor, the water beneath us quieted miraculously and the passengers came back to life.

When I entered our cabin, I found that Father had lost some of his ashen color and sat dressed in his shirt and pants, putting on his shoes.

"My God, what an appalling experience. I think I would rather have died." He looked up at me. "I have never been so ill in my life."

"I am glad you have recovered. If you don't mind, I should like to change my dress as soon as you are ready. In the meantime, let me put these things"—I gestured to the closet—"in my trunk."

"There is plenty of time," Father said. "It will be at least an hour before we arrive. I'll be dressed in a moment, and then I'll leave the cabin to you. A brisk walk in the fresh air should straighten me out. God, what a voyage!"

"Father," I said, "I plan to return to England as soon as possible. I wonder if I could leave my trunk on board. I suppose the *Antonia* will be returning to England. Do you know when?"

"You are not returning to England," Father said.

"I certainly am," I said. "You could not possibly imagine that I would stay with you after—after what happened on deck that night."

"Whatever do you mean?"

"You intended to push me overboard. Why didn't you do it?"

"Push you overboard? Why, whatever gave you such a notion? When did I try to push you overboard?"

"The night you told me there were flying fish. There were no flying fish."

"Not when we were looking, no. But there were before."

"You were going to push me over. I felt you start to."

"I was *holding* you so you wouldn't fall."

"It doesn't matter. I am not going to stay in New York."

"I think you have very little choice," Father said, leaning back in his chair and looking up at me.

"I have all the choice in the world. I am returning to England. I am going home on the first available boat."

"How do you expect to pay for this voyage?"

"Surely you will pay for it? You can't expect to keep me here against my will. Uncle Andrew will reimburse you if necessary."

"That will not be necessary because you are not going anywhere. You are staying here with me—with your father, where you belong."

"But I don't *wish* to stay here with you."

"Nevertheless, you will stay."

"I won't! I'll cable Uncle and ask him to send the money for my passage. And then I shall go."

Suddenly he smiled broadly and said, "Oh, now, Louisa, you will be perfectly safe. I promise you that. What more can I say? Stay and enjoy your experience. Not every girl has the chance to visit New York." He smiled again. "Pack your things now and join me on deck. It is a marvelous harbor."

As we steamed past the Statue of Liberty, New York City reflected my cheerlessness. How congested and grim it looked—its pyramid of skyscrapers crammed together on the narrow island.

Nor did Mrs. Harris lighten my mood. She and two other passengers from the captain's table stood at the rail a few yards away from us. I could not hear what she said to the man and woman, whom I had not met, but I knew by the sly looks she cast at me and the shocked glances of her companions that she was telling them about my "illicit relationship" with my father.

I tried to convince myself that this did not matter—that Mrs. Harris had gone out of my life, and that I would never be required to have anything further to do with her.

This was not quite true. Later, after the confusion of disembarking, as we stood waiting for the customs men, Mrs. Harris ran toward us, her arm extended, diamond rings flashing.

"I just wanted to say *au revoir,*" she said, when she stood breathless before us. "Never good-bye. It is such a *tiny* world that we are certain to meet again. And I could not go off without saying farewell to my two *favorite* people. You are such dears, both of you—sweet, darling child and our shining star of the stage. Oh! There is the customs man. I must fly!" Then she ran back toward her trunks and her maid, calling to us, "We will come and see the play."

After that I turned my back on her—hoping I would never see her again.

I do not wish to think about those wretched two weeks in New York with my father, so I will not dwell in detail upon the deterioration of our relationship and the state of his mind and health. But I must describe the end of that stay with him, because what happened then prefaced the appearance of Stuart, himself.

Chapter Fifteen

Briefly, then, we stayed at the Ritz-Carlton Hotel, where Father engaged an expensive suite. Why did I remain with him so long? First, I had only a few pounds. I cabled Uncle Andrew from the desk at the hotel to send me money for my passage home. When after a week I had received no reply from him, I cabled Lyle and asked him for the money. I waited another week for his reply, but I heard nothing from him either.

Meanwhile, some of the maids at the Ritz-Carlton had heard me "rehearsing" the mad scene from *Flannagan's Daughter* with Father to test his lines and had spread the story that I was crazy. I know this sounds incredible, but it is exactly what happened. Because of this, Father threatened to have me committed to a mental institution if I left him! I didn't take this very seriously, but it was most uncomfortable having everyone at the hotel staring at me.

So I waited patiently for Uncle and Lyle to reply to my cables. And I attempted to induce Father to give me the money to return to England by being disagreeable—criticizing him, complaining, and acting in as shrewish a manner as I could.

Meanwhile, he attended rehearsals of *Flannagan's Daughter*. The leading lady, Julia Marlow, had had a small part in *Melantius*, the play that had been such a disaster at the Drury Lane because of Father's drinking. To protect herself, she determined to make Father's experience in *Flannagan's Daughter* so unpleasant that he would either leave the cast or return to drink. He did the latter and was sacked.

His reaction to being dismissed was to go on a spending spree. He spent all his money on clothes and jewelry. During these days he drank more and more heavily. I was revolted by his behavior, and so was the management of the Ritz-Carlton. After a particularly drunken scene in the dining room one evening, we were asked to leave the hotel.

We moved to Bixby's Hotel on the Bowery, just south of Hester Street. Bixby's Hotel was an ancient and dilapidated three-story frame structure, which had been the Ram's Head Tavern for more than a hundred years before Mr. Bixby bought it.

Father engaged two small rooms on the third floor under the pitched roof. They were directly across the corridor from one another and were identical—each lighted by a window in a tiny dormer. But Father's room looked out on the Bowery, while mine looked out at the barren dirt yards and rotting board fences of buildings facing Elizabeth Street, on the other side of the block.

After we had been shown to our rooms and two ragged, dirty little boys—Mr. Bixby's sons, I supposed—had carried our bags and trunks to our rooms and left us, I walked to the doorway of Father's room.

"It is so hot up here," I said to him, "with the sun beating down on the roof. And stuffy! No air can get through that tiny window. I can't bear it."

"Can't bear it?" he said. "I think you have no choice but to bear it. Did you think we could live in luxury forever?"

"I did not expect such squalor."

Father did not answer me. He stood bending over the window, looking down at the street. "Couldn't we at least move to the floor below? It would be cooler there."

Father fetched his whiskey bottle, poured some of the whiskey into a glass, and then turned the faucet.

No water came out. "Blast!" he said.

He took a gulp of whiskey neat. Then he returned to the window.

"I'll go and see if Mr. Bixby has rooms available downstairs," I said.

"We'll stay where we are," Father said, without looking at me.

"In this oven?" I cried. "Do you think I'll let you subject me to misery like this? If you must keep me here, let me be comfortable. Otherwise let me return to England."

Father looked at me then. His eyes were very red. He had been drinking heavily before we left the Ritz-Carlton, and he was more intoxicated than I had imagined. His look was one of intense annoyance.

"Go, then" he said. "Go!"

I walked into the room toward him, held out my hand, and said, "Thank you, Father. If you will give me the money for my ticket, I'll go to the Cunard office this afternoon and buy it."

He began to laugh. His laughter grew from an almost silent chuckle to a roar.

"Stop it!" I cried. "Stop it! You have no intention of giving me the money. You think I'll remain in these squalid surroundings while you drink yourself to death. That is what will happen. You will never set foot on a stage again. No one wants a disgusting, filthy drunkard. You are finished! It is the gutter for you."

He lunged and struck me hard across the mouth. The rage on his face frightened me. As soon as I had recovered from the shock of the blow, I turned from him and ran into my room.

Father followed me. "I haven't any money," he said. "I need some."

"I haven't any either."

"You must have *something*."

"I tell you, I don't."

As I spoke, I backed slowly away from him, without thinking, toward the chair on which my purse lay. Father saw it, and before I could stop him, he ran past me, grabbed my purse, tore it open, and began to rifle through it.

I ran to him and tried to wrench it from his hands, crying, "Stop it! You have no right!"

But before I could pull it away from him, he had found my money. I snatched at the notes with both hands, but before I could tear them from his grasp, he swung the fist that clutched them and struck me on the side of the head. The blow thrust me backward onto the bed.

He picked up my bag and searched it further, removing three coins that lay at the bottom.

"There is a penny there," I said. "Be sure to take it too."

"I'll pay it back," Father said. "I am only borrowing it until I pawn my stickpin."

"You have no right to touch it! You! With all your grand ideas—throwing money away in every store in New York. And now you steal ten pounds from a woman. You must feel very proud of yourself."

He did not reply, because at that moment a man appeared in the doorway.

"Ah, Sewer!" he cried. "Here you are, then. Well, well. Not exactly the Ritz, eh?"

"Yes, well, come along," Father said, rushing to the doorway. "Let's get out of this heat. I'll buy you a drink."

"Easier on the pocket though, eh?" the man said, as Father pushed him out into the corridor.

They walked toward the stairs then, and I heard the man mumble something. Then they were gone.

Tears of anger and frustration leapt to my eyes as I rose from the bed. I would not spend another minute with that man. I felt no love for him, not even pity, only loathing. There was nothing I could do to help him, even if I wanted to. No, I would leave him and go to the British consulate. They would help me. And if they wouldn't, I would find a way to exist somehow until I had heard from Uncle Andrew or Lyle. Perhaps I could find a job for a few days until I did.

But I was penniless. I didn't even have bus fare to the consulate. Then it occurred to me that perhaps Father, because of his intoxication, had left some money in a pocket of one of his suits. It was possible.

So I walked into his room, closed the door behind me, and opened the door of his closet. No suits hung there. He had not unpacked. I searched his handbag, which stood on the floor. This contained shirts, underclothing, and such, but no suits.

Then I turned to his trunk. For a moment I was afraid that he might have locked it, but he had not; the lid lifted easily. There lay his suits, tossed into the trunk and hardly folded. I searched each garment, finding fifty cents in the pocket of the last suit coat.

I was about to toss the mass of clothing back, when the edge of an envelope caught my eye. It lay in the trunk beneath a thick, leather-covered book. The envelope might contain money, I thought. So I lifted the book from the trunk in order to reach the envelope beneath it. The book was so thick and heavy that instead of laying it aside, I opened it to see what it was. It was Father's scrapbook, with newspaper clippings carefully pasted on its pages. I flipped the pages, reading a sentence or two here and there.

I found that the reviews at the beginning of the book were long and filled with praise. One read: "Mr. Kean's acting was without trick or ostentation. His performance was powerful yet subtle—wholly convincing."

But as I continued, the newspaper clippings became shorter and less complimentary. One, for his performance in *The Second in Command* in Bath read: "The author must feel indignation for Mr. Kean's weak, vacillating style in representing Sergeant Parks." The review of Father's performance in *Melantius* read in part: ". . . a shocking display. Mr. Kean's performance could in no way be considered acting. One can only conclude that he was ill and should not have appeared."

After that the pages of the book were blank. Three or four clippings had been tucked into the binding, however. These merely mentioned Father's name toward the end of a list of the play's cast.

The scrapbook was a record of alcohol's destruction of an artist. *Flannagan's Daughter* had been Father's last chance to regain his reputation in the theater. But alcohol hadn't allowed that.

I shut the book in disgust, laid it aside, and picked up the letter. Its envelope was addressed to Raoul Sewer, Esq.

The name was familiar; Father's friend had used it a few minutes before. I had not thought much about it at the time.

Immediately I drew the letter from the envelope and read:

October 12

My dear Raoul,

I have just read the review in the *Times* of your performance of Romeo. I knew you would act the part well. It is almost as if the Bard had written the play especially for you, as I have told you. Those lines: "O, that I were a glove upon that hand,/That I might touch that cheek!" I can hear you saying them with that mixture of intensity and pathos that you summon up so well. I must come up to London before you conclude your appearance in the play. I would not miss seeing it for the world.

I am so very proud of your magnificent progress in what is truly the most sublime profession. This success is far distant from those first attempts at Rugby. But even then in *The Castle Specter* and *Revenge* (do you remember how you could not memorize the lines?), I knew that you possessed the talent that would bring you to the zenith of our profession.

Work hard, study, and above all—watch. Watch! And evaluate and understand what you see. You may then, my dear boy, become one of the great names in the history of theater. I truly hope so.

All goes well here at Sheffield—a promising season. You must return and appear.

I pray for your continued success. As always,

Your affectionate
Father

The letter mystified me. Father had mentioned that his father had managed a theater—first in Newcastle and then in Sheffield. And the letter had been written to Father.

Father had spoken about appearing in those very plays when he was at Rugby. And the successful appearance as Romeo could only have been Father's.

But why had the envelope been addressed to Raoul Sewer, Esq., and the salutation been, "My dear Raoul"? It would not have been, "My dear Richard," as Richard Kean was Father's stage name. But why was it not, "My dear Harry"? Who was Raoul Sewer?

Perhaps Father's trunk contained other letters that would help me answer this question. I examined the contents of it and discovered that if it did, the letters would probably be among the pile of loose photographs. The rest of the trunk was filled with clothing, shoes, and copies of plays.

I searched through the pile of pictures and discovered two other letters, still in their envelopes. And, lying on the very bottom of the trunk, I found two folded pieces of yellow paper.

I opened them at once. They were the Western Union forms on which I had written the cables to Uncle Andrew and Lyle. I had given them to the man behind the desk at the Ritz-Carlton to send for me. Father had arranged, then, that any messages I send be given to him!

But I was much more interested in the other two letters I had found. Both were addressed to Raoul Sewer, Esq. The first of the two was in the same handwriting as the letter I had already read and also closed with, "Your affectionate Father." In the letter his father begged Raoul to come to Sheffield and act in his theater, which was doing badly and needed a famous performer to attract patrons.

The second of the remaining letters had been mailed from India and read:

GOVERMENT HOUSE
Calcutta, February 20

My dear Raoul,

Word has reached us, even out here in India, of your repeated successes. The *Times* is full of it. How I wish I could get back to London on leave to see you perform, but I am afraid that cannot be for some time yet. Montagu is out in "the stirrup," as we used to say, and we can't tell when he will return.

And there is great unrest here, especially due to this absurd principle of dyarchy, which I have never agreed with. And as you probably know, the Muslims and Hindus are at each other's throats. And with Gandhi in jail, well . . . So we all stand ready.

Julia and the boys are in excellent health, and she sends her affectionate regards.

Then he spoke of the heat, the lassitude, and the boredom, and ended with:

So, old boy, if you could spare forty or fifty pounds or so, it would make this deuced life out here bearable. It is simply impossible to live at all on what the government pays us. That's a good chap, and we are eternally grateful.

Your affectionate brother,
Edward

I had just come to the end of this letter when I heard the door open behind me. I turned and saw my father standing in the doorway. He did not move. He was too astonished, I suppose, at finding me standing before his open trunk. Then without speaking, he began to walk toward me—a crooked, intoxicated smile on his face.

"You are Raoul Sewer," I said.

He stood still, examining me. As he did so, an even broader smile spread slowly across his face.

"Yes," he said finally. Then he shrugged his shoulders. "You would have found out sooner or later. There is nothing to steal there, or were you looking for entertainment? Those pictures should—"

"I have no interest in them," I said. "You are Raoul Sewer!"

"Yes!" He said this triumphantly, joyously. Then he began to laugh. "Yes, Raoul Sewer. Isn't that a name? Can you imagine: '*Romeo and Juliet*, starring Raoul Sewer'?" He seemed to find this extremely amusing. His laughter became almost convulsive for a few moments. While he laughed, he staggered to the bed and sat down. "They called me Foul Sewer at school when I was little. *Foul Sewer!*" Now he laughed even harder, holding his stomach as he did so.

I waited until he had quieted, and then I said, "Then you are not Harry Little."

"No," he replied, still chuckling.

"Then you are not my father."

"No, I am not your father," he said. His eyes narrowed then. "If I was, I'd have a daughter who showed some respect. I'd never have a bloody shrew like you."

"But you said you were my father."

"Well?"

"And you knew all about Mother—everything that happened to her during all those years."

"A fabrication—I made it up," he said.

"You made it up?" I asked. "You couldn't possibly have."

"Some of it, I did. Enough to connect things. The rest was from plays I've been in. *Anna Dure* and *A Wayward Child* gave me most of it. And then the bit about Morris was true; he did keep a woman out there, and his father never knew about it. Wasn't it superbly done?"

"I don't believe you," I said.

"Superb! Masterful! Perfect! My finest performance. If only it could have been done on the stage instead of just for three or four people."

"And Mrs. Schultz?" I asked.

He chuckled. "Mrs. Schultz? She did my laundry for me when I stayed at Mrs. Barker's."

"She didn't live in Manchester?"

"No." He laughed. "She'd never have been out of Soho in her life." Then after a pause he continued, "I was told some true things and I made the rest up."

"You were *told*? Told by whom?"

He did not answer.

"*Who* told you?"

Still he gazed at me silently with that inscrutable smile.

"You won't tell me?" I asked.

"I would hardly be fool enough to do that."

"Why not? It is all over now."

"And have him find out? God knows what he might do to me then."

"He couldn't do anything."

He did not reply to this. Instead he raised an eyebrow and glared at me.

"*Why* did you do it?"

Now he reached into a paper sack, drew out a bottle of whiskey, and drank. "For money," he said, when he had wiped his mouth with the back of his hand. "I did it for money. I had none. I couldn't appear in New York in rags. Richard Kean must *look* like Richard Kean, not like some shabby pauper. Don't look so bloody horrified. I've done you no harm. You owe your *life* to me."

"My life?"

"One little push and you would have gone over the rail that night. Just think about *that* sometime. Think how it would have been—all alone in the Atlantic, watching the ship sail away."

"Why didn't you do it?"

"I couldn't."

"Is that why you've kept me with you—so that I wouldn't return to England. So that I wouldn't return from the dead?"

"Yes. *Yes!*" he shouted at me. "And I wish I'd done it. I wish to hell I'd pushed you over. Then I wouldn't have had you clawing at me all the time—making my life miserable. I could have taken it if it hadn't been for you." Tears glistened in his eyes now. "I could have endured Julia Marlow, but not the both of you. *You* are responsible for this. I wish I'd thrown you over. I wish I'd never seen you. I wish I'd never had any part of it."

"Who paid you? Tell me!" I cried.

Again he smiled that crooked smile. I thought he would not answer me, but presently he said, "Someone who has a lot to gain. A lot to gain."

"Who?"

His smile disappeared now. He said nothing, but the expression on his face made a chill go down my spine. Beneath the bravado he was afraid.

Then I held up my cables to Lyle and Uncle. "I suppose you told Mr. Wheeler to give you anything like this. That was to keep my existence from being known in England, I suppose."

His eyes narrowed as he gazed at the forms. Then after a moment he looked up at me and said, "Why bother to send them? He's here in New York."

"Who is here in New York?" I asked.

"Lord Hartley. He is staying at the Ritz-Carlton."

"How do you know that?"

"Wheeler told me. He's due this afternoon. He would certainly want to see you. We couldn't have had that, could we?"

I stared at him in astonishment for a moment. Then I said, "I am going to him, and there is nothing you can do to stop me—*Mr. Sewer.*"

I ran from the room and across the corridor to my own. Then I hurriedly put on my hat and, taking my gloves and bag, I dashed toward the stairway. Mr. Sewer did not attempt to stop me. I glanced into his room as I left my own and saw him sitting still on his bed, looking at me. I ran out of the hotel and was fortunate to find an empty taxi passing by. I hailed it and told the driver to take me to the Ritz-Carlton Hotel as quickly as possible.

As we drove through the city streets I thought about Lyle. Oh, how much I wanted to see him! I wanted him to hold me in his arms. He would take me back to England—back to the rectory where I would be safe. Would he have arrived yet? It was just after one o'clock. If he hadn't, I would wait in the lobby for him.

Safe. I had thought I would be safe when I left Ledington with my father. How wrong I had been. Stuart had almost had his way; if Mr. Sewer had had the courage to push me overboard that night on the *Antonia*, I would be dead. It was Stuart who had hired Raoul Sewer to impersonate my father and to kill me. He was the brute who had masqueraded as Mr. Throckmorton and had threatened Miss Broughton. And it was he who had told Mr. Sewer all about me. No wonder Mr. Sewer was terrified!

· But *why* did Stuart want to kill me? Not merely because we had quarreled. No, Mr. Sewer said that Stuart had a lot to gain. What could he gain by killing me?

What had he gained by killing Nanny Thompson? What had he gained by killing Lord Bude? Something terribly strange had happened at Compton Hall a long time ago. It had had something to do with the late Lady Bude and Stuart's mother. It was more than Elizabeth's refusal to marry Lord Bude—much more than that. And somehow, I was connected with it.

If I knew what had happened then, I would know why Stuart wanted me dead.

Mr. Wheeler saw me as soon as I had stepped into the lobby. And as I hurried toward him, he looked at me, I thought, with a mixture of astonishment and alarm.

"I should like to see Lord Hartley, please," I said to him when I had reached the desk. "Has he checked in yet?"

"I beg your pardon?" he said.

"I should like to see Lord Hartley," I repeated.

"Now, Miss Kean," he said. "Try to be calm. I do not believe I know of a Lord Hartley."

"He is a guest here at the hotel. He has a reservation and is expected to arrive today."

"I don't believe we are expecting anyone by that name. One moment please, let me check." He glanced through some papers on a table behind the counter. "No, we have no reservation for Lord Hartley. Perhaps next week— perhaps if you return in a few weeks' time."

"You are expecting him then?"

"No, not exactly, but one never knows who will write and request—"

"He is arriving *today*," I cried, much too loudly.

"Miss Kean!" he hissed. "Where is your father? You and he are no longer guests here, you know."

"I came to see Lord Hartley. He will be staying here."

"You can glance at the register yourself," he sighed. "You will see his name written there if he is staying at the hotel."

Lyle's name did not appear there.

"He is not here, then?" I said to Mr. Wheeler. "You are not expecting him?"

"No, Miss Kean, we have never heard from Lord Hartley."

I did not wait for him to finish. I turned from the counter. But as I began to walk toward the street, two things happened: a group of noisy men trooped out of the elevator and streamed into the lobby, blocking my way; and on the far side of the room a man ran into the hotel from Madison Avenue. The man was Stuart.

He was in a hurry, and there was an air of determination about his movements that sent a chill down my spine. As he entered the hotel, he glanced purposefully about as if looking for someone.

Startled though I was, I was able to move quickly, crouching behind a cluster of potted palms. Had he seen me? I peered through the branches of the plants and watched him. No, he had not. He strode through the group of men straight toward Mr. Wheeler at the desk.

Mr. Wheeler was looking at the palms where I stood in astonishment. If he continued to do so, he would surely draw attention to me. I had to act; so I darted along the side of the room to another bunch of palms near the door. I paused behind them for a moment to look back at the desk. Stuart was talking to Mr. Wheeler. I dashed toward the doorway. When I reached it, I glanced back across the lobby. Mr. Wheeler was pointing triumphantly at me. Stuart faced me. Our eyes met.

Immediately I ran through the doorway and out onto Madison Avenue. The sidewalk was crowded. I ran as fast as I could through the pedestrians, across Forty-seventh Street, up Madison Avenue to Forty-eight Street, and turned left. Presently I reached a narrow alley separating two buildings and dashed into it.

The alley was partially blocked by a stack of packing boxes. At once I darted behind them and stood there catching my breath, while I peered out to see if Stuart had followed me.

As I watched for him, I realized that Stuart had gone to the Ritz-Carlton looking for me. Mr. Sewer had probably told him where to find me. Needless to say, I couldn't return to the Hotel Bixby.

As the minutes dragged by, I began to feel certain that Stuart had not been able to follow me. After perhaps a quarter of an hour, I felt sure of it. Leaving the alley, I walked north.

Chapter Sixteen

THE LIVERMORE MANSION STOOD ON THE corner of Fifth Avenue and Seventy-seventh Street. It was an enormous, ornate, five-story white granite building in the style of a French chateau. Two tiers of balconies looked out over Central Park. It was a terrifying house; it seemed to loom on the corner waiting to pounce upon anyone who dared approach it without the proper social qualifications.

I walked bravely up to its pillared portico, facing Seventy-seventh Street, and approached its paneled door. I rang the doorbell and stood waiting for perhaps half a minute before the door was opened by Mr. Livermore's butler.

"Is Miss—" I began.

"It is *Mrs.* Cartwright whom you wish to see," the butler said. He held his head so high that I wondered if he could see me at all from beneath his lowered lids. "Mrs. Cartwright is the housekeeper here. However, she is not engaging anyone at present."

He was about to close the door, so I said quickly, "I wish to see Miss Livermore."

"On business?" he asked.

"No. Certainly not."

"Miss Livermore is not at home." The butler stepped back then, allowing me to enter the vestibule. "If you would care to leave a card?" He gestured to a silver tray which lay on a table against the wall.

"I have no card," I replied. "Do you know when Miss Livermore will return?"

"I could not say, miss."

"This afternoon? This evening?"

"I could not say, miss."

"I see." I paused then, desperately trying to decide what to do while that haughty man examined my clothes. Would there be any use in leaving a message for Salvia? I could not even tell her where to find me. No, I would simply leave. As I crossed the portico, I heard the door shut behind me.

I walked quickly along the wrought-iron fence that edged the areaway beside the house toward Fifth Avenue and the park beyond it. But I had walked only half a dozen steps when I heard a noise as if someone were tapping on a pain of glass. I looked up. Someone was indeed banging on the glass, and that someone was Bertha Bailey!

I stood staring, unable to believe that it was really Bertha. Immediately Bertha began to tug at the window from the inside, and in a moment she flung it open.

"Louisa!" Bertha cried, as she leaned out of the window.

"Bertha!" I replied. "Whatever are you doing here?"

"Where have you been? I didn't know where to find you. What has happened?"

"I can't very well tell you about it standing here on the street."

"No!" Bertha cried. "Come in and I'll make you a cup of tea. Down the stairs under the stoop." She pointed. "Wait there and I'll go down and let you in."

I did as she directed, and in two or three minutes Bertha rushed out and hugged me. Then she grasped my hand and pulled me along behind her into the house, down a long corridor, and into the kitchen.

"The kettle is on and we'll have our tea. Mrs. Cartwright is out, so we can talk as long as we like."

As Bertha got out the pot and cups, we began to tell our stories.

"Did Mr. Salt come and get you, then?" I asked her.

"Yes!" Bertha popped her eyes at me in that old familiar way.

"When? How long have you been here?"

"Since a week ago—July twenty-fourth. Paul and me

were married by the captain of the *Mauritania*." Again she popped her eyes, gauging my reaction.

"How exciting! And have you been in New York since then? Did Mr. Salt finally convince Mr. Livermore?"

"Yes! They were up in Sussex, staying at Ardsley Castle with Sir Robert and Lady Swindon when Mamma passed away."

"Oh, Bertha—No!"

"Well, you know she wasn't well. Dear Mamma. But it was a blessing. She passed away in her sleep on July twelfth."

"I am so terribly sorry," I said. "Of course I didn't know."

"No," Bertha replied. And without pausing, she continued, "Mamma passed away on the twelfth—she just slept away with the most angelic expression on her face. Well, after the funeral, on Thursday, I got to thinking about things, and I wrote to Paul. I knew he was staying at Ardsley Castle because I had received a letter from him the Monday before telling me where he was. That was the Monday after you left Ledington.

"Well, I wrote to him and told him about Mamma's death and how I didn't know what I would do, and lo and behold on Saturday he arrives at the Hall! Out of the blue, there he was! And he says he's taking me to America. Just like *that*!"

"Mr. Livermore had agreed," I prompted.

"Yes! They were leaving Ardsley Castle on the seventeenth and sailing for New York on the Mauritania on the eighteenth. He refused to go back to America with Mr. Livermore. He wouldn't go without me. So I had one day to get everything together. Mrs. Merrymede was an angel about it, and I promised her I'd behave until we were married."

"How is she?" I asked.

"In very low spirits. It was the murder, of course. Oh, Louisa, the funeral—you have no idea. The flowers! And the people! They kept coming and coming, and Mrs. Merrymede cried and cried."

"Please! Let's not talk about it," I begged. "I can't bear not having been there. How are you? Are you happy?"

"Yes! Oh, yes. Except when Paul is in the country and I'm left here. He's at Rhineland now. That's Mr. Livermore's mansion on the Hudson River. I was there with him until I had to come back here for a week or two. They're already preparing for the wedding. They'll be coming back early—in September, I suppose."

"Salvia is going to be married?"

"Yes. She is going to marry Prince Robinsky. They met at Ardsley Castle."

"Oh? Then she is at Rhineland with her mother and father?"

"Yes, but not this week and maybe not next. Mrs. Livermore and Miss Livermore came down on the train yesterday morning. Now Miss Livermore said she would have luncheon here, but she hasn't come back. Everyone is worried to death about her. But I'm not. She can take care of herself."

"You don't like Salvia?"

"Oh, yes. That is, I don't dislike her. But she can take care of herself. I wouldn't worry about her. But now you. What happened to you? How is your father? Tell me about the play."

I told Bertha most of what had happened to me since I had left Ledington, but I did not tell her about the attempt on my life by Mr. Sewer or about seeing Stuart at the hotel. She sat listening in amazement, hardly interrupting at all until I had finished.

Then she said, "How horrible! Oh, you poor dear! What you have been through! Why didn't you come sooner?"

"I didn't know you were here, of course. If I had, I would— Is that someone? Listen!"

"It is probably Miss Livermore. I'll go and see."

Bertha jumped up and left.

Two or three minutes later I heard quick footsteps in the corridor and then Salvia appeared, followed by Bertha.

Salvia cried, "Louisa! Oh, how marvelous to find you *here!*" Then she turned to Bertha and said, "You were right, Bertha. It *is* Miss Little."

"Bertha and I are old friends from Ledington," I said. "We grew up together. I was so surprised to find her here in New York."

"Yes. She is an enormous help to us," Salvia said. "And we are *most* appreciative. Thank you, Bertha." Then she turned to me. "But you must be famished."

"No," I replied. "I'm really not hungry."

"Well, I am. Have something to keep me company." She extended her hand to me and at the same time moved toward the doorway. "Come."

I thanked Bertha for the tea, and then I followed Salvia upstairs to the gilded, mirrored, dining room, where an astonished and still hostile butler helped us to be seated and then hurriedly set a place before me.

Salvia did not speak while this was going on, but she examined me closely. Finally when the butler had left to fetch our soup, I looked directly at her as though inquiring about this.

She said candidly, "I was wondering if you were as beautiful as I remembered you. Sometimes memories play tricks. Your English weather—that's what's responsible for your marvelous complexion. I shall never forget that misty afternoon in— What was the name of the little town below Compton Hall?"

"Ledington," I said.

"Back in Ledington."

"I am so awfully sorry about—"

"Don't be. *I* was delighted. I couldn't have been happier. It was marvelous not to marry Lord Hartley. Of course, Mother was terribly upset. She had set her heart on it. But you see, you really did me a terrific favor."

"You mustn't think badly of Lyle," I said. "He is completely sincere." Salvia's eyebrows rose in an exaggerated fashion. "He asked me to marry him, but I could not accept his proposal."

"I should hope not," Miss Livermore said, her eyebrows

still elevated. "I won't risk offending you by saying anything more. But no, of course you couldn't."

The butler entered the dining room with our soup then, and we were silent.

When he had left the room, Salvia smiled at me, tasted her soup, and said, "Mother and I came into the city for a few days. There is so much to do! And it was imperative that I see my dressmaker. Now tell me, what on earth are you doing in New York?"

"I came with . . ." I began. "Salvia, I've had a ghastly experience."

Salvia questioned me with her eyes, but did not speak.

"I came to New York," I continued, "with a man who pretended to be my father." Then I told her briefly what had happened, holding back nothing.

"And you think Lieutenant Compton hired Mr. Sewer to murder you?" Salvia said.

"Yes, I am sure of it."

"But that's ridiculous! Why should he hire anyone to murder you?"

"I don't *know*. I have tried and tried to figure it out, but I can't. He did, though. And he is here! Here in New York, and now he is searching for me. It was all arranged that he find me at the Ritz-Carlton, and then— Heaven knows what would have happened if he had caught me."

"You must be imagining it," Salvia said finally.

"No, I am not imagining it," I said. "I didn't know what to do. The only thing I could think of was to come to you. Will you help me? Will you help me return to England? Lend me the money for my passage? I'll return it to you, I promise."

"Of course!" Salvia cried. "Of course I'll help you get back to England. And don't worry. You are with *me* now. But why didn't you come right away?

"Don't give it another thought. You poor dear! What you've been through! Men are such beasts. If one is clever, one has nothing to do with them—ever. Did Bertha tell you that I am going to be married?"

"Yes."

"To Prince Robinsky. Karl, eighth Prince Robinsky, actually. Mother is determined that I marry a title of some kind, and I just can't fight her any longer. I may as well be a princess as anything. He's Austrian. Really old family. Castles on the Danube and all that. And he's nice enough, I suppose. We met at Lady Swindon's—at Ardsley Castle. Father had him investigated, of course. Genuine, but impoverished."

"I am so happy for you," I said. "Where is Prince Robinsky? In Austria?"

"No, he is at Rhineland. Mother said we couldn't have him tagging along with us here when we have so much to do, thank heaven."

"Isn't your mother having lunch?"

"She is lunching with Mrs. Cornelia Finch. Something about a benefit for St. Luke's Hospital. But *you*. Where are your things?"

"They are at the Hotel Bixby. But I can't go back there for them."

"Why not?"

"Because Stuart might be there. He knows Mr. Sewer and I are staying there, and he will be waiting for me."

"Oh, but surely not."

"No, Salvia, he will be. I know he will be, unless..."

"Yes?"

"Unless he is on his way here. He knows we have met."

"Then we will go to Rhineland. You will love it! The *Albany* is at Twenty-fifth Street. That's Father's yacht. Captain Innes will take us up to Rhineland. It's a marvelous cruise up the river. If this man is chasing you, he'll never find you there."

At that moment I heard a movement behind me and turned.

Mrs. Livermore stood in the open doorway of the dining room. She stood there imperiously, watching us—her enormous bust flattened by a tight corselet. As I gazed at her, she thrust her glasses to her eyes, squinted through them, and frowned.

"Look who's here, Mother," Salvia called gaily. "Louisa! She will be staying with us. Isn't that *marvelous*?"

"Oh?" Mrs. Livermore said. "How nice to see you again, Louisa. You will be staying the night? Wakely is here, but half the staff is at Rhineland. However, we will do our best. We had no idea you would be coming."

"Thank you, Mrs. Livermore," I said. "It is so good to see you again. I hope you have been well. And Mr. Livermore?"

"Fatigued. We are all perfectly exhausted after President Coolidge's visit to Rhineland. We had hoped for a week or two of complete rest. And then of course there are all the arrangements for the wedding. I am quite dizzy at the prospect. But you mustn't mind that." Mrs. Livermore turned to her daughter then. "Salvia dear, have you shown Louisa her room? I suppose the blue bedroom is prepared? I had no idea that we would have a guest so soon after our exhausting weekend and with the house all but closed. But do take Louisa up and then come down at *once*. I want to talk to you."

Salvia and I left her mother, and when we had climbed the staircase to the second floor of the house and, so, could not be overheard, I said, "I don't think your mother is very happy to see me."

"She is tired," Salvia said, "but she will be fine tomorrow. She was awfully nervous about entertaining President and Mrs. Coolidge. It was really exciting, but a strain for Mother. So she is a little depressed. But don't worry about it. After all, she doesn't have to *do* anything. We've still lots of servants. Here we are."

Salvia gestured to an open doorway on our right. Then she said, "You'll want to wash. Then come down. I'll go see what Mother wants."

As I descended the stairs a bit later, I heard Salvia and her mother.

"That girl!" Mrs. Livermore cried.

"Oh, no," Salvia moaned.

"You know very well what she did to Lord Hartley."

"She didn't do anything to Lord Hartley," Salvia said.

"If it hadn't been for her, you would be Lady Hartley now."

"Won't Princess Robinsky be better?"

"Salvia! You talk as though this were a game of some kind. I am only thinking of your future, and I don't want her to spoil it again."

"But Karl would not be in the least interested in Louisa, Mother."

"I've seen the way he looks at other women, even if you haven't."

"I *have* seen the way he looks at other women. You know perfectly well he won't be attracted to Louisa."

"She is nothing! A nobody! She is an orphan! Nobody knows what she came from, and yet she acts as though she were a duchess. She's a troublemaker! She will ruin everything."

"Nonsense!" Salvia exclaimed. "How could she?"

"We cannot have her at Rhineland. You must spend your time with the prince. You pay so little attention to him as it is. He is getting bored and—and dissatisfied. He is about to call it all off."

"And throw away a million dollars?" Salvia cried. "Don't be absurd."

"A man wants more than money, Salvia. He wants companionship and love. And children! Children are *important* to Europeans. Heirs! He is no longer sure. He is changing his mind!"

"Don't be ridiculous!"

"It is not ridiculous to spend your time alone with your future husband before your wedding so that you won't lose him. I don't care what you do afterward, but don't spoil it! Don't you have any feelings for me at all? Why, I would be a laughing stock if anything happened. That girl will not come to Rhineland. She must go! And I intend to see to it that she does."

Pretending a cough, I strode into the drawing room.

That afternoon, while Salvia napped, I wrote to Lyle.

August 1, 1927

My dear Lyle,

I am coming home! I can't tell you what a terrible experience I have had ever since I left Ledington. Your advice was terribly wise. I should have followed it and never have come to New York.

I shan't go into it all, except to tell you that Mr. Kean is not my father, but an imposter paid to act the part. The rest would only worry you, and there is no point in doing that because it is all behind me. I am now visiting Salvia Livermore at her home on Fifth Avenue. She has promised to lend me the money to return to England, which I shall do at the earliest possible opportunity.

How I long to be at home! And oh, how I wish everything could be the same as it was before.

And I long, more than I can say, to see you again. Then I'll tell you everything that has happened, and I know that if I need your help, you will give it to me.

Until then, dearest Lyle,

Yours most sincerely,
Louisa

Then I wrote to Aunt and Uncle, but I did not tell them about Mr. Sewer. I simply told them that I was coming home, and that I would be so glad to see them. Then I gave my letters to Salvia, who gave them to Wakely to post.

I knew that I must not go to Rhineland. Stuart might find me there. And it was a country house—probably isolated. I would be even more vulnerable there than in the city. No, I must go back to England and put the whole Atlantic Ocean between Stuart and me, back to Lyle where I would be safe.

The following morning, Mrs. Livermore found me sitting alone at breakfast.

"Salvia is not down?" she asked, as she entered the dining room.

"Good morning, Mrs. Livermore," I said. "No, she hasn't come down yet."

"Good! Louisa, I have some things I wish to say to you."

I smiled up at Mrs. Livermore. "Yes?"

Mrs. Livermore did not sit down. Instead she grasped her glasses, which she wore on a chain around her neck, clamped them to her head with a jerk, and stood staring down at me.

"I can't tell you," she said, "how pleased we would be to have you visit us at Rhineland."

"Thank you, Mrs. Livermore," I replied.

"But I think it would be too tiresome for you," Mrs. Livermore continued. "We entertain rather less at Rhineland, preferring to enjoy ourselves quietly—just the family, you know."

Now Mrs. Livermore sat down in the chair across from me and poured herself a cup of coffee. She held her back straight, her bosom high. But stern and formidable though she looked, I noticed that her fingers worked ever so slightly over the handle of her cup.

"This is not an ordinary autumn for us at Rhineland," she said. "On the contrary, it is a very busy one—making all the arrangements for the wedding and, of course, entertaining my daughter's fiancé, Prince Robinsky."

"Yes," I said. "Salvia told me about her engagement. I hope she will be very happy."

"You do?"

"Yes, of course."

"Then I know you want these—precious days before their marriage to be as happy and as—*genial* as possible."

"Certainly."

"I think I should tell you, Louisa, that I am troubled. I hope I can count on your discretion."

"Of course."

"The prince is concerned about my daughter's affection for him."

"Oh, dear."

"He has not told me that in so many words, of course, but he has indicated it unmistakably. I have tried to reassure him, but he is still concerned. He feels that Salvia is not spending enough time with him—not paying enough attention to him. You can't know how impossible men can be sometimes. Now, I am sure you have not been in the least aware of this, but now that you are, I know that you will want them to be alone together as much as I do. I am very concerned. I believe that this is quite imperative, or else . . ." Mrs. Livermore shut her eyes and gave her head a quick little shake from side to side.

"Oh, I agree entirely, Mrs. Livermore," I said. "Salvia is such a dear. She would spend far too much of her time entertaining me when she should be with the prince. Anyway, I can't stay here. I must go home to England. Some terrible things have happened—"

"Salvia has told me all about it, Louisa. Yes, you *must* go. You may be in extreme danger here, and we really cannot accept the responsibility."

"But I have no money. How can I buy a steamship ticket?"

"Salvia will lend you money if you ask her for it."

"I have and she has refused. I asked her last night, but she wouldn't hear of it. She said she wouldn't allow me to go all that way alone. She wants to take me with her and the prince to England after their wedding."

"On their honeymoon?" Mrs. Livermore shrieked.

"Yes."

"Oh, my dear God! She must be mad!"

"And my passport is in my trunk."

"I never interfere. Salvia must lead her own life as she chooses. I *never* interfere in the slightest. But this is appalling! I will give you the money, Louisa. Where is your trunk?"

"At Bixby's Hotel, but I can't go back there. Lieutenant Compton will be waiting for me."

"Which hotel?" Mrs. Livermore asked. "Whixley's?"

"Bixby's. On the Bowery, just below Hester Street."

"How did you ever find it?" Mrs. Livermore murmured, grimacing. "Well! There is only one thing to do. I will go and get it."

"But then he will know where I am."

"Don't worry about that. I shan't tell anyone who I am. There are ways of doing these things."

"But you will have to tell Mr. Sewer who you are. He will never let you have my trunk if you don't. And then he will tell Lieutenant Compton. No, please don't. I can get a new passport, and the clothes don't matter."

"That would take time," Mrs. Livermore said. "You are in danger! The sooner you are on a ship traveling to England, the better. No one will know who I am."

"But how can you—?"

"With pieces of green paper, Louisa. They are called dollar bills. They accomplish miracles."

As I watched her stride across the sidewalk to her car an hour later, I wondered how many dollar bills Mrs. Livermore carried in her purse. She wore a dress of gray silk. Her hat and gloves and bag were gray too. She reminded me of a warship, sailing inexorably across the pavement to her black Cadillac limousine. She was indomitable.

Augmented by her chauffeur, a huge man, and another manservant, Mrs. Livermore would return with my trunk. I had no doubt of that.

Shortly after she left, Salvia and I sat talking in the parlor, when a car drew up outside.

"It can't be your mother," I said, walking toward the window.

It was not. From behind the lace curtains I watched Stuart jump out of a taxi, slam the door shut behind him, and stride toward the portico. The doorbell rang.

"It's Stuart!" I said.

"Here?"

"You are not at home. Nobody is at home. Send him away!"

"We can't do that. He would only come back."

"But he mustn't know I am here!"

"Of course not. I'll see him." Salvia squinted shrewdly. "Let me take care of this."

She turned from me then, and marched out of the room, leaving the door wide open behind her. I ran to it at once and closed it. But then I opened it a crack to listen. I heard Wakely speak to Salvia, telling her Stuart's name, and then Salvia said, "Lieutenant Compton?" I could not see her, but she had evidently decided to speak to him at the vestibule doorway.

"I apologize," Stuart said, "for calling at this unusual hour, Miss Livermore. But I have urgent business which can't wait."

"What can I do for you, Lieutenant?" Salvia said.

"Is Miss Little here?"

"Miss Little?"

"Yes."

"I don't believe— Miss . . . Little?"

"Miss Little. From Ledington. You met her when you were visiting Compton Hall."

"Louisa?"

"Yes."

"Here? Louisa? Good heavens, *no*! Whatever gave you that idea?"

"Have you seen her?"

"No, not since—the day I left Compton Hall, I believe. Is she in America?"

"Yes. I thought she might be here. I am sorry to have bothered you."

"No bother at all, Lieutenant Compton. If you should see Louisa, please ask her to call. I should so like to see her again."

"I shall, Miss Livermore. Thank you."

"You are welcome, Lieutenant. Good-bye."

I heard the entrance door close. Then I ran to the window and watched Stuart climb into the taxi. As he closed the door and the car began to draw away from the curb, Salvia entered the parlor.

"Well?" she said, smiling broadly.

"You were *perfect*!" I said.

"Was I?"

"Yes! I don't know how you did it. You sounded so surprised—so mystified."

"Yes. I should have been an actress. I have always wanted to go to Hollywood and be in the movies. You don't think he suspected?"

"Never!"

"Good. Then that's the last we'll see of Lieutenant Compton. He will search for a little while and then go back to England."

Mrs. Livermore returned a half hour later. Salvia and I watched from the window as she directed the men to carry my trunk into the house. We heard her booming voice and then she threw open the door to the parlor and stood there gazing at us triumphantly.

"The *Aquitania* sails on Thursday at eleven A.M.," she proclaimed. "I have sent Wakely for a ticket."

"Mother!" Salvia cried.

I rose from the sofa and walked to Mrs. Livermore. "How can I ever thank you?" I said.

"It is entirely unnecessary, Louisa," Mrs. Livermore said. "We must do what we can to help those—in less fortunate circumstances than ourselves."

"Mother, how can you?" Salvia cried.

"What, my dear?" Mrs. Livermore said to her daughter.

"Ask Louisa to leave. You said you wouldn't interfere."

"Louisa has asked for my help, Salvia. She wishes to return to England."

"Please don't be angry, Salvia," I said. "But I have explained it all. I must go."

"Oh, very well!" Salvia cried. Then she stamped out of the room.

"Pay no attention, Louisa," Mrs. Livermore said. "Salvia is emotional."

"Thank you for fetching my trunk for me," I said. "Was Mr. Sewer there?"

"Mr.—Sewer had left the hotel and had taken all his belongings with him."

"Oh? When did he leave?"

"Yesterday afternoon, according to the manager."

"You didn't tell him who you were?"

"I told him I was your aunt. No name. Just your aunt."

"Did he object to your taking my things?"

Mrs. Livermore smiled craftily. "When I offered to pay your hotel bill and relieve the man of your things? And then laid a twenty dollar bill in his perspiring palm in the bargain? Hardly, my dear. Not a peep."

By lunchtime Salvia appeared to have recovered her good spirits. She seemed convinced that I would not be able to visit Rhineland. I wondered why she had been so insistent about my accompanying her to the country. After all, I hardly knew her. Why this determination?

She ordered the car for us, and we went out for a ride.

It was delightful to be out of that big, gloomy house and into the fresh air. I took a deep breath and gazed at the greens of Central Park. Beyond the stone wall the grass in the sunlight was almost chartreuse. A few people strolled along Fifth Avenue and sat on the benches lining the avenue.

On the bench nearest the corner of Seventy-seventh Street a man sat reading a newspaper. I didn't notice him until we had settled ourselves in the car and Sam had driven us to the corner and turned onto Fifth Avenue. I started.

"That man," I said. "The one reading the newspaper."

"What about him?"

"It's Stuart."

"How can you tell? You can't see his face."

"I saw his eyes a moment ago. He was not holding his newspaper so high. It was Stuart!"

"It can't be! He is sitting there completely unconcerned. It is an utterly strange man reading his morning paper in the park—that's all. Really, Louisa, you can't imagine every man you see is Lieutenant Compton."

When we returned from our drive, we found Mrs. Livermore waiting for us in the drawing room.

"He came back!" she said. "Lieutenant Compton came to the house again at a quarter past two. He called to see *me* this time. Wakely got rid of him. He said that we had left for a cruise along the coast of Maine aboard the *Albany*, and that he had no idea when we would return. I think that was terribly clever of him, don't you?"

I was not so sure of that. Had Stuart belived Wakely's story?

Wednesday morning was hot and humid. When I looked out of my window before going down to breakfast, the other side of Fifth Avenue was half obscured behind a scrim of milky haze. The street and sidewalk were deserted except for a black sedan parked a little way up the avenue on the park side of the street. All of its rear windowshades were drawn.

It was still there when I returned to my room after breakfast. I sat down by the window and looked out at it. I had nothing better to do just then. Salvia was probably still sound asleep, and I was too excited to read. One more day and I would be aboard the *Aquitania.* Tomorrow morning I would be on my way home!

When Salvia came to my room at half past ten, the sedan was still parked there. And it was still there when she came to fetch me for luncheon.

I had spent the later part of the morning going over the clothes in my trunk.

"Oh, darn!" I said, just as Salvia walked into my room.

"What's the matter?" she asked.

"A run! It's ruined, and this is my last pair."

"We'll buy you some more, then. We've all afternoon, and you can't go off without stockings. Is there anything else you need?"

"No, I am all right on everything else. I'm not sailing to impress anyone, you know."

"Lord and Taylor has just gotten in some silk pajamas which look absolutely *marvelous* in their ad. I'll buy us both a pair. And some stockings for you, and who knows, maybe we'll find some other goodies. Won't that be fun?"

"I don't think I should go out, Salvia. Suppose Stuart—"

"Louisa! Not in broad daylight. He wouldn't dare! And Sam will be there. We can't mope about here all afternoon. It would only be from here to the car and from the car to the store and back again. This is New York, Louisa. A big city! Millions of people everywhere. What could he *do*?"

"Of course. You are perfectly right, Salvia. That would be wonderful. Thank you so much."

I glanced out of the window then at the car. Salvia must have noticed that I was disturbed because she asked, "What is it?"

"There is a car parked out there. See it?" When Salvia had come to the window and looked out, I said, "Do you suppose Wakely or somebody could go up and look inside it?"

"Whatever for?" Salvia asked.

"I think maybe Stuart is hiding in the back of it."

Salvia laughed. "You can't be serious!"

"Well, he could be, you know."

"You're just jumpy. Come to lunch."

Sam dropped us off in front of Lord and Taylor. He said he would park the car nearby and wait for us at the store entrance.

Once inside, Salvia bought me half a dozen pair of stockings, including a pair of green ones to go with my green velvet dress. And then she bought a pair of pajamas for herself and a pair for me. It was much too frivolous a garment. What on earth would I do with black silk lounging pajamas? But she insisted, and I didn't have the heart to object. I would much rather have had a new petticoat. There were some lovely silk ones with lace inserts in one of the cases, which I examined while Salvia wandered off to look at the bathing suits. And I liked the dress on the mannequin at the end of the counter. It was a tennis dress. I did not intend to play tennis, but I thought it would be attractive to walk in on deck aboard the *Aquitania*. It was of white cotton, sleeveless, with a square neckline and a pleated skirt.

As I stood in front of it, dreaming of wearing it, I felt, rather than heard someone coming. I glanced behind me. Stuart strode straight toward me. I was too astonished to think clearly, but somehow in a brief instant I was able to examine his face. How pale he was. How tightly the skin was drawn across those prominent bones. How deep and dark the hollows around his blazing eyes.

He stood before me.

"Louisa," he said quickly, "I must talk to you."

He glanced anxiously about the store with a desperate, hunted look, like a cornered wild animal. Where was Salvia? The floor was empty.

Stuart's hand shot out and gripped my arm. I tore myself free. I ran!

Stuart sprang after me. I ran toward the elevators. But I realized I could not wait for one to come. Then I saw the red light above the open doorway, and I ran toward the stairs.

But I never reached them. Stuart caught me before I did. He grabbed my arm tightly, and as he swung me about to face him, I saw the lighted elevator rising from the floor below.

"Let go of me!" I cried. "I'll scream!"

Stuart saw the elevator too. Instantly he thrust me toward a door in the wall a few feet away. As he opened it, I screamed. He thrust me through the doorway, slammed the door shut, and clamped his hand over my mouth.

It was pitch black. I fought, scratched, pushed, kicked, and struck at him.

"Now, you little—" he began.

My hand felt a belt or strap hanging down from above. I pulled it. Then as the door of the little room was thrown open, the very ceiling seemed to fall upon us.

I thrust masses of fabric aside and ran through the doorway through the group of people who had gotten off the elevator and now gaped at us, into the store.

"He tried to kill me!" I shouted back at the man who

had opened the door. Then I saw Salvia. I grabbed her arm and pulled her toward the stairs. "Run!" I cried.

We ran down the stairway and out into the street. Sam stood beside the doorway. Salvia thrust her packages into his arms and said, "Hurry, Sam!"

He was astonished, but he did not question her. He followed us on the run around the corner and then led us to the car. We got in, and in a moment the huge engine roared to life. The car pulled out into Thirty-eighth Street and sped down the block toward Sixth Avenue.

"What happened?" Salvia asked.

"It was horrible!" I said. "He dragged me into that little room. And then he very nearly strangled me."

When we arrived at the house, the black sedan was no longer parked on Fifth Avenue. I remarked about this that night when Salvia came to my room to say good night.

"He *must* have been in it," I said. "He must have hidden in the back of that black car and followed us."

"Now, don't worry," Salvia said. "Wakely makes the rounds after everyone has gone to bed and makes sure all the windows and doors are locked for the night. Don't worry! He won't break in—not here. Are you frightened? Don't be. I'll stay with you tonight."

"No, I'll be all right, Salvia."

I had been sitting on the side of the bed. Now Salvia jumped out of her chair and came to me.

"Dear Louisa, you must be exhausted," she said. "Stand up now, and take off your robe, and climb into bed. I'll turn out your light. And you will *not* worry anymore about it."

She helped me off with my robe, and when I had gotten into bed, she walked to the lamp on my bedside table and turned it out.

It took a few moments after that for my eyes to become accustomed to the darkness. I had not heard Salvia move, nor had she said good night. When I was able to see her dim form, I realized that she still stood beside my bed, looking down at me. She sat down on the bed beside me.

"Now you will sleep like an angel," she said softly, gently brushing a lock of hair from my forehead. "You mustn't worry about a thing." She leaned over me and kissed me on the mouth.

I pushed her away from me. "Good night," I said. Then I turned my back.

Salvia stood, and after a moment or two I heard her stride across the room, closing the door behind her with a sharp crack.

In the morning Sam and Wakely carried my trunk down to the car at about half past nine. Then Mrs. Livermore, Salvia, and I got into the limousine, and Sam drove us to the Cunard Line pier at the foot of Fiftieth Street.

The *Aquitania* was a much larger ship than the *Antonia*. We could see the liner's four, enormous black stacks rising above the buildings even before we had crossed Tenth Avenue. Smoke rose from her funnels. She was anxious to sail.

I was terribly tense, and I found myself looking anxiously from one face in the crowd to another, searching for Stuart.

As soon as the porter had loaded my trunk onto his little cart, Mrs. Livermore handed me an envelope. "Here is your ticket, Louisa," she said. "And a little spending money besides. It should take you home quite nicely."

"How can I ever thank—?"

"No." She held up her hand. "No, I told you that isn't necessary. It is our pleasure. We have so enjoyed having you. But it has been for such a terribly short time. Oh, if you could only have stayed longer, but of course you couldn't. You don't mind, my dear, if we don't see you to the ship, do you? I have a terribly important luncheon engagement, and Salvia is coming along. So we really must dash. Have a splendid trip." She hugged me quickly. "Just up those stairs there and along to the gangplank. You will see it. Now we must fly! Come along, Salvia."

She turned away quickly, Sam opened the door, and she got into the car.

Salvia gave me her hand. "Have a good trip," she said without smiling.

Then she followed her mother. As the Cadillac pulled away from the curb, Mrs. Livermore gave me one quick wave. Then they were gone, lost in the traffic on Twelfth Avenue.

I climbed the stairs at once and hurried along the pier toward the gangplank. As I walked, I opened the envelope which Mrs. Livermore had given me and drew out forty dollars and a steamship ticket enclosed in a Cunard Line folder. On it in large letters was printed, Tourist Class.

Far from being disappointed, I was delighted by this, my wardrobe was hardly adequate for any other class aboard the *Aquitania*, and tourist class would get me to England as quickly as First.

The ship's officer directed me to my stateroom on B deck. I was, I discovered, to share it with three other passengers, none of whom was there yet. It was a pleasant enough stateroom. And all would be well if only we sailed on time and Stuart did not appear.

I strolled on deck, looking at everyone who passed me and the people crowded at the rail, but I did not see Stuart. Finally a voice called over the loudspeaker several times: "All ashore that's going ashore." And then after about fifteen minutes and several blasts from the ship's whistle, a murmur rose from the crowd at the rail. I saw that the gangplank had been removed. The ship's lines were being untied one by one. Then as the liner and her tugs spoke their whistle language together, the pier began slowly to recede, and the stretch of water separating us from it widened. We were moving!

It was then that I noticed a figure running along the pier toward the doorway where the gangplank now lay. It was a big, broad-shouldered man, and he stopped in the opening and stood, gasping, staring up at the ship.

Chapter Seventeen

IT WAS STUART. I HAD LEFT HIM BEHIND. I was safe.

Had he seen me? Oh, how I hoped he had. I wanted him to know that I had escaped. We seemed for a moment to be looking straight at each other. But I doubted that at that distance he could have picked me out of the hundreds of people along the rail. Still, I had left him behind. I was safe!

But then, almost instantly, I realized that I was not safe at all. This was only a reprieve. Now that he knew where I had gone, he would follow.

All during the voyage this thought lay at the back of my mind. And even after we had docked, as the taxi carried me from the Outer Quays to Southampton's Terminus Station, I wondered when Stuart would arrive in England.

At the station I found that my train for Bridgehampton left at half past eight. Since it was seven o'clock then, I had plenty of time to have a pot of tea and a sweet bun in the refreshment room and ring up Aunt Grace and Uncle Andrew to ask if they would have Patrick meet me in the Bridgehampton station.

But then I decided to send them a telegram instead, thus avoiding lengthy explanations over the telephone. I had my tea and finally boarded my train.

It was dark when the train pulled out of the station and it had begun to rain. And the nearer we drew to Bridgehampton, the harder it rained—the wind hurling water at the windows of our compartment at times in sheets, almost as if from a gigantic bucket.

On time, the train slowed noticeably as it approached Bridgehampton station. I rubbed a clear circle in the fogged glass so that I could look out through the rivulets of water running down the outside. Bridgehampton was terribly dark; the lighted windows of its houses seemed barely able to penetrate the blackness outside. And the rain pelted down as hard as ever.

As soon as the train stopped, I opened the door to look about. There seemed to be no one to fetch my trunk. But then I saw Patrick running toward me. But no, it wasn't Patrick. It was Lyle.

"Lyle!" I cried. "What on earth are you doing here? Why, you are soaking wet!"

"Never mind that," he said, grinning at me. "Run for cover. I'll get your trunk. Hurry!"

I dashed for the shelter of the station's wide overhanging roof while Lyle ran to the luggage van.

I thought then of that sunny afternoon a little over four weeks ago when I had waited on the opposite platform with Mr. Sewer for the London train. How filled with excited anticipation I had been at the prospect of traveling with my father. I had no idea then when I would return to Bridgehampton. I certainly had not dreamed that I would be standing on the other side of the tracks in a shivery rain on a chill August night, those awful experiences in New York behind me, while somewhere out in that black world Stuart stalked me.

But now at least, I was no longer alone. Here on the station platform was Lyle, the man I most counted on to help me. He appeared a half minute later through the train smoke, followed by the porter with my trunk. In another minute my trunk had been loaded into the back of Lyle's car, and we drove away from the station toward Ledington.

"How did you know I was coming?" I asked. "Lyle! You are shivering. You're chilled!"

"I'll be all right," he said. "A good-sized brandy, a change of clothes, and a fire will take care of it. And I suggest the same for you."

"I would rather have a hot cup of Mrs. Moore's tea."

"I'm afraid she won't make it for you."

"Oh? Of course she will."

"She's not there. Your aunt and uncle aren't at the rectory anymore."

"Not at the rectory? Where are they?"

"In Weymouth—with Mrs. Cuttlebuck's sister. They *couldn't* stay here, Louisa. I did everything I could. I tried every way I knew to smooth it over. But you know how furious Colonel Fitzcroft was. And then Mr. Denby, and Lady Hewingham, and Miss Ormsby, and God only knows how many more. They were outraged! The whole church— I had to do it. I hated to, Louisa, but your uncle had to go. It would have been constant open warfare if he hadn't."

"Oh, Lyle."

"It wasn't my fault. He did it. One must expect to take the consequences of one's acts in this world."

"I suppose so. Is anyone at the rectory now?"

"No. We're waiting to find someone."

"And Mrs. Moore and May?"

"I don't know."

"How did you know I was coming, then? I wired Aunt and Uncle from Southampton."

"I got your letter on Saturday, and Mr. Bankside rang me up about your telegram."

"Could you drive me to Weymouth?"

"Tonight? In this?" Lyle gestured to the rain pounding on the windshield. "We would never get there. You'll stay at the Hall, of course." Lyle concentrated then on driving a winding stretch of road. Presently when the road straightened out, he said, "Why didn't you write? You might at least have told me you were all right. Not a word. And then your letter on Saturday. What happened? What terrible experiences? If Kean is not your father, who is he?"

Then I told Lyle as briefly as I could all about Mr. Sewer—how he had tried to kill me and everything that had happened in New York until I left him at Bixby's Hotel.

"He admitted that someone had paid him?" Lyle said,

when I had finished. "He admitted it to your face? Who? Who paid him?"

"I told you, he wouldn't say. Only that it was someone who had a lot to gain. He was too frightened to say anything more. He was frightened of what that person would do to him if he told me."

"It's fantastic! I can't believe it."

"It's true. And of course you know who did it."

"Compton?"

"Why do you think so?"

"Who else? Can you think of anyone else who would have done it?"

"Yes, it was Stuart. I knew it even before I got back to the Ritz-Carlton Hotel." Then I told Lyle about narrowly escaping Stuart at the hotel and going to Salvia's.

"Why the Livermores, of all people?" Lyle asked.

"I couldn't think of anything else to do."

"Did you tell them? About Kean and Compton?"

"Yes, I had to."

"Anyone else? Mr. and Mrs. Cuttlebuck? *Anyone* else?"

"No, I wrote, but I didn't tell them. Not even Bertha. She is in New York working for the Livermores now. No, I haven't told anyone else. Why do you ask?"

Again Lyle had to concentrate on the road.

Then he said, "Just wondering. But because Compton was at the hotel, doesn't mean—"

"He tried to kill me." Then I told Lyle in detail how Stuart pursued me and attacked me at Lord and Taylor.

"It was Compton, all right. It must have been," Lyle said. "But why? Do you have any idea? Why should he want to kill *you*?"

"I don't know. I've thought and thought. Something that happened a long time ago—between your mother and his mother, I think. I thought you might know. Or do you suppose he is out of his mind?"

"Possibly," Lyle said. Then after a few moments he continued, "We're almost there." He smiled at me. "I'm afraid you'll find things changed at the Hall."

"Oh?" I said.

"Yes. I've closed it."

"Closed it? Why?"

"Have you any idea how much it costs to run a place the size of Compton Hall?"

"Well, no. How could I?"

"Forty thousand pounds a year. Forty thousand pounds! That is a little over thirty-three hundred pounds a *month*. And I have no clear idea yet of the financial condition of the estates. Harrison was a bungler—I do know that. And a thief as well. He was stealing my father blind. The first thing I did was sack him." He paused for a moment. "I don't quite know what I'll do now. I can't bear the place . . . after Father. Anyway, it's in rotten repair. Practically falling down. Perhaps I'll move to a more modern house— nearer London somewhere."

"But what of the servants? What about Keating and Mrs. Merrymede?"

"Keating was far too crippled to go on working. I pensioned him off just after you left. He lives with a niece in Scotland, near Paisley. And is very happy there too. And after Father's death, Mrs. Merrymede was only too glad to go live with her sister. I gave the rest notice—with a sizable bonus to each, of course."

"Everyone?"

"I've engaged a butler, a good enough fellow named Chitley, and a housemaid to look after the place. Griffith and his wife are still there. They have a cottage, out beyond the wood behind the glasshouses. And Herbert and Anna in the lodge, and Rodger and a groom in their quarters in the stables."

"But you can't possibly manage with only a butler and a housemaid," I said.

"It won't be for long—only until I decide what I am going to do and Winterthorn has read the will."

"He hasn't read it? But it has been weeks."

"I know. I spoke to him over the telephone yesterday and he said he'd come down toward the end of the week. Deuced offhanded, I thought. At first he was away, and then he was ill. One excuse after another. I think he's gone senile. I'd hate a dustup over it, but if he doesn't come by the weekend, I'll have to do something. I mean, after all . . ."

He smiled at me then and slowed the car. "Nothing to worry about." Quickly he leaned toward me and kissed my cheek.

"Lyle, you are trembling! You are shaking with cold. Never mind, you will have your brandy soon. We have only to climb the hill. Look, there is St. Clement's."

It was not the church that brought tears to my eyes as we drove past it; it was the rectory that made me cry. The house stood as it had when I had left it. But no lights shone now in its windows. It looked sad and empty and cold. I wished then that I could run to it and find everything as it had been: Aunt Grace in bed in her room and May and Mrs. Moore in the kitchen. But a new rector would live there now, and it would all be changed. "We can't go back," I remember saying to myself as we left the rectory behind. "All we can do is go ahead, in spite of what lies in store for us. The past can't be changed and I don't suppose the future can be, either."

The immediate future was to bring Herbert running from inside the lodge to open the gates of Compton Hall for us. Then we drove toward the house. Though it was still raining, I lowered my window to see it as we approached. Compton Hall loomed ever larger before us—a giant black shape against the sky. It was totally dark. Surely it was deserted.

But it was not. Almost at once, as we pulled up before the house, the vestibule light was switched on and the door was opened by a young man. He turned out to be Chitley.

An hour later, as we sat at the table in the dining room eating dinner, I said, "He is too young to be a butler. He seems too high-spirited somehow, and he could not have had much experience."

"Perhaps," Lyle said. "But it was better to have someone than to cast about aimlessly for the perfect man and have no one. He seems to make every effort, though, don't you think? And June too. Here we are seated at dinner, fires warming both our rooms and one in here, dressed in dry clothes, and restored with excellent brandy in perhaps an hour's time. I should say that was something of an accomplishment."

"Yes, I suppose so. But I don't think she is very experienced either. And certainly not a cook. Stewed tomatoes, boiled potatoes, and omelets for dinner? Is this an omelet?"

"I don't know what you would call it, but fear not, madam. Mrs. Merrymede made some inquiries and discovered a Mrs. Meacham, who has agreed to come up and cook for me if I need her. Do you know Mrs. Meacham?"

"I know her by sight. She is a Methodist, I believe. Then you are to have a Methodist menu?"

"If her food is as good as Mrs. Merrymede seemed to think it would be, perhaps I shall become converted: Go thou into all the world and spread the gospel of the Methodist menu."

We laughed at this. And I wondered when had been the last time I had laughed.

"What is it?" Lyle asked.

"I was wondering when was the last time I laughed," I said. "I'll ring up Aunt and Uncle in the morning and tell them I'm coming."

I slept late on Wednesday morning. Lyle slept even later, not coming down to the breakfast room until I had finished eating and sat gazing out of the window, drinking my second cup of coffee.

Suddenly from behind me he appeared and said, "Beautiful morning, isn't it? Sleep well?"

"Yes," I replied. "I was sitting here, thinking how lovely our English greens are—American trees and grass are sharp, too garish almost, in comparison—and putting off the duties of the day."

"And what are the duties of the day?" Lyle walked to the sideboard, rubbing his hands together in mock anticipation. "What delicacies have we here? Cold toast . . . and what are these?"

"Cold omelets, I believe."

"Ah, the ever-present egg. The fountainhead of life."

I smiled at Lyle. "Do you suppose June realizes that they eventually turn into chickens? Perhaps a chicken salad for luncheon? But no, probably not. I must ring up Uncle."

"What will you tell him?"

"Why—that I'll be arriving in Weymouth later. When could you drive me there?"

"Could they have you?"

"Well, I don't know. Surely Aunt Maud could put me *somewhere*. I'll ask, but of course she will."

"You won't tell them about Richard Kean?"

"Heavens no! Not over the telephone."

Having helped himself to some toast, Lyle sat down opposite me. "Do you think you should tell them at all? Anyone?"

"I am certainly not going to brag about it, but there is no reason to keep it a secret."

"I don't think you should tell anyone about it. If I were you, I'd simply let the matter drop. Your father has a busy schedule, and you've returned. That's all."

"Why do you say that?"

"Hasn't it occurred to you that if it is incredible to us—his perfect impersonation, I mean—it would be totally unbelievable to other people? What will they think? That you pretended this strange man was your father so that you could go off with him. Or even worse."

"I never thought of that. Yes . . . I suppose the less said, the better. Let me go ring up Uncle."

It was Uncle Andrew who answered the telephone when I got through to Weymouth.

"Hello, Uncle Andrew? This is Louisa. I'm home!"

"Louisa?" he said. "Where are you?"

"In Ledington—at Compton Hall. Lyle was good enough to put me up for the night. I didn't know you weren't here."

"No. I suppose he has told you everything that has transpired."

"Yes."

"Needless to say, none of it would have happened if you had remained in Ledington and married Lord Hartley as Grace and I advised you to do. 'Bow down thine ear and hear the words of the wise,' Proverbs 22:17."

"I don't see how that would have— How is Aunt Grace?"

"Not well. Not well at all, I am afraid. I must say, Louisa, that your willful and foolish manner has caused both Grace and me great pain and unhappiness, in spite of our unstinting efforts on your behalf."

"I am awfully sorry," I said. "I didn't mean to hurt you."

"That very willfulness has lost me my living at St. Clement's parish. Since you were determined to leave Ledington, Lord Hartley saw fit to vent his anger upon me, making vile and unjust accusations to disguise his real intent."

"He wasn't angry at you, Uncle. He told me so. But we can talk about that later. How is Aunt Maud? When can I come to Weymouth? Lyle said he would drive me."

"Naturally we would enjoy seeing you, Louisa, but I am afraid that now would not be the most appropriate time for a visit. Perhaps later."

"I didn't mean to visit, Uncle. I can't stay here. If I can't be with you, what shall I do?"

"Call upon the Lord for help, Louisa. 'For it is God which worketh in you both to will and to do of His good pleasure.' He acts in strange ways, and we are not to question them or interfere with them. This is as it should be. God gives us experiences to teach us while we are upon this earth. Always remember Galatians 6:7. 'Be not deceived; God is not mocked: for whatsoever a man soweth, that shall he also reap.' "

"I see. Aunt Maud couldn't have me with her?"

"I am afraid that is out of the question, Louisa. We would like to help you, but it must be obvious that we are no longer in a position to do so. I'm afraid you will have to manage independently now. That seemed to be what you wanted, wasn't it?"

"Yes. Well, give my best to Aunt Grace and Aunt Maud. And I'll see you all soon."

"God bless you, Louisa, my dear, and—"

But I did not wait to hear more. I replaced the receiver and then I leaned against the wall for perhaps a minute, thinking, before I returned to the breakfast room.

"They can't have me," I said to Lyle. "I suppose there isn't room enough."

"Wonderful!" Lyle said. "Don't look so woebegone. You will stay here with me—where you belong."

"I can't stay here."

"Why not? I'll send Chitley down for Mrs. Meacham, and then after—"

"But I couldn't! What would people say? It would be terribly improper. And this is the first place Stuart will look for me—Ledington, I mean. He will come straight here. No, I can't stay here, not even for a little while."

"I mean permanently, Louisa. As my wife."

"Oh, Lyle. Do you still want me?"

"More than ever. If you knew how I've thought about you these past weeks. Dreamed about you. Seen you in every room—so intensely that you were actually here. Marry me, Louisa! Father can't object now. We're completely free. I love you! More than I've ever loved anything in the world. I'll make you happy. And as for Compton, he wouldn't dare come here. He wouldn't dare set foot in England, let alone Ledington. He is wanted for murder. Detective Inspector Huff of Scotland Yard is on it. He is staying in Bridgehampton when he is not in London. Do you know him?"

"No, how could I?"

"I thought you might know *of* him." Lyle paused a moment, thinking. "He solved the Newton Mews murders, and he was responsible for the conviction of Howard Dentwood, and many others. I'll go into Bridgehampton this afternoon and tell him all about Compton and how he wants to—how he has been after you. Inspector Huff will know what to do. He will certainly want to know where Compton is. You won't have anything to worry about as far as Compton is concerned."

Lyle reached across the table, covered my hand with his, and said, "Marry me. When Winterthorn has read the will, which will be any day now, we'll be married. We'll go directly to Italy, if you like, on our honeymoon. And browse about there until Compton has been caught. *Will* you marry me, Louisa?"

I gazed into Lyle's intense eyes for several moments before I answered him. "That was all I thought about, Lyle—all the time I was away. I want to get home, I thought, and be with Lyle. I want to marry him, if he'll still have me. He will keep me safe." I smiled sadly. "And now here I am, and that is exactly what you have done. And . . ." I couldn't continue. I was not smiling now.

Lyle returned my gaze and waited. Finally he took a cigarette from his case and lit it. "And now you can't bring yourself to say yes. Is that what you're trying to tell me?"

"Lyle, I am so confused. I can't think clearly. Not with Stuart wanting to kill me. Not knowing why. Not even being able to go home, and be quiet, and think! I can't think, Lyle."

It seemed a long time before Lyle spoke. "Try to imagine this as home, my darling," he said at last. "Relax. Compton is far away and you will never see him again. Relax now, and think. And then let me know. Will you do that?"

I agreed.

I tried to do just that. Lyle was terribly considerate. He left me alone after breakfast, saying that he had work to do in his study. I wandered about the house for a while and then I went upstairs to my bedroom and lolled about, thinking that I might collect some things to wash and thinking about Lyle.

That was when I saw Mrs. Meacham walking down the drive toward the house and went out to meet her. Ordinarily I need not have done that, but since Chitley had left for the village to ask her to come to the Hall, I had not seen him anywhere about. Someone had to show Mrs. Meacham where to go and what to do.

I remember thinking as I left the house and walked toward her that I had not seen either June or Chitley for hours, and I wondered what they had been doing. I was sure there had been nothing lazy or malicious in their disappearance. They were simply young and irresponsible.

Mrs. Meacham wore a long black coat that reached to the ground and a black hat with a wide brim, and she carried a satchel and an umbrella, which I thought strange, since the sky was cloudless. She was followed, rather reluctantly I thought, by a plain-looking girl in her early teens.

"Mrs. Meacham?" I said. "I am Miss Little. It was so good of you to come."

She must have seen me looking at her umbrella because she replied, "Always carry an umbrella in case it rains. Only God knows when that will be. This is my niece, Nancy. She's going to help me. Well, I couldn't do it all alone. Where's the kitchen?"

I led them along the drive where it bordered the kitchen wing of the house to the larder at the far end. "I am afraid I can't help you very much in finding things," I said. "June, the housemaid, might be able to. She has been cooking for his lordship."

"I'll find things," Mrs. Meacham said. "I can't promise much for lunch. It depends on what's here. Mrs. Merrymede has put things up, no doubt. It will have to be at half past one. Mr. Budley is bringing a lamb over from the farm this afternoon. I saw him in the village this morning. And I'll need money to pay for things from Sweet's at the end of the week."

"Yes, of course."

"And I want his lordship to know that this is only for the time being—until he makes arrangements. I'll cook the meals and go home at nine o'clock. And I don't care if he sacks me like he did the rest. I'm only doing it to help out, and I'm not afraid of him or nobody."

"I understand."

"He shouldn't have done that. Give them notice like that. Some of them was with his old lordship for years. It ain't Christian."

She said no more—even when we arrived in the kitchen. Nancy never spoke at all. She stood pouting in the corner while Mrs. Meacham removed her coat and hat, hung them on a hook near the door, tossed her satchel on a chair, and hung her umbrella on the back of it. Then she opened her bag, drew out an apron, put it on, and began to open the cupboards one after the other to see what they contained.

I left her then and had no sooner arrived in the loggia and climbed halfway up the stairs toward my room when I heard a car on the drive. My heart leaped to my throat; it was Stuart. The car door slammed, and then a moment later the doorbell rang. But then I realized that Stuart couldn't possibly have gotten to England so soon.

As Chitley was nowhere about, I went to answer the door. It was Police Inspector Greg.

He did not seem at all surprised to see me. "Good morning, Miss Little," he said. "Is Lord Bude at home?"

"Yes. Won't you come in, Inspector Greg?" I said. "I'll go and see— Oh, here he is now."

Lyle ran down the stairs, a wide smile on his face, his hand extended. He shook hands with the inspector. "A pleasant surprise, Inspector," he said. "To what do we owe the honor of this visit? Nothing unpleasant, I hope."

"Not at all, not at all, Lord Bude," Inspector Greg said. "Just passing by and thought I'd look in to see if everything was all right."

"Very good of you, I'm sure," Lyle said. "As a matter of fact, I was going in to Bridgehampton this afternoon to see Detective Inspector Huff. Now you've saved me the trouble. Won't you come up to the drawing room? Miss Little and I have some rather important things which we feel you and Inspector Huff should know. Perhaps you will be good enough to pass them along to him."

When Lyle and I sat together on a sofa in the drawing room and Inspector Greg stood before us (he had declined to be seated), Lyle continued, "Miss Little has only just returned from the States, Inspector."

"Ah," Inspector Greg said.

"Yes. I have asked Louisa to become my wife, and you are the first to know, Inspector."

"Ah," Inspector Greg said, rising on his toes.

"Yes." Lyle took my hand and smiled at me. Then he turned to Inspector Greg. "Inspector, Louisa has had a particularly harrowing experience which you should know about. Do you know where my cousin, Lieutenant Compton, is now?"

"We have our sources of information about things of that nature, Lord Bude. One can not be too careful about discussing official business, you know, but I can say that our investigation is going along satisfactorily."

"He is in New York, Inspector. He was in New York at the same time Louisa was. He harassed her there. He made an attempt on her life."

"Indeed?" Inspector Greg said. "Where and under what circumstances did this attempt occur?" Inspector Greg asked, looking at me.

"In a department store where—" Lyle began.

"We will have it from Miss Little, if you don't mind, Lord Bude."

"Yes," I said. "But before that—"

"Tell Inspector Greg," Lyle said, "everything that happened *after* you arrived at the Livermore's house. Louisa was staying with Mr. and Mrs. Gerald Livermore, Inspector, and their daughter, Salvia."

I told the inspector then what had happened from the time I arrived at Salvia's until I sailed. He listened patiently.

When I had finished my account, he said simply, "That is everything?"

"Yes, everything I can think of, Inspector."

"Good. Then I shall pass this information on to Detective Inspector Huff." He looked at Lyle. "Was there anything else, Lord Bude? Everything all right hereabouts?"

"No," Lyle said. "That is all. But I think Louisa's experience in New York is significant, don't you, Inspector? Yes, everything is fine here."

Inspector Greg left us almost at once and drove away.

"I don't know what I expected of Inspector Greg," I said to Lyle at luncheon. "But some reaction, further questions, some . . . *interest.*"

"Yes," Lyle said. "I never did think much of Inspector Greg. Pompous, dull little man. But he will tell Huff, and that is the important thing."

"What is he like? Have you met him?"

"Inspector Huff? Sly, cruel. Only interested in his own advancement. Wants to add another jewel to his crown, dramatically solve the Bude murder and create a sensation. Ambitious. Too much ambition is dangerous—not to be trusted. I don't like him. But he is shrewd—brilliant mind. I wouldn't underestimate him."

"You didn't want me to tell about Stuart's hiring Mr. Sewer, did you?"

"It wasn't necessary. Why embarrass yourself for nothing?" Lyle grinned at me. "One attempt on one's life is enough to fascinate the authorities, don't you think?"

"Yes," I said, dipping into Mrs. Meacham's hot, clear soup.

The soup was followed by slices of baked ham, fluffy mashed potatoes, vegetables, hot biscuits, a delicious tossed salad, and, finally, preserved peaches and coffee. How she managed it in such a short time was a marvel to me.

The meal lightened my spirits considerably, and when Lyle asked what I would like to do during the afternoon, I said, "I'd like to go to the stables and see Samantha. I should take her for a run, I suppose, but I don't want to go alone. Will you come? How are you feeling? Did you catch a chill last night?"

"Perhaps a little," Lyle said. "Nothing to worry about. No, not for a ride, but I'll come see her with you."

"Shouldn't you stay indoors?"

"We won't be long, and I'll wear a sweater."

So Lyle and I visited Samantha. We took the shortest way to the stables, walking across the lawn from the breakfast room past the corner of the maze. As we passed one of its entrances, I thought how delightful it would be to explore it. I had never seen the miniature pavilion in the maze's center, and I was curious about it. As we returned to the house, I suggested we go into it. But Lyle said it would be chilly in the shadows of the hedges, so we did not.

"Then walk to the rosery with me," I said, when we had almost reached the breakfast room doorway. "And let's go to the bower and make believe it is early June and that Arthur and John will soon come with lemonade and sandwiches."

"You go," Lyle said. "It will be windy out there, and I should take a little care. I'll wave from the library windows."

So I left Lyle and walked alone across the lawn toward the rosery. Even in those few weeks the gardens had changed; hedges needed trimming, and the lawns should have been cut. Already leaves were falling, and they lay upon the long grass, blown this way and that by the wind.

Lyle did wave to me from the library window. I turned as I approached the bower and saw him standing there. I waved back, and then when he had withdrawn from view, I turned and entered the bower. I could not sit there now because the chairs of June had long since been taken away. So I stood looking about at the ramblers that covered the little structure—no flowers bloomed there now—and at the long grass beside the rosery paths, which not long ago had been a smooth, green carpet.

And I tried to recapture the glory of that early June day when Lyle and I had sat there, but it would not be June for me. It was well into August, and not very long before the roses would begin their winter's sleep.

I traced our footsteps of that day then (I did not care if Lyle saw me do it), leaving the bower, walking down the walk beside the hedge, and through the opening in the wall to the lake. There Compton Hall stood mirrored in the water as perfectly as it had on that June day. It was a beautiful house—just as beautiful now as it had been almost three months before. *Why*, then, did it seem so changed?

It was not only Lord Bude's death, the dismissal of the staff, and the closing of the house that made everything seem so terribly different, I thought, as I walked on toward the honeysuckle and clematis vines upon the wall. It was not simply that it had been June when I found the Hall and its gardens so enchanting, and now it was August. I stood against the vines and remembered the way Lyle had kissed me there. No, it was because Lyle had seemed enchanting then and now he did not. If I married him, the rest of my life would be the end of a summer, and I longed for the sweet, vibrant beginning of it.

That was when I knew I would never marry Lyle.

He had finished breakfast by the time I came down in the morning, but he kept me company while I ate. And when I was almost finished, he suggested we walk out onto the terrace into the morning air.

"Bring your coffee," he said. "It's incredibly fresh out there. The rain has washed everything in the night. Did you hear it?"

So I walked out onto the terrace with Lyle, and we stood together there, looking out across the lawn at the flower beds, and the shaggy maze hedges, and the glasshouses.

"Shouldn't the grass be cut?" I asked. "And the flowers need weeding badly."

"Yes, but I don't think I'll keep the place, Louisa. And who knows what the next owner will want to do with it."

"You *couldn't* think of selling it."

"You love it, don't you? Then I won't if you'll marry me. Marry me, Louisa."

He put his arms around me then, and I set my coffee cup on the railing of the balustrade before he drew me to him and kissed me.

Then holding me away from him, Lyle asked, "Will you marry me—ever?"

"Lyle, this isn't the time—"

"I think it *is* the time, Louisa. It will have to be the time sooner or later. Will you keep me in suspense forever?"

"No, of course not."

"Then make it now, please."

I gazed into Lyle's beautiful brown eyes for several moments then, while I asked myself if I was truly sure of my answer.

Then I said, "No, Lyle, I can't marry you. I don't love you—as a man. I love you as a friend, and I need you. And if anything should happen to you, I think I would die. But I cannot marry you."

He stood still, gazing into my eyes for several moments, his thoughts unreadable. Then he turned, and without a word walked into the house.

"I am afraid I shall have to leave you to your own devices this afternoon," Lyle said, as soon as we had sat down to luncheon. "I won't be any longer than I need to be. I've found something disturbing in the account books. It is something that should be investigated as soon as possible."

"But surely it doesn't have to be done today," I said.

"These things cannot be allowed to go unattended, Louisa. The consequences could be disastrous. My father owned extensive commercial property in Deptford. It was handled by an agent there whose name is, or was, Leopold Shenk. I can find no references to either the property or Mr. Shenk after the thirty-first of December two years ago anywhere in the account books or in my father's papers and notes. It is as though they have both vanished into thin air. It is important to find out about this, and especially what has happened to those revenues which amounted in previous years to more than twenty thousand pounds. No, I'm afraid this cannot wait. It is most suspicious indeed."

"I see. May I come with you?"

"Deptford is a grim, dangerous area. The docks are no place for a woman. You will have Chitley and June, and Mrs. Meacham. You will be perfectly safe here."

So Lyle left Compton Hall shortly before two o'clock that afternoon. I watched him drive off, and then wandered into the library to see if he had left the *Times* there.

The *Times* was not there. Where was it? And where was Chitley? Where in heaven's name was he? Without him about and with Mrs. Meacham away in the kitchen and June having disappeared as usual, Stuart could march into the house, strangle me, and leave without even having been seen.

This angered me, and I determined to find Chitley and have a word with him. I discovered him in one of the bedrooms with June. From outside in the corridor I heard her giggle as he spoke to her.

"Chitley," I called.

"Yes, miss?" he said, when he had run out of the room to me.

"Wherever have you been, Chitley?" I said. "I have been looking everywhere for you."

"I was helping June move some furniture, miss," Chitley said.

"I hope that you have finished helping June, and that from now on you will remain within hearing distance of the bell in the event someone should call. It is important that you be at the entrance if someone should.

"And would you kindly go and find today's *Times* and bring it to me in the library?"

But I couldn't read. Instead I gazed out of the window, sitting in the chair that Lord Bude had used when we had read together.

How things had changed since then! If it could only be any one of those days before Stuart arrived—before that long black Bentley drove up the hill through the mist toward me. Ever since that day he had pursued me. He would not let me be. Even now, at that very moment, he was drawing nearer; I could feel it.

I knew that this time, if he found me, I would not escape him. What could I do? Leave Compton Hall. Leave Ledington. Go! Yes, but not today, not quite yet. Tomorrow, maybe.

Thinking back, it is clear to me that I should have left Compton Hall the following morning and gone to London. The ominousness in the air that morning should have warned me to leave, and to leave quickly. I sensed a strange quality of unrest. The park outside and the house lay beneath a blanket of hot, moist air. And an odd, orange-gray color seemed to glaze everything.

Chapter Eighteen

I DID NOT LEAVE COMPTON HALL THAT DAY. I did not wish to be confronted again so soon with strange people and places. Compton Hall was familiar to me and comforting. And I felt that possibly Lyle was right; Stuart would not come back to England. And if he did, I would certainly have a few more days before he arrived.

So I convinced myself that I was temporarily safe. I believe I was more worried that day about Lyle than about myself. How moody and glum he had become since I had told him that I would not marry him. He seemed to realize that my decision was final. He had not argued with me, or tried to change my mind. On the contrary, he had been terribly considerate and kind. He had told me he would always love me, and had offered to help me in any way he could. But it was clear that I had hurt him. I had made him unhappy. And because he was unhappy, I was unhappy too.

The day passed slowly, one endless minute following the endless minute before it. I washed two or three underthings and some stockings during the afternoon. Then I sat huddled in Lord Bude's chair at the library windows trying to read until dinnertime, not caring if I wrinkled my green velvet dress, and loathing the melancholy stupor I had fallen into.

Because of Mrs. Meacham, dinner was now at seven o'clock. It was a dreary meal. Lyle and I tried to seem cheerful. He asked what I would do now, and after I said that I hadn't decided, we said nothing much more to each other.

Immediately after dinner Lyle went up to the study and I walked out to the drying yard behind the laundry to take my wash off the line. Shortly after that Miss Ormsby arrived with her alarming news.

It was just as I had finished taking the last stocking from the line that I heard it. It was a birdlike, almost cuckoolike sound—a high, then a lower note: "Hoo-hoo." Then it was repeated: "Hoo-hoo."

But it was not a bird calling. The call had been made by a human voice. As it was repeated, a woman's face peeped out from around the corner of the laundry at me. Then Miss Ormsby's entire figure appeared, and she minced hurriedly across the grass toward me.

"Oh, Miss Little," she cried, as she approached. "I knew I would find you somewhere. There is no one else *anywhere*. I rang and rang."

"Miss Ormsby!" I was utterly surprised to see her. "However did you get here?"

"I walked! There is nothing like a bracing walk on a summer's evening. We must have our exercise, you know, and walking is simply the most marvelous exercise of all."

"Yes. Well—won't you come into the house?" I began to walk around the house toward the front entrance, and Miss Ormsby walked beside me. "What a pleasant surprise. Did you know I was here?"

"Yes! Mrs. Meacham told me in the village early this afternoon. I was simply delighted. But when did you arrive? No one knew!"

"Tuesday night, quite late. After dark."

"And you are—ah—staying *here*?"

"Yes. Lyle has asked me to marry him, and . . . we have the servants, of course, and—"

"Where is your father?"

"In New York."

"He is such a charming man. He is well?"

"Yes, quite well."

"And the play?"

"Not a great success, I am afraid, though by no means a failure. Of course, it involved an enormous amount of effort to prepare for the opening of it, and theatrical life is exhausting. Such hours—always getting to bed in the wee hours of the morning. Quite impossible. I did have the pleasure of visiting Mrs. Livermore and Salvia at their house on Fifth Avenue."

"*Really?*" Miss Ormsby said wide-eyed. "But I would not have thought— I mean, after . . ."

"Oh, yes! They were most hospitable. I returned to England aboard the *Aquitania*. It is so awfully good to see you again, Miss Ormsby. You are looking so well!"

"Am I?" she said, as I opened the vestibule door for her. "Where is Lord Bude?"

"In the study. I think he would prefer not to be disturbed unless it is something important."

"Oh? Well, I have some distressing news. I am sure he should know about it, but let me tell you first and then we can call him in."

"Very well, Miss Ormsby. Won't you come up to the parlor? We will be more comfortable there."

"Isn't it warm!" Miss Ormsby said, when we had almost finished climbing the staircase together. "Ominous! I knew it boded evil even before I went to Bridgehampton this afternoon. And so close! There will be thunderstorms—I can feel it. Oh, this is a day when evil hovers about us on huge black wings. Don't you feel it?"

"I don't know about the black wings, Miss Ormsby, but it is terribly warm."

As I said this, we passed through the hall opposite the library doorway. I remember wondering at the time if Lyle had heard Miss Ormsby and me. I was quite sure he had not. If he had, he would have left the study, which was off the library, and come to the library door to see who was with me.

We passed into the rear hall then and entered the oval parlor at the far end of it. We seated ourselves opposite each other. Miss Ormsby had fallen silent.

"What was it you wished to tell me?" I asked, when we had made ourselves comfortable.

"Can you imagine whom I saw in Bridgehampton this afternoon?"

"No," I said, a little shiver of apprehension running up my spine. "Who?"

"Mr. Graves was going in at four o'clock and kindly offered to take me with him. He had shopping to do for Mrs. Graves, and then he was to visit briefly with his sister who had fallen down a flight of stairs and broken her fibula. I was to meet him at Hobbson's at half past six for the drive home. Well, I had finished up earlier than I had expected and sat on one of the benches outside Lane's, watching the passersby. But then when there weren't many people about, I thought I might have a pot of tea at the Red Lion and watch who arrived on the six o'clock train. I can always get one of the tables by the window at that time. Well, I was sitting there having tea and a trifle, which I always have there, when the Southampton train came in. And *who* do you suppose walked down the stairs from the platform?"

"Who?"

"Lieutenant Compton!"

"You must be mistaken," I said.

"No! I was not mistaken, Miss Little. I know Lieutenant Compton when I see him. I have good cause to remember him well."

"You are absolutely certain?"

"Positive! I watched him walk down all those steps and pass along opposite me and walk through the tunnel toward Hobbson's, as large as life. I am positive. He was in a great hurry. Inspector Huff asked the same thing. Do you know the Inspector?"

"No."

"A *charming* man—utterly attractive." Miss Ormsby giggled. "A hero! One would place one's life in his hands. Of course, I help him whenever I can. I went directly to him and told him all about it. 'Are you certain it was Lieutenant Compton?' he said. And I said, 'I am positive, Inspector Huff.' "

"What did the inspector say then? Did he seem surprised?"

"I don't think he believed me. I don't think he believed me at all. I told him how I had been sitting at the window in the Red Lion eating my trifle when—"

"Listen!" I said. "Is that a car?"

"Yes, I believe so," Miss Ormsby said.

"No, don't get up," I said, rising from my chair. "Please don't trouble yourself. I'll go and see. I'll only be a moment. It is probably only Rodger with the car for Lyle."

I was not at all sure that it was only Rodger, and after I had left Miss Ormsby in the parlor and run through the hall to the front of the house, where I could look out onto the drive, I was certain that it was not.

Three men had driven up to the house. A young, pimply-faced ruffian stood by the car while two other burly men walked across the gravel toward the entrance door of the Hall. The man in the lead was Stuart.

Instantly I flew to the railing of the staircase to look down and listen. As I did so, the library door opened, and Lyle dashed through it and ran to my side.

"Who is it?" he asked breathlessly. "Did you see them?"

"It is Stuart and his henchmen."

"Henchmen?"

"You didn't think he would come alone, did you? Listen!"

From below I heard Stuart's voice. "Where are his lordship and Miss Little?"

"If you would care to wait, sir," Chitley said. "Who shall I say is—?"

Stuart and his accomplice dashed to the stairs and began to run up them toward Lyle and me.

Lyle grasped my hand and began to pull me toward the library. "Come into the study with me," he whispered rapidly.

Just as Lyle pulled me away, I caught a glimpse of both men bounding up the stairs.

"You take Hartley, and I'll get Louisa," Stuart called to the other man.

"No," I cried to Lyle, wrenching my hand from his. "Run and hide!"

I had already begun to run. I ran back toward the parlor, and as I passed through the doorway into the rear hall, I glanced back at the stairs. Stuart had seen me and was running after me.

I dashed through the rear hall, past the parlor, to the rear stairs, and down them. I flew down the narrow, wooden stairway making as little noise as I could. But when I had gotten halfway down them, I heard Miss Ormsby scream. I stopped, shocked by the terror in her voice.

He has killed her, I thought in a flash. She is quiet now. I had forgotten all about Miss Ormsby. I should never have left her alone. But if I had gone back to her, he might have killed us both.

But I had no more time to think about that, because I heard Stuart's heavy footsteps running across the floor above me. He rushed to the dining room, then to the drawing room doorway.

I'll run to the stables, I thought as I raced down the rest of the stairway. I must get to Samantha. She will carry me to safety.

I ran straight to the breakfast room then, across it, wrenched open the door to the terrace, and dashed outside. Then without pausing, I ran as fast as I could out onto the lawn and across it toward the corner of the maze and the stables beyond.

He will never find me now, I thought as I ran. He is still searching the house. He will never dream that I have run outside into the dusk like this. I slowed my pace then and looked back toward the house. And as I did so, Stuart darted out of the breakfast room doorway and paused on the terrace, looking in my direction. Then he bounded after me.

I did not look to see more, but concentrated on running away from him as fast as I could. I had almost reached the corner of the maze, so I was almost halfway to the stables. But I could not run as fast as he. I knew then that my only hope of escaping him was to dash straight into the maze. He would never find me there.

But before I could do so, something sped through the air near my head, and almost at the same time, I heard an explosion behind me—a loud, sharp report. He had shot at me! Even before I had fully realized this, he shot at me again.

I dashed into the maze. I ran between those walls of hedge, turning always first to the right and then to the left, as Lyle had told me to do, in order to reach the center. In half a minute I scurried through an opening into the little center yard of the maze. There before me in the deepening twilight stood the tiny, columned pavilion.

I stood still then, looking about, catching my breath, and listening. For a moment the air was still. Then I heard a distant rumble of thunder, and off in the eastern sky saw a glimmer of pulsing light. Then there was silence.

The silence lasted for only an instant before I began to hear footsteps nearby in the leaves. Stuart had followed me into the maze. He stopped to listen, and then he began to move again, stealthily. But his were not the only footsteps. Other shoes pummeled the lawn outside the shrubbery, drawing relentlessly nearer. His accomplice, I suppose, had followed him.

"Louisa!" Stuart hissed. "Answer me! Louisa!"

Did he think me a fool? Did he imagine I would answer him? I could not stay where I was. Suppose Stuart's mother had told him the secret of the maze. In that case I should not stay at the pavilion. I should hide in one of the culs-de-sac near it.

Stuart had now paused again to listen. But his accomplice had not. He seemed to have entered the maze. I thought I heard his footsteps close by. And I thought I heard someone else running toward the hedges. Was it one or two persons who now approached? Could it be Lyle? Lyle and who else?

In a moment the others had entered the maze too. Now several persons crept about in it. But no one spoke. I could hear only footsteps and loud breathing.

Then a voice called from outside the maze, "I say! Hello? Is someone there? Has something happened?"

"Sh-h-h!" a nearer voice hissed.

The first voice was a young one—the young ruffian, probably. He had heard the shots and come running.

It was now imperative that I leave the center of the maze; so I stole to the entrance of the little yard and, hearing a movement, peered cautiously around the corner of the hedge into the dusky passage. A dim figure appeared at the end of the corridor and crept stealthily toward me. As he approached, I could see the man's eyes glint savagely in the twilight. It was Stuart . . . and he was moving directly toward me. His mother *had* told him the secret of the maze.

I drew back a bit, held my breath, and waited. He was so close that he would hear me if I moved. He paused, looked into a passage on his right, then continued toward me. In a moment he would be upon me. He would surely see me standing there.

But then, miraculously, he stopped, looked into a corridor on his left, turned, and vanished into it.

At that moment I heard, "Hoo-hoo. Hoo-hoo."

"I say," the younger voice said, "what kind of bird is that?"

"Sh-h-h!" the older man hissed. "That's no bird. It's that woman. Go get her! Get her out of here. I don't care if you have to strangle her."

The maze was ominously quiet then, but on the lawn outside I heard footsteps as still another person ran toward us from the direction of the house. This and a nearby clap of thunder prompted me to act. I had to do something, perhaps sneak out of the maze if I could, while the others were occupied inside it. Then I could dash to the stables. It was almost dark, and it was already difficult to distinguish objects about me. I might now creep past the others unseen. If I waited much longer, it would be completely dark and I would not be able to see my way.

As quietly as I could, peering intently about me, I stole

along the passages of the maze, reversing the formula—turning to the left and then to the right.

Then a voice cried, "Your lordship! Your lordship, wait!"

So Lyle *was* here somewhere. If only I could find him. Was it he who now brushed the yew branches in the passage in front of me?

No, it was Stuart. "We will never find her if we go on wandering about like this," he said. "Now, if—"

A clap of thunder crashed down upon us then and a flash of lightning lit the sky. As if to answer the thunder, a pistol shot shattered the air with a deafening roar from beyond the hedge.

At the same time, Miss Ormsby screamed, "You've killed him! You've killed him!"

I could think only of Lyle then. Stuart had shot Lyle! I must go to him. I ran in the direction of Miss Ormsby's voice. As I turned a corner of the hedge, I saw a dim group of figures. Lightning flashed again, illuminating them. Miss Ormsby knelt over a prone figure on the ground. The young ruffian bent over it too. And there, in front of them all, stood Stuart. At that moment he glanced round and saw me.

In one quick movement he leaped at me, his arm extended. I turned and ran. He was much too close to outrun now, or even to lose in the maze. In a moment his hand would grasp the back of my dress. But I had to run anyway. I darted through an opening in the hedge.

As I did so, I heard a heavy thud and a grunt directly behind me. Stuart must have tripped and fallen. I looked back just in time to see Mrs. Meacham withdraw the shaft of her umbrella from under Stuart's legs. Bless her, she had tripped him with it.

Before Stuart could leap to his feet, I bolted down the passage before me, turned, and ran out of the maze onto the lawn. I was free!

But I did not stop running. I ran into the gathering darkness. It was not enough to be out of the maze. I must get to the stables and Samantha. Lyle was dead. I couldn't help him now. I must save my own life. In a flash of lightning, I discovered that I had left the maze from the south side. So I ran toward the topiary figures. I would have to run through them and on to the stables that way.

The storm was upon us now—lightning flashed and thunder crashed and wind whipped my hair and skirt. And it began to rain. As I felt the first large drops, I heard running footsteps behind me. Was it Stuart? Could he see me? Surely he could in the flashes of lightning. I ran faster, not daring to look back, hoping the pain in my side would not grow worse.

I ran on for perhaps half a minute and had almost reached the first topiary figure, when I had to stop for a moment. I looked behind me then, as a long bolt of lightning streaked the sky. Stuart *had* seen me. He was bounding toward me. Seeing him so near gave me new strength. I dashed behind the topiary lion, and between lightning flashes dashed behind several of the other figures. I hoped that Stuart had not been able to follow my erratic movements in the darkness. I remained crouching behind the hippopotamus before dashing quickly to the three ladies.

There I stood among them—erect and still. My green dress was almost the color of the yew from which the figures had been clipped. I prayed that in the darkness, I would appear to be one of the sculptures. If I remained still, Stuart might not find me. I could not hope to reach the stables. This was my last chance.

He was near. I could hear him move, but I dared not turn my head to see where he was. And as the seconds passed, his movements became louder. He was looking among the sculptures for me. Yes, I could see him now out of the corner of my eye, standing behind the kneeling camel.

Then he strode directly toward the group of ladies where I stood. He stared straight at me as he came. I was about to bolt when he paused not three feet away to stare at something on his left. He was so close I could have reached out and touched him. I held my breath. Then my heart sank; lightning flashed as bright as daylight. If he should turn his head . . . Would the lightning never stop?

Finally it ceased. Stuart turned from me and began to walk away. He hadn't seen me. His footsteps became softer. I turned my head slowly to look for him. But I could not see him now in the darkness, nor could I hear his footsteps.

I listened intently for several moments, but I heard nothing except the raindrops on the shrubbery. He must have gone back to the maze. I was alone. It was raining hard now. The wind on my skin made the rain feel so cold. I shivered. I could not stand there any longer, so I left the topiary ladies and crept among the other sculptures until I reached the standing bear at the far edge of the group.

There I paused to listen, standing against the beast so as not to be easily seen. I thought I heard a movement nearby. I stood very still, holding my breath and listening. Then I felt the icy fingers touch my throat. Instantly the hands squeezed my neck, cutting off my breath. I tried to scream, and at the same time I pushed at my assailant with all my might. I struck at him, kicked him, and struggled wildly, trying to wrench myself from his grasp. But it was useless; he held me too tightly. Now my chest felt as if it would burst. My neck burned like fire. A numbness began to spread through me.

Suddenly, in a flash of lightning, I saw his face and the wild look in his dark eyes.

I remember nothing more.

Chapter Nineteen

I REMEMBER NOTHING MORE UNTIL I FELT myself being carried in someone's arms and then laid upon a bed. But I remember this only vaguely. I do not believe that I knew at the time precisely what was happening.

My first clear recollection was of Mrs. Meacham bending over me, saying, "She's coming around now." Then I remember her turning her broad back on me and saying, "I'll take care of it. Dry clothes and bed. Go along. Leave us be."

"Who is it?" I asked.

"Don't worry," Mrs. Meacham said, "and don't talk. Save your strength!"

She helped me out of my wet clothes and into a dry nightie and a flannel robe. Then she turned down my bed, removing the coverlet, which was damp where I had lain on it.

"Into bed and keep warm," Mrs. Meacham ordered.

"I really don't think—"

"You don't want to catch your death, do you?"

I climbed into bed. But I did not remove my robe. I wore it because I knew I would soon have a visitor.

Mrs. Meacham left me then, returned in a few minutes with a pot of tea, and poured some of it into a cup. I drank it eagerly. I had almost finished it when someone knocked on my bedroom door. Mrs. Meacham went to it and, after a whispered conversation, opened the door wide and left the room, as Stuart and the man who had come to Compton Hall with him that night stepped in.

"Louisa," Stuart said, "this is Detective Inspector Huff of Scotland Yard."

"Has someone been hurt, Inspector?" I asked.

"No, miss," Inspector Huff said. "When one finds a pistol pointed at oneself, it is wise to drop to the ground. For some reason, this caused Miss Ormsby to become hysterical. I trust that is what you mean?"

"Yes," I said. "Where is she?"

The inspector sighed deeply. "She has gone home," he said. Then after a pause, he continued, "I am afraid I must ask you a painful question, miss."

"Yes?" I said.

"Do you know who attempted to strangle you a short while ago? Did you see him?"

"Yes, Inspector," I said. "It was Lyle—Lord Bude. I saw his face plainly in a flash of lightning."

"And would you be willing to swear to that in a court of law?"

"Yes, Inspector. But how did I—?"

"That is all I want to know. Thank you. Now, if you will excuse me, I will say good night. We have your assailant in custody, and we must remove him to the jail in Bridgehampton. Nothing to worry about. You will be perfectly safe now."

"Do you need help?" Stuart asked the inspector.

"No," Inspector Huff said. "Sergeant Biddle and I can manage him nicely. He won't give us any more trouble, thanks to you."

Then Inspector Huff turned and stalked out of the room, leaving Stuart and me alone together.

"What did you do to him?" I asked.

"Hartley?" Stuart said. "I beat him half to death."

"You rescued me from him?"

"Yes." Barely pausing, he continued, "Louisa, there are some things I must tell you at once."

"I think I know what they are."

"Oh?" Stuart raised his eyebrows at me and smiled.

"Yes. Lyle killed his father, didn't he? And he killed

Nanny Thompson. And he hired Richard Kean to kill me. Do you know about that?"

"Yes. You seem to have fit the pieces together nicely."

It was seeing Lyle's face—out there in the storm—that told me. But why, Stuart? *Why?* Do you know why?"

"Yes. But you have been through a terrible—"

"Tell me. I must know. Do you think I could sleep without knowing? Wondering?"

"All right then, I'll tell you a bedtime story." Stuart sat down in a chair, smiled broadly at me, and began. "Once upon a time, there lived in a large country house a British peer, whom we shall call, simply, Frederick. Frederick had two sons, William and Charles. Nearby lived two young ladies, whose names were Elizabeth and Anne—daughters of a local, wealthy squire.

"Both Elizabeth and Anne fell in love with Charles, Frederick's younger son. Though Elizabeth and Anne were identical twins, Elizabeth was by far the more attractive, both in beauty and in personality. And while Elizabeth was strong, Anne was sickly. It is not surprising, then, that both sons, William and Charles, fell in love with Elizabeth. Elizabeth chose Charles, and they were married. Naturally both Anne and William resented this terribly. In a fury, William proposed to Anne, she accepted, and they were also married.

"Because of their unsuitability to each other and their increasing unhappiness together, their resentment of Elizabeth and Charles turned quickly to bitterness and then to hatred."

"Are you speaking of your mother and father?" I said.

"Never interrupt a story—especially a bedtime story," Stuart said, frowning at me and then smiling. "Because of William's and Anne's hatred of their brother and sister," he continued, "the two couples became entirely estranged.

"In spite of this, William and Anne learned that Elizabeth had given Charles a healthy baby son. Anne's children, on the other hand, had both been daughters and had died soon after birth. This set of circumstances did not in any way ameliorate the feeling of enmity that William and Anne felt for Charles and Elizabeth. Indeed, it deepened it."

Stuart paused, as if considering how to continue. Then he resumed his story. "Soon Anne was with child again. This time the local doctor told William that if Anne survived the birth of her child (her previous confinement had been a difficult and dangerous one), she must never have another. Now, girl babies had been so much the rule in Anne's family that William feared this final baby would be another daughter. If the child was a girl, William's title would then pass to Charles, if Charles survived him. If he did not, the title would pass to Charles's son, Stuart."

"But—" I began. Stuart's look of displeasure silenced me. I decided to allow him to finish his story without further interruption.

"His title passing to his brother or his brother's son was utterly repugnant to William," Stuart continued. "And, of course, he wanted a son to inherit his beloved country house and estates. So William took steps to insure that his child would be a son. He arranged for Anne to have her baby at Wignore House, his house in London, under the care of an eminent physician, a Doctor Malcolm Fitzpatrick.

"Actually it was Doctor Fitzpatrick who was to assure William of a son. In return for William's gift of twelve thousand pounds—which would build a magnificent new surgery onto his Harley Street residence—Doctor Fitzpatrick agreed to substitute a baby boy for Anne's child if she should bear a daughter."

"How could he possibly do that?" I could not help asking.

"With the help of a Miss Blunt, the secretary of a hospital for poor and unfortunate women in London. Miss Blunt was to receive one hundred pounds for her role in the affair if a substitution were necessary.

"There were usually a few babies at the institution who were not wanted by their mothers, prostitutes or working women to whom a child could only have been an inconvenience. These babies were kept for the first few weeks, for adoption, and then were turned over to an orphanage affiliated with the hospital. It was hoped that one of these babies would be a healthy male of about the right age. He would be substituted for William's daughter.

"Soon, as William had feared, Anne gave birth to a daughter. The very day before, a woman of various occupations and pastimes, whose name was Nancy, gave birth to a healthy baby boy at the hospital. Nancy had not wanted the child. She refused to have anything to do with it—even to look at it. She wanted only to be rid of it.

"Two days later Miss Blunt gave Nancy's baby boy to Doctor Fitzpatrick in exchange for William's daughter. Preparations had been made to take William's infant daughter to the hospital for the exchange. William had hired a nanny to carry the child and care for it during the trip, and also to care for Nancy's baby boy when Doctor Fitzpatrick returned with it to Wignore House.

"The nanny was Nanny Thompson. Miss Blunt was sure that she would go along with the scheme, because of her involvement in the Bainsborough child murder. Miss Blunt, since she had known Lady Angela Bainsborough and had arranged for her to have her child at the charity hospital where she worked, assured William and Doctor Fitzpatrick that Nanny Thompson was entirely trustworthy, competent, and innocent of any wrongdoing.

"So, shortly after the boy was taken from the hospital, Miss Blunt obliterated the sex of Nancy's baby from the records with a blot of ink, and William returned to the country with a son.

"In the meantime, however, Nancy had changed her mind about her child. Now she wanted it. When she demanded her baby, she was given William's daughter instead. Nancy had never asked whether her baby was a girl or a boy.

"By the time the girl, whom Nancy had named Louisa, was six years old, William, having become more and more conscience-stricken over what he had done, finally decided to trace Nancy and find out the circumstances of his daughter's life. When he had done so, he was so horrified that he arranged, by paying Nancy a large sum of money, for Louisa to be brought to the rectory in the village below his country house and installed there as a sort of foster child of the rector and his wife. At that time, he questioned Nancy about the existence of a husband or anyone who could possibly lay claim to the child. There was no one.

"This seemed to William to be a perfect solution to the problem of Louisa. The rector was of a good family, well-educated, childless, and poor enough to need the living. William had endowed the living, and though the rector did not relish the responsibility of bringing up a six-year-old child, he dared not refuse William's request, even though William had refused to tell him why he wished this to be done, and had cautioned the rector to keep his involvement in the matter a secret."

Now Stuart sat gazing at me in silence, waiting for my reaction to what he had told me.

"Have you finished?" I asked.

"Yes. The story isn't finished, but—yes."

"Is it true, Stuart? Is it a true story?"

"Yes, Louisa."

"How do you know?"

"Because after Hartley—Little, his name is. I mustn't keep calling him Hartley. Lyle Little. Because after Lyle killed my uncle and I read about it in the newspapers, I went straight to Inspector Huff and proved that I was nowhere near Compton Hall that night. Huff asked me to help him. We went to see Mr. Winterthorn together, and Mr. Winterthorn told us the whole story. It is all written down in a codicil to your father's will. Evidently your father never liked Lyle very much. And when he found out that Lyle was planning to sell the estates after his death, he left everything to you, Louisa. And he explained the whole story."

"I don't believe you," I said. "You've invented it all. Why?"

"No, the story is true, Louisa. I swear it. Think about it. Why were you brought almost halfway across England from Manchester to Ledington? Why did Mr. and Mrs. Cuttlebuck take you in? Did you feel they ever really *wanted* you? Of course it's hard to believe. What your father did was monstrous—abandoning his daughter like that. And what you have had to endure because of it was appalling. My poor Louisa."

I gazed into Stuart's eyes for some moments then, reading in them that what he had told me was the truth. "Then Lord Bude was my father," I said.

"Yes. And you are Lady Louisa Compton."

Stuart remained quiet, not interrupting my thoughts. Finally I said, "I suppose Lyle planned to prove the codicil false because I had gone away with my 'father.' Then he would have inherited the estates."

"That seems to have been the general idea," Stuart said.

"When I returned, he had to kill me to keep me from telling everything. Or marry me—one or the other. He would have had control of the inheritance if he had married me."

"Yes."

"Why did you come to New York, Stuart?" I asked, after I had thought a moment more.

"To find you. I was worried out of my mind. I thought Kean might have killed you."

"I should have known. I should have suspected Lyle from the beginning. He was always too nice. No one is like that. No one is everything nice."

Stuart grinned at me. "Not little boys, anyway," he said. "That's not what little boys are made of." But then he suddenly became serious. "Louisa, people are nice only when they have something to gain by it."

"You don't believe that."

"It is true. Not everyone, but most people. The nicer they are, the more they want."

"I am nice, and I don't want anything from anyone."

"Don't you?"

He came to the bed then and sat down beside me.

He did not speak. Instead, he bent and kissed me long and passionately on the mouth.

"What do *you* want?" I asked.

"You."

"Nothing more?"

"No," he said solemnly.

I slid my arms around his neck then and drew him to me.

"Stuart," I said. "Hold me!"

He crushed me to him until I could scarcely breathe. I was safe. And I knew that it would always be that way, that he would never let me go.

Epilogue

THOUGH STUART HAD TOLD ME MOST OF what I needed to know about my father and what he had done, and I had been able to deduce from this many things that had puzzled me, a few questions remained. So Stuart and I went back over it all in detail late the following morning as we strolled together in the sunshine on the lawn before Compton Hall.

"When did Mr. Winterthorn arrive?" I asked Stuart.

"Last night after you were asleep. His car broke down this side of Maiden Newton. Did he tell you?"

"Yes, before you came down. What a ghastly experience. And no mechanic within miles."

"He was to meet us here at eight o'clock. It was Huff's idea. Mr. Winterthorn was to read your father's will to you and Lyle in front of Huff and me. And let the chips fly where they may."

"What do you mean by that?"

"Huff knew what Lyle had done, but he couldn't prove it. There was no evidence to convict him. So it was all arranged as a last, desperate attempt to trip him up, so to speak."

"But Lyle must have known what was in the will," I said.

"Of course he did," Stuart replied. "Do you know when he found out about it?"

"No. When?"

"During the dinner party for the Livermores here at Compton Hall—while you were charming Mr. Winterthorn with your piano playing. Your father knew that Lyle planned to sell off the estates after his death, so he summoned Mr. Winterthorn to Compton Hall to draw up a new will. Lyle knew this and left the room shortly after you had begun to play, not to care for your father, but to go into Mr. Winterthorn's room and read the new will. Mr. Winterthorn found his papers disturbed when he returned to his room that night."

"Then Lyle went to London," I said, "and using the name Throckmorton examined the hospital's records. *Lyle* was Mr. Throckmorton."

"Yes," Stuart said. "He read the records, but remember that the records contained no proof that you were Lord Bude's daughter—primarily because of Miss Blunt's ink blot. And Lyle was unable to discover the whereabouts of Miss Blunt."

"At least he did not have to worry about Nancy Little. He knew she was dead."

"But she is not dead," Stuart said, "nor is Miss Blunt."

"How do you know that?" I asked.

"Because Inspector Huff has talked to both of them. But that gets ahead of your story. Go on."

"Well, then Lyle decided to marry me. If he could not inherit my father's wealth, he would gain control of it by marrying me. That was why he held the ball and invited you to it. He would announce our engagement during it and so put an end to your attentions to me. I was as surprised by his announcement as you were."

"I know that now, but I didn't know it then."

"I went to the manor house to tell you, but you had gone. Where were you?"

"In Scotland—on Skye. Licking my wounds."

"Of course I refused to marry him. Not only because I didn't love him—"

"You didn't?" Stuart said, grinning at me.

"I loved you from the beginning, you know that. From that very first day at the millpond."

"You were not very sure of that for a while."

"I was too! It—it wasn't only because I didn't love him, but because I had a strange feeling about him which made me uneasy. Now I know what it was. It was that Lyle reminded me of his mother, Nancy Little, and of her cruelty to me as a child."

"My poor darling."

"Then since he couldn't marry me, Lyle decided to find another way to obtain the inheritance. I think he decided to prove he was Lord Bude's son in spite of the will and codicil. He thought he could prove that the codicil was a lie—the vindictive trick of a vengeful father. Then the will would be found invalid. Even if it wasn't found invalid, I would be dead, because Lyle had employed Kean to impersonate my father and then kill me in the middle of the Atlantic. Lyle knew all about me by then. He and Kean must have written Kean's letter to me together. Anyway, after I was dead Lyle would inherit everything as Lord Bude's son. After all, Doctor Fitzpatrick must have written Lyle's name on the birth certificate as Lyle Anthony Stephens Compton. And no doubt it was recorded that way in the birth records. What happened to Doctor Fitzpatrick? Is he still alive?"

"No. He was killed during the war when a German shell hit a field hospital near Verdun."

"Fortunate for Lyle, but not for Inspector Huff. To get back to Lyle's strategy, to prove the codicil a lie, Lyle would produce the man whom he would claim was my true father, Richard Kean. It would be obvious, then, that if my father was Richard Kean, Lyle's father must be Lord Bude. But he talked to Nanny Thompson first. It was Lyle who visited Nanny Thompson the afternoon she was murdered. He crept back to Ledington and no one knew it. He wanted to find out where Miss Blunt was."

"Of course," Stuart said. "He was terrified that Miss Blunt would appear. She was the one person who could prove that you were Lord Bude's daughter. After all, she had switched the babies."

"But Nanny Thompson knew all about it. Why did she come up to the Hall to see you that night? Did you know her?"

"No. I told you I didn't. She didn't come to see me; she came to see my uncle. And when I told her Lord Bude was dining out that night, she refused to believe me. She became hysterical. She must have been nearly senile."

"She was old," I said, "and she was peculiar. But she was terribly sensible at times. Lyle knew this, and when he discovered that she had come to the Hall to see Lord Bude, he had to murder her to keep her from telling my father that Lyle knew the whole story. Lyle must have realized then that it had been a mistake to question Nanny Thompson. And then, of course, she was a witness to the switch of the babies. So Lyle would have had to kill her sooner or later anyway. That poor, dear woman."

"You thought I had done it, didn't you?" Stuart asked quietly.

"What else was I to think? Did you once kill a man, Stuart?"

"So you heard about that. Yes, but I didn't mean to. He was a low scum. He came at me with a knife. It was either he or I. I hit him on the side of the head and it killed him."

"It was Lyle who tried to drown you at Cambridge, wasn't it?"

"Yes. He told you it was the other way around? I might have known."

"Yes, he twisted it all around. Everything about him is twisted and horrible. It's no wonder my father did everything he could to keep me from marrying Lyle. Why didn't he simply *tell* me everything, Stuart?"

"How could he? How could he tell you to your face what he had done to you?"

"I suppose you're right. At any rate, the last thing in the world he wanted was for me to marry Lyle—for my sake and the estates'." I paused then, thinking. "And he was terribly conscience-stricken about what he had done to me. The costume I wore to the ball was my mother's. He came upon me when I was trying it on one afternoon here at the Hall and he thought I was Elizabeth returning from the dead. He cried out then that 'she' was all right, and that she would get everything. But I didn't know at the time what he meant."

"My poor darling," Stuart said. He hugged me close to him then and kissed my cheek.

"Chitley will see," I said. "And so will June."

"Let them. Lord Bude will rest now that you are going to marry me."

"Will he?"

"Yes. And you will, won't you."

"Is that a proposal of marriage?"

"It is."

"Yes, I will," I said, smiling at Stuart.

Tears filled my eyes then, but I quickly blinked them away. We walked along for a minute or so in silence, holding each other very close.

Finally I said, "We are first cousins. Will that matter?"

"Prince Albert and Queen Victoria were first cousins," Stuart said. "It didn't matter to them, did it?"

"No, they were very happy until— Oh, Stuart, there has been so much death—so much poison. If only my father could have lived. If only we could have known each other as father and daughter. And it was my fault. I was responsible."

"For what?" Stuart asked, startled.

"For his death. Don't you see? If I hadn't shown him Mr. Kean's letter, Lyle would not have had to murder him. But once he knew about the letter, Lyle had to kill my father to keep him from exposing Mr. Kean and ruining everything."

"We can't blame ourselves for things done out of ignorance, Louisa. And anyway, Lyle would have killed your father sooner or later. Each murder is easier than the last, they say. And Lyle was getting in deeper and deeper. Very convenient to blame his killings on me, I must say. And it almost worked."

"Lyle must have worn big shoes," I said. "And it is obvious that he disposed of the miniature himself. I hope he hasn't destroyed it. Perhaps he has hidden it somewhere. Do you think he would ever tell what he did with it?"

"I doubt it. But it may turn up—stuffed in a stovepipe, perhaps, or some such place. It's really not that important, but I should have liked to have had it."

"And the cuff link? Will you have that back after the trial?"

"Oh, yes."

"Where did Lyle get it? I know Nellie Linton stole it from you when you were staying here, but she gave it to Mrs. Merrymede, and Mrs. Merrymede gave it back to you."

"No, she *didn't*," Stuart said. "She gave it to Lyle to return to me, as was proper. But Lyle never gave it back, which was an indication of his true character. Returning the cuff link to me would have been doing a little kindness to someone he hated. Lyle could never have borne that. So he kept it—threw it into one of his drawers.

"Later, Nellie, on another stealing expedition, saw it in Lyle's chest of drawers, but of course she left it there. Huff traced Nellie, and she admitted that she had seen it long after I had left the Hall."

"Was that after you had come down from Scotland?" I asked.

"Yes."

"What happened then?"

"Huff and I went to see Mr. Winterthorn, and he told us all about the codicil and the will. Then, of course, the pieces all fit together. Your father had mentioned to Mr. Winterthorn that Miss Blunt had a mother in Penzance who was desperately ill about the time you were born and needed constant care and expensive doctors. That was why Miss Blunt needed money so badly. She is still there. And Huff traced Nancy Little to Liverpool. But while he was doing that, I was off to New York to find you."

"How did you find me? I was never so shocked as when I saw you come into the Ritz-Carlton."

"By looking for you at the better hotels," Stuart said. "Finally I found that you had stayed at the Ritz-Carlton and that you had moved to Bixby's Hotel. But when I got to Bixby's Hotel, Mr. Kean told me you had gone to the

Ritz-Carlton. So I rushed back there only to have you run away from me."

"To the Livermore's."

"Yes. I went back to Bixby's. Mr. Kean had checked out, but your things were still there. So I waited for you, even taking a room there, but you didn't return. The next morning I thought of the Livermores. I believed Salvia's story, but when I got back to Bixby's, Mr. Bixby told me that someone had come for your luggage, someone in a Cadillac with the initials G. L. on the door.

"So I checked the Livermore's garage and found that it had been the Livermore's car and that you must be staying with them after all."

"Did you sit on a bench reading a newspaper?" I asked.

"I wondered if you had recognized me. I had to find out if you were really there. Then I had to talk to you. I couldn't get into the Livermore's house, so I hired a car and followed you to Lord and Taylor." Stuart hugged me to him and grinned down at me. "I had a lot of explaining to do to prevent them from calling the police."

"But how did you know I was sailing on the *Aquitania*? I saw you run out onto the pier as we sailed."

"Bertha told me. I wrote you a note and went to give it to her. But she told me that you had left for the boat. I just missed you. So I cabled Huff about it and told him that I would arrive yesterday on the *Leviathan*. Thank God we got here in time."

"Why do you say that?" I asked.

"I presume Lyle asked you to marry him again. Did you tell him you wouldn't?"

"Yes. How do you know?"

"Because he sent a radiogram to the *Leviathan* asking if I was among the passengers."

"Why should he do that?"

"Think."

"So that was why he said he was going to Deptford. He was really going to London to send the message."

"He would have killed you as soon as he knew I was in England. He knew I had pursued you in New York?"

"Yes," I said. "He made a special point of telling Inspector Greg about it and asking him to pass the information along to Inspector Huff. If he had killed me, the story would have made it seem all the more as though you had done it. Stuart! He might have killed me! I was alone with him here."

"Huff knew that," Stuart said. "That was why he sent Inspector Greg out to look things over. But when Greg heard that you and Lyle were to be married, he reasoned that you were safe enough."

"We *weren't* to be married. Lyle said that he had *asked* me, that was all. Thank God you got here in time."

"Huff hoped that additional things would happen to improve his case. And they did, unfortunately."

"I should say they did. It was Lyle who shot at you and me as we ran across the lawn yesterday, wasn't it? He had to kill me, and by then he had to kill you too. It was unfortunate for him that he was such a poor shot."

"I think he was shooting at me," Stuart mused. "I think he planned to shoot me and strangle you. Then he could say that he had come upon us as *I* was strangling you, and that he shot me, but not in time to save your life. Of course, he might have been shooting at both of us. He could have put the gun in my hand quickly and said that I had shot you and had then shot myself. There were several possibilities. But you can be sure he wanted us both dead."

I thought for a moment, and then I said, "What exactly did happen yesterday afternoon?"

"After you ran away from me through the house? I ran after you, and when I got to the parlor, I found Miss Ormsby standing there. She screamed when she saw me. Then I searched the other rooms for you. Meanwhile Inspector Huff had left Lyle and run to the parlor to see who had screamed. While he was quieting Miss Ormsby, Lyle got his gun from wherever he kept it, ran after us, and shot at us. Then I followed you into the maze, and Lyle followed me, and Huff followed Lyle, and Miss Ormsby followed Huff . . . so that she would not be left unprotected, and probably also out of curiosity. I guess we had disappeared into the maze by the time she reached the breakfast room doorway, so she had no idea I was there.

"I tried calling to you, but then I realized Lyle had arrived and that would be dangerous. Miss Ormsby missed Huff and began to wander about, looking for him. The whole thing was such a comedy of errors that it would have been funny if Lyle had not been so desperate to kill."

"Horrible!" I said.

"Well, then Sergeant Biddle arrived," Stuart continued. We had left him at the car on the other side of the house, and he heard the shots and came running." Stuart smiled at me. "Then the fearless Mrs. Meacham joined us."

"With her umbrella," I said, smiling back.

"Anyway, when Lyle heard Huff and Sergeant Biddle and me talking, he knew where we were. When the lightning flashed, he shot at me and then ran off quickly so he would not be seen. When Miss Ormsby became hysterical, he thought he had killed me. She thought it was Huff who was dead, because when Huff saw Lyle and his gun, he dropped to the ground. The rest you know."

"Yes," I said. "I've been wondering if Lyle followed us when you were chasing me through the topiary figures. If he did, he must have thought you were Inspector Huff. Or did he come upon me later, having crept about longer in the maze?"

"We shall probably never know," Stuart said.

"He must have been a little mad."

"Undoubtedly."

"There is just one other thing I have been wondering about."

"What is that?" Stuart asked.

"Did your mother tell you about my father's exchanging Lyle for me when we were babies? Did my mother know? Did she tell your mother when she was dying?"

"No, not to my knowledge. I don't believe Mother knew anything about it."

Stuart and I walked on a little farther without speaking, each lost in his own thoughts.

Finally I sighed and said, "Well, that is the end of the story."

"Not the end," Stuart said. "We have yet to be married . . . and have children. And we will live here at Compton Hall, happily—"

"You will not restore the manor house?"

"No, not now. I would have done it for Mother. She would have liked that. But now I have someone else to love. . . Happily ever after."

The magnificent staircases
were overgrown with ivy.
Her hostess was gone without warning.
Her host was grown sullen and coarse.
And David Field, a tall, broad-shouldered stranger,
seemed to know her at once,
though they had never met.

What had befallen the castle?
What part was Mary to play?

A fear surged within her
such as she had never known
—and something stronger, a rapturous love,
that called to her very soul.

She knew now that she belonged there—
to share the tortuous destiny of

**CASTLE
CLOUD**

ELIZABETH NORMAN

Avon/50062/$2.50

CLOUD 2-80